PRAISE FOR TERRY GAMBLE AND
The Water Dancers

"A beautifully woven story . . . crafted so well that readers will feel the work that went into every page yet find the reading effortlessly enjoyable."
—*Tampa Tribune*

"Luminous. . . . Gamble imparts a remarkable sense of place while launching a searing indictment of prejudice, all the while demonstrating a restrained, understated lyricism that only serves to heighten the novel's power."
—*Booklist* (starred review)

"Gamble's voice is often fresh and assured, yielding a first novel that bodes well for her second."
—*New York Times Book Review*

"A mixture of Louise Erdrich, Hemingway, Fitzgerald, and Sherman Alexie."
—*Lansing City Pulse*

"[An] elegantly written, handsomely constructed debut novel . . . Gamble draws all her characters so skillfully and with such depth that no matter how much you'd like to take sides, it's impossible."
—*Cincinnati Enquirer*

"An exceptional first novel. . . . Gamble's writing is hypnotic."
—*Grand Rapids Press*

"Gamble manages to represent many of the racial, economic, and political complexities of Native American community life without preaching, and her prose is . . . capable of evoking strong images. Her graceful style achieves its ends . . . making *The Water Dancers* a vivid reading experience that, to its great credit, never becomes predictable."
—*BookPage*

"Class, race, love, betrayal—they are all here in this passionately told tale. I loved it."
—Lynn Freed

"Readable and fresh."
—*Kirkus Reviews*

"This rich northern Michigan tale starts slowly and expands gradually, as the author builds a memorable story of family, tribe, racial bias, and the enduring love of land and water."
—*Ann Arbor News*

"Well-drawn characters and engaging prose."
—*Library Journal*

GOOD FAMILY

ALSO BY TERRY GAMBLE

The Water Dancers

HARPER PERENNIAL

NEW YORK • LONDON • TORONTO • SYDNEY

GOOD FAMILY

TERRY GAMBLE

HARPER ● PERENNIAL

A hardcover edition of this book was published in 2005 by William Morrow, an imprint of HarperCollins Publishers.

P.S.™ is a trademark of HarperCollins Publishers.

FIRST HARPER PERENNIAL EDITION PUBLISHED 2006.

Designed by Claire Vaccaro

The Library of Congress has catalogued the hardcover edition as follows:

Gamble, Terry.
    Good family : a novel / Terry Gamble.—1st ed.
        p. cm
    ISBN 0-06-073794-8
        1. Inheritance and succession—Fiction.   2. Conflict of
generations—Fiction.   3. Michigan, Lake, Region—Fiction.
4. Mothers and daughters—Fiction.   5. Women—Michigan—
Fiction.   6. Vacation homes—Fiction.   7. Summer resorts—Fiction.
8. Rich people—Fiction.   I. Title.

PS3607.A434G66 2005
813'.6—dc22   2005041469

ISBN-10: 0-06-073795-6 (pbk.)
ISBN-13: 978-0-06-073795-5 (pbk.)

06 07 08 09 10 ❖/RRD 10 9 8 7 6 5 4 3 2 1

This one's to Peter

And in loving memory of my parents, Jim and H.

ACKNOWLEDGMENTS

First, my deepest gratitude to my real-life family, who indulged this project with good-natured enthusiasm—my sister Tracy and my extraordinary cousins who over the years have bestowed upon me the gift of solidarity, humor, and love.

And to the ladies—the "girl-pies" as Suzanne says—bound by more than words, true sisters all: Alison Sackett, Mary Beth McLure-Marra, Suzanne Lewis, Sheri Cooper Bounds, Phyllis Florin, Elissa Alford, and Linda Schlossberg. Thanks for your honesty and your tenacious faith.

Once again I am blessed to work with Jennifer Brehl, brilliant editor, and Carole Bidnick, agent and friend, whom everyone should have in their lives.

Peggy Knickerbocker, Tamara Hicks, Maria Hekker, Hathaway Barry, and Peter Boyer for invaluable feedback.

To Mary Pitts for unfailingly finding loveliness in plainness.

And always to my husband and children—Peter, Chapin, and Anna—who have grown accustomed to sharing their world with imaginary people and mythical places.

ADDISON FAMILY TREE

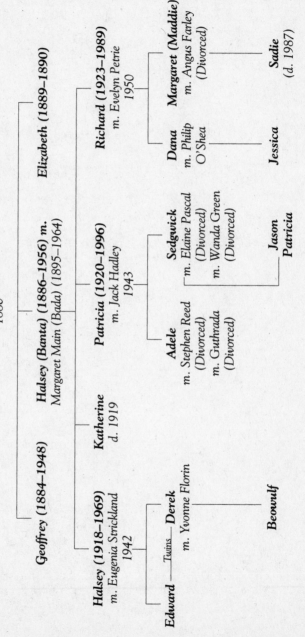

Edward Addison m. Sadie Boothe
1880

Geoffrey (1884–1948)

Halsey (Banta) (1886–1956) m.
Margaret Main (Bada) (1895–1964)

Elizabeth (1889–1890)

Richard (1923–1989)
m. Evelyn Petrie
1950

Halsey (1918–1969)
m. Eugenia Strickland
1942

Katherine
d. 1919

Patricia (1920–1996)
m. Jack Hadley
1943

Edward — Twins — **Derek**
m. Yvonne Florin

Adele
m. Stephen Reed
(Divorced)
m. Guthrada
(Divorced)

Sedgwick
m. Elaine Pascal
(Divorced)
m. Wanda Green
(Divorced)

Jason
Patricia

Dana
m. Philip
O'Shea

Margaret (Maddie)
m. Angus Farley
(Divorced)

Beowulf

Jessica

Sadie
(d. 1987)

PART ONE

ONE

In the years before our grandmother died, when my sister and I wore matching dresses, and the grown-ups, unburdened by conscience, drank gin and smoked; those years before planes made a mockery of distance, and physics a mockery of time; in the years before I knew what it was like to be regarded with hard, needy want, when my family still had its goodness, and I my innocence; in those years before Negroes were blacks, and soldiers went AWOL, and women were given their constrained, abridged liberties, we traveled to Michigan by train.

Summers began with our little group clustered, my father presiding on the platform, the tinny train-coming smell that electrified the air. Weeks before school let out, the steamer trunks had been brought up, followed by the ritual of packing. In June, we boarded the Super Chief, pulling out of Pasadena, my mother and father, my sister and I, Louisa our nurse, my grandmother and her parakeet, her chauffeur, her cook, and two maids who had parakeets of their own. My grandmother, Bada, who was my father's mother, visited with us in the club car and viewed the dresses our mother had bought—appliquéd beanstalks meandering up one side, Jack at the hem, the Giant at our shoulders. Bada smiled and patted our heads and gave us sour candies. Then Louisa pulled us away to the dome car, where we watched the rocks and sand and cactuses of Arizona glide by.

Like Louisa, the porters were Negroes. They called my father "sir," and he called them "sir" back, but I knew it wasn't the same. My father was a tall man with a proud nose and a bearing bred from Choate and Princeton and World War II. He seemed to stand taller than anyone in the Chicago train station. I shook off Louisa's hand, my Mary Janes clacking upon the tiles as I ran through a vast cavern rife with cigars and diesel until I found my father's hand and grasped it. *Can't you keep hold of her?* my mother hissed at Louisa when they caught up to us. My father laid his long fingers on my shoulder as if he was going to embrace me. Instead, he prodded me toward my mother.

From that time on, I was put on a leash. They strapped me into a sort of vest I could not undo, and Louisa grasped that leather rope as if her life depended on it. After I grew up, my mother told me it was only one summer I traveled to Michigan at the end of a leash, but if my memory serves me, I traveled like that for years.

Now it is blackness below—acres of woodland, lake, and river. The inside of the plane is barely lit, and even though the seats are full, no one talks above the engines. It is late, and everyone just wants to get there. Except for me. I want the plane to turn around. I press my forehead to the glass until I vibrate, becoming one with the engines, scanning the landscape for that one place where gravity takes me as if nothing else exists. Finally, I make out a band of lights on a smudge of land, the dots of moored boats in a harbor. Below on that island huddle forty or so summerhouses. Some of them are silent with sleep. Others have people sitting on porches, drinking their nightcaps. In more than one, someone is playing bridge or charades. Someone is dancing. Someone is making love.

But not in our house. In our house, my brother-in-law has nodded off beneath his book, and my sister, if she's awake, is knitting. Upstairs, in the front room—the good room facing the lake—my mother, too, is sleeping, as she has slept for months, her eyes not quite closed, unable to move, her snore penetrating the board-thin walls.

I am not returning because of my mother. It is my sister who calls me back. We are descending now, the runway traced by a pale, blue glow. The plane lurches, stops. The passengers rise, their heads ducked beneath the low ceiling. I grab my bag, waiting my turn to push out the door into the humid sweetness of the Michigan air.

E xcept for the bars, Harbor Town is dark. It is late, and even the ice-cream store has been mopped up, the chairs stacked on tables. It's been eleven years, but I know that in the daylight, colored awnings will flank the streets, shading boxes of petunias and impatiens—red, white, and violet. From every lamppost, American flags imply that the Fourth of July, already one month gone, is just around the corner. The airport van has dropped me off. Standing beside my luggage on the pier, I fix my eyes on the humpbacked island less than a half mile offshore. It looks the same. It always looks the same. For a moment, dread gives way to the anticipation that I felt as a child after a four-day train ride when we first saw the lake, the ferry, heard the gulls, smelled the rotted essence of fish.

I ring the old brass bell that has hung for over a century. From across the harbor, the rhythm of a chugging propeller grows louder until I make out the gleaming teak lake boat of my childhood. The driver is young. He wears a guard's uniform and a change maker on his belt, but he doesn't charge for the ride. After he docks and loads my bags, I sit in the cockpit, crossing the channel that, like the river Styx, divides one world from an-other. The faint strands of U2 coming from the driver's radio seem jarring, and I don't know the driver's name, but I give him mine, whisper it like a password, a name that passes unnoticed in New York. But here, the name is currency, and I feel a prick of shame and pride as I use it—Maddie Addison—and he motors me across, politely calling me "ma'am," which irritates me. At least he doesn't say, *Addison, like the cough medicine?*—but why would he? Half the denizens of Sand Isle have names that read like major brands.

The carriage isn't running tonight. One of the horses threw a shoe. The ferry driver tells me I can use the wagon my sister left, or he can bring my bags in the morning. Taking him up on his offer, I shoulder my carry-on and set off down the boardwalk. There are no cars on Sand Isle. With the exception of a golf cart added ten years ago to deliver groceries, everything and everybody else travels the island by foot, by bicycle, by boat, or by the clomping, bell-hung horse carriages full of old people and children who know all the horses' names.

Voices drift down from some of the porches, but mostly it is quiet. A man and a woman ride by on a tandem bicycle. The woman has hiked up her dress, and the man snaps at her to stop leaning out so far, and she throws back her head and laughs loudly, saying, "I'm glad *you're* steering." They glide by as if I am a tree. Perhaps I am, in my dark clothing, so unlike the woman in her bright patterned dress, something I would never have in my closet, even as a teenager when my aunt insisted that "*everyone* has a Lilly Pulitzer!"

I'm nearly out of breath when I arrive. One yellow bulb burns on a porch two stories up, but our house still dazzles me—the mere physical fact of it. The word *loom* was created for this house, rising as it does four stories—a "cottage" that, built before the turn of the century, continued to grow as more rooms were needed for children and staff and friends. Four generations—five with the niece and nephew who'll be arriving soon, along with the cousins.

There are ghosts in this house. We've known it since we were children. Most of us think we have seen them, except for my sister, who resolutely hasn't. But what she hasn't seen, I've seen in spades—twice the sightings of anyone in our generation, and if it's imagination or madness or too much drinking, who cares? Ghosts there are, and they're watching me now.

I start up the first flight of steps and stop underneath the ship's lantern on the landing. Something scurries in the eaves. I switch my bag to my other shoulder, catch my breath, feeling addled by the smell of the lake. It is redolent of fish, and the air is so heavy, my lungs strain for oxygen. In a few days, the living room will be filled with relatives. My sister will be complaining about the help, and my mother, if she's talking at all, will be ordering her nurse. When I saw her last fall after her stroke, my mother's bark had been replaced by a whisper, but the tone was still there, imperious and demanding, the last surviving Mrs. Addison.

I drop my bag at the front door, walk around the widow's walk to the porch overlooking the lake. Someone says, "Hello?" and I stiffen. If I listen carefully, I will hear the clicking of needles. My sister says knitting calms her mind, but compared to me, she's as serene as a windless lake. Perhaps she's thinking about her daughter or how to construct a menu for ten. Perhaps she's thinking about Mother and wondering, as I wonder, how long this will go on.

I step out of the shadows and see her by the lamp. Her profile is lovely and even. She has cropped her hair since last fall. It looks easy to manage and, while it would make me look severe, seems to suit her. Neither of us is letting the gray come in the way our mother did when she was only in her thirties. Mine, I am keeping a honey sort of blond. Dana's is dark, as it's always been dark, the two of us like bookends—slender girls, unremarkable, with moments of prettiness, some would say beauty, I with my father's nose, she with my mother's.

"Dana," I say.

"Ah!" She drops her knitting and rises. "There you are."

She reaches for me. As we embrace, I take in her smell—our smell—the smell synthesized from a chromosomal likeness of blood and skin and guts, the smell my child would have had.

"Mother?" I say to my sister.

"Asleep. All day." Dana pushes away from me. "You must be exhausted."

"And you! You never stay up this late."

"It's the excitement."

I look around. I can't imagine a less exciting place in the world. The lulling lake, the dull-leafed trees, and rocking chairs all evoking the benign calmness of a sanitarium. From the window above, the drone of a snore.

"Have you talked to hospice?"

Dana pushes back her efficient hairdo. "I have. They want to come out. But I'm afraid it's going to upset her."

I look up at the window and wonder how Mother would even know. For nearly a year, a hired caretaker has seen to her. We are neither of us nurses, my sister nor I. Besides, Mother wouldn't want us to bathe her, change her diaper or bedding. We have never been a family for sharing nakedness, much less our effluence.

"She hasn't spoken for days."

I turn back to my sister. Almost ten months since my cell phone rang, Dana's words—like a blood clot—moving unstoppably east: *Mom's had a stroke, Maddie. You'd better come.* And though I immediately joined them in California in October, it's been more than a decade since I've come to our summer place in Michigan. Now that I'm finally here, Dana looks happy. She has been waiting up, longing to find in me hope and solutions. It is August, and her summer can begin, and all the things we have to tend to. Calling hospice, checking with the doctors, setting up the kitchen for when the cousins arrive.

"Look," I say, "I'm tired."

I see her face fall in the porch light, but what can I do? Five minutes, and I'm craving solitude. I wish I could call someone. Ian, perhaps. But there's only one phone in the house—at the base of the stairs—and my cell phone doesn't work here.

"What room am I in?" I say.

"Your old room," she answers, her voice slightly bruised, and I tense, wondering if she means the nursery in which I slept as a child. "The Lantern Room," she adds.

I relax. We refer to rooms by themes. A painting of a boat hung on the wall designates the Schooner Room. The room looking west becomes the namesake of an iron Jack Russell doorstop that was a house present in

1890. In my twenties, I slept in the Lantern Room, called so because of the base of a lamp.

Dana says, "You're the first one here, you know."

Later, lying under a quilt, I listen to the house. My mother's snoring has subsided, but she still breathes. I have looked in on her. Against the pillow of the hospital bed, her face appeared ancient, twisted to the side. I touched her arm through the sheet. I did not kiss her.

I am engulfed by the dark honey of cedar walls. A toilet flushes, the squeak of mattress springs as someone gets into bed. Already, I can taste the rain and know that tomorrow will be spent indoors. The house groans. The ghosts are waking.

T W O

I have always woken early on Sand Isle. There is a bird that calls out just before light, and then the yardman begins to sweep down the cobwebs. The melancholy church bells toll across the channel as the island comes to life: the competing trills of doves, a distant motor droning, the rustle of sheets. There is a tipping point when it all comes together, when I could still drift back into oblivion or rise instead, becoming a daughter, a sister, a mother.

Lying very still, I allow my body to sink into the mattress. Sometimes I imagine someone coming into my room to check on me—the reincarnation of Louisa, perhaps, as my mother's nurse. She will feel my forehead, take my pulse. Perhaps she will inject me with something. I know it is an addict's fantasy, but in this house, it comes to me vividly and unbidden. The last time I was here, I was beyond redemption.

Now—oppressed by the weight of blankets—I throw them off, pull a sweatshirt on over my nightgown, and head down the hall. My mother's room, once that of my grandmother, looks out upon Lake Michigan. On bright, sunny afternoons, the color of lake seeps through the windows and turns the room a dreamy blue.

"Mother?"

She cannot turn her head. Ever since the stroke, she's been immobilized. The nurse has propped her on a pillow, put one of those half doughnuts around her neck that keep people's heads from dropping sideways on airplanes. With her neck brace, her hair combed back from an ashen, once-lovely face, she looks almost Elizabethan.

During my early childhood when my grandmother was alive, this room smelled of Addison's Sweet Rose Hand Cream and Joy perfume. Now cigarette smoke clings to the window sheers along with newer emanations related to bedsores and incontinence. Even so, it is still the most beautiful of rooms. The southeast corner above the card room opens into a round sitting room of a tower looking out on an oak tree my father climbed as a boy, scaring my grandmother half to death. A screen door leads to a sleeping porch overlooking the lake. The mahogany bed has been replaced by something leased from the hospital. There is a folded wheelchair leaning into a corner, but according to my sister, it hasn't been used since they arrived in July.

She won't go out, Dana told me. She's pulling into herself.

I study my mother's face. I am fascinated by this pulling inward, one eye open, perhaps seeing, perhaps not. Her left side is drooping, but when I saw her in California right after her stroke, her right side still had that way of crinkling at the nose. Now everything seems sunken and waxy—even her beautiful throat. If I have barely touched her in years, I am even less inclined this morning.

"So," says a voice behind me, "you came."

I turn. "Hello, Miriam."

Miriam is wrapped in a pink chenille robe. She hasn't yet put on her wig, and her black hair is oiled and pulled rigidly into a net. She hasn't penciled in her eyebrows, either, and I realize she's no spring chicken. At the very least, she's over sixty, less than ten years younger than my mother, yet she's the one who bathes and dresses her, dabs her mouth as gently as a lover. Miriam's arms are crossed, and she gives me a long, steady look as if she's wondering why I'm here after all this time, and I realize there is no Louisa in Miriam. I stare back, refusing to back down from the gaze of an old, black home-care nurse, even if she *is* the one who wipes my mother's bottom.

"Wake up, honey," she says to my mother. "You won't believe who's come."

My mother's eye wanders briefly to the left. There is no movement in her fingers or her mouth. Only her chest rises and falls.

"I can't stay long," I say for my mother's benefit as much as Miriam's. "I'm here to help Dana get ready. Besides," I go on, trying to sound upbeat, "it looks as if she has everything she needs."

"Oh, she has everything she needs," says Miriam, pressing her lips together.

I push open the window so I can listen to the waves. In the distance, the drone of a motorboat. I wonder if my mother hears these things, if she hears the cawing of gulls or the sizzle of heat bugs after the rain.

"Miriam," I say, "do you think she can hear me?"

"She hears you all right."

I lean against a bureau and look down on her. Her head has dropped to the side in an almost coy fashion is if she is flirting, but I'm convinced she can't see me. Wouldn't she say something? Wouldn't she mouth my name?

"How do you know when to feed her?" I ask Miriam.

Miriam's eyebrows are drawn together with vicious precision. "I feed her," she says, matching my intonation exactly, "when she's hungry."

Yes, of course, when she's hungry. But how would Miriam know? I fix my eyes on my mother. "I don't know what to say to her."

Miriam sticks a straw into my mother's mouth. My mother's cheeks work vigorously as her eyes roll toward me like a curious child's. I wonder if Miriam has spiked the drink, and if that's why my mother is sucking so earnestly. "Why don't you tell her about your life?" Miriam suggests.

I laugh quickly and turn away. My mother stopped asking me about my life ten years ago, so why should I inflict it upon her now? Would she really like to hear about being single and thirty-nine in New York? Or would she like to hear about the documentaries Ian and I make—obscure narratives about obscure people who have spent their lives pursuing arcane interests? Or how I met Ian in grad school; how he got me into treatment and AA when I was starting, it seemed, from scratch? We had held each other's hands at the close of my first meeting, both of us averse to touching, each of us refusing to say the Lord's Prayer, our hands clutching afterward like survivors on a raft, both of us knowing we had found a kindred soul.

"She doesn't want to hear about my life."

"How would you know what she likes to hear about?"

"I wouldn't even know how to ask."

Miriam dabs at my mother's lips. "She likes music. You like music, don't you, Evelyn?" My mother's eyes are intensely locked on Miriam. She doesn't nod. Instead she makes a clicking sound, apparently with her tongue.

"What's she doing?" I ask.

"She's telling me she's had enough."

Oh, dear God.

"You can sing to her," Miriam says to me. "You know how to sing, don't you?"

"If you consider a two-note range singing."

Miriam looks at me as though I'm beyond the pale. Her look reminds me of Louisa, and I think of how, when we were growing up on Sand Isle, the black help and the white help had different nights off. The memory of it embarrasses me now, like that picture of that little girl on the steps of an Arkansas school. I suddenly want to let Miriam know that I'm not of this place—that I've moved light-years away from here. I mention that I have a friend who sings scat in Harlem.

Miriam purses her lips. "I don't think Evelyn would appreciate *scat*."

"How can you stand it here, Miriam?"

Miriam smoothes my mother's hair and begins tucking in her bed-clothes. "Keep your apologies," she says.

I cross to the bed and join her, making hospital corners by my mother's feet, folding them like handkerchiefs. My mother's right hand grasps the sheet; her left lies limp. The nails on both hands are clipped down to the tips, pitifully naked and colorless.

"Miriam," I say, jerking my head toward the window, where there's a clear view of the lake, "can't we move her over there?"

Miriam briskly adjusts a pillow, then squirts some lotion into her hand and starts massaging Mother's arms.

I persist. "It's so stuffy in here. She might like the breeze."

Miriam pulls her brows together, but she seems resigned. "You hear that, Evelyn? You're going for a ride." She rubs the rest of the lotion into her own arms and gives me a nod. Together, we heave the hospital bed across the room so that the breeze coming through the window can touch my mother's face. She's had so little touching in her life. My theory is that she went to the hairdresser every week because someone would run his fingers across her scalp, massage her temples. Breathing from the exertion, I drag my hand across her forehead. Her open eye closes with the touch. At this moment, I wish I could sing to my mother, sing her something low and soulful to ease her way, but I have only a two-note range and can't find the words.

I an?" I almost whisper into the phone.

"Oh, my God! The prodigal Maddie! Have they locked you up yet?"

I make a sound like *oy*, something vaguely Jewish just to make me feel like I'm back in New York. "It's not just my family," I tell him. "It's me. It's like having your childhood smack you across the face and say, 'See! *This* is who you are!' "

"Yes, but have the cousins arrived?" The thought of my cousins makes Ian almost rapturous—poor only-child Ian from Minnesota who grew up a voluptuary in the midst of Lutheran pragmatism. No thespian, coke-sniffing cousins for Ian like my cousin Sedgie; no paint-encrusted heartthrobs like Derek; nor any who, like Adele, believe they are the reincarnation of Mary Magdalene. "A-*dele*," says Ian, his voice lascivious, evoking Sedgie's glamorous sister. "Is she there yet?"

"Ian," I say, "I've got to book an earlier flight. I want to get back to work."

Ian, my partner in film production, ignores me. "You've got to tell me what she's wearing."

I sigh. "No one's here, Ian," wanting to add, *For which I am grateful.* "It's quiet, for once."

Ian starts incanting, "MaddieAddieAddison. It's only a place."

But what does Ian really know about Sand Isle? I have tried to paint for him a picture of exclusivity that doesn't allow for much variation in race or religion. The dour descendants of Anglo-Scottish ancestors purged their souls with bracing morning swims, retired to prim, sober sleep each evening after vespers. Only at the turn of the century were non-Presbyterians allowed. By then, the climate was distinctly less sober, especially during Prohibition when the denizens had their own bootlegger who came by rowboat after dusk. My great-grandmother, famous for having lost her mind and regaining it, ascribed this to pernicious Episcopalian influences, but before she succumbed to cancer in 1935, the Catholics had appeared, about which Grannie Addie was aggrieved. Since then, interfaith marriages (Presbyterians to Episcopalians, Episcopalians to Catholics) became de rigueur, and, for the first time ever, a divorcée was allowed to take title of the cottage she had inherited from her parents.

Sexual orientation? Ian had inquired after hearing all this. *Do they care if you're queer?*

Now I hear someone coming out of the kitchen. I tell Ian I will call him back. Hanging up, I stare at the wall. Bead-board is a hallmark of these cottages. Some owners have painted theirs in an attempt to "brighten," some have Sheetrocked over the studs. Our house is mostly intact, the dark wood in front of me a gallery of framed pictures. Some are tens of decades old—nameless and yellowed. There is my grandfather as a boy in bloomers sitting in a rowboat, his long, blond curls falling past his shoulders. There is my grandmother, droopy-bosomed even before she was middle-aged, three children—four, if you count the one who died—two boys and one girl who would each go on to have two children of their own. Postwar babies who

arrived after my uncle and father returned from Europe, toddling on the
knees of aunts whose saving graces were their sisters-in-law and the army of
maids in my grandmother's staff. We are the cousins, and there is ample
documentation of our ever-expanding family. Nineteen forty-nine—the
first one, Adele, followed by the identical twins Edward and Derek, who had
to endure the scrutiny of four grandparents and two sets of aunts and uncles.

The rest of us were born in the fifties—almost the sixties, in my case. Ike
was president, Elvis was singing "Love Me Tender," and the low rumblings of
sex, drugs, and rock and roll were beyond the curve of the earth. *That* world,
consisting of two kinds of people—relatives and friends—was my Eden, pristine and blank, unfettered by truth before knowledge first touched my lips.

Nineteen-sixty is the first family photo where we're all together. Edward
stands off to the side almost in premonition of his absence. The other
cousins are crew-cutted or pixied, three of us fair with Scots-Irish blood,
three of us dark—the mysterious gypsy genes—our expressions ranging
from confident to surly, our beaming, Coke-fed faces betraying nothing of
what came later. There is no hint of multiple incarnations in Adele then.
Or of Derek's artistic bent. And the smaller of us—Sedgie, Dana, and
me—we are scooped into our mothers' laps or leaning against our fathers'
legs, our grandmother, now widowed, anchoring the center. It is here at the
Aerie that we all come together, our yearly pilgrimage that defines and
gives us meaning. No one looking at this picture would see anyone alcoholic or oversexed or neurotic or delusional. Dana, on my father's lap, looks
slightly worried, her eyebrows furrowed even then. And me? I am the youngest, hardly yet formed, a lump on my mother's knee, as raw and unpro-
tected as a just-hatched chick.

When Dana comes into the dining room, I am looking at the
place I marked twelve years ago behind the door. Eighteen
inches above the floor, the initials *S.A.F.* Sadie Addison Farley. She was fifteen weeks old. We held her up to the wall as if we were taking a mug shot.

Sadie's wrinkled face was red with baby acne, and she looked like a cranky old man in need of a bowel movement.

Penciled into the same soft bead-board, initialed and dated, is the mark of Aunt Pat at age five, already tall for her age. Below and above it are those of my father, barely two feet in '23, shooting all the way up to six feet two inches in '55. The whole wall looks like a Rosetta stone of growing children. Some of the initials are difficult to read. Some have changed with marriage and divorce. Next to an aunt in 1920 is a great-nephew in 1984. Same height, two generations later.

"Did you check on Mom?"

"Hmm," I say.

"So what do you think?"

How, exactly, to phrase my response? Do I say that it's an abomination that our mother is lying bedridden in a diaper, drooling out of the left side of her mouth? That she can no longer walk or talk coherently or smile or give any indication of what she's thinking, or if she thinks at all?

I touch the mark on the wall and stand up.

"The guard brought your suitcase, and Dr. Mead is coming over," Dana says. "This afternoon." She pushes her glasses up on her nose, looks from me to the wall, but doesn't ask. I was hoping to go swimming this afternoon, but the rain I predicted last night is waiting to drop, and the lake is a forlorn gray.

"Did hospice call?" I say.

"Still waiting." Dana looks exasperated as she says this. "The phone's been tied up," she adds in a tone as if she's been stewing over something for the longest time, and that this particular transgression, which should have been obvious, is left to her to rectify.

"It was Ian," I reply evenly. "We're in the middle of a project." I know she won't ask, *What project?* That would acknowledge a world outside of this one, one that involves productivity and colleagues. It is a threatening, tainted world, and the borders of Sand Isle are sealed.

"Does Mother want to see her?" I ask, referring to Dr. Mead.

Dana crosses her arms. "I thought *you* might want to."

I know where she's going with this. Already, I am feeling sucked in, asphyxiated. I want to say, *It has* nothing *to do with me*. Mother and I have made our truce if not our peace. Rain has started to beat against the dining-room windows. I wonder if Philip will cut his sail short. "Okay, okay," I say, backing against the wall of initialed heights. "I'll see the doctor."

My sister reaches forward, lays her hand on my head. It is as if she is giving me a blessing, but I'm sure she's only measuring me.

A half a day, and I've avoided the nursery. There's no reason to go back there other than my therapist's suggestion that it may be (A) edifying and/or (B) cathartic. Dr. Anke, dispeller of bogeymen and tainted memories. She asks relentless questions about my parents. She makes me go into rooms I would dearly prefer to avoid.

In the Lantern Room, I turn on the faucet. Most of the bedrooms have their own sinks from the days when water closets were sequestered, and bathtubs had their own cells. In houses like these, plumbing was an afterthought. The faucet sputters and burps, coughs out a liquid that is insidiously brown. I let it run for a while, waiting for the cold, rich stream of hard water to erupt from its artesian source.

When it runs clear, I splash some on my face. I've learned to control my panic attacks. *Breathe,* Dr. Anke told me. *In and out.* I can walk through the bathroom to get to the nursery, or go down the hall and enter it from the west. Two doors—one in, one out. Like breaths.

There is a buzzing in my ears. If only I'd adjusted that baby monitor. I envision the crib. I breathe.

D r. Mead has been tending my mother since the year before she had her stroke. Dr. Mead is the only one other than Miriam who, as far as I can tell, talks straight to her. Two years ago, Mother had gone over to the hospital in Chibawassee for some complaint—plaque in the eyes, a slight blurring of vision—and lucked into Dr. Mead moonlighting in the ER. Dr. Mead had checked my mother's vitals, moved a pin light around her eyes, examined her skin for bruising.

How much do you drink, Evelyn? Dr. Mead had inquired, yanking her stethoscope out of her ears.

Oh, my mother had said airily, *a couple of cocktails around dinner.*

Your liver's enlarged. You don't get that kind of liver without knocking back a lot of booze. And you have emphysema. You're going to stroke, Evelyn, if you don't cut this out.

Dana, who had accompanied our mother to the doctor, braced herself for one of Mother's withering responses that she gave to taxi drivers or hairdressers when they were too familiar. But my mother's nose crinkled conspiratorially as if she and Dr. Mead were sharing some delicious joke, and after that, she and Dr. Mead were friends.

It wasn't Dr. Mead, however, who was scoping my mother's carotid at Cedar-Sinai last fall when she threw the clot to her brain. They knew instantly my mother was stroking. First she vomited; then her hand went rigid. The operating room filled with people trying to revive her, to keep her heart beating, her blood flowing. When she finally came to, her mouth drooped and she could not speak.

The doctors went on to fill her with anticoagulants and antispasmodics and antidepressants and antibiotics whenever she ran a fever. She won't have a year, they told Dana, so when June came, Philip and my sister brought her back to Sand Isle via private jet loaned by a friend.

Now we are sitting at the kitchen table with Dr. Mead. I have risen twice to refill our coffees, offered butter cookies from a flowered tin.

"She refuses to move," Dana explains to Dr. Mead. I notice that Dr. Mead is about my age, but she seems older. She certainly has a more attractive hairdo, her hair swept up from her face like that. "And," Dana adds, her voice pinched with disgust, "Miriam is giving her vodka in the Ensure."

"Very practical," I say.

My sister shoots me a look. At the very least, given my own history, Dana feels I should exhibit at least a modicum of outrage concerning our mother's alcohol intake. But what can I tell her? That I might do exactly the same, given the circumstances?

"Under the circumstances," says Dr. Mead, "I don't see that as a problem."

I try not to smile, although I feel vindicated and even further allied with Dr. Mead. Dana, who has never so much as taken a hit off a joint, done a line of coke, or had a major hangover, doesn't quite understand the exquisite pleasure of leaving one's body. But I know. I know it as my mother knows it.

"These doctors in California," says Dr. Mead, leaning in toward the two of us. "What's with all these meds?" I had noticed Dr. Mead picking up all the little orange containers on my mother's bedside table, reading their contents. "Anti*depressants?*" she says.

"Well," says Dana, "she's depressed."

"Of *course* she's depressed," snaps Dr. Mead.

"Agoraphobic, too," I say, avoiding Dana's eyes. *What would you know about Mother?* she could say. *You've been AWOL yourself.*

"Well then, maybe these drugs would have done her some good ten years ago." Dr. Mead shakes her head. "Now they're just dragging out a process that can't be pleasant for anyone. Least of all, your mother. Your mother"— she beats us down with eyes that have seen it all— "just wants to die."

I have decided Dr. Mead is the sanest person I have ever met. Her candor is like a drink of springwater. I want to ask where she buys her clothes. She looks neither resort-y nor JCPenney-ish, which are about the only choices in this area. She resembles a sister of mercy. But just as I am about to ask her what we ought to do, Philip pushes through the kitchen door.

"Hey," Dana says to her husband in an unnaturally cheerful voice. "We're talking about Mom's meds."

Philip pulls off his hat. Either he has gotten caught in the rain or is sweaty with humidity because his wildly curly hair is plastered to the top of his head. There is a priestly quality to Philip having to do with his black-Irish genes—a whiff of Erin go bragh and *Father forgive me*. "Maddie," he says, nodding as if he just saw me last week. "Good trip?"

Before I can answer, he turns to Dr. Mead. I expect him to firmly request a change in the treatment, to say with pastoral conviction that something should be done, that this whole sorry mess was because of doctors in the first place. Instead, he says, "Enough's enough, don't you think?"

Philip rarely speaks without careful consideration of his words. Words, like money, should be sparingly allotted rather than spent, lest they become as unruly as his nemesis hair.

Dr. Mead brings her coffee to her lips, sips it daintily. "It's *your* decision," she says, looking at each of us. "Yours and Evelyn's."

Flinching at the implication, I back-paddle frantically. "It's just that I'm not going to be here in Sand Isle very long, Dr. Mead."

"No?" she says to me, her eyebrows heading north in a familiar way that gives me the willies. "You might want to reconsider that."

The alliance I formed with Dr. Mead evaporates like the steam from her coffee. It is my sister's turn to suppress a smile.

Our porch sits high in the trees. Maples, mostly. An occasional curly-leafed oak. Below, the hill falls away to the beach—a sandy dune anchored by Virginia creeper, poison ivy, and blackberries. Mixed in are the sunflowers and lilies and black-eyed Susans our great-grandmother once planted, attempting a garden down to the beach. That's when there were three gardeners to tend it, cutting back the overgrowth, trimming the trees, repairing the boards in the walk that switchbacked to the shore.

Dana has been in a foul mood for the last hour because the cook she has hired called to say she won't be available, that there is a family illness. "A better offer, more like it," Dana says. These days, we have only the yardman who sweeps, and the flowers and boardwalk have all but disappeared.

"We should trim those trees," Philip says.

"Amen," I say.

"And what will that cost?" says Dana.

But I agree with Philip. The view is the most spectacular feature of this house. You can see the whole bay, the lights of Chibawassee, and to the right, the open lake—a glacier-carved gash of blue in the middle of the industrial wasteland and cornfields of the Midwest.

"So," I say, "shall we tell Mother?"

We are all three sitting in rocking chairs, staring at the lake in a perfect line as if we are onstage, looking back at the audience. It's five in the afternoon. Mother, as usual, is sleeping. In years past, this would be her cocktail hour. She would have napped from three to five, risen and made a drink, started to get dressed for the evening. Now the naps merge into other naps, semiconsciousness into sleep.

Philip takes a long, contemplative sip of beer, but says nothing. Dana shifts her weight. She is uncomfortable with the notion of taking our mother off all medication except painkillers. It is unclear to me if it's religious conviction or that she doesn't want to let Mother go. Dana converted to Catholicism when she married Philip, and though I don't think of her as fervent, she seems to express more zeal than Philip, who describes himself as lapsed.

"You want her to go on like this, Dane?" I say. "What kind of life is this? Lying up there like that, having everything done for her. It's one thing when you're a baby and you're cute, but this is a horror story—"

"Oh, thank you very much," says Dana, interrupting me. "Thank you for explaining to me just how awful the situation is, and how ghastly Mom's life is, and what it takes to care for her and do the things that have to be done, and resist the urge to put her down like a dog."

I take a long, calming breath. "Fine, fine, fine." I do not want to argue with her—not really. Besides, Dana's righteousness always trumps mine. She is the designated repository of virtue in this house, the good daughter who stayed home. I, on the other hand, left years ago, and thus saved my life. Were Dana any less virtuous, any less responsible, it would not have been possible for me to do so. This I know—not because of any personal insight on my part, but because it was pointed out to me by my therapist, Dr. Anke.

"Besides," I say, "it's not as though we're pulling the plug. Just no more heroic efforts. It's what she wants."

Philip clears his throat. "Will she get plenty of morphine?"

I can never be sure what Philip's position is on any of our family. Does he regard my mother as a burden? Me as an annoyance? The cousins he endures every summer the way he endures inclement weather on the lake. Yet I believe that, lapsed or not, his concern about my mother is sincere, that his musings about morphine aren't malevolent in any way.

"Who's going to tell the cousins?" Dana says.

The cousins. I have purposefully avoided asking who's coming and when, as if my lack of interest renders more probable my exiting sooner rather than later. "I think we should tell Mother first."

We all three start to rock in unison. It is late afternoon, and no one has done anything about dinner. Miriam is upstairs tending Mother. No one else is going to help us. There are some eggs in the refrigerator and a wilted head of lettuce. My offer to make scrambled eggs and salad is gratefully accepted by my sister and brother-in-law.

"I'll go to the market tomorrow," I say.

"I'll try to find another cook," says Dana.

"Forget it, Dane. We'll do it ourselves. We'll make a list about who does the shopping, the cooking, the cleanup," I say to Dana as the sunset bleeds out. "Charts. Matrices," I add with a flourish. "A whole organizational system of labor rotation."

Philip slaps a mosquito and eyes me warily, gauging the distance between sarcasm and sincerity.

My sister's eyebrow rises again. Dana can practically conduct a symphony with her eyebrows alone. "Adele?" she says.

"Depending on the incarnation," I say, holding up my hand like the open palm of Buddha, "even her."

. . .

I 'm staying," I say to Ian in the phone at the foot of the stairs.
"I knew this would happen," he says. "I knew it."

His voice burbles for a moment, as if he is underwater. Then I hear
honking and sirens in some far-off place—discordant in contrast to the
rustling leaves, the trilling bells on the horses of Sand Isle.

"Where are you?" I say.

"Forty-fourth and Madison." More honking, and I hear Ian say "sorry"
to someone, not me. He might as well have said Forty-fourth and Jupiter.
"So let's clarify this point. You get there. In about two minutes, you're
climbing the walls. You can't breathe. You can't think. And now everything's cool?"

I drop my voice. "Dana needs me. And we're taking Mom off the blood-
pressure medicine. The Coumadin. Everything."

There is a long, static-y pause at the other end, and I wonder if we've
lost the signal. Finally, Ian says, "You're letting her go? Just like that?"

But Ian should know all about letting go. *Let go and let God.* How many
times had we heard it at AA meetings—the sanctimonious if correct response to our shared frustration about the inability to control our lives? Ian
calls his higher power Betty. *Let go and let Betty,* he says.

"Yeah."

"This makes me very, very uncomfortable."

"You?" I'm indignant. "She's not *your* mother." But having listened to
me describe them in detail over the years, Ian has always felt proprietary
about my family.

"Maddie," he says, "this makes me very sad."

And I realize that's what I've been trying to get to. The sadness of it all.
My father is dead, and my mother is dying, and none of this is going to last.
All the clichés like *This Too Shall Pass* really are true, and I hate it, because
it means the good as well as the bad. You have to feel it, and I never wanted
to, none of us did, anything but that. So here's Ian, a thousand miles away,

on the way to pick up his corned-beef-and-rye. I can see him now. His Adam's apple going up and down, his pale Lutheran hair thinning, his narrow shoulders stoically immune to any attempt at getting buff. He is dodging someone on the sidewalk, graceful as a dancer in the coursing midtown river, a universe away, but essentially here and with me in this gloomy, old dining room, explaining to me the best he can that my mother's death evokes sorrow.

"Thank you, Ian," I say as I hang up the phone.

THREE

As I unload bags of groceries onto the kitchen counter, Dana tells me who is coming and when. On the wall in front of me is my cousin Derek's drawing of Louisa, childhood nurse and guru of the kitchen, long dead, sorely missed. I make a note to construct a little shrine to Louisa before the cousins arrive, something involving chocolate chips and butter. I have gone to the IGA grocery, where I have found and chosen to ignore plastic-wrapped produce as withered as the lettuce in our refrigerator. Instead, I have loaded up on toilet paper and cereal, six-packs of Ensure, and the strawberry-flavored Snapple that Miriam drinks, bottle after bottle, saying, *Sweet Jesus. This weather.*

Jessica's coming tomorrow, Dana tells me. In her voice, I hear resignation, trepidation, even longing. I want to ask about Jessica's current state of mind and if the two of them are talking again. Instead, I ask about Adele, object of Ian's fascination. Older than I by ten years, Adele—the most beautiful of the cousins—married young and frequently.

"Open-ended," says Dana, telling me that Adele's current incarnation doesn't allow for making plans.

"What about Sedgie?"

"Maybe. Maybe not."

Sedgie has had a tenuous career in the theater. Now he is going through his second divorce, though this one, like my marriage, hardly counted, so brief was it, so obviously influenced by cocaine and a rebound from the actress he'd lived with for seven years.

"Why didn't he just marry that actress?" I say.

"If he'd married the actress," Dana says evenly, "he'd be on his third divorce."

I stare at the can of Campbell's soup I hold in my hand. "Have you ever read these labels?"

Still, mushroom soup goes with everything, and I'm determined to make this cooking process seamless and not too taxing. Ian calls the Midwest "The Land of Creamy Mushroom and Mayonnaise," and as if to prove his point, I've bought three bags of Ruffles potato chips and dip to match.

"Who else?"

Derek on Wednesday, she tells me, with or without his French wife. I try to focus on the small-print recipe for creamy mushroom chicken thighs. Derek, artist, seer of cousins, translator of truth and beauty, real or imagined, maker of worlds. His name still evokes in me a mixture of giddiness and nausea.

"But Beowulf, for sure," Dana adds, referring to Derek's ostentatiously named son.

It strikes me again how much time is spent at Sand Isle discussing people and their plans—not only those of our family, but the arrivals and departures, the ramifications and nuances of our friends' and neighbors' lives.

As if she is reading my mind, Dana says, "You remember Larry Hobson? He's getting divorced."

I haven't seen Larry Hobson for years. Still, that anybody other than someone from *our* family should get divorced on Sand Isle attracts my keen interest.

"Why?" I ask against my will, not wanting to be drawn back in, but fascinated, nonetheless. "Surely no one's having an affair with Larry *Hobson?*"

Dana shrugs. "His wife is asking for the cottage."

"The Hobsons' *cottage?* She's crazy. It'll never happen."

"Things change," says Dana, ominously. "You wouldn't believe the things that are happening."

"Try me."

"The Dusays, for instance."

The name sounds familiar. "The Midland Dusays?" I say, suggesting a family from downstate whose fortune was made from plundering farmland to erect brightly colored, postmodern shopping malls.

My sister nods. "Richer than God. They've built a huge house. Huge. Tore down the Bakers' place *and* the Hewetts'."

"And built something *new?*"

Nothing new has been erected in Sand Isle since 1890. I'm alarmed it could happen.

"Totally mansionized," says Dana.

"Is it"—I look at her slyly— "tasteful?"

Tasteful is one of our code words. Our aunt Pat taught us this. She would say, "NOCD" for "not our class, dear," or categorize a wedding present of indeterminate description as a "Shovunda"—meaning it should be "shoved under" a bed. She could assess decor with a beady eye and dismiss someone's efforts by saying, *Lovely drapes.*

"Jamie's here," Dana says. She says it as casually as she would have said, *Mail's here,* but I am not deceived. It is her way of testing the water, using her toe before jumping in.

"Well," I say, using my own forced version of a casual tone, "why wouldn't he be?" Jamie's family, after all, has been here almost as long as ours. Jamie of the colorless hair and chiseled face. "Still married?"

"Still is."

"Two kids, is it?"

"Three."

I silently ponder the tastefulness of having three children.

"Philip says everything's changing," Dana goes on.

Snapping the last of the paper bags shut and flattening it out, I remember Louisa once saying, *Oh, nothing much changes around here.*

Dana picks forensically at the edge of the kitchen table where the swirly blue veneer has started to lift and curl. "We should probably do something about this linoleum."

I think, *Oh, please don't start with the fixing up.* It's been peeling for decades. No one has bothered to replace it. Although we have our inheritance, it is not so huge that we might want to fling it away on dry rot and cracked linoleum. And there is a generalized family aversion to gainful employment. Certainly no one has gone into the family business for generations. Addison & Sons has as little to do with us as the Scottish town from which our ancestors came. All we have is this name—like petrified wood, stone hard and calcified, long after the wood has rotted.

B y midafternoon, I have dusted and swept the living room, the dining room, the porch, as well as the deck. I've pulled my hair straight back and dug up an apron my mother gave Louisa, KISS THE COOK emblazoned on the front. *Don't even try,* Louisa used to say, waving us away, dodging our lips, but she rarely took that apron off.

The kitchen seems beyond my capabilities, so I have moved on to the downstairs bedrooms. In point of fact, I have little aptitude for this work. I have gleaned what skill I have from watching housekeepers over the years or by Ian explaining to me about working top down. *Ceiling to floor. Dust first, sweep last.*

When my grandmother was alive, I shadowed the housekeeper as she cleaned, carried along by the smell of lemon oil and beeswax. Did I, like most children, think that my world would always smell the same? A stock simmering in the kitchen, the smell of biscuits. After my grandmother died, the men started smoking cigars. It thrills me still to pick up that scent evoking afternoons when the ladies were napping and the children were left alone.

At night, the heady perfume of my mother and the aunts, the talcum of my grandmother. Even today, the smell of mildew, like that of bourbon, is as viscerally charged as one of baking popovers or chocolate cake.

I move on to the Love Nest, so called after my cousin Adele and her first husband, Stephen, took the guest room off the living room—a peculiar choice since the walls were thin, and anyone staying up for bridge or Parcheesi could hear the little groans behind the door. I run my duster across a bureau, one that has been painted so many times the drawers can be opened only by bracing one's legs and tugging hard. Every surface is cluttered with a potential yard sale of knickknacks. Crocheted doilies anchored by porcelain boxes and figurines. Ashtrays and ivory brush sets, tattooed with unreadable monograms.

On the desk by the window I find a box with decoupaged lid—a relic of my mother's efforts in summers past. A large letter A from a children's book (two elves dancing cheek to cheek) is glued to the center, around which ladybugs and mushrooms, butterflies and pixies are arranged in an artful composition. *You have to cut the paper like so,* my mother said when I expressed an interest, showing me how to hold the scissors at an angle in such a way as to shear a perfect edge. Each leaf, each lock of hair had to be precisely separated from the background so that it could be lifted, glued into place, and varnished over. Once, I saw my mother cry after the scissors slipped and the wing of a butterfly she'd been working on for half an hour fell to the floor.

Lifting the lid, I find postcards and newspaper clippings along with parchment-fine stationery with a faded scrawl. I pick up one of the letters.

Dearest Sarah, the ancestral cursive begins in a correspondence from my great-grandmother to a friend. *Let me tell you about the house.*

I sit on the edge of the mattress—a saggy invertebrate that barely holds me.

We placed the schooner you shipped from England upon the mantelpiece.
The boys are delighted with the rigging lines and the tiny ship lantern, but
I fear they shall break them in their zeal.

I remember that ship in a forlorn heap, my mother's efforts in the sixties at "brightening."

We are going to call the cottage "The Aerie," sitting as it does high up on the bluff over the beach. We are surrounded by dunes and a clutch of oaks out of which I can carve a cutting garden. Lilies and Passion Roses. Bachelors' Buttons and Cosmos. Edward is having a wooden walkway built down to the beach so that we can comb for rocks. Your Clarence would be amazed to see the Devonian fossils, and could certainly hold forth on the fauna of the Pleistocene. Edward promises to teach me how to use the canoe. And, Sarah, did I tell you we have a piano?

When Dana finds me, I have curled into the bed, pulled the covers up. The feather duster lies beside me like the carcass of a bird. "What are you doing?" she asks.

I run my finger across the final paragraph in my great-grandmother's hand in which she describes how they went into the woods and dug up trillium to plant along the edges of the house. She herself had planted the garden that overlooks the lake, plotting out sunflowers and hollyhocks, bushes of lilacs, summer roses, lilies, and yarrow. She signed her letters *As always, Sadie.*

Sadie. The name of my child.

"The telephone," I say, "is truly a mixed blessing."

"What do you mean?"

I hold up the sheet of stationery. "This is from Grannie Addie to her friend Sarah. You and I would have had this conversation on the phone, and then . . . pffft . . . no one would know or care."

Dana's sideways glance. I can tell she is thinking, Why would anyone care what we said in the first place? So I read to her the piece about the schooner and the curtains and the trillium, and soon she is lying on the bed next to me on the swaybacked mattress while I read aloud the words of our ancestor. It was a forest then. No manicured lawns. The beach was a rocky, wild place from which they would launch canoes, the women in their long dresses with their parasols, the men mustached and grim, their shirtsleeves pulled up for their two-month hiatus from industry.

"Her baby died," Dana says after I stop reading. "Banta's little sister. She got scarlet fever and died."

I know this—our grandfather's sister who died as an infant, the insidious infections that haunted the country in the late nineteenth century, how my great-uncle, too, had almost died, yet lived, never to have children, but to ride through Turkey on a camel. Our grandfather was sent away to someplace less septic, and when he returned, his sister was dead, his brother living, his mother dressed in the black rags of grief. I have known this, but forgotten, or at least not thought about it for years. Perhaps I've blocked out the dead infants in our family, the legendary bereavement of my great-grandmother.

The Aerie, my great-grandmother wrote in 1887, *shall be a place of respite. When you come, dearest*, she penned her friend Sarah, *we will sit in the trees and paint whatever vista suits us. At night, we shall read poetry.*

Poetry, painting, and prayer. My great-grandparents came to Sand Isle with the best of intentions. Their fortune had been made—first by a cough remedy, later by sops and cures for headaches and lice, bad breath and sore throats, constipation, arthritic fingers, and aching teeth. My great-great-grandfather Josiah—Civil War soldier, repairer of roofs—was the embodiment of the philosophy that it's better to be lucky than smart. The pine tar of his trade had a number of attributes, not the least of which was its medicinal value when combined with peppermint. Later, his son—my great-grandfather—imported eucalyptus from California, where it had been imported from Australia, apocryphally for railroad ties, but more than likely to prevent erosion on denuded hills. Structural lack of integrity aside, eucalyptus proved effective when its vapors were inhaled.

In 1875, Addison's Curatives, as it was then called, employed Dr. Reginald Sedgwick, an English physician who had traveled to India and Turkey, returning with an antidote for constipation involving almonds, fenugreek, and caffeine, along with a cure for postbellum malaise using mustard and, as with many Addison products, alcohol.

My great-grandfather Edward succeeded in his courtship of Sadie Boothe (later to become Grannie Addie), a missionary's daughter from Dayton who was prone to musings about the occult—particularly after the death of her daughter, Elizabeth. I can imagine my great-grandfather in 1880: Edward Moore Addison, son of a particularly prosperous maker of remedies, dressed in a waistcoat at a Sunday picnic along the banks of the Ohio—a river that curved through the limestone bluffs of southern Ohio and northern Kentucky, freezing chastely in winter and turning turgid in the spring as the runoff from rain and snow leached into the Ohio River Valley. By summer, the river was a slow brown snake, steamy and sultry, laden with catfish and water moccasins, not to mention garbage from the factories that were growing up along its shores. The condensed air of the valley, the clammy evaporation of the river—all conspired to render the humidity nearly one hundred percent, and the air so cloying, it bound clothes to skin, curled your hair, and made it hard to breathe.

Especially with a corset and three layers of petticoats.

Hand me your handkerchief, Father. I am feeling faint.

Or giddy? Had she noticed my great-grandfather—a fine example of Presbyterian righteousness (prone to stuttering, but attractive nonetheless with those deep green eyes, that finely cut coat that he insisted on wearing even in that heat)? If she'd looked closer, she might have noticed that, fine fellow though he was, he'd had a sip or two—discreetly, of course—of Kentucky bourbon. Her father, the traveling missionary from Dayton, a hero in his own right having lost an eye at Gettysburg, saw the opportunity in the piety and tipsiness of young Edward. A pragmatist—my great-great-grandfather, the missionary, who crawled off the fields of Gettysburg with one eye intact and all of his limbs. Crossing with similar resolve the sea of checkered clothes and now-folded parasols and newly lit lanterns, he presented his handsome but introverted daughter who read too much and lived in a world of her imaginings to the minister of the Cincinnati First Presbyterian Church, who in turn presented her to my great-grandfather. The introduction thus made, the tantalizing blink of aroused fireflies began in the dusky Ohio sky.

Miss Boothe?

Mr. Addison?

Fade in to a shot of my great-grandfather with his mustaches, my great-grandmother with her center-parted hair, their expressions dour in the daguerreotypes that hang on our walls. The spring before my grandfather was born, construction began on the Aerie. My great-grandmother's letters from those days wax hopeful about the prospect of shared poetry and piousness—a gentile reprieve from the manufacturing and marketing of medicines. Besides, no one could *breathe* in those industrial river valleys with their sweaty summers. Sand Isle was parceled off and sold to a covey of like-minded people whose social, moral, and spiritual values were aligned. At which point, my great-grandfather, if he harbored any notions of bourbon before bed, was sorely disappointed. The bylaws of the association read that no alcohol was to be served on the premises of Sand Isle, a rule that remained until 1945 (Addison's Cough Medicine excluded). Thus alcohol went underground. It was hidden in log piles, in the Bible holders of wicker chairs, behind the curtains, beneath the mattresses; it was smuggled by train and ferry. In 1896, a renter was barred from future rentals by the board of directors after openly serving wine at supper.

So, too, were fishing and the playing of games on Sunday prohibited. As for swimming, "suitable attire" was required between the hours of 6 A.M. and 9 P.M., leaving one to assume that after 9 P.M., these Presbyterian paragons could, with impunity, cast off their clothes and swim flagrantly in their birthday suits beneath the cover of darkness.

Even in my moviemaking imagination, I find it challenging to envision my great-grandmother cavorting nakedly. In every picture—even those on the beach—Grannie Addie is fully skirted, her collars starched, her hair done up, a little hat perched jauntily beneath a parasol. The remains of these outfits are now costumes in a box. The last time Sedgie opened a parasol, it exploded in a puff of dust and rotted silk.

But back to Sadie and Edward and the construction of the Aerie. Fast-forward the men reshaping the dune with shovels and plows, the carpenters laying a foundation on the stumps of felled trees. Up goes the house in a matter of seconds—studs, bead-board, shingles, shiplap, more shingles, and the obligatory garlands above the windows. The house is painted a sober green, and—behold!—my great-grandparents, along with their first son and my infant grandfather, waving from the porch.

According to Grannie Addie's letters, the house originally had no kitchen. All meals were to be taken communally at the clubhouse—what was later to become the yacht club. Neither was there any plumbing; thus, the Byzantine pipes that came later. And it wasn't until 1900, after the kitchen was built, that Sadie Addison started writing down her recipes for tripe and tongue. By then, she had lost a daughter and, allegedly, her mind. Infections of the time killed more than a third of American children before their fifth birthdays. Statistically, Sadie and Edward's family was right on the money. One child out of three succumbed.

H ospice has come to show us how to help our mother die. Two mild-faced women at the door. They remind me of Mormons. I resist the urge to open the door and say in a Lurch-like voice, *You rang?*

Dana and I invite them into the living room. They are winded from the stairs. *So many stairs,* they say. *How do you sweep them all?*

"We don't," I say, pouring tea.

Dana beams the two women an earnest smile. Perhaps *they* hold the possibility of a solution. "Our mother," she begins. The two women lean forward. "She hardly eats. Ice cream, vodka. I try to get her to talk to me, but she won't."

One of the women purses her lips, reminding me of my current shrink, the eternally patient Dr. Anke. Dr. Anke nods in response to all my rants of victimization. She eggs me on. *Your mother,* she says. *Why was your mother always napping?*

Dr. Anke is my third therapist. The first two were abysmal failures—more my fault than theirs. I wasn't even sober. I moved back to New York and, within a year, got into a program. When I got out of treatment, the hospital referred me to Dr. Anke. I liked her name. It was like the Egyptian sign for life.

Are you Egyptian? I asked her.

Swedish, actually. She had long, blond hair swept back in a ponytail. She wore glasses to make herself look older, but she was smarter than her age. Together, Dr. Anke and I have mapped out the terrain of maternal pathos—a long-forgotten garden choked in weeds. *Why was your mother not supportive?* With pruning shears, we've attacked my mother's drinking, the way she took to her bed. Hack, hack. We pulled back wayward ivy and thorny stems. *Do you think your mother was happy with the choices she made in her life?* Hack, hack, hack. *What do you think she would have done differently?*

The first time she asked me this question, I considered it carefully. I even stroked my chin. But Dr. Anke's eyes bore into mine until I finally said, *My mother's choices were limited to marriage and children, and after we were grown, what? Garden club and bridge? Martinis at lunch?*

I then added what I already believed to be true: that my mother simply lacked interest.

That's very sad, Dr. Anke had said.

"It's very sad," one of the women from hospice says in response to Dana. "But death is a natural part of life. Without death, life would have no meaning."

I want to dispute her on this point. What about work? The meaning of friends? But her statement carries the finality of one of my mother's needlepoint sayings.

"It's all about contrasts," the other woman says. "Letting go. It's quite beautiful, really."

Let go and let Betty.

Dana says, "So you think you can help her?"

"Normally, we work with people who are terminally ill with cancer. But in this case . . . because she *is* terminal, according to Dr. Mead . . . we can help you cope. At least, we can tell you what to expect."

One of the women begins to hand out brochures. These, she tells us, will explain the process of dying. An infection may occur, taxing the lungs. Or, in the case of a stroke, brain capacity shuts down, compromising organs. "The body dies slowly," she says.

I want to tell her she is wrong. The body can die in an instant, that it can be breathing one second in the nursery upstairs, the fontanel pulsing with life, and in the next moment, cease to breathe. Simply stop.

"Ultimately," the hospice woman goes on, apparently having read my mind, "the breathing simply stops."

I look at the woman sharply. She is older than I, maybe fifty. Her hair is gray, while her friend has dyed hers assertively red. The gray-haired one keeps putting on her reading glasses as she cites passages in the brochure, then taking off her glasses and staring at Dana and me. She earnestly wants us to get it. She is an interpreter of death. Like my father's secretary, when I turned twenty-one, laying before me spreadsheets and columns, interpreting the numbers of what my grandmother had left me, making sure I understood. It meant nothing to me at the time. A number, fixed in ink, nothing plastic that could be reshaped or adapted. A sentence, not a choice.

"So," I say. "How long?"

The two women exchange glances. I have the feeling my question is predictable, unenlightened. And like Dr. Mead, they look at me a little regretfully. If they pat my hand, I'll scream. But they do not touch me. Instead, they say it will happen in time—in the body's time, in Evelyn's time. We will see the changes, though. The subtle blue in the extremities, the irregular breaths, the fixed stare. Things will become very focused. Our world will become small.

Don't tell me about small, I think. Don't tell me about death. I've been there, ladies, and I'm not thrilled to go again. I ignored the baby monitor, and Sadie stopped breathing—and now you're asking me to sit and wait and gauge my mother's breaths as she creeps out of life on her own damn time?

"Well, then," says Dana. "We'll just have to keep her comfortable."

Leaving their brochures spread all over the coffee table, the two women ask to look in on Mrs. Addison.

"Certainly," says Dana, rising.

"Go ahead," I say. "I'll be up in a minute."

After they leave, I pick up a pamphlet, but I can't concentrate. I want to believe my unspoken declaration to Miriam that *I'm not of this place*, but the letters in my grandmother's hand say otherwise. Her letters from the time the house was completed in 1887 up until 1890, the year of Elizabeth's death, are demure examples of Victorian optimism. They never speak of money. They never mention my great-grandfather's surreptitious drinking. They are sunny letters that begin with cozy and familiar wording such as *Let me tell you about the house*.

But in the summer of 1890, after Elizabeth's death, the tone of her correspondence changes. Curling up in a wicker chair, I read the letter she wrote to her father, the one-eyed Presbyterian:

Weeks have passed, and though the weight is still heavy in my chest, I have taken your words of comfort to heart. Indeed, as you say, God sends children to cleave us to the world while teaching us not to love too much. In my weaker moments, I wonder why He would expect us to strike so precarious a balance. Perhaps the measure of our lives rests on such a fulcrum. That He loves her as we do, I have no doubt, and possibly she was spared a greater unhappiness by avoiding the burdens of adulthood. Yet I shall always wonder who she would have been. So, too, shall I miss those dear brown eyes that reflected the world in innocence.

You may tell me not to dwell on these things—that my duty now is to my sons. But please indulge me my despair, for her short life was the bitterest sweetness, longer in my womb than under this too bright sky. I take care not to expose my weakness to my husband, but hopelessness contaminates this house as surely as the fever that went before.

Please keep us in your prayers because, at this moment, I cannot offer mine.

One might think that, with a thirty percent mortality rate, parents of the time would be better braced for the loss of a child. Who would risk becoming fond? The photos I've seen of Elizabeth show a fat-cheeked infant with brown eyes drowning in cascades of ruffles and lace. The tintype in the oval frame on the dining-room wall displays her seated in the lap of my grandfather, my great-uncle looking on. Two weeks later, she started crying, exhibited a rash and a fever and, within three days, was gone. Scarlet fever wasn't an epidemic in 1890, but there were outbreaks. In 1887, each and every one of the children in the village of Harrison, Ohio, perished. Perhaps one of the maids in Cincinnati brought it to Sand Isle. Perhaps another child.

I can imagine my forebear kneeling by nine-month-old Elizabeth's crib—the same crib, perhaps, in which my daughter, Sadie, died. The original Sadie Addison, in her cotton skirts and silk blouse, prayed in the confines of her summerhouse, where she and her husband have planned their Elysium far from the shores of the Ohio River. Surely, the vicissitudes of life—the dank pollution, the rotting, sulfurous air—can't reach them here. The child's cheeks are flushed—not with health, but fever. Elizabeth's eyes glisten, the brown eyes of the child's matching those of my great-grandmother.

There is no poetry left in my hand, she writes. *I am bereaved beyond words*.

Reeling, I return again and again to my great-grandmother's letters until my mind is suddenly on gardens. I start thinking about gathering flowers to put in vases in the cousins' rooms. Surely something can be resurrected from the weeds below the porch. Cornflowers for my niece Jessica. Sunflowers for Sedgie. Black-eyed Susans for Adele. Roses or cosmos for Derek.

I will hack away and excavate them from the overgrowth, the grasses and brambles that have smothered them. From beneath the campanula gone to seed, the opportunistic tendrils of myrtle, I will ferret out the leafy remnants of my great-grandmother's garden, breathe new life into them, finger them for a pulse.

FOUR

"Ready about!" I say as I come around a corner.

My father bought the Malibu station wagon new in 1964, and at one time, its lines must have appeared sleek and modern. Even so, it has less than ten thousand miles on it because it only gets driven in summer—airport runs, the IGA, and, when we were teenagers, long, winding drives out the shore. After I turn the wheel, seconds seem to pass before the rest of the car decides to follow. Like a cartoon limousine, it snakes around curves.

Jessica's plane was due in at 3 P.M., but planes seldom land on time this far north. Some flights are canceled for days. *But the Baileys' cocktail party!* Dana groaned when she heard that Jessica would be delayed for hours. At which point I offered to pick up my niece, relieved for the excuse to dodge my parents' friends whom I haven't seen in more than a decade. Their questions, good-natured and wholehearted, inevitably gloss over their true opinions of my absence.

It is raining, and the wipers barely make a dent. I take back-country roads, coasting past farmland and orchards separated by islands of deciduous woods. When I finally arrive at the airport—a cinderblock building and an asphalt strip in what would otherwise be a pasture—the rain has lifted, and my hair is curly with the humidity. I could spend hundreds of dollars in New York to get this look. The downside of all this humidity is the perspiration on my forehead, the little pimple forming next to my brow. Nearly forty, and I still break out.

I get out of the car and search the sky, blooming with thunderheads, for Jessica's plane. Pulling my mildewed foul-weather gear tight, I lean against the door—anything but go inside, where stubble-chinned teenage boys play Doom or Mortal Kombat in a haze of greasy hamburgers.

"Maddie?"

A figure is coming toward me, calling my name. I push back my hair and squint into the wind.

"Jamie," I say. "Wow." My old boyfriend, whom I haven't seen in twelve years, still looks the same. I, on the other hand, have frizzy hair and a zit.

We awkwardly kiss at each other's cheeks. It seems a perverse gesture for two people who have once been so intimate. Jamie has a Burberry raincoat slung over his shoulder and a briefcase, and his hair is slicked back, which, in my opinion, looks a little eighties, yet on Jamie, undeniably attractive. No gray in his blond. Darkly tanned. I smile inanely and try to expunge the image I have of him in my college dorm room, completely naked, his bath towel dangling from his erection like the white flag of surrender. The last I'd heard he'd become president of his family's company. They'd made their money in plastic garbage bags, later expanding into a wider panoply: bags that zipped together, bags that withstood heat, bags that burped.

Thank God for trash and leftovers, I used to say to him, but the forty-four-year-old man standing before me looks humorless compared to the boy of my college memories, and I doubt the old joke would amuse him.

"I didn't know the flight was in," I say, noticing he still has that mole on his cheek. "I'm waiting for my niece."

Jamie scans the sky. "North-worst," he says. "They're always late."

I used to wish Jamie and I had met for the first time when we were in our thirties instead of when we were kids. If only we'd done some living prior to meeting each other, our timing would have been perfect. But looking at him now, I suspect I was wrong. My life is leagues away from Jamie's—like sailboats whose courses diverge by one degree and end up on separate continents. The last time I laid eyes on Jamie, it was from a distance. He was standing on a dock. He had slicked his hair straight back from his face, and was running his hands over it, back arched, his elbows splayed. It was an exquisite gesture—something out of F. Scott Fitzgerald or a Brylcreem ad. I felt I was seeing him through water, like a face on a boat you see as you slip below the surface and sink.

"You heading out, then?" I ask him.

"Just got in," he says, jerking his head toward the tarmac where the private planes are parked. There used to be a line of single-engine prop planes, the occasional twin engine. Now there is a fleet of Learjets and Gulf Streams, one of which appears to be Jamie's. Ever so faintly, I hear Aunt Pat's voice saying, *You didn't try hard enough.*

Jamie cocks his head. "Haven't seen you around here for a while. Why the honor?"

Eleven years exactly. "My mother."

"I'm sorry."

"Well, you know," I go on, doing something spastic with my hands, "Dana's here. The cousins are arriving. The typical scene."

Jamie smiles. Again, I have that sensation of being submerged. For the first time, I notice his teeth are unnaturally white. His eyes I can't read.

"It's a great family," he says.

I fail to suppress a hiccup-y sort of laugh. I can't tell if I'm nervous or merely incredulous. "A great family," I repeat, looking away. "That's for sure."

"And you?"

"Oh, I'm great, too."

"I mean, where are you living?"

"New York. For years now."

He nods, and I see a flicker of that wounded, wary look he used to give me. "Well, then."

"Yeah," I say, giving him a little wave. He turns and walks away. Remembering my manners, I call after him, "Say hi to . . ."

He turns back, a questioning look on his face. "Fiona," he finishes for me.

"Yes," I say. "Fiona. Give her my best."

But the plane drowns out the last of my sentence, and I start toward the cinderblock building. "Jerk," I mutter under my breath, more to myself than Jamie.

J essica, her hair shorn and bleached stark white against her olive skin, tosses her duffel bag into the back of the Malibu.

"Nice tattoo," I say, noticing the newest pattern encircling her wrist.

Jessica beams, ignoring my sarcasm. "It's Celtic."

"That's appropriate," I say, mentioning that the Addisons are Scots-Irish from way back.

But Jessica looks about as Scottish or Irish as Miss Saigon. Half-Vietnamese, half-Caucasian, she was given up for adoption as an infant. Dana and Philip, who had tried for several years to have a child before being told they couldn't, seized the opportunity in spite of our mother's dubious response to Jessica's Asian roots. *It's not that she's Oriental,* our mother had said. *I just worry she might not fit in.* Given that our mother was ostracized for having red nails and being from Missouri, she felt qualified to speak on the subject. But disparity in bloodlines notwithstanding, Jessica and I have a bond. Her wary dark eyes are not unlike my gray ones at her age.

She slams the door, and we drive off, Jessica cracking the window, lighting up a cigarette.

I cast a sideways look. "Yes, I *do* mind if you smoke."

Jessica rolls her eyes, draws once more on the cigarette, and flicks it out the window. The stark white of her current hairdo replaces the sinister burnt orange of last fall.

"Great," I say. "Start a fire."

She sticks out her tongue where a gold stud is planted like a pea. "Thanks, Mom."

Jessica was the most enchanting and squeezable of babies. Whenever I was in Pasadena, I'd rush to see her, watching her progress from black-haired toddler to sure-footed soccer star, her serious brown eyes beneath blunt cut bangs. Then came high school.

"Kick the Ecstasy habit?" I say, trying another angle, but the look on my niece's face says, *Don't.* Sullen and closemouthed on the subject, she turns away from me and looks out the window at an orchard speeding past.

I release the steering wheel and hold my hands up. "Scout's honor. Our secret."

Now she's in college. According to Dana, she rarely calls home.

Jessica shakes her head and changes the subject. "You haven't told me who's coming."

So I begin the litany: the ambiguous arrival of Adele, as well as the questionable status of Sedgie, whose grown kids are employed and, thus, have limited time to travel.

"*Real* jobs," I say to Jessica, with a meaningful look. Derek's wife, Yvonne, is climbing Mount Kilimanjaro, but Derek, who has flown in from Paris, is due in this week along with Beowulf. "They're driving."

"Beowulf," says Jessica wistfully. "And you think *I'm* the drug addict?"

It's almost seven now, an escaping bit of evening sun casting a sharp blade across a cornfield. We push on. The State Road turns into the Lake Road, and we descend into Harbor Town and, finally, to Sand Isle. I park the car in our spot, and Jessica loads her duffel into the ferry that is waiting at the dock. The ferry driver—the one who called me "ma'am" the other night—unties the lines, pushes off. He glances at my niece, but says nothing. His radio is turned off tonight. "Ma'am," he says again, but I don't mind.

"What's your name?" I ask the driver.

"Mac."

"Do you carry a gun, Mac?" I say, indicating his guard's uniform. His eyes flicker briefly—long enough for me to believe he does. I exhale, close my eyes, think of Jamie with his jet and his Burberry coat. The channel is patterned with the reflections of clouds and smells of gasoline and fish. Reaching the other side, Mac helps us onto the dock.

S edgie has called to say he will be getting in late. He is driving from upstate New York, where he'd partied with the cast after the close of their Sondheim review, and now he's somewhere northwest of Lake Erie, concerned that his car might break down, seeing that there's no Citroën mechanics in Canada, but I point out he's not far from Quebec, and surely there must be someone.

"Your geography sucks," he says.

"So when are you getting here?"

"Days. Weeks. What room do I have?"

I remember how he used to call dibs for sleeping in the bunkroom and needed to keep the bathroom light turned on. When he was a kid, he had freckles like red ants swarming on pale skin and was the first to run screaming if a bat flew down from the attic. Now he walks onstage in front of hundreds of people, invisible behind the footlights, exorcising his fears by becoming someone else.

"The Anchor Room," I say, naming a room that used to have anchors on the curtains and bedspreads until Aunt Pat replaced them with now-faded chintz.

"Not the Love Nest?"

"Taken."

"By?"

"Derek's coming tomorrow."

"Derek, Derek, Derek."

I wait for Sedgie to ask about my mother, but he doesn't. Mostly, Sedgie thinks about himself, which is why he's driving alone in a Citroën across Canada.

"So, babe," he says, "stick some Stoli in the freezer, and I'll see you in the—" His cell phone cuts out before I can tell him we'll leave the wagon at the ferry and not to wake us.

Dana and I finish picking up the kitchen, tossing the plastic containers from the take-out burgers and fries. There is something sad and despairing about such a meal in a kitchen that used to turn out standing rib roasts and beef Wellingtons. Even Jessica commented on the dinner, saying it was pathetic and she could do better. *Great*, said Philip, *why don't you?*

Dana, Philip, and I are bone-tired from that day's errands and chores. The boats had to be inventoried, dragged down to the beach. Canoes, the sailfish, some obsolete Windsurfers. Even the blunt-nosed rowboat that always sinks stakes a claim on the shore.

And then there are the linens. Most of the blankets are moth-eaten, the sheets torn and stained. The beach towels are threadbare, and the bath towels, once an upbeat color like coral or cherry, have faded to a bland, fleshy salmon, sandpaper-rough and stiff.

"Really pays to get here first," I say as we tie up the garbage, but Dana flashes me a look that makes me wish I could take it back. I have no cause for complaint. When you disappear for years, you abdicate your right to an opinion.

Furtively, I have read the brochures left by hospice. They tell us how to keep our loved one comfortable. They talk about grief. I turn this pebble of a word over in my mouth. It is a hard thing, rough at the edges, yet small enough to swallow and pass unnoticed through one's gut unless it sticks in your craw. Sometimes I think my grief is stuck so tightly, I will gag on it. But you can't vomit grief. I've tried. I've shoved my finger down my throat or swallowed tequila between retching so that I might retch again.

I've heard it said you don't get over loss, but that grieving shifts when you wake up one morning and it isn't the first thing you think about. When did I wake up and not think of Sadie, first and foremost, the tug on my breast?

I drag the swollen trash bag two stories down to the wood room. It is cool and vaguely insidious, yet comforting with its familiar dank smell.

I open the trash can, shove the bag into its mulchy gut. For a moment, I am transfixed by darkness. I remember hiding here during a Sardines game more than thirty years ago. How long had it been before Dana found me? I was braver then. I relished the dark.

"Maddie? Are you in here?" I jump, turn around. It is Jessica standing in the door. "What are you doing?"

"Trash," I say.

"I thought I'd make a fire," she says, jerking her head toward the woodpile.

I switch on the light. Someone has replaced the old yellow bulb with one of those fluorescent, long-lasting things. It casts us in a faint blue glow, illuminating the wall of stacked logs. Together, we start loading wood into a canvas bag. Jessica's eyes are heavy-lidded, and she seems quieter than usual. "Glad to be here?" I say.

She looks at me, and there's something knowing in her look. We share a moment of mute acknowledgment—that heaven, limbo, and hell, like the center of a compass, are all really the same place, depending on how you look at it.

"I want to ask you something," she says.

"Shoot."

"Did you ever want to have a child?" She looks hard at me.

The moment drags out. Something is pressing against my chest, and I can't make a sound.

"I mean," she adds quickly, "*another* child?"

One by one, the rocks slide off, and I can breathe again. So many years have gone by, twelve months per year.

"I'm almost forty," I say.

And she, only half my age, says, "I'm thinking about it."

I don't even know what question to ask. I am the one she called when she hadn't slept in three days because of the drugs. I am the one she almost—almost—tells the truth to, although she rarely speaks the truth at all. Even this—a notion so ridiculous I can't put words to the possibility—may or may not be true. Ever since she turned fifteen, Jessica has spoken her whims just for the shock value, their impact like a punch to the face. Her own parents are numb from her whims, sometimes acted upon, sometimes not.

"I thought it'd be, you know, cool."

"Cool?" I stare at her incredulously, the word curdling in my mouth. "Do you know what it takes to raise children? Money, for one thing. And patience. And maturity. Oh, and a partner. Have you thought about that?"

A sudden longing for the clear rightness of my father gives way to feeling provincial and stodgy. I can't see Jessica's eyes clearly in the semidarkness, but I can feel her become defensive. "I don't *need* a partner."

I suppose she doesn't. Sometimes a partner is a liability. Sometimes it's better to be on your own. "Easier to get a puppy," I say as I reach for the canvas bag.

The sound of a toilet flushing. It is still dark. Sometimes I wake up like this—between two and four in the morning, flooded with anxiety, too late to take a pill. Dana tells me that it will get worse in my forties, that sometimes she doesn't sleep at all. She worries, she tells me. Constantly. I wonder if soon I, too, will have that hard line between my brows.

Dana never slept well after they adopted Jessica. First there was the crying in the night, the feedings. Then came the night terrors or Jessica's climbing into bed because she was lonely or frightened. And during those few years when Jessica *did* sleep, Dana lay awake, wondering if there would be intruders. Or a fire. Or an earthquake. For the last few years, Jessica has been going to raves, staying out all night. We had all hoped that when Jessica left for college, Dana would sleep, but she lies awake nonetheless, wearing her vigilance like a straitjacket.

Compared to Dana, I sleep like a baby. Me, whose own child stopped breathing for no reason at all. Perhaps I sleep because I find Sadie in my dreams and, for a moment, it comforts me.

I wonder if it was Dana who flushed the toilet. Maybe I should go to her door, whisper her name. I will tell her about my life, make her listen. I will say, *Do you know your twenty-year-old daughter is thinking about having a child?* Dana will become a grandmother through adoption or artificial insemination or because of some obliging male. And then it will start all over again—a new heartbeat to fret over.

How different it is for Jessica. My mother and my aunts were not yet twenty when they met the men who were to be their guiding forces for the next forty or fifty years. That's what college was for—to meet your husband. And from my aunts and mother, life asked the following: go forth and be fruitful; and when you are done, hire a nurse. Go on thereafter to acquire jewelry, redecorate, join the garden club. Should you have problems along the way—say a hot flash, a pill problem, a philandering husband, breast cancer—treat it lightly and without care. Too much emphasis can make those bogeys real, and it's best to affect a fey sort of detachment, even if your children bring it up. *Especially* if your children bring it up. Eventually, your husband will be dead, and you'll have at least ten good years of doing whatever you damn well please while maintaining the myth of marriage and motherhood. Try not to drink too much.

Those of us who grew up in the sixties and seventies seldom dated. We went around in groups or met in coffee shops to debate Zionism and apartheid, the Pill vs. the IUD, the poetry of Leonard Cohen vs. that of Dylan (Bob or Thomas, depending). If we met someone decent like Jamie, we were suspicious. We would find ourselves in our thirties, the sun showing itself in lines around our eyes, often childless, often husbandless, but for the lucky ones, well employed.

I wish I had a kaleidoscope so I could take all the pieces of my mother's life, the pieces of mine, throw the shards together, find a pretty pattern that I could hold up to Jessica and say, *Here, this is how you do it.*

Someone is standing in my doorway.

"Hey, cuz," he says.

"Sedgie?" My voice is bleary. I ask him what time it is, if he found the wagon. Feeling for my glasses, I come across the scattered pages of my great-grandmother's letters strewn across my bedspread.

"You forgot the Stoli."

I half sit up. From the look of him lurching in the doorway, it seems he found it anyway. Sedgie is here, and soon they will all be coming—the cousins—and the house will start to awaken. It will yawn, groan, stretch its bones. Like a transfusion, the family will invigorate it. Consanguinity. The ties of blood.

"I'm shit-faced," says Sedgie. "Where's my room?"

Sighing, I gather the letters together, stack them on the bedside table, and rise. The dull ache of sleeplessness and anticipation presses against my eyes as I lead my cousin down the hall, show him where to sleep.

I t is midmorning, and Sedgie hasn't risen. Jessica and I have pulled out bowls, softened butter, and are now cracking eggs in an attempt to resurrect Louisa's perfect tollhouse cookies. The kitchen is filled with golden light, sifting through the forest like brown sugar. Miriam wanders in and pops a Snapple, telling us that Mother has had a hard night, and our cackling would wake the dead.

After Miriam leaves, Jessica stares at the breakfast dishes that Miriam hasn't so much as looked at. "Doesn't she help around here?"

In a whisper, I tell Jessica that Miriam is a nurse, and that when Dana hired her, Miriam made it very clear that her duties were limited to caring for our mother. No cleaning. No cooking. Don't bother to ask. Instead, we wait on Miriam the way we would a high priestess who cares for our temple and speaks directly to God—in this case, Mother, with whom our communication has ceased. It is Miriam who tells us if Mother's had a difficult night, if her bowels are congested, if she is peaceful or restless, happy or sad. Like a reader of omens and tea leaves, Miriam has the sight.

Jessica thinks this over, scoops a handful of chocolate chips into her mouth. Both of us, in our addicted way, are hitting the chocolate. Less than three days, and I can feel my body swelling. Mayonnaise and chips. Butter.

The phone rings in the dining room. I wait for Dana to pounce on it. Finally, on the sixth ring, I rise.

"What . . . is going on?" says Ian on the other end after I pick up.

"Oh, it's you."

"You said you would call. Who's there?"

"Sedgie," I whisper, cupping the phone to muffle my voice.

"The movie star? How's he look?"

In point of fact, Sedgie has only been in one movie, in which he was cast as the long-suffering husband of a bipolar Amish woman whose manic break sent her running to the streets of New York. Sedgie's big scene was when he climbed onto his buggy, stalwartly declaring he was going to retrieve her, but before he could even pull onto the Pennsylvania turnpike, a storm kicked up, wetting the roads, making it impossible to see—especially in a broad-brimmed hat—and Sedgie, buggy and all, ended up in the ditch. It seems like a sad and not far-fetched metaphor for Sedgie's life.

"He's still asleep," I say. "No, wait. I hear him."

Sedgie, stubble-cheeked and dressed in his boxers, stumbles down the stairs and past me into the butler's pantry, where he starts fishing around for a coffee cup. He is wearing sunglasses, and the way he paws through the china gives him the appearance of a blind man trying to find his way.

"Christ," says Sedgie, picking up and putting down one chipped cup after another. He reaches to the farthest shelf, finds what he is looking for, blows in it to get the dust out, and staggers to the coffeepot. Armed with coffee, he makes his way back to the dining-room table. I watch him, trying not to laugh. He takes a gulp, makes a face.

"It's two hours old," I hiss from the phone desk, pantomiming gagging.

"What?" says Ian.

"I was talking to Sedgie."

"So how does he look?"

Ian, who's had a little crush on Sedgie ever since the Amish movie, maintains Sedgie has Harrison Ford potential. I can't quite see it, especially this morning with the bed head and the beer belly and the white, freckly skin that only comes out at night.

"He has sunglasses on," I say in the hushed tone of a mourner.

Sedgie must have noticed my whispering because he suddenly bellows out, "Who the fuck died?"

I tell Ian I have to go.

"Mother has had a hard night," I tell Sedgie in a calm, steady voice. He screws up his eyes at his cup. I recognize that cup from our childhood, one of the six our grandmother painted by hand. I thought they all had broken over the years, but here is Sedgie's still intact, his name in red cursive on the side.

"Where the hell am I?" He looks around the dining room, mutters something about culture shock. I remind him he only came from Pough-keepsie, which isn't exactly a cultural hub, but I know what he means.

"It's all relative," I say.

"Relative-zzz," says Sedgie. Then—as if it just occurred to him—he blinks at me. "Maddie," he says, "MaddieAddieUnderpants. When was the last time *you* were here?"

It still makes me flinch—how Sedgie had found my underwear I'd stuck in the trash after I'd peed during a game of Sardines. He'd strutted around with them on his head, a towel trailing down his back, proclaiming himself "Lawrence of Sand Isle."

Dodging the question, I go on the offensive. "So, how's the divorce?"

Sedgie's eyes, bloodshot, pale, gaze back at mine over the rim of his childhood cup. His forlorn expression seems to say, *I am Sedgie Hadley, the only son of Jack Hadley and Patricia Addison. I was supposed to be a lawyer, a doctor, a banker, anything but an actor, but here I am—a semiemployed, quasi thespian, burned out, wasted, going through my second divorce.*

His expression says (or I think it does) that nothing prepared him for this, that his Andover yearbook's prediction of success along with all that was promised by halcyon summers spent on Sand Isle have come to naught, that his childhood fear of the dark was, in fact, prescient, and that no matter how much vodka he drank, women he went with, coke he stuck up his nose, life has proven to remain scary after all.

"She's taking me to the cleaners," he says dolefully.

Even Ian predicted it. I remember my lawyer saying years ago that I had to give my ex-husband money, and though I countered that we'd been married less than two years, my lawyer said, *But you have all the cookies.* It was a strange and offensive concept to me—that someone could pry off part of you and claim it for himself.

What does it mean to you, this money? Dr. Anke once asked.

I laughed flippantly. *Oh, you know, groceries, rent.*

But her eyes bored into mine, and she said, *But you have much more money than that, don't you? Rent and groceries aren't the concern.*

But they are, I thought. They are if you're not sure you could do it on your own, if your only stabs at employment have been acceptable jobs like babysitting or wrapping presents at Christmas. And what does it mean to have someone go after you like that, demanding restitution, as it were? How do we get *our* restitution—we who hold all the cookies? How do we get compensated for that sly comment about cows when we were pregnant, or for the slap to our face when he called us an ungrateful bitch? Where's our remittance for the time spent apologizing for the way we looked, for the way we acted, for the friends we chose (or didn't)? If we have all the cookies, our only choice is to give them away. People rush into our lives like tides stripping a beach of its sand. It's the way the world works. We can make no other contract. Maybe Jessica has it right, doing it all on her own.

I gaze back at Sedgie, wondering if he noticed the sunflowers I put in the splatter-glaze vase by his bed. His once-red hair is dulling to gray. Hadn't he realized I peed in those pants? I touch his hand, but he flinches. I want to tell him he's worth more than this, that he deserves better, but at this moment, with his reddened eyes, the chipped cup in his grip, Lawrence of Sand Isle looks like a derelict, as resourceless as a bum.

FIVE

My mother, it seems, has thrown nothing out. Miriam has told me to fetch a bed jacket, and now I am entranced by an archive of my mother's fashion life. Looking at the remains of her wardrobe, I remember the time, dressed in an evening gown, she walked straight into the lake. She was wearing peach chiffon.

That particular dress is now Permasealed in a Saks Fifth Avenue bag, wedged between a Lanz of Salsburg bathrobe and a shift patterned with flowers of shocking pink. I pull down a powder-blue jacket of quilted satin and return to my mother's bedside. Ever since we have taken her off the majority of her meds, she has seemed less agitated. It's not the morphine, which Miriam administers in moderation, careful not to overmedicate. This new serenity seems to be related to us ceasing any attempts to get her well. She can now relax into her invalidism. She can languish unmolested. For a moment, I envy her.

"Mom," I say, "we're going to dress you up a little. The cousins are starting to arrive. They'll want to see you."

Her eye darts to mine, and I read trepidation. Ambivalence, certainly. *Leave me in peace*, she seems to say.

"Mom," I persevere, "you *know* you like to look good."

She cannot deny it. In years past, she'd have gone to her grave dressed for the Queen, but the stroke has made grooming, much less dressing becomingly, nearly impossible. Miriam gives her a comb-out every day, washes her hair once a week in a bowl. But sponge baths and adult diapers are hardly the stuff of an extravagant toilet.

I lift her hand, feel the bas-relief of veins, the knobby fingers once adorned with red nails and beautiful rings. Miriam raises her from the pillow, and I thread her arm through a sleeve, arrange the jacket behind her. Miriam does the same with the other arm. Delicately, I tie the bow beneath my mother's chin. She smells of baby powder and looks almost pretty now—her pale blue eye alert. Dr. Mead has explained the physiology of the stroke by analogizing the death of oxygen-starved cells to a movie screen gone blank.

You mean she can't move her left side because it's paralyzed?

No, answered Dr. Mead. *Your mother can't move her left side because, as far as she's concerned, it simply isn't there.*

Miriam and I prop Mother up. I set her hands in her lap. "Lovely," I say, though my enthusiasm is met with silence.

Miriam beams at me across my mother. "Sometimes I dress her up nice. Put on her jewels. You like wearing your things, don't you, Evelyn?"

She should, I think. She's earned every one of them.

"Her circle pin, for instance," Miriam goes on. "Perks her right up."

"So why don't we put on some of her jewelry?"

Miriam smiles more than a little conspiratorially this time. Crossing the room to my mother's underwear drawer, she returns with a white satin box engraved with the initials *EPA*. After our mother had her stroke, Dana put the better pieces in the safety-deposit box, but there are still a few pins, her sapphire-and-diamond engagement ring, her scarab bracelet, some strands of pearls, the thin band from Tiffany our father gave her for their fortieth anniversary.

"And look at this," says Miriam, pulling out a gold signet ring engraved with a winged lion.

"A griffin," I say.

"She told me it was her college ring."

My mother appears to be half smiling. She went to college for a year during the war before telling her father that it was a waste of money, that there was a war going on, and that she was going to get married anyway. She dropped out at nineteen, was married the following year.

"She loved art history," Miriam says fondly. "Monet just sent her."

I look from my mother to Miriam and wonder when they had this conversation. My mother never told me she studied art history. As far as I knew, the zenith of her college career was being the queen of the May festival.

"What else?" I say to Miriam.

"Music," says Miriam with a nod. "She said she got more out of her music-appreciation class in one semester than in ten years of studying piano."

I gape at this. I had absolutely no idea. "She hardly ever played."

Now it's Miriam's turn to stare. "That upright downstairs? Didn't she ever play it for you?"

" 'Heart and Soul,' " I shrug, remembering the way her nails clicked and scratched the wood behind the keys. " 'Chopsticks.' "

"No, ma'am," says Miriam. "Your mother studied Mozart."

M y God," says Dana, finding Miriam and me in our mother's clothes and jewelry—me in a Pierre Deux jacket turned up at the cuffs, Miriam in the pink flowered print. Mother, herself, is dressed in the peach chiffon, diamond circle pin at her throat.

"We were having a bit of a drag fest."

I can tell from her expression that the three of us must look like refugees from a yard sale. Miriam, who's on the heavy side, can't zip up the shift, but the pink of the flowers offsets her skin in a way my mother's pallor never did.

"You remember this dress, Dane?" I say, fondling the silky peach of Mother's sleeves. "Remember when she went swimming?"

"Your wedding," Dana says, her mouth puckering as if she's just eaten something sour.

I nod, remembering the way our mother had headed toward the lake at the end of the reception on the yacht-club lawn. It was Labor Day, ninety percent humidity and ninety degrees in the shade. The toasts had been made, I was a married woman, slightly nauseated, and my husband had disappeared with his best man. There was an abrupt, awkward pause after the band took a break. The light from lanterns strung across the dance floor lit up the lake, and my mother, drink in hand, suddenly turned and walked into the water, her peach dress billowing around her like a gossamer jellyfish. Soon, everyone followed her. In ones and twos, we all ended up swimming.

"I thought she threw that dress out," says Dana, suspiciously eyeing our mother as if to say, *What else haven't you told me?*

A queasy, uncomfortable feeling rises in my chest at the subject of my wedding. My marriage—brief and unhappy—was an embarrassment to my family. I had married a liar and an opportunist, but I was worse. An unfit mother; an unfit wife.

I decide to change the subject. "Look," I say, holding out Mother's hand. "Mom's college ring." Dana's mouth is set in a thin line, her eyebrow still raised at Miriam's and my invasion of Mother's closet. "Whatever happened to that boyfriend whose ring you pitched into the lake?"

"Bruce Digby?" Dana rolls her eyes. I wonder if Dana dwells on Bruce Digby the way I dwell on Jamie. She's been married to Philip for two decades now and, unlike me, Dana isn't the type to languish in nostalgia or regret. "That was the worst summer of my life."

"I couldn't believe you did that."

She casts me a sideways look. "Did what?"

Miriam is humming something I discern as "Für Elise." I pull the lapels of Mother's Pierre Deux jacket together. It smells of cedar and mothballs. "Pitched his ring."

Dana sighs. "It wasn't the least of it." Without bothering to elaborate, she turns and leaves the room.

. . .

M addie?"
     I look up dreamily. I've fallen asleep in the hammock, lulled
by the madness of Mrs. Rochester, a copy of *Jane Eyre* gaping beside me. It
is as I've always imagined—waking up to the solicitously handsome face of
a prince who can truly see me, but try as I might to sit up in this web of
rope, I can't make traction and fall stupidly back.

"Derek?"

He holds out his hand to brace me. Awkwardly kicking my legs off the
hammock, I come to my feet. His eyes—green pools within pools plumbed
by observation and contemplation—study mine.

"Maddie." He says it so softly, it's as if he holds a bird. No lover has said
my name like this. Not even Jamie. Certainly not my ex-husband, who
only used my surname. Derek says it in a way that makes me feel that he
has traveled across mountains and deserts to find me, like the source of the
Nile. For a moment, I totter, lost in those eyes, and I think, I would follow
him anywhere.

I rouse myself. "I thought you weren't coming until tomorrow."

"We sped."

"We?"

"Beowulf," he says, telling me he had his son with him—as if traveling
with one's child was as rare and privileged an experience as being accepted
among nomads.

Derek is not tall. Forty-eight, and his cheekbones are still reminiscent
of the exotic masks he collects from Africa and New Guinea. The rough-
ness of his hands speaks of his more recent work—the tree carvings chiseled while roped in twenty, thirty feet up (ancestral, totemesque faces
peering down at whoever chances through that particular *bois ou forêt*), the
granite stacks constructed in the middle of rivers, painstakingly photographed, left to the elements to wash downstream. "And you?"

It is an impossible question begging uncharted territory. He won't accept my usual answer of *Fine, fine, fine,* so I think of saying, *You got about a year?* But he'd probably answer yes.

"Yeah, well," I say, my eyes drifting upward. "You know about Mother?"

Not missing a beat, he says, "She's choosing this, you know."

I look skeptical.

Derek nods. "She wants to be touched, cared for. It's exactly what we have to do."

I feel the same frisson of annoyance as I did with the hospice ladies and their know-it-all manner. "A little extreme. She could have hired a masseuse."

Derek cocks his head. Again, those fathomless eyes. When he cups my cheek in his hand, I flinch, but Derek's hand stays with me. "Haven't you ever been touched, Maddie? Deeply?"

This from him. The screeching of crows grows louder. A squirrel runs up the trunk of the oak just off the porch, and the air smells faintly like skunk. "You're in the Love Nest," I tell him, hesitating a second before I remove his hand.

From the kitchen, a burst of laughter. Something is cooking. Not chocolate-chip cookies, but something healthy. Tofu, I think. Broccoli. Following the scent and the laughter, I find Jessica seated at the table, leaning on her elbows, her head inclined toward a young man as ravishing in his own right. The last time I saw Beowulf he was gangly and brooding. I remember Jessica's allegation about Beowulf's drug addiction and wonder if it's true. Dana sent me a CD of some of the songs he's composed while at Oberlin—track after track of unrequited love. Drugs. Longing. Even the enchanted son of Derek is prone to the most prosaic of despairs.

Now he reminds me of Edward at that age, although Aunt Eugenia's darkness is even more exaggerated in her grandson, whose prominent nose and searing smile have more to do with the genes of his French mother than anything Addison. The look he gives me is unfocused, as if he doesn't quite know who I am. When I kiss him, he looks embarrassed. He also smells faintly of pot. I eye the tofu frying on the cook top. "So what's so funny?" I ask.

"This," says Jessica, holding up an ancient and deteriorating leather-bound book. "It's Grannie Addie's recipe book from 1900. She wrote the whole thing by hand. Listen." She flips through pages filled with an elegant if faded scrawl. "Tripe à la Mode!" she says, gesturing grandly. "Sweetbread Havanese!" More fingering. "And then there's . . . Pigs' Feet." Jessica fights to keep a straight face as she reads aloud how the forefeet are the best, how they have to be soaked under running water throughout the night, then cooked for an entire day in order to be edible.

"An entire day!" says Beo, hiccuping as if he can't quite believe it.

I glance at the lovely handwriting, recognizing it from the trove of letters I have found in the Love Nest. One by one, I am reading them, tumbling into the past of a long-dead woman who nearly lost her mind.

"Someday," I say, "*your* grandchildren will be undone because you ate tofu."

This sends them.

Grannie Addie, the minister's daughter who married a wealthy man. In her letters, she never mentions money other than to allude to her children's allowance, yet they were rich enough to have their own train car and a staff of seven in Cincinnati, along with founding several hospitals, a high school, and the Addison Seminary outside of Dayton.

When Beo asks me if I'd like to join in their meal, I say, "Sure, why not?"

We stand together in the kitchen, each with his plate of tofu and broccoli on Grannie Addie's gold-trimmed Worcestershire, one of several sets of "summer china." Once there were uniformed cooks and maids bustling around this kitchen, ladling soup, garnishing twice-baked potatoes.

"What would Louisa think?" I say, conjuring ghosts.

The thought of our old cook Louisa eating tofu makes Jessica and Beo again scream with laughter.

. . .

J essica and Beo are really stoned," I tell Dana. We are sitting on deck chairs on the porch extension, trying to sun our legs.

Dana pushes her sunglasses up on her nose and peers at me. "I hate when they do that."

"We-ll," I say. After all, substance abuse has been an honored Addison-family tradition for several generations.

"With Mom right upstairs," she adds.

But Mother probably wouldn't mind. If she'd been born in our generation, she might have tried everything. Lucy in the Sky with Diamonds. She would have taken lovers. Put flowers in her hair.

"She doesn't know," I say.

Dana turns to me. "Maddie . . . how do we know she's really dying?"

The question has been hovering for days. The hospice ladies would make no prediction, only describe the signs. It could take weeks, months. It could take years.

"I hope it goes quickly," Dana says, adding hastily, "for her sake." Then she is embarrassed for having said it, like some dreadful swearword that will cause our father to wash our mouths out.

After a heartbeat, I say, "So do I."

The sun feels like a loving embrace upon my legs. It is a drug, this sun. I can feel my skin tingling, the DNA's vain struggle to produce a tan on my still-freckly skin. Dana is wearing a hat with a brim to protect her face, but I, taker of risks, expose my face brazenly. We used to consider it a job—working on our tan. I'll pay for it in my forties, but for now that seems as far away as thirty-nine once did to my twenty-year-old self.

Any day now, Adele is coming—the last of the cousins expected. I've made lists, changed the sheets. There are flowers in almost every room.

"Listen," says Dana.

I hear the distant strumming of a guitar. "Jesu Joy of Man's Desiring." The dulcet tones of Beowulf.

"Bach," I say, wondering if Mother can hear it. I mostly remember her listening to Percy Faith and the Boston Pops. What would she make of the segment Ian and I did on the musician from Hoboken who played the electric fugue?

Out on the lake, a fleet of sailboats races to the mark. They move in silence, but I can imagine shouting, the metallic bleat of winches. I can almost hear my father barking orders. *Derek! Edward!* The scrambling of bodies. Whenever we sailed, I somehow ended up in the wrong place. Or was I the wrong child altogether? A daughter, not a son as my parents had hoped. A pale, feather-plucked girl whose mind was prone to wandering. *Maddie, get out of the way!* Stay the course. Know your purpose. Would that I had been able to grasp the tiller so firmly and without question.

"Listen," says Dana again.

Bach has been replaced by a voice that sounds like one of the Indigo Girls—at once soaring, earthy, and tremulous.

"That's Jessica," says Dana with pride.

"She's incredible."

Dana pulls off her sun hat and runs her fingers through her blunt, no-nonsense hair. "It always feels like everyone else is at a party, know what I mean? Like there's something delightful and wonderful going on, and I'm not part of it."

I stare at her. Dana of the boyfriends and the beer parties and the fraternity rings. Perhaps I should feel smug, but instead I feel the wrench of her loss and disappointment.

"You were always so popular," I say.

Chagrined, she blinks at me. "Maddie," she says, "that was *so* long ago."

Adele has called to say she isn't coming because her Ascended Master has said this is an inauspicious time.

"Translation," said Dana. "No cook."

Now the phone has rung again, and Derek is in the dining room, saying "mmm-hmm" and staring with deep-water eyes at the pictures on the wall. From the kitchen, I watch him as I did when I was young. According to Dana, his marriage to Yvonne isn't going well.

This time it's different, Dana said. *This time she's gone off with another man,* adding, *and he doesn't want to talk about it.*

Derek, I notice, is stabbing the phone table repeatedly with a Bic pen. Finally, he says, "Aunt Ev's passing over, Adele," and a final "okay" before he hangs up the phone. He glances at Dana and me standing in the kitchen door. "Adele's coming."

"When?"

"That," he says, stroking his chin, "is still subject to debate."

Derek and I stare at each other. I find physically beautiful subjects such as Derek problematic to film, but for now I linger on his tangled brow and lashes that, at fourteen, I had coveted for myself. That his wife may be leaving him I find amazing, but I keep my curiosity to myself.

Back in the kitchen, peeling carrots, Dana says, "Adele probably has to throw tea leaves."

"The *I Ching*."

"What?"

"You throw the *I Ching*, not tea leaves."

Dana looks askance as if such trivial knowledge is the intellectual equivalent of junk food. Dana is the kind who folds her underwear and lines it up by color, categorizes pencils, erasers, and paper clips into divided plastic trays. Like our mother, she is partial to crafts, especially knitting, the counting of stitches, the preordained pattern with little left to chance. She says, "As if we don't have enough to think about."

It's part of the problem of Sand Isle, this not having enough to think about. I pick up a carrot and start to hack. "I saw the Dusays' new house," I tell her, running the blade away from me and flinging a fine curl of peel into the sink.

"What did you think?"

"We-ll." The word *massive* comes to mind. Well-proportioned, beautifully chosen materials, ballroom-size porches of stone and wood. "It sort of misses the point," I say, scooping a fistful of carrot peels out of the sink and tossing them into the trash. I wonder how much a garbage disposal would cost.

Dana sniffs. "Exactly," and I feel a wave of affection for her, just as I feel a wave of affection for this old place with its crooked floors and redundant hallways, doors slung like drunkards in off-kilter jambs. It is a house that has had to adapt to circumstance. If it burned down, no one would rebuild it. Who would choose to build a house without rhyme or reason, a complete lack of plan?

In the living room, someone is banging on the piano with the gusto of a child. The noon whistle in Harbor Town begins to wail. Sedgie, carrying a book, pushes into the kitchen with the offended air of a cat that has been doused. As he slumps down at the table, I glance at the title under his arm.

"Ibsen?"

"We're playing Buffalo in the fall."

"Cheery combination," I say, running water down the drain.

"As a matter of fact," Sedgie goes on, "I need someone to feed me my lines."

"Sorry," says Dana quickly, telling him she has plans for a swim.

"What about you?" says Sedgie, as if seeing me for the first time. "You work with actors."

"I work with *people*." Thirteen years since I graduated from film school, and my family still hasn't a clue. "How about Jessica? She's dramatic."

"Ah, the enigmatic Jessica. Sappho or Aphrodite?"

"What's that supposed to mean?" says Dana.

I pick up another carrot and, studying Sedgie, bite into it. "Sedgie is being pompous."

Again from the living room, a cacophony of notes.

"Jesus," says Sedgie, who goes off to speak to Beowulf.

"I never know what he's talking about," Dana says. She has made a big bowl of tuna salad with plenty of Hellmann's. After smearing another dollop on individual slices of bread, she starts to scoop the tuna onto them. "So what do you think?"

"About?"

"Jessica?"

Weighing the pros and cons about coming clean with my concerns regarding my sister's daughter, I pop a bag of Ruffles, dump the contents in a bowl. "She seems fine."

"She lacks direction."

"Didn't we all at that age?"

Dana fingers her ring. "I was practically married."

I look at Dana and wonder how we ended up so differently. Bolstered by knitting and religious conversion, she has set her point, followed it. "You were the exception."

"Good little Dana," she says, making quotation marks with her fingers.

In her earlobes, she wears the diamond studs Philip gave her for their twentieth wedding anniversary. I try to imagine that degree of marital consistency.

She finishes the sandwiches, cuts them in half, slices off the crusts, and places them on an old Minton platter. From the piano in the living room comes Mozart's *Dies Irae*, followed by the booming sound of Sedgie's laugh.

A fter lunch and a desultory sort of cleanup, the cousins drift to their rooms to put on swimsuits and head for the beach. On the way to the Lantern Room, I look in on Mother. Her bed shoved up to the window, she is propped up against the pillows wearing her bed jacket. One eye is closed, the other open. Her profile is still regal in her collapsed face. I want to lean forward, push it all back into place, and, with a drink and a cigarette, settle in with her, ready to share the gossip. She always liked a story at someone else's expense. *It's not gossip*, she would explain to our father. *It's exchanging information.* Thus she would exchange information with the aunts over drinks, with Dana in her bathroom, with her friend Bibi Hester at the club.

"So, Mom," I say, "everyone's here but Adele." I sit on the edge of her bed, opting to talk to the open eye. She seems to regard me, though her face is slack and still as the morning lake. "I don't know what to do about Jessica." She listens silently. "She's even more impulsive than I was. If Dad were alive . . ." I trail off. Perhaps it's better he's not around to see where the shifts in the wind have taken us. Ten years ago, he suddenly dropped to the ground after a bubble burst in his brain. We couldn't believe it. How many times had our mother threatened that something we might say or do would kill him? Then suddenly and without warning, our father was gone. No preparation. No pronouncements. And for the first time in more than forty years, our mother was free to swear with impunity. She could have colored her hair, grown out her nails. She could have taken up with a gay man as she'd always threatened. But she didn't. Instead, she started wearing ill-fitting clothes with high polyester counts. Many days, she didn't put on lipstick. She sat for hours at the kitchen table, smoking and making lists. Dana would come over and take her to the store, but for years she drank only consommé and vodka for lunch. During that time, my mother and I hardly spoke because, as she put it, I'd killed my father.

Now she can't move. I stare into her open eye that fixes back on me. "Dana doesn't know this, but Jessica's thinking of having a baby. She's not going to even bother with a husband. No fuss, no muss. No messy divorce and custody battles or shuttling the kid back and forth." For a moment, my mother's eye and mine seem to duel. She can't say anything. Perhaps she's not even appalled. Perhaps that side of her that's beyond numb has finally snuffed out all semblances of moral indignation.

The last bit of closeness I had with my mother was right after Sadie was born. For the brief duration of Sadie's life, my mother became involved with selecting a layette, talking about cradle cap, producing a silver mono-grammed brush with the softest of bristles. That summer in Sand Isle, I wouldn't let Mother smoke in the house, so she'd stand on the porch, then come inside to hold Sadie. I made a video of her dancing with the baby, my mother's creased cheek nestled against Sadie's, the two of them dancing to music only my mother could hear.

I rearrange her hands on the blanket cover. It is scalloped, piped in the same blue satin as her initials on the white piqué. "I'll tell Beowulf to keep that racket down," I tell her. "He thinks he's the new Shostakovich." I rise to leave. To my surprise, on my mother's lips I see the faintest of smiles.

I t is what my father would have called "a Michigan day." The lake is impossibly blue, competing with the sky. A steady breeze, the hyp-notic lapping of waves, the heat from the sand warming the beach towels. I make a frame with my fingers and view it all through filmmaker's eyes, panning the triangle of white that is our sailfish sail as it cuts out toward the middle of the bay, flops to a reach, scurries parallel to the shore with the wind behind it. I have planted myself alongside a wide circle of football-size stones, carefully arranged by Derek in what appears to be the genesis of an art project. Holding up my imaginary camera, I zoom in on the frenetic arm thrusts of Dana, who is swimming to the bay buoy.

Sedgie has camped away from the water, closer to the dunes and the shade of scrubby beach pines. He is in a lawn chair, wearing a Panama hat, sunglasses, smoking a cigar, and reading Ibsen. Wrapped as he is in beach towels, the effect is that of a Mexican in a serape. My camera focuses on his hand holding the cigar, the way he turns the page. Then my lens drifts across the scraggly pines, pulls back, zeroes in on Jessica and Beowulf, rolled onto their tummies, lying side by side. Beowulf is examining Jessica's wrist. I wonder if he's telling her about his father and mother's marital problems; I wonder if Jessica telling him *her* parents don't even have a clue. Or, being twenty, do they even think about their parents? If I were to interview them I might say, *Do you think your parents don't have lives?* I focus tightly on Jessica's newest tattoo, linger there.

Now I go for scenic footage. In sepia tones, I imagine documenting summers past—even the long-ago ones of parasols and ridiculous swimsuits, the skirted ones Dana and I wore as children, my mother's first two-piece, the briefest gash of belly appearing between the bra and culottes. My mother holds on to her broad-brimmed hat with one hand, waves at the camera with the other. The film is silent, but I can see that she is telling Dana and me to wave as well—two skinny girls with pixie haircuts under rubber bathing caps, jumping up and down for the camera.

The image fades, segues to the shore. The beach is coated with stones as my great-grandmother described in her letter—a geological treasure trove of fossils, metamorphic and igneous rocks, tiny shells, beach glass, and fish bones that fill the frame for a moment before I pull back for a shot of Derek's embryonic Stonehenge. Fade to black. Cut. I squint at the sun-drenched lake to make out Dana's distance. She has turned around and is swimming back. Derek, his sail eased, is cutting in behind her. From my left comes the high-pitched wail of a Jet Ski. Like a megaton mosquito, it works its way toward us, seesawing over waves. My film-editor eye takes in the distance between the sailfish and Dana, the tempo of Dana's strokes, the velocity of the keening engine. *Eee-yaw, eee-yaw, eee-yaw.*

I rise to my feet, seeing that Jessica and Beowulf are also scrambling up. Simultaneously, we take off toward the lake. I start to yell while Jessica reaches down to grasp a fistful of stones. Soon we are all picking up rocks and throwing them at the Jet Ski, screaming at the top of our lungs. Dana doesn't seem to hear. Her stroke is intense and purposeful. Our shrieking is drowned by the whine of the engine; our missiles fall short. I wade into the water just as Derek maneuvers the sailfish between the Jet Ski and Dana. Seeing Derek and the boat, the Jet Ski veers off, circles back toward where it came from, our catcalls and expletives chasing after it like angry bees.

Dana reaches the shore, rises up from the waves, and slicks back her hair. Seeing all of us standing there but unable to read our faces, she says, "What?"

"Whoa, Aunt Dane," says Beowulf, "you almost got chopped."

Jessica starts toward her mother, and then stops, her worried expression hardening into one of annoyance. My heart pounding, I stand among the stones. Derek, again the hero, is pulling the sailfish up on the beach. A low-flying plane zooms overhead. Looking up, Sedgie says, "Lear" the way we used to call out species of birds.

Sedgie has taken charge of the kitchen. It is a talent I didn't realize he had. Tonight we will have leg of lamb just like Louisa made. New potatoes. Mint jelly. Even blueberry pie. Between sips of sherry and a clatter of pots and pans, Sedgie is barking orders. He is wearing Louisa's old "Kiss the Cook" apron. I wish Ian were here to see it.

Standing next to Jessica scrubbing potatoes at the sink, I am overcome with that midsummer sanguinity born of good food and fresh air, the sting of the day's sun, and lots of noisy company. In spite of myself, I feel almost happy.

"So," I say to Jessica, who is brown as chocolate, "do you really think you're ready for a kid? They puke and poop and keep you up all night. Worst of all," I say, "they'll turn out just like you." I say this with affection.

Jessica is up to her wrists in blueberries as she mixes them with sugar. "Mine will be different."

We all think we're different—that the fruits of our labors or our loins are in some way exempt from the banality of other people's reality. We think that we can produce something loftier, transcendent. No pettiness in our marriages. No shallowness in our kinder. Our work will have impact and meaning.

Jessica licks at her fingers, leaving a cockeyed mustache of blueberry above her lips. At moments like this, she looks vulnerable. Even the tattoos and the piercings and the unlikely colored hair seem more childlike than menacing. I spit on the towel and make a move toward her face.

"Yuck," she says. "My mother used to do that."

"You and your mother," I say. "When are you going to give her a break?"

"When are *you?*"

"Fine, fine, fine." We stare each other down.

"It's different now," says Jessica, the first to shrug. "It's just that . . . when I was a kid, I felt like I, you know, belonged. Like all those marks on the dining-room wall had something to do with *me*. I thought I could trace *my* ancestors back through those names to grandfathers and great-grandfathers and great-greats."

"Well, you can. Sort of." I eye her, thinking about the significance of those gouged feet and inches, the Faustian bargains we made when we signed on the dotted line. "Your mark's up there. You're stuck with us. Besides"—I give her a meaningful stare—"your parents got to *choose* you. The rest of us were just the luck of the draw."

Philip, just up from the dock, pokes his head in the kitchen. "Everything under control?" he says in a jovial sailor's voice before disappearing, presumably to my grandfather's former office, commandeered by Philip, whose sole client is a very old, very rich woman in Pasadena.

Under her breath, Jessica says, "Dad will of course kill me."

"That's the difference between our fathers," I say. "I always thought everything I did was going to kill *him*."

Jessica finds this funny, but it occurs to me as if in a revelation that my father is really, truly dead, and that nothing I do now can affect him. I feel both bereft and liberated. No one to assess my progress or flinch at my failures. Drying my hands on a dishtowel, I consider the ramifications.

I an," I say, fingering the photograph of my grandfather hanging over the phone table. "What would you say about me having a baby?"

"You're kidding, right?"

It is six o'clock in New York, same as here. Ian has just woken up from a nap. Tonight, he will go to an art opening and, later, meet up with the musician from Hoboken we befriended while filming him. His evening sounds foreign, illicit even. Here, Dana is organizing a game of charades after dinner.

"I'm not old," I tell him, my eyes grazing a picture of Dana and me on our mother's lap.

There is a pause at the end of the line. I picture Ian in his boxers, the ones his friend gave him printed with lipstick kisses, sitting at the edge of his Philippe Starck bed, his face scrunched up the way he does when he's considering a proper edit. "Who's the lucky guy?"

Ian isn't a prude, exactly, but he's old-fashioned. He believes in the convention of marriage, if not necessarily a heterosexual one. He believes children should call adults Mr. and Mrs. unless invited to do otherwise. He believes, with the fastidiousness of a penitent, in washing your hands each time after peeing and wearing shoes to dinner. "Ian," I say, "have *you* ever thought of having children?"

His answer comes quickly, almost urgently. "Okay, so you *are* losing your mind. It's not healthy for you, Maddie, to be there alone. This line of thinking, for instance."

"I'm not crazy. Don't tell me I'm crazy."

"Listen to me. It's the *place*." He stops. I can hear the sound of drawers being opened and shut. "Okay," he says. "Okay. I want you to call the airline tomorrow. I want you to get a ticket."

"I'm not crazy."

"Get a *ticket*, Maddie."

Sedgie is moving through the house, clanging a large triangle we use to call everyone to meals. Behind him, Jessica, looking like Helen of Troy bearing the fruits of war, carries a platter steaming with lamb and potatoes. Everyone gathers in the dining room, oohing and aahing over Sedgie's fare. Whatever Ian says is drowned out by the din. I cup my mouth to the phone and tell him I have to go.

S edgie takes a sip of his drink. "So, Derek, when's Yvonne coming?"

"Yvonne never comes, Sedge. You know that."

"I thought with the family and all." Sedgie stabs a potato with his fork and misses, sending the potato across the table. "Whoops," he says.

The first time I met Yvonne was just before she and Derek were married. She had been his model at Yale, and he followed her to France, bringing her back almost like an offering or as evidence that his life was continuing elsewhere.

"Perhaps she finds us odd," I say, feeling a budding rekindling of my old allegiance to Derek. "What do *you* think, Philip?"

Philip gives me an appraising look from beneath black brows. "Nothing that the rest of us can't handle," he says, although no one points out that he's the only in-law left among us.

Dana, I notice, seems edgy. When she again suggests charades after dinner, everyone protests, but Sedgie comes to her aid by insisting it's a *wonderful* idea. Looking gratefully at Sedgie, Dana takes a sip of wine, turns to Beowulf, and asks him about school.

"School," says Beowulf, "is a temporal sop to the sublime."

Dana has told me that Beo is going to join a rock band if his composing doesn't work out. I notice he is eating with his fingers. Jessica's eyes are fixed on him. The various colored clips in the form of butterflies dotting her hair give the effect of a tangled, albino bush upon which insects have landed.

Beowulf turns to me. His ponytail has come loose. Beneath his lower lip is a little patch of facial hair I have an urge to wipe off. He says, "I saw that piece you did about Bene Sadah. It was really fine."

The ten-minute clip on the musician in Hoboken. "You're kidding," I say. It never occurs to me that my family would actually *see* any of the films or segments Ian and I produce.

"Who's Bene Sadah?" says Philip.

In a patient voice, Beowulf says, "An *awesome* syntho-fuguist."

"That sounds obscene," says Dana.

"Bene Sadah, Bene Sadah," says Sedgie dreamily, tapping his pointer fingers together in anticipation of charades. "Two words. Second word . . . sounds like . . . We could act out *sodomy. That* would be fun."

"I want Sedgie on *my* team for charades," says Jessica, her eyes dancing, the butterflies threatening flight.

H aving Sedgie on our team turns out to be less of a boon than expected. By the time the dishes are done, he is tanked. He stretches out on the floor, proceeds to fall asleep. Stepping over him, I curl up in a corner of the couch. Beowulf has drifted to the piano and has begun to play, while Jessica is busy shredding paper and tossing the pieces into two bowls, one for each team—Dana, Jessica, Sedgie the unconscious, and me on one, Beowulf, Philip, and Derek on the other.

Hand over hand, Beowulf strikes an eerie progression of notes. The day that started out so vividly blue has shifted suddenly as an evening storm blows in. Michigan weather is like that. *If you don't like the weather, wait five minutes* is the tired old joke. Already we can hear the sound of distant thunder as Beowulf 's hands come down hard on the first few chords of the *Appassionata*.

It's in our genetic code, this playing of charades. We know all the gestures describing movies or quotations or plays or songs or books. We could do it in our sleep, as Sedgie will demonstrate. We write on our slips of paper, huddled conspiratorially, gloating with shared sadism as we plot to stump and baffle.

"How about *Titanic?*" says Dana.

"Too easy," I say.

"*Big Sur and the Oranges of Hieronymus Bosch?*" says Jessica. "*In Watermelon Sugar the Deeds Are Done and Done Again as My Life Is Done in Watermelon Sugar?*"

"*Oranges,*" I say. "Everyone knows the Brautigan."

"I've never heard of it," Dana says.

Sedgie gives a loud snore.

We go first. Jessica bravely crosses the living room and plucks a piece of paper from the basket Philip thrusts at her. Her brows knit together, then I see a tiny smile form upon her lips. Clock starts. Jessica cups her left hand around her eye, makes circular motions with the right.

Film!

Soon she is on all fours, prancing around like a dog, lifting her leg on a chair. She *is* a dog. *Reservoir Dogs! Straw Dogs!*

No! *Dog* is the first word of . . . *three* words. Second word, little word. A . . . *the* . . . *at* . . . *to* . . . *in* . . . *IN!*

Dogs in . . .

Dogs in . . . heaven?

"*Dogs in Space!*" I shout out, jumping up, and Jessica shrieks and hugs me. We are brilliant; we are staggeringly awesome.

"Dogs in . . . space?" repeats Dana, mystified.

I glance at Beowulf, who looks gratified. "That is *so* obscure," he says.

"Australian punk band," I explain to Dana, while Jessica hoots, saying, "Oh, man, I never thought they'd get that!" Except for Sedgie, our team high-fives all around.

Now it is their turn. Philip steps forward and draws a slip. We all peer at it while he mulls his strategy for *The Elegant Universe: Superstrings, Hidden Dimensions, and the Quest for the Ultimate Theory.*

"No problem," he says under his breath.

Even I have to admit Philip is good. In a whirlwind of acting out *book, thirteen words, elephant* (forming a trunk), *universe* (like sky, but big, bigger, biggest), I think of Mother upstairs, our hilarity percolating up, intruding upon her peace. She, who sat staring out of windows for years before her stroke, can no longer avoid the fact of our family.

Now Philip is acting crazy, going after the word *demented* for dimensions, but no one gets it, so he moves on to the gesture for *sounds like*, then fondles his chest to rhyme with *quest.*

But Philip's team stares at him blankly, and finally he throws up his hands in disgust as Jessica calls time.

"The Elephant's Universal Lunatic?" Derek ventures, but when Philip tells them, they all cry foul.

"Bestseller," I say.

"Okay, okay, okay," says Philip, fixing on me. "Now it's your turn."

I get up, stretch, and sashay over. Covering my eyes, I reach in, choose a scrap of paper, unfurl it. Folding the paper back up, I wonder whose suggestion it was. Everyone on the opposing team looks smug. I wheel around and face my team. Jessica's almond eyes, Dana's softly out of focus, Sedgie's shut. I make quotation marks with my fingers and indicate fourteen words. I point at all of us, make a gesture as if gathering us together.

All of us . . . family.

I nod. I think of my mother upstairs. I act out the second word and start to smile inanely.

Crazy? says Dana.

I shake my head.

Happy?

Yes!

I act out the seventh and tenth words by mimicking crying, then ponder how to convey the fifth, when Sedgie suddenly stirs, raises his head like a turtle, gapes fuzzily at me, and, holding up a finger, recites, " 'Happy families are all alike; every unhappy family is unhappy in its own way,' " before slumping back into oblivion.

I yelp while everyone else gawks at the sodden Sedgie. I turn to see Philip's bemused expression. Evidently, it was *his* idea to use the Tolstoy. I give a little bow, and wonder why he chose it.

The evening waltzes on. *Priscilla, Queen of the Desert. Middlemarch.* We act out *lizard* and *sisters* for *Lysistrata*. The rain has started falling in big, splatty drops, and Dana says we should cover the porch cushions and close the windows. Already, doors are slamming around the house. *Bam, bam!* I wonder if Mother is sleeping through this Wagnerian shift in the weather. Everyone dashes to his room to batten down the hatches, when, suddenly, the lights go out.

Of course, none of the flashlights work. Like blind men, we paw through drawers, groping for batteries. The best we come up with is matches, and soon the house is glowing in a golden combination of votive, beeswax, and birthday candles, while the thunder comes louder and faster. Miriam has shown up in her hairnet and bathrobe, saying that the storm was agitating Mother, but now she is drugged and sleeping.

"What kind of drugs?" says Beowulf.

Sedgie stirs like Lazarus from the dead. "A séance!" he announces in a surprisingly sober voice. "Given the Gothic circumstances." Miriam gives him a long, incriminating look as if he has suggested something illegal. "Come on, Miriam, you're not afraid of a couple of ghosts?"

This from Sedgie, of all people.

"Some things are best left alone," says Miriam. Her face by candlelight looks sharply planed as she tells us she's had her share of the spirit world while taking care of the dying. "Why go conjuring?"

Miriam sweeps out of the room in a penumbra of candlelight, but

Sedgie is not to be dissuaded. He insists we all gather in a circle around a cluster of candles on the living-room floor. Philip excuses himself to go down to the beach and check the boats. We all take a deep breath. Except for the sound of the rain and the wind, the house is quiet. Candlelight has honey-coated the room with its cedar walls and shelves crammed with knickknacks and books. In the glow, I can barely make out their spines—*The Indian Drum* and *War and Peace*, some obscure novels from the forties, a couple of Agatha Christies, and a dog-eared Harold Robbins. We still have the record player and the cherished albums, though they haven't been played in years. The bongo drums are new—maybe Derek or Beowulf's. I close my eyes.

Someone starts to giggle. Sedgie makes a groaning sound—something borrowed from *Macbeth*, but Jessica says, *Sssh, listen!*

I don't know if I am expecting the room to fill with light, but there is an unmistakable sense of a new presence.

"This isn't funny," says Jessica.

"Shhh!"

A creaking board. The tread of footsteps. A thump. The front door flies open. We scream in unison.

In the doorway stands a cape-clad figure, starkly silhouetted. Sedgie, his voice no longer bold, says, "Jesus Christ!"

"Close," says Adele, throwing back her hood to reveal a shockingly hairless head. "At *least*," she says, her billowing cape reminiscent of countless dramatic entrances, "you could have met me at the ferry in this bloody rain."

PART TWO

SEVEN

My grandmother Bada died in the autumn of 1964. Aunt Eugenia and Uncle Halsey moved into Bada's bedroom the following summer. Aunt Pat and Uncle Jack took the Schooner Room; my parents were in the Lantern Room. We younger cousins slept in the back bedrooms that had been added, twin beds stuck any place they could fit, bunk beds built into the eaves.

"I call the single bed in the bunkroom," said Sedgie, who was the loudest, brashest of the cousins, but everyone knew he was afraid to sleep alone.

After Bada died, my mother surveyed the living room, cast her eyes on the decomposing ship model on the mantelpiece, and said it was time to brighten the place up.

"What do you mean, 'brighten'?" my father asked.

She slapped the back of the couch, sending up a poof of dust. "I mean some color other than menopause green."

After dinner, the grown-ups sat on the porch drinking, smoking, plotting change. We could hear their voices, but not their words. The smell of tobacco crept into the living room, a smell unknown in my grandmother's time. I wondered if the fabric festooning the card room in the tower would come down. The walls were draped like a fortune-teller's tent with silk damask acquired in Turkey by my great-uncle who had ridden around on a camel. It had been a scandal in the family—not that he brought back the silk (along with several carpets and a hookah), or that he had been in such proximity to WWI without actually *fighting* in it—but that he'd been in so unseemly and unchristian a country in the first place. To my great-grandmother's horror, he insisted the silk be used in the summerhouse, and there it continued to drape, a swagged indictment of the family pariah.

"Louisa," I said later as she helped me brush my teeth, "what do you think will change?"

"Oh," said Louisa in her lilting drawl, "nothing much changes around here."

Being the youngest, I was to sleep in the nursery. It was a tiny room in the farthest reaches of the top floor, big enough only for a twin bed, a crib, and a bureau. For the first years of my life, Louisa had slept in the bed, me in the crib. But my mother, feeling it was time for me to sleep alone, decided to promote Louisa from nurse to cook and move her to the help's quarters beneath the stairs.

"Sleep with me, Louisa," I begged. "Just tonight."

"Say good night to your mama," Louisa said sternly, but I could see she was pleased.

Later, she lay next to me on the narrow bed, talking in her slow sentences about her life in Ohio. She had left two daughters—"love children" she called them—with her own mother when she came to work for my parents in California. "Summer nights in Ohio was heavy cream, baby girl. And you knew God was watching you. You knew 'cause you could see His eyes."

"What do God's eyes look like, Louisa?"

"Have you ever seen fireflies, child?"

Soon, Louisa was snoring, and I, too, must have drifted off because I jerked awake to a sound in the room. Thinking it was my mother coming to evict Louisa, I pretended to be asleep, but the room seemed to fill with the scent of lavender. I slowly opened my eyes. The moon-brushed trees pressed against the window in front of which I made out a form bending over the crib.

"Mommy?" I said, but the woman who turned to me was not my mother. Her narrow face and deep eyes looked familiar, but her clothes were strange. She was wearing a long, black dress, cinched at the waist, ruffled at the hem, and puffed at the shoulders. Louisa was pressing against me, making it difficult to breathe, so I shoved her away, sat up, and said, "What?"

The woman turned and left the nursery.

Barefoot, I followed her. Her skirt rustled against the floor and, oddly, I wasn't scared. Perhaps it was her Addison features (the mouth turned down at the edge), perhaps it was the sadness of her face, but it seemed natural to tag after her as she went from room to room, gazing in on my sleeping parents, drifting through the sour-milk smell of the bunk room, gliding downstairs. We went from one bedroom to another, pulled along in a cloud of lavender. She spoke to me, and I knew what she was saying, even though the words, when I tried to make them out, sounded like the beating of moth wings against a screen. "Ta, ta, ta," she said, telling me who slept in each room and why it was built, the guest who had visited, how long they stayed. Weeks. Months. "Ta, ta, ta."

Finally, we came to the living room. The old damask in the card room cascaded exotically, conjuring windswept deserts on moonlit nights. The woman strode over and began to tear down the silk. I could hear the fabric shredding. *Stop,* I wanted to say, but nothing came out.

The next morning, I told Louisa what had happened. "It was a dream," she said, shaking her head.

When we came downstairs for breakfast, I looked into the card room to see if the silk had been torn down, but it remained. Then I saw the crumpled wreck of the ship model lying in a box.

"What are you doing?" I said to my mother, who was drinking tea at the dining-room table.

Bleary-eyed, she set down her cup. "That awful relic."

I did not tell her about the woman I'd seen. Louisa, however, told my mother I wasn't sleeping well, that I seemed fussy and disturbed. My mother relented in letting Louisa stay with me, but moved us to another room down the hall.

The upholstery and curtains in the living room were replaced by flowered chintz. The Turkish silk and the hookah in the card room, however—once controversial, now revered as tradition—stayed intact. Three years later, Uncle Halsey was diagnosed with cancer. After my uncle's death in 1969, my father took over as head of the family even though his sister, Aunt Pat, was older. Aunt Eugenia eventually remarried. Screens were added to keep out the bugs. My mother insisted we get rid of that ghastly light fixture in the dining room. Every three years, the house was repainted the same dark green. The boardwalk down to the beach was repaired. It was a huge shock when one of the oaks had to come down, but other than that, Louisa was right about nothing much changing, although by the time I stopped coming to Sand Isle, Louisa herself was gone.

EIGHT

Ev. Evelyn. Ev the Elegant. The line of her throat as she lifted a cigarette to her lips. She was a small-town girl who wore bobby socks—a fourteen-year-old smoker who went on to become a glamour puss who loved martinis and who threw up in a revolving door at the Ritz. She had grown up alongside the Missouri River in a house that had stood on stilts. Every house on her street, she told us, was waiting for the river to rise.

My mother's pride was her nails—sharp red talons totally unsuitable for manual labor. When she and the aunts took up decoupage, they would spend days with manicure scissors, littering the floor with clippings as they pored and snipped through illustrated books with an eye toward a compelling image—a tendril of campanula from *The Flowers of the World* or a little girl holding a bucket from *A Child's Garden of Verses*. I would watch, fascinated, waiting for the shellac to dry so Aunt Pat and my mother could go to work buffing. No speck of lint, no air bubble was too small to escape their scrutiny. My mother was especially zealous. She would pick up whatever she was working on, hold it up to the light, take a drag on her cigarette, and say, *Hmmm*. The she would set down her cigarette, pick up the sandpaper, and begin to rub in a frenzied fashion as if the Holy Spirit itself was moving her.

"There. You see?" Aunt Pat had said when the sandpaper chipped the nail on my mother's right ring finger. "And you're denting the varnish with those claws."

The truth was, my father's family didn't approve of makeup. My mother's red polish alone was something of a scandal, not to mention her jazzy California fashions that were in sharp contrast to the demure wraparound skirts, the monogrammed blouses, and circle pins of my aunts. My mother liked to try different styles—orange-and-pink shifts in geometric patterns. Wide-brimmed hats that tied beneath the chin. Huge, square sunglasses that came with matching plastic bracelets. In the midsixties, she even tried to wear a frosty white lipstick, but she tossed it aside after my father told her she looked dead.

I remember one night Dana, Sedgie, Adele, and I were sitting on the floor in front of the fireplace playing war. In the card room, our parents were deep in a game of bridge with Aunt Pat and Uncle Jack. Below the card table, disemboweled of their images for decoupage, the books were stacking up. My father had raised the bidding to two hearts, Aunt Pat passed, and it was my mother's turn again. My mother fingered the corners of her card, looked hard at my father, who stared back at her impassively, then waved her fingers and, with a shrug, said, "Pass?"

"The contract is two hearts," said Aunt Pat, briskly smacking down a card. Our aunt was known as a "mean bridge player," but whether that meant she was clever or cruel, I couldn't be sure.

My parents were facing each other across the table surfaced with a nautical chart. My mother had her hair pulled back in a grosgrain bow and was wearing an oxford-cloth shirt with the collar turned up, fastened at the wrists with cuff links and tucked in at the waist. She was, I decided, more beautiful than the other aunts. She had what one of my uncles described as a Greta Garbo profile, legs that went on forever, and glossy black hair that later would turn suddenly, almost violently gray. She laid her cards down on the table, faceup, crossed her arms, and beamed proudly at my father.

There was lovely tension in the air as the grown-ups went on to play their hands. The fire sputtered as a breeze came down the chimney and thunder rumbled from the horizon. Somewhere out on the big lake, a storm was moving toward us. The skies had turned crabby that afternoon, making the air so electric, our hair stood on end. In the tented card room, the edges of the Turkish silk were fraying.

Earlier that week, the riots had started in Chicago, and now the cops were beating the protesters. There was no TV in our house. My father disapproved of television in the summer and, besides, reception in northern Michigan was poor. The neighbors, however, had put an antenna on their roof just so they could watch the convention.

"Can you blame the cops?" Sedgie said. "I mean, if someone had thrown piss in your face?"

"They're protesting the war," said Derek.

"I'd kill 'em," said Sedgie.

Adele got up and put on Bob Dylan. The record player and the shiny new rack that held the albums looked odd and out of place in this room of dark wicker. Anything that had been brought into the house after the forties had that air about it—a temporary feeling as if it were a slightly embarrassing houseguest.

"Jesus H. Christ," Uncle Jack yelled, "turn off that racket."

My father shot Uncle Jack a look. My father had a very clear position on swearing. Never, never, never was swearing permitted. If he caught any of us using bad words, he would wash our mouths out with Addison's Astringent Rinse that was touted for its ability to cure sore throats, canker sores, and, as far as we knew, obscene language. For years, I couldn't swear without the sensation of that sharp, minty taste.

Adele lifted the arm of the Victrola, sending a loud scratch across the vinyl. My cousin Sedgie, owner of that particular record, said, "Shit, Adele!"

All eyes turned to my father, but he didn't seem to have heard. The wind had picked up the way it does before a squall rushes in. My father's jaw worked tightly. He was looking at my mother.

"Evelyn," he said flatly, "my bidding two hearts was forcing."

The lightning was coming faster now, the thunderclaps close together. "I had an ugly hand, so I passed," my mother said lightly, flinching from the thunder. She reached for her drink.

My father continued on in his low, tight voice, snapping down each word the way he would a card. "You had a *void*." The way his lips were quivering, we knew this was significant. "I could have slammed this hand against the wall and made four hearts."

I recognized the tone in my father's voice. It was the tone he used with all of us if we parked the bikes incorrectly or sloppily folded the sails.

My mother's red-tipped fingers tightened around her glass. I fixed my eyes on her face as she tried to keep smiling, wanting her to pitch her cards or her drink, stare my father down, and say, *Don't speak to me as if I'm a child.*

But she said nothing.

The rain beat harder. Lightning lit up the room, and the cousins shrieked. Aunt Pat put her hand on my father's arm and, in the preening older sister voice she often used with him, said, "Now, Dickie, at *least* you made your contract."

It turned into a whopper of a storm—a real "lollapalooza" as Louisa would say. Late that night, woken by thunder, I left my room, heading to the Lantern Room, where my parents slept. I could hear voices and what sounded like my mother crying. My father was saying something like, "If you're going to play bridge, do it right," and my mother said, "Fine, fine, fine. Just don't lecture me in front of your sister."

I was sure she was in her nightgown, pacing and smoking, the wind rattling the windows. The vein in my father's neck would be pulsing, his mouth drawn into a crowbar of disgust. No doubt they were avoiding each other's eyes.

And then my father said, "Damn it, Evelyn!"

I couldn't wait to tell Dana. My father had not only sworn, but sworn at my mother. But then to my surprise, I heard my mother's rich, low voice.

"You Addisons," she said. "You think your shit doesn't smell."

The floor creaked, and I froze. Right then I decided it was better to tell no one, to pretend I hadn't heard. I tiptoed down the hall. Through the window, the strange blue light from the neighbors' TV hovered ghostlike in the trees.

The next morning, my mother came down to breakfast and held up her naked hands for everyone to see. With her nails shorn, she looked as defenseless as the hairless Samson. There would be one less thing for my father and Aunt Pat to criticize.

"Happy?" she said.

The following summer, my father bought a television to watch the Eagle landing on the moon, and my mother took up needlepoint, stitching pillows with slogans like *Where there's a will, there's a relative* and *Golf is a good walk spoiled*. After the decoupage period, she began to dress more sedately. No more plastic jewelry. No more unseemly polish. The chichi Mexican skirts gave way to Lilly Pulitzer pants in the seventies. She gave up on fashion in those years after the moonwalk, surrendering to the belts decorated with silhouettes of whales, the matching sweater sets, the strand of pearls.

NINE

D erek and Edward, the sons of Uncle Halsey and Aunt Eugenia, were twins, nine years my senior, physically alike, but of different temperaments. Both were slightly built and dark, prone to sinewy muscles that developed quickly over a summer of balls whacked, lines trimmed, strokes swum. Derek was an artist with a thoughtful, sexless quality that emanated virtue, while Edward was moody and volatile and, thus, more intriguing.

Once, Adele had arrived, her sneaker blossoming with blood after playing mumblety-peg with Edward. "I'm going to die!" she kept screaming. "He's cut off my toe!"

It was the first time I'd felt jealous of my gorgeous, older cousin Adele, whom Edward followed whenever we played kick the can. I wished Edward had chosen *me* instead of Adele with her stigmatized foot. I would have stared him down, dragged my foot to where the knife landed, daring him to nick me, and later borne my wound with pride. I wouldn't cry like Adele. I could almost feel the pleasure of the blade striking my flesh, the blood trickling down.

Uncle Halsey had died the year before, Derek had a year left in college, and Edward, claiming there was no point in anything after his father's death, had dropped out. To console herself, Aunt Eugenia had taken a trip to Ireland, bringing back presents for everyone. That summer, she'd given me a loosely knit sweater she'd acquired abroad. A fisherman's sweater, she told me. I wore it with everything—shorts, jeans, even on hot humid days when everyone else was wearing a T-shirt. I would sit on the back steps coming down from the kitchen and call my chipmunk, Chippy, by making "tch tch tch" sounds with my tongue. It had taken me weeks to gain his trust by strewing peanuts from the tree where he lived through the myrtle leading to the foot of the kitchen stairs. I would sit very still. Chippy would emerge, grab a nut, dash back to his bunker beneath the tree. Soon, he was feeling more brazen. Two nuts closer. Three. Eventually, he was eating out of my hand. I could feel his weight, the damp, clinging prick of his paws. I spent hours with Chippy, cupping him in my palms, his cheeks cartoon-ishly swollen, his beady eyes reflecting what I took to be fondness. Appre-ciation, certainly. *You don't know how much easier you're making my winter,* he seemed to say.

But my sister and the rest of my cousins had no interest in Chippy. Dana, sixteen, was having one of her rare summers in which she was tan-gling with my parents. She was shaving her legs and had taken to perfum-ing herself heavily with Jean Naté. She and Sedgie were around only for meals, and sometimes not then. They ran with a shadowy gang of kids who had access to ski boats and their parents' cars. I had heard my father's stern voice, the slammed doors, the tears, but it was an exclusive world of hor-mones and budding breasts, and I didn't qualify.

Edward had removed himself from the rest of us by throwing a mattress on the floor of the boat storage and cordoning it off with bedspreads. Whether he'd withdrawn from college or was kicked out wasn't exactly clear, but with his college deferment gone, he'd been drafted. There was some talk of producing evidence of a physical or mental malady so he could get 4F'd and avoid serving, but Edward actually seemed pleased to go into the army. After all, his own father had received a Purple Heart in the

Second World War. Pitching his knife and listening to music, Edward seemed to be readying himself. Sometimes we smelled marijuana if we circled around the basement of the house, but Edward would lean out of the window and tell us that there was poison ivy and we should "keep the fuck away."

"Nice, Edward," Dana had said, but she knew enough to sense the danger of telling our father about Edward's pot smoking or his language.

"I was ROTC when I was your age," my father told him one night at dinner. "Graduated in my uniform from Princeton in three years and went straight to Fort Sills."

"Are you scared, Edward?" Sedgie asked him.

Edward, who rarely smiled, smiled then. He went on to tell us that, no, he wasn't scared, and I realized it was the smile of someone who looked forward to being in the jungle.

Derek, who was studying art at Yale, leaned across the dining-room table. He spoke so softly that you had to strain to hear him. "They're not gooks, Edward," he said to his twin. "They're people."

But Edward only laughed.

Unlike Edward, Derek was gentle, otherworldly. Derek's skin had tanned to the color of an old penny. He took walks with me on the beach that summer, gathering stones, studying their patterns—the swirl of minerals, the fossilized lace. "All things are connected," Derek said, showing me how certain rocks, when broken open, contained a jewel box of crystals. He was trying to teach me, with little success, how to skip stones. "The flatter and broader the better," he said, caressing a stone the way he caressed his paintbrushes.

The first time Derek drew my portrait, we were sitting on the beach. I could feel him looking at me, studying my face as if it were a building or a tree. Backlit, the golden hairs on his arms betrayed the tiniest halo. I wanted so badly to see how he saw me, what I really looked like, but he held his tablet close, smiled occasionally, and, when he was done, said, "Thank you, mademoiselle!" with a flourish that made me blush.

But even Derek was indifferent to Chippy. Alone, I spent hours on the damp, mossy stairs, occasionally moving aside as Louisa trundled up and down with the garbage, or when the grocery man arrived—old Wade, who took nips from everyone's liquor cabinet before climbing back into his one-horse dray and saying, "Git!"

"Training chipmunks, are ya?" Wade said as he stepped over me to haul up boxes of cereal and milk. "You watch it, now. Those things are rabid."

"Not Chippy," I said. I could hear Aunt Eugenia calling Edward from the other side of the porch, something about a sailboat race and my father. A few minutes later, I heard the squeak of a kickstand. Then Edward was standing over me, leaning on his Schwinn.

"What?" I said uncomfortably, pulling my fisherman's sweater over my knees. Edward kept staring at me as if he had never seen me before. I rubbed my cheek on the sweater. I could see Chippy on the root of his tree, see the perky way he stood on his hind legs as he spotted me and began to dash along his crooked route, greedy for a nut.

In an instant, Edward spotted him, too. "Holy shit," he said as the chipmunk climbed into the sleeve of my sweater and crawled up my chest. "What the hay . . . ?" He reached down and touched the front of my sweater, grasping for the chipmunk.

"Cut it out," I said, crossing my arms.

"Tch tch tch," said Edward, speaking Chippy's language, but the screen door slammed above us, and down came Wade, reeking of alcohol. Edward withdrew his hand. Wade stepped over me, wobbling slightly, but managing a straight course as he headed down the path. Then he stopped, turned around, and leveled my cousin with a stare.

"Nice chipmunk," Edward said as he pushed off on his bicycle.

Wade just stood there until Edward was gone, then he tipped his cap and climbed back onto the dray. "Rabid," he muttered. "Like I said."

That night I smelled marijuana from beneath the porch, but there was no one around to tell. Our parents were at a party, and even the neighbors' house was dark. We'd added a deck onto the porch that year—punched it out into the treetops so we could sit under the open sky, search it for shooting stars, the aurora borealis. Sedgie and Dana were on somebody else's beach, drinking beer. Adele was with Stephen, her fiancé. Even Derek was gone. Louisa had retreated to her tiny room beneath the kitchen, and I was alone on a chaise longue, staring upward. I wanted somebody to talk to—Derek, preferably, who would look at the night sky with me, discussing time, dimensions, the infinity of space. How can something have no end? Surely there were other stars, other planets that had begotten life. Bacteria, at least. Insects. Maybe even intelligent life, more enlightened than ours. A peaceful civilization with no war, only virtue. They would be up there, looking down, studying us sadly, hoping for the best.

Reveling in the possibilities, I heard a creak behind me. The faintest scent of pot. I bunched myself up on the chaise, willed myself to be invisible, but a hand laid itself on my head.

"Pretty stars," I said, but Edward said nothing.

But I knew enough to feel nervous when Edward said, "Do you let that chipmunk of yours climb into your sweater every day?"

I didn't hesitate. I jumped to my feet and pushed past him, ran upstairs to my room. It was the little room in the farthest corner of the house. Slamming the door, I locked it, breathing hard, waiting for the footfall that never came.

The next morning was bright and dewy. Louisa was making waffles, setting them on heaping platters on the buffet by the dining-room window. My father and Uncle Jack had joined us for a few weeks' vacation, and now they sat, steaming cups of coffee in their hands as they read the *Wall Street Journal* and rarely spoke.

"That McGovern," muttered Uncle Jack.

My father grunted.

I helped myself to waffles. The teenagers were still in bed. From the bedroom beyond the Love Nest, I heard the faint tones of Derek's recorder. Outside, the gardener was sweeping the porch, and on the lawn below, I made out Edward swinging a golf club, practicing his stroke.

"What are you up to today, Bug?" my father asked.

I shrugged. I knew he didn't really want to hear about the book I was reading or the fort I'd made in the attic or how Chippy could sit on my head. I downed my waffles, raced through the kitchen, giving Louisa a pinch, and headed down the steps.

"Tch tch tch," I said, and waited. "Tch tch tch."

But Chippy didn't come that morning. I waited for hours. The woods were still except for the cry of chickadees and the whoosh of Edward's swing.

TEN

In the summer of 1974, Dana and I picked up an Indian woman who was hitchhiking down from Sturgeon. Dana was driving the Malibu—a wantonly profligate and clandestine act given that (A) gasoline was rationed, and (B) Dana was grounded. Our parents were at a cocktail party, so Dana had sneaked the car out so we could drive up the coast of Lake Michigan and listen to music while she smoked cigarettes. We strained to hear Elton John, but the radio this far north was faint and given to polkas, and sometimes we listened to nothing at all.

"B-B-B-Bennie and the Jetssss," I sang.

"Oh please, dear Lord, can someone buy me an eight-track?" said Dana, jamming the radio buttons. She was nineteen and dating a tennis player at UCLA and was going through a cocky patch that raised eyebrows and voices at dinner. She was always perfectly dressed in an alligator shirt with the collar turned up, khakis and a belt, her hair pulled into a tail of chocolate brown. I was in awe of her nails, not unlike our mother's—the way they held a cigarette, the imprint of lipstick upon its tip.

"See that tree?" She nodded as we meandered through a curve. "That's where Tad Swanson totaled his car."

Tad Swanson's father had made a fortune in curtain hardware. *Where there's a swag, there's a Swanson* was his motto, but my mother always called him the Drape Man.

"How fast was he going?"

Dana drew on her cigarette. I was relieved when she put both hands back on the wheel. "About ninety," she said, exhaling. "Wrapped it around completely."

I whistled. Mr. Swanson's boat, *Swan Song*, was a shiny new fifty-footer. Full of amenities and polished chrome, it made our boat look like a tub. The gleaming *Swan Song* would surge by us almost immediately in races, but my father would coax the best out of the *Green Dragon* and, when the race was over, console us with *Winning is one thing, but losing builds character.*

Dana and her friends had taken off ahead of Tad. They didn't know that, less than a mile back, Tad and his girlfriend were hurtling at ninety miles an hour toward a nonnegotiable curve, an oak tree sentry-tall and proud. Three weeks later, you could still see the skid marks. Tad's Firebird was flimsy as silk when the tires left the road. They pried the two kids out of the car, the gory details percolating into the cocktail chatter of Sand Isle. And guilt by association being what it is, Dana was immediately grounded.

I looked back at the tree as if it was a talisman.

"She was pregnant," said Dana. I noticed her hands were shaking. On the pinkie of her right hand, she wore the gold signet ring of our girls' school, its motto, *Virtute et Veritas*—Virtue and Truth—engraved at the center. On her neck, she wore a chain with her boyfriend's fraternity ring. By the end of summer, she would take that necklace off, fling the boyfriend's ring into the lake.

The air grew delicious with rumor and secrecy. I was seldom taken into Dana's confidence. Mostly, she ignored me, but since she was grounded, I was the dregs to which she resorted. Not that I minded. I slurped up details of Tad Swanson and Deb Bailey's ill-fated lives the way my parents and their friends slung back cocktails.

"Life is short," said Dana in a wise, knowing voice.

"Really short," I said, though I was not yet fifteen. I decided I'd better seize upon the intimacy of the moment, given that I was usually invisible. "If I die, Dane," I said solemnly, hoping my voice sounded poetic, even tragic, "I want you to know I've had a good life."

Her eyes slid sideways as if to say, *You poor, dumb fool.* I eyed the fraternity ring around her neck, thought of what she'd said about Deb. Pregnant was bad. One girl we knew had been taken out of school the year before, suddenly and without explanation. And then there was the scandal of Libby Strauss, not only pregnant, but by a black guy. That almost did our mother in. She announced one night at dinner, fixing her eyes on each of us, that *it would . . . KILL . . . your father.*

We had come through the curvy, densely forested part of the shore, out to the pasture stretch before the town of Goodhart. Queen Anne's lace edged the side of the road, beyond which a field was swathed with thistle.

"Why didn't she have an abortion?"

Dana sighed. "Tad was really confused."

"Tad?" I said. "How about *Deb?"* Now Deb was dead, along with Tad and what I assumed was his baby. Tad was twenty. Deb was seventeen. She had gone to a girls' boarding school in the East, was headed for Sweet Briar in the fall. Girls like that didn't have babies they didn't want. Abortion was legal as tobacco now. No more furtive trips to Mexico or ill-explained forays to Sweden. Girls didn't have to bleed out or become sterile or be packed off to homes for unwed mothers like some criminal. "Hey, Dane," I asked, "you'd go on the Pill, right?"

Again, that look. "I don't need the *Pill*," she said, her eyes narrowing. I knew better than to ask more questions. I was too intoxicated by having the inside story on Tad and Deb to jeopardize my position now. Besides, we had to get the car back before our parents got home.

We sped down the road. I thought about asking Dana for a cigarette, but the only time I'd smoked, I coughed till I threw up. Dana had Coke bottles filled with butts on the little porch off her bedroom in the Aerie. I had been demoted back to the nursery, while Dana upgraded to one of the

guest rooms next to the Love Nest, which would soon be inhabited by
Adele. Adele was going through her first divorce and was arriving in August, along with Edward, who had spent the last three years in Southeast
Asia. Derek had been here for a week and was wearing sandals and draw-
string pants that resembled pajama bottoms. Night after night at dinner, he
and my father tangled.

This burning-your-draft-card business—, my father would begin as he
carved the roast. *It doesn't sit well with me. I was scared. Sure, I was scared.
But we knew what mattered then. We knew where the line was drawn.* As if to
illustrate his point, my father drew the blade of the knife with one sure
stroke between the ribs of the meat. Juice poured out. *Your father,* my father
said, invoking Uncle Halsey, who had received a Purple Heart, *was a hero.*
He jabbed the knife at Derek. *How could you not serve your country?*

At this, Derek seemed to flinch. He had finished graduate school the
year before, just as the war ended, and had set up a studio in one of the
spare maid's rooms. In response to my father's question, he tugged on his
longish hair. *What is* your *definition of service?* Derek asked as Louisa delivered our plates, a look on her face like she'd heard this all before. *What is
your definition of* servitude?

When I was your age, I was laying lines across the Rhine River.

The virtuous war, Derek shot back. I couldn't tell if my cousin was being
respectful or sarcastic. They could sound the same in our family. *Vietnam
was different.*

You think there's no virtue in stopping the spread of communism?

But we were invaded in 1941, Derek said.

At which point, Uncle Jack jumped in. *That's true. If it weren't for the
Japs, Roosevelt would never have gotten us tangled up in that mess.*

If it weren't for Roosevelt's decision, our father replied brusquely, *Western
Europe would be speaking German.*

If it weren't for the Japs, persisted Uncle Jack, who had stayed home from
the war because of his bad back.

Derek ignored him. *Vietnam was a racist war. Look who fought in it.*

Dana, who had been avoiding the conversation by reading a book and chewing absentmindedly, sighed. Sedgie took a knife and wedged it into the seam of the table leaves. Louisa circled slowly.

Were there any blacks in your regiment? said Derek.

I had started prowling around Derek's studio whenever he let me. Sometimes I would go in when it was empty. The smell of turpentine and linseed oil was an elixir.

There were *blacks in the army,* said my father. *There was a whole mix of men. Jews, Mexicans—*

Jews, Mexicans in your *regiment,* Derek interrupted. *But no blacks.*

Edward's not black, I said, but no one seemed to hear me.

We were all *Americans,* said my father. He was trying to control his voice. Louisa set down a plateful of potatoes. The china made a little clink as it hit the table, but there was an unnatural, heavy silence, as if the room had frozen.

My mother, who was usually a little tight by the end of the meal, lit a cigarette and shook her head. *This Patty Hearst,* she said, as if she had been holding her own private conversation all this time, *calling her parents pigs.* She looked at each of us around the table as if to say, *You wouldn't do that, would you?*

Finally Derek spoke. *She was locked in a closet and raped, Aunt Ev. She thought she was going to die.*

But the disgusted expression on my mother's face said, *Regardless of the circumstances, you don't call your parents pigs.*

I had felt an allegiance to Derek that night—a tingling excitement as if he heralded some yet-to-be-articulated change. With my fifteenth birthday weeks away, I was feeling both abandoned and imprisoned by my family. Derek, with his clear conscience and his artist's eye, prophesied escape.

Now it was a few days later, and Dana and I were doing some escaping of our own in the stolen Malibu, gliding along the bluff, discussing Tad and Deb. "Will you look at that?" I said as we passed a figure wrapped in a blanket, arm extended, thumb jerking for a ride. I couldn't make out the

woman's age, but her face was clearly Indian. My own experience with In-
dians was limited. Many of the names of towns and roads in the area were
Indian, and we knew all the legends—the Sleeping Bears, the Manitous.
But actual Indians were few and far between. They stuck to themselves.
Some of them lived in the woods we called Indianville behind Harbor
Town. When we were kids, we would walk by their houses, stare one another down, the Indians silent and suspicious upon lopsided porches. *Woo
woo woo*, we sometimes said, smacking our palms against our lips. *Woo woo
woo*. We never knew what they said about us.

I touched Dana's arm. "Let's pick her up."

But Dana didn't let up on the gas pedal. She glanced in the rearview
mirror, exhaled. For a moment, it occurred to me that her smoking of cigarettes, her stealing of cars were puny and insignificant acts of rebellion
compared to Derek's pronouncements about war and injustice. Having
watched Derek for the last week stand up to my father, hearing the passion
in his voice, I wanted to be so much more than a privileged white girl.

"Dana," I said, "stop!"

She slammed on the brakes, her face set straight ahead. She was more
than irritated; she was seething.

"Back up," I insisted, feeling the same tingle of excitement as I did
when Derek took on our father. "Come *on!*"

It was the first time I'd exerted my will on her. I began to see a chink in
her armor. Reluctantly, Dana reversed the car. As we pulled up alongside
the figure, I could see it was a woman's face, old and weathered. I rolled
down the window. A wise face, I decided, without much dental care. She
hesitated, looked back up the highway as if another car might be coming—
a better car with more to offer than two teenage girls, one of them smoking. "Get in," I said, adding, "It's okay."

Dana said nothing, but my heart was pounding with the audaciousness
of the act. If our mother knew. The woman smelled like root vegetables
and grass. Dana was gripping the steering wheel, but I was twisted around,
trying to get a look at our passenger. When the blanket dropped away,

I searched her wide, flat face for the poetry of the indigenous, her mane of hair for the shrill song of chants. She held a paper bag in one arm, and with her free hand, she pawed in the direction toward town.

"That's where you live?" I asked.

Lake Michigan spread endlessly to our right, the shadows of islands off to the west. They used to come in canoes—all these tribes, gathering for the hunt. You could see signs of them on the roadside—little stands selling beadwork and leather, billboards painted with feathered braves. Next stop, Michillamackinac! You could take a ferry, buy a box of fudge, join the horde of tourists wandering the paths where Indians once tracked deer. *Woo woo woo*, we'd say.

"Where are you going?" I said as we headed down the highway.

I had no idea what was in the bag, didn't want to ask. The Indians we saw in Harbor Town came out of the bar, started up the bluff, lay down on the bench halfway up, and fell asleep.

"Ask her if she has an open container," Dana said. I noticed Dana was creeping along at about twenty miles an hour, taking no chances.

"What'd you buy?" I asked in a nonchalant voice.

"Cookies. You girls want a cookie?"

I was disappointed. I wanted her to have bought tobacco to summon the spirits, herbs for a remedy. "What kind?" She peered into her bag, pulled them out. They were shaped like little windmills. "Van de Kamp," I said.

She smiled. Her teeth weren't great, but the ones she had looked solid and rooted, like they could take on any kind of tooth decay and stay put. Suddenly she yanked her head around, pointed at a road we'd driven past. "That's my turn!"

Dana was trying hard to maintain her composure. "Like I'd know."

"Turn around," I said.

Dana turned, but not without giving me a look first that promised a slow and painful death. The station wagon dropped off the highway onto a road that was barely a road, leading through the woods. It began to dip and twist down the side of the bluff until we came to a collection of shacks that made Indianville look like the Riviera. The tar paper nailed to the sides seemed to be the only thing holding them up. I started to open my mouth to say, *Are you sure you want us to leave you here?* but Dana had slammed on the brakes and was waiting for the woman to get out.

"Well, then," I said.

The woman sat there for a while, looking pleased to have arrived home in a car. Perhaps she had been gone for weeks. Perhaps she had set out like a fur trapper, hunting for pelts to warm them in the winter, returning instead with cookies.

I took one from the box she offered.

"No thanks," said Dana, staring anywhere but at our passenger.

The woman heaved herself out of the car, pulled her blanket close, clutched her bag, peered back in at us. "You know them astronauts?" We stared at her blankly. "The ones that went to the moon?" Dumbly, we nodded. "You can *see* how the weather's gone all wrong." This was a statement.

Dana and I looked at each other. Nothing strange about the weather as far as we could tell. The summer had been a little dry and windless, but Michigan weather was always changing.

The woman lifted her right hand, spread her fingers wide, palm up, and gestured at the sky. For a minute, I thought she was going to say, *So long, Kemosabe.* Instead, she said, "So it's them *astronauts*." We looked up, then back, but she was heading down the road into the forest.

We sat there for a minute, the motor idling. Dana said, "Shit, Maddie. Shit, shit, shit. We could have been killed. She could have knifed us and hidden the bodies and made off with the Malibu."

But I was tingling with adrenaline and the headiness of risk. I took a hard bite from the cookie. "No," I said, shaking my head, my mouth filling with ginger, "she's just kind of crazy."

We drove off, leaving the forest and the pastures behind us and heading toward town. It had been five years since our father had caved in and bought a TV so we could watch the moon landing. The image had been fuzzy and broken, but we had seen the footprint they made. A proud moment for all

Americans—except for those who lived in the forest, under a pristine moon. If you had no TV, you couldn't see the One Giant Leap. But we'd seen it. We'd gathered in front of our set as if it were a campfire around which tales were told.

Dana obviously felt relieved, having expelled our passenger. Had Tad Swanson with his reckless bravado and his belly full of beer seemed as remotely foreboding and threatening as the Indian woman, perhaps Deb would not have gotten into his car. But she had grown up with him, trusted him. There was nothing strange or exotic about Tad.

I felt solemn and ennobled. My back was a little straighter. I would tell Derek what had happened. Perhaps I would tell Louisa we picked up an Indian woman. It was fine and good, and I was somehow different from my father.

We were almost back to Sand Isle. I could feel Dana's thrill at returning the car undetected as we pulled into the parking lot alongside the ferry dock. She was getting away with something—a rebel in her own right. The sky was darkening. Perhaps our parents had left the cocktail party, perhaps they had gone on to dinner. Tomorrow Dana would brag to her friends about her transgression. She might even tell about the Indian woman—*You know them astronauts?*—but, like Eve and the apple, I was the one who'd eaten the cookie, and Dana had refused.

ELEVEN

I began posing for Derek in his studio below the kitchen. The room was tucked between a stair landing and two bathrooms—the kind of room that appears in dreams when you thought no room was there. The walls were papered with studies of nudes he'd done at Yale. An old woman's pendulous breasts. A man splayed on a stool, his penis drawn as carefully as his hands.

"*I* was the one who wanted to pick her up," I said, telling him about Dana's and my hitchhiker.

Derek was holding a paintbrush at arm's length as if to measure my features. He blinked one eye, then the other, until he seemed satisfied and made a dash of charcoal across the page.

"Me," I repeated, studying Derek, mimicking him. Each time I alternated blinking eyes, he moved slightly left, then right. If I blinked really rapidly, it appeared as if he and Edward were standing side by side.

"Stop blinking, please," said Derek.

Derek was a masterful draftsman, using the chiaroscuro of charcoal and chalk to good effect. Tacked to the wall were several studies of a voluptuous nude, the terrain of her curves exquisitely rendered. "What's her name?" I said, lingering on the smudge of charcoal between her thighs.

"Yvonne."

"Is she your girlfriend?"

Derek looked like Edward, yet not Edward. It was as if someone had taken Derek's features and gently rearranged them like one of his portraits, primitive yet artfully capturing some essential quality. I wondered what quality Derek would find in me, but I suspected there was nothing of interest to exhume. I was teeming with impulse but little substance.

"And the sun shines down like honey on our lady of the harbor," Derek sang as he moved his hand across the page.

After Dana and I picked up that Indian woman at the end of July, the mood of the summer had shifted. Adele arrived the beginning of August, thin as a toothpick and wearing leather pants along with a macramé shirt, huge fortune-teller earrings, her black hair pulled straight back from her face. With her sunglasses on, she looked like someone who would hang out with Andy Warhol or Roman Polanski. She had left her husband for an Italian and had just come in from Florence. Her Italian, she told me, did things to her she never dreamed of, using his tongue, his hand, his knee.

His knee? I said, trying to imagine that one. For years, Adele had taken a sporadic interest in me, though I was about as exotic as cornflakes. Like Derek and Edward, Adele was olive-skinned, but her eyes were more topaz. Angling for her allegiance, I reported what Aunt Pat and my mother were saying about her terrible mistake divorcing Stephen, who was a bright light in his Cleveland law firm and who came from such a good family.

"Stephen," Adele had told me, eyes flashing, "is the world's most boring person."

I had taken this to mean that Stephen was *not* adept at using his knee. Spouseless, Adele commandeered the Love Nest and the phone, talking to her Italian, ignoring my father's demand that she reverse the charges because why should *we* pay for her adulterous conversations.

"And she's touched your perfect body with her mi-ind," Derek continued, singing the Leonard Cohen song.

Possessed by a new bravado, frozen in a pose, I continued to examine Derek's studio. Dibs and daubs of color—detonations worthy of Pollack—graffiti'd every surface. The floor was strewn with drawings passionately tossed aside.

"Derek," I said, "would you like me to take my shirt off?"

I suspect he heard me, but he busied himself with a knife and a charcoal pencil, filing its tip to a point. I undid the backstrap of my halter. As it slid to the floor, I was suddenly aware of the thinness of my arms, the pronounced line of my clavicle. In spite of all those times I'd willed it otherwise in the mirror, my breasts were barely formed, pink-tipped as rosebuds. Thrill gave way to doubt as a breeze came through the window, and I shivered violently. Derek, his back to me, hacked at his pencil silently. I studied his neck, discerning a spot of color. Then all at once he turned.

"So," he said.

I continued posing over the next two weeks. Midmornings, I went to the studio below the kitchen, sat in a wicker chair. I would unbutton my shirt, fold it neatly, then pose primly or languorously, depending on what he wanted. It became like a game of hide-and-seek—going off to a secret place, hoping no one would find us.

"See that pattern on your belly?" Derek pointed to the shadow made by the lace curtain. He touched my back. I thought he might kiss me, but even when he stared with a frankness that took me in, he always returned to his sketch.

And what was I to do? After the initial thrill of sitting in the nude wore off, I had to acknowledge my incipient boredom. My legs grew tired. My neck itched. So I fantasized, using the prose I'd read in novels to conjure lurid yet unspecific scenes of romance in which I was seduced—not so much against my will, but without my awareness, thus absolving me of any

incestuous transgression, real or imagined. Why such obtuseness appealed
to me became a subject of discussion with Dr. Anke, but at fourteen, my
idea of romance had everything to do with it being inadvertent as well as
overwhelming.

"Think of it—" Derek said one morning while he was measuring
me with the brush. "Our exalted civilization. We could be sitting in a café
reading poetry, and Nixon tips off the Cold War. A nuclear blast, and we're
annihilated. Reading Pablo Neruda one minute, and the next we're fused
to our seats. Eyes, hair, flesh gone. Bone becomes rubble." Derek spoke with
alluring moral authority. It was the middle of August, and Nixon was going
down. I was about to say that it was probably as good a time as any for the
Soviets to invade our country while all of us were preoccupied with Water-
gate, but when I opened my mouth to speak, Derek said, "Lift your chin,
Maddie. Imagine yourself on a throne."

But why would I want to imagine myself away from this perfection with
my cousin focused on me?

E dward came back from Vietnam the second week of August. He
returned twitchy and preoccupied. Ever since he was a teenager,
Aunt Eugenia had been wary of him, circling around like a mama bird as-
sessing the viability of a chick that had fallen from the nest. He had a way
of staring at mirrors as if he was falling into them. We knew better than to
ask. Even so, we overheard things—the way he talked to Louisa, for instance, as though she was the only person who understood. With a smile
that could swallow the waning moon, Louisa spoke low and steady to Edward, spoke to him about nothing. Edward watched as Louisa cracked eggs
and chopped vegetables and chattered on about the heat and "them nasty
raccoons strewing the garbage again."

Edward had reclaimed the old boat room, where he'd slept before going to Vietnam, making it into a spartan sort of camp. A cot mattress. A
candle by which to read. He'd taken to burning incense. Its smell would

insinuate into the rest of the house, permeating the rooms with the sweet fragrance of overgrown temples and deep-jungle statuary with slanted eyes. *Weird*, Sedgie said. *Edward's just plain weird*. But then, he'd always been a little off. If you looked at him funny. If you looked at him at all.

He didn't smoke pot anymore. He was living clean. *Survival*, he explained to me one morning when I saw him drinking something green and thick as pond slime. It *could* have been pond slime, for all I knew. Adele told me that Edward had survived an ambush by breathing through a hollow blade of grass beneath the surface of a river.

"Did you really do that?" I asked him. I wanted to envision what it looked and smelled like, the sounds of the jungle, the taste of the swamp.

Edward stared at me over his sludgy drink. While Derek's hair was long, Edward's was strange—short but uneven as if he hadn't used scissors. I was almost fifteen, now. My braces would be coming off at Christmas. Emboldened by my new stature as a muse, I decided to press further. Had fear electrified his nerve endings in a steady burst? Or had it stuck in his throat?

"Did *what?*" The tone in which he said it made the question itself seem dirty.

I hesitated, then said, "Sucked air through a straw?"

"*Sucked?*" Edward laughed. "Sure. Want me to show you how?"

Things had been unraveling in the house ever since Dana and I had taken our clandestine Malibu drive. The ferry driver, it seemed, had reported us. My parents were informed. Now Dana had been double-grounded. She would drag the phone from the dining room into her bedroom, its long cord snaking around the landing and through another hall. We could hear her muffled voice as she described this purgatory to her boyfriend, who at first was sympathetic, then bored, and, finally, indifferent. When it became apparent Dana no longer held his fascination, she took it out on me. If we hadn't picked up that Indian, we would have made it home unnoticed. And now Bruce or Buck or whatever his name was wouldn't return her calls. Doors slammed. Sobs ensued. My mother's voice was firm as she tried to comfort Dana. Once, after a tearful scene in which

Dana threatened to drop out of school, I overheard my parents arguing, my mother telling my father that Dana was *his* daughter, too, and why didn't he step in?

I, in the meantime, was invisible to my parents. If my mother even noticed me, it was with mild surprise as if I was a book she had set down or misplaced, then forgotten altogether. After her fight with my father, I had found my mother playing solitaire in the card room. Flipping a card and scanning for an ace, she had drawn on her cigarette and said, *Promise me when you have a problem, you'll spare us the hysteria.*

"So what do you do in there anyway?" Edward asked over the rim of his glass. "Derek got you cleaning his brushes?"

Ignoring his question, I mustered my courage. "So what *was* it like?"

Edward slowly set down his glass, licked a fleck of green from his lower lip, and sat back with his arms crossed. Like Derek, he was dark, but his lips were fuller, almost girlish, so that when he sneered, it looked faintly pornographic. In spite of the antipathy I felt for him, I was curious.

Edward seemed to weigh my intentions. "The weird thing—" He leaned toward me across the table. I found myself pulling back a little, just in case. "The *weirdest* thing," he continued, "is that I'd rather be stuck on a hill with the slants shooting at me than holed up here with a bunch of prepsters worried about scoring beer and whether Mommy and Daddy are going to come through with some bucks. Know what I mean?"

In some nascent, unformed way, I did.

D erek, in the meantime, was taking peyote and studying rocks. I found him on the beach one evening before the sun went down. Sitting together on the cool mound of sand, we watched the lake turn to slate. There was a dark bank of clouds along the horizon boding evil weather, but for now the sky above was clear, soon to be pricked with stars.

"Matter is an illusion," Derek said. "Do you have any concept of the distance between atoms?"

I edged a little closer to him. Ever since Uncle Halsey had passed away in the winter of 1969, Derek had taken on the pastoral quality of a handsome priest. Derek was awestruck, not cynical like Edward. I so much wanted to emulate him, but my fear was that I was more like Edward, prone to sourness and a jaded eye.

"Have you ever taken peyote, Maddie?"

I shook my head. Psychedelics made me think of Jimi Hendrix and Art Linkletter's daughter, the stove flame that blossomed into a flower in the antidrug film we'd seen in school.

"If you did, you'd see things. Really see them. My father—" he broke off. For a long moment, he regarded the lake. My memories of Uncle Halsey were dim recollections of a thin-faced man, peevish with cancer, unkind to his sons. Derek's green, spaced-out eyes took on a keen sort of focus. He fondled the rock. "All these connections. There's poetry in these rocks, Maddie. If you could only see it."

Y our cousin," my mother said, yanking a red strand of yarn through needlepoint canvas, "seems to be having difficulties."

"Which cousin?" I said.

She stared at me over her glasses. She was wearing Ben Franklins now, looking more and more like my aunt Pat in cable-knit sweaters and Liberty print skirts. "Who do you think? That Edward, of course." She sniffed. "He was always strange. Even as a child."

We were sitting in the tower room, me with my book, my mother with her needlepoint. I had been reading a Harold Robbins novel till my mother found it and took it away. I had dog-eared some of the sex scenes, marveling at how my thighs tingled from merely reading the printed words. Now I was reading a copy of Anaïs Nin I'd purloined from Adele.

"Maybe he was in the Green Berets, Mom. He could have seen women and children butchered." I sighed dramatically.

"Even so," said my mother. "He's odd."

Which was exactly what drew me to him. I had previously found him repugnant; now I was enthralled, as with the Indian woman and her store-bought cookies, her notions about the moon. Edward *was* odd, and his oddness held promise. Even Derek, who was my idol with his artistic vision and his noble sense of justice, had lost some of his luster to the taboo allure of Edward. While Derek might take peyote and find poetry, Edward, drug-free, saw demons.

My mother, who had given up on Dana's moroseness, took longer and longer naps, and I was left mostly to myself. Soon, the summer would be winding down, and I would be back to my sophomore year. In two years, I would get my own school ring, *Virtute et Veritas* engraved around the edge. But for now, I was savoring the last of the August evenings, already heralded by a dented harvest moon.

It could have been a Friday or a Tuesday night. All the nights in summer bled together with little to distinguish them. Most of the family was out, including Dana, whose detention had expired. Even Adele had gone on a date, wantonly disloyal to her Italian as well as her husband, and I was left alone on the porch swing to contemplate a partially eclipsing moon. Above the shrill of crickets, I could hear the faint threads of a dance band at the yacht club. I pushed the swing back and forth, immersed in Anaïs Nin's voluptuous self-exposure. Deep in the house, Edward was listening to Asian music in his own private reverie, facing his demons or casting them out. At one point, the music stopped, and I thought I heard him pacing, but no one came onto the porch, and when my solitude proved too unbearable, I went upstairs to my monk's cell in the recesses of the fourth floor.

Soon, I was nestled into my bed. The nursery was pleasantly musty and barely bigger than the closet where the geranium fabric hung. Dead moths were tangled in the yellowed sheers; there were corpses of wasps on the sill. I had slept in this room with its narrow bed and old-fashioned crib off and on since my childhood, discerned distorted faces in the grain of the cedar bead-board, made up stories and games when I was left alone for hours. Now that I was nearly fifteen, the room seemed close. My legs and breasts felt bruised from growing. And I ached in some mysterious way—a delicious, throbbing midriff ache that spread downward to my thighs.

I must have slept. In the narcotic slumber of an oppressive night, I dreamed of tall, thin houses by a lake. Restless, I threw off my sheets. My breaths took on the rhythm of the waves. When the footsteps came, I lay very still.

What were you thinking? Dr. Anke would eventually ask me.

Explanations fail me. Was I excited? Scared? The door closed behind him, he crossed to my bed and sat down. In the darkness, I could barely see his face, just the ragged silhouette of hair. He touched me—not on my breast, but on my braces. He ran his finger across them, then his tongue. He tasted of toothpaste. With Adele's Italian in mind, I had dreamed of passion. I had imagined Derek, but it wasn't Derek. The darkness leached out what subtle differences they had; Edward became Derek became Edward again.

"I saw the pictures," Edward said. "The ones he drew of you."

Something flickered in my stomach. *It's not what you think*, I started to say, but I was riveted by the all-seeing look in Edward's eyes.

"Don't you get it?" he said, touching my face. "You think they see you, but they don't."

Edward sighed as if it should have been obvious. *You're bottomless*, Anaïs Nin wrote. *You're unfathomable*. When he lay down next to me, I took Edward's face in my hands. I could have lain like this all night, but Edward gradually grew agitated. *Shh, shh, shh*, he said as he rubbed his Levi's against my nightgown.

Uck, I thought, still trying to read Edward's face, praying he wouldn't kiss me.

Somewhere on a beach, Dana was crying. On the Baileys' porch, Adele leaned in for a kiss. In another house, my mother blew smoke, lifted her drink, while my father, watching Nixon, shook his head. Edward's breath quickened. Tearfully, Dana snapped that chain from her neck and flung her boyfriend's ring into the lake. Edward shuddered, whimpered, became still.

I could not move. On the back of my tongue, the bitterness of bile. I knew that I had brought this on myself with my prurient fantasizing. That Edward, as well as Derek, was my cousin entered my senses with latent if obvious clarity, and I felt sick. I wanted him to say something more. I could already taste the abandonment, but, unlike my sister, I had no ring to toss extravagantly away. When morning came, I would go to Derek's studio, find those drawings, and tear them up.

TWELVE

My mother sent me to Harvard with three pieces of advice: wear clean underwear, take music appreciation, and look up Jamie Hester. The Hesters had been friends of my parents since before they were married, Bibi Hester being the one person my mother could count on to get even more sloshed than she did at a party. Bibi Hester was resolutely blond, her hair teased into whatever was that summer's version of a beehive, her lips and nails ranging from coral to pink. My mother liked to tell the story of how Bibi had blackened the eye of another bridesmaid at my parents' wedding in an attempt to catch the bouquet.

And she was already married to Huntley! exclaimed my mother.

Except for the underwear, I blew off my mother's suggestions, signing up for literature courses like Love and Eroticism in Poetry and History of Politics in the Novel. I altogether ignored Jamie Hester, who was in his first year at business school, but my mother and Bibi were in cahoots, and Jamie eventually gave me a call. Up till then, Jamie had been a pale-haired boy with brown legs leaping over tennis nets or rooster tailing behind ski boats, the son of my mother's boozy friend. When he showed up in my dorm room, he affected the cocky manner of a boy who'd avoided the draft and whose future in bags was set.

"You'll want to move into an apartment next year," he said with an air of authority. "No one stays in the dorms."

Although I agreed with his assessment, I shot back, "It's not so bad."

He took in my roommate's side of the room—her Happy Face decals on the closet door, the fake fur throw pillows, the "I am I, and You are You, and If By Chance We Meet, It's Beautiful" poster. Jamie's eyes drifted back to mine, an amused eyebrow arching slightly. We both laughed and then and there, like our mothers, became co-conspirators and friends.

Soon, he was dropping by all the time. My roommate, who was prone to promiscuity, often stayed out nights with the hockey player of the week. It was on these nights that Jamie would appear in my room with his guitar and a bottle of wine. He had a birthmark on his cheek, the only flaw in an otherwise perfect face. The more I sipped, the more gorgeous he became with his thin ponytail and single earring. Gradually, he began to take on more significance than the son of my mother's friend. In his slow, stoned voice, I gleaned spiritual depth that needed only to be teased out by some-one with a more evolved social conscience. Perhaps I could talk him into using his graduate degree for something loftier than commerce. When he played his guitar and sang Neil Young songs, something stirred in me. *Old man, take a look at your life . . .*

"You're not like your family," I told him.

"And *you*," he said slowly in a wine-thickened voice, "are definitely not like yours."

I took a sip from his glass. "Which means?" I said, trying to decode his stare.

Seeing the look on my face, Jamie chucked me on the chin and strummed a few more chords. "The crazy Addisons," he said.

One January evening, Jamie found me in the library reading Proust. It had been snowing hard all day. "You can't even *see* the sidewalks," he said, insisting that he walk me back to the dorm, helping me to navigate the snowdrifts that challenged my California sense of balance. It was a wild ocean of a storm. Snowflakes like frenzied fairies danced around the streetlamps of Cambridge. Breathless, we arrived at the dorm, icy-cheeked, our clothes powdered with snow. "If you'd grown up in the Midwest," he said, watching me shiver in my blue jeans and insubstantial coat, "you'd know how to dress."

"I *know* how to dress," I said, slapping snow off my skimpy jacket that was soaked clear through.

Jamie helped me off with my coat. Outside, all of Cambridge was cloaked in white. "Do you know how to *un*dress?" he said, nuzzling my neck.

My first reaction was to laugh. My second was to stand perfectly still. I had never had a lover. In the minute that followed, I considered my prior yearnings. Now, as Jamie backed me up and lowered me onto the bed, I looked up into his eyes and tried to interpret what I saw.

"You're beautiful," he said. I knew I wasn't. Still, I hung on his words as though they held the possibility.

For weeks, I told no one, not even Dana. That my lover was someone I had grown up with struck me as slightly incestuous. But Boston was a different longitude, far from my family in California, farther still, in many ways, from the Aerie and Sand Isle. Meeting in cafés, going to bars, listening to his guitar in my room, I pretended that our relationship had nothing to do with our families, that it was freshly honed, that Jamie was a man who could see me for myself. Hadn't he looked delighted when I told him about the Indian woman we once picked up?

"The aunts will be delirious," predicted Jamie, and I could just imagine Aunt Pat sizing up the situation. We all knew about the Hester tiara that was moldering in a safety-deposit box—a nineteenth-century crustacean that yielded up diamonds whenever one of the Hester men became betrothed. I had seen Hester-tiara diamonds mounted as solitaires, nestled between smaller diamonds, offset by colored stones on the knuckles of Jamie's aunts and cousins' wives. Jamie's mother, the boiled Bibi, had a stone the size of a prune on her left hand.

"You're late for economics," I said as Jamie rolled over and lit a cigarette. He looked for all the world like someone who was in love. His pupils seemed to expand when he saw me.

The roommate had moved out permanently by April, and because it afforded more privacy than the apartment Jamie shared with four other guys, we made my dorm room into our own little world. We rarely saw anyone else. We went to our classes, hurried back. The midday sun streaked through curtains onto the Formica desk. The floor was strewn with books and clothes and empty Mateus rosé bottles. On my bedside table, an ashtray I had stolen from the Aerie, monogrammed with the initials of my grandmother, was filled with the stubs of Marlboros and Virginia Slims.

"I could *teach* that class," said Jamie, who had spent his childhood dinners talking about profit margins in the bag business.

"So come to class with *me*." I was madly in love with poetry and was trying my own hand at it to poor effect.

He shook his head and smiled, ran his finger down my cheek as if it were the finest porcelain. Not infrequently, I compared him to Derek, searching for some scrap of the artist or poet in Jamie's soul. And every now and then, I compared him to Edward.

I grabbed his hand and kissed it. "*I stood on the balcony dark with mourning like yesterday,*" I said, " *. . . hoping the earth would spread its wings in my uninhabited love.*"

"Maddie's sad poetry," said Jamie, pushing my hair away.

"Neruda," I said.

That our world became very small, that Jamie overtook me like the sea seemed only natural. To this day, I remember feeling his beating heart through his frayed cashmere sweater.

When I finally told Dana, she said, *Aunt Pat's going to pop a vein.*

. . .

By June, the dewy newness of my affection was giving way to annoyance. Mannerisms that had struck me as charming eccentricities began to irritate me—Jamie's proclivity for putting on a brocade bathrobe after sex; his aloofness toward waitresses; his fastidiousness about his hands. He was constantly scrubbing his nails. And then there was his elitism. *We are the American aristocracy*, he said to me one night over a glass of wine. Thinking this over, I felt my ardor cooling. *Jamie*, I said, *even if aristocracy was worth aspiring to, you shouldn't confuse it with selling a lot of bags.*

Everything changed when we returned to Sand Isle and the adhesive presence of our families. Cornered by Aunt Pat, who advised me that Jamie was a good catch and I should be careful not to lose him, I started to squirm. *He's from a good family*, Aunt Pat said.

My mother started referring to Jamie as the Mole because of his birthmark. It was to be the first of her many disparaging nicknames for the boyfriends I brought home. As the years progressed, they would be called the Chinless Wonder and the Criminal, the latter being the pot dealer I dated senior year.

Why was your mother so dismissive of your boyfriends? Dr. Anke asked. *Did she cause you to break up with Jamie?*

But it wasn't my mother who was behind my disenchantment. It was through Edward's eyes that I began to perceive Jamie as just another young scion marching unquestioningly down his path. Edward would size up Jamie's clothes and grooming. *A country-club boy*, Edward would pronounce him. *A prepster.* Good family or not, there was neither poet nor swamp in Jamie.

"Don't you ever feel like doing something different?" I asked him one night. We were sitting on the end of the yacht-club dock. We were both pretty drunk, and Jamie was talking about his future in the family business. After more than a couple of glasses of wine, I had become brittle and argumentative. "Don't you *ever* want to break away?" Feeling expansive and intoxicated with the possibility that there could be more to life than the obvious path, I swept my hand across the panoramic view of twinkling mooring lights.

Jamie pushed a yellow lock from his eyes, lit a Marlboro, passed it to me. Where Dana had failed in teaching me how to smoke, Jamie had succeeded. It would be years before I quit. "No," he said. "Not really."

And I, less secure in the happy providence of manifest destiny, suddenly realized that Jamie's principal act of rebellion for his entire life would consist of the length of his hair and the earring he wore in college.

The next night, Jamie tried to make love to me in the Aerie. My parents were playing bridge, and whatever cousins were around were locked in combat over Scrabble or backgammon. Jamie grabbed my hand, looking pleased by his own daring, and led me to the nursery on the top floor. It still had its geranium curtains, its solitary bed.

"C'mon," he said.

"No. I mean . . . this is not the place."

"C'mon, Maddie. No one will find us."

A feeling of revulsion. I pushed him away with a newfound ferocity. How could I tell him that there were no secrets in this house, that someone *would* find us, that there were ghosts?

Something evaporated in Jamie's eyes that evening. The rapture gave way to the recognition that I wasn't the girl he had perceived. There was a flaw. My sense of whimsy that he so admired betrayed potential instability. "God, Maddie," he said, looking at me the way someone would a piece of coal they had mistaken for a diamond, "what is *wrong* with you?"

For years to come, men would ask me this question in their own way. Even if I'd known, I couldn't have answered. Besides, I had found something that could kill the pain. A glass of wine washed away that gritty feeling inside my head and stopped that impulse to scream. Two or three made it possible to feel lighthearted, to act like everything was fine. If I could just tamp down the boredom, the self-contempt, the despair, the loneliness, one of these relationships might work. The right amount of alcohol, and I would become the sunny, fair-haired girl my family had raised me to be.

Our final argument was on the beach. Jamie had persisted in finding opportunities to have sex in the Aerie or on the beach, in someone's boat, in someone's car. "Goddamn it, Maddie," he said, flinging a rock into the lake. "You're fucking crazy."

I wanted to tell him that there was nothing wrong with me—nothing at all—but his assertion had taken root, and I couldn't deny the possibility. I left him on the beach, tossing him away as Dana had once tossed her boyfriend's ring—certain that the world held a plenitude of Jamies—lovely boys, but with deeper spirits, more soaring hearts. I walked back to the house on the boardwalk under a dusky sky. It was August, and except for the black-eyed Susans and baby's breath, the garden was looking frayed. I passed Edward's boat room, empty that summer, came up the back stairs, found Louisa in the kitchen making cookies. Sitting me down at the table, she felt my forehead. When I was tiny, Louisa would open cupboards, find me inside, and shriek. *Miss Maddie, you know that drives me crazy!* She had always maintained I had a dark nature. *Still water,* she said, *runs deep.*

"Girl," Louisa said now, studying me closely, "you look like you seen a ghost." The taste of butter and sugar was comforting. I pressed my palms into my eyes and tried not to cry. Later, Aunt Pat would look both exasperated and pleased when she told me in front of my mother, *You should have tried harder.* But Louisa, seeing my face, pulled me into her chest and spoke to me in a voice she had used with Edward. "You are special, child. Special, special, special."

THIRTEEN

After I broke up with Jamie, my heart took on a sharp edge like a nicked tooth. I dared anyone who got to know me to really *see* me—and if they did, to love what they saw. Dr. Anke's theory is that I was trying to subvert my father's virtue and my mother's passivity by cleaving to the inappropriate man, but virtue comes in many forms. Jamie Hester had said I was crazy, and I was sure it was true. I had seen that glimmer of trepidation in my mother's eyes when she looked at me, and had done nothing to dispel her doubts. With my subsequent lovers, I was chipped glass.

In 1984, I moved to New York for film school. I seemed suited for it with my appraising eye, my urge toward reinterpretation. At NYU, I discovered how to burn my own reality onto film. I could choose my shots, control my angles, and run the credits in any order that I pleased. As Dr. Anke says, *Beware the revenge of a child whose tongue has become her own.*

For the most part, I avoided the other students. I found it easier to sublimate my social needs by drinking a bottle of wine each evening while watching the news and *Family Feud*. Besides, the male students talked too much—mostly about themselves. They seemed to want reassurance about their precocity, but their puppyish need irritated me, and the women weren't much better.

And then I met Angus.

Angus Farley had a well-developed eye for film, an almost Man Ray–esque vision for setting scene. Not so much for his films, which tended to be derivative, but for others in which he could perceive flair, talent, even genius. He shadowed me for weeks—sitting beside me in a class on film noir, pretending to run into me by accident, lingering in the classroom after we'd critiqued a three-minute sequence of my train film.

"What do you think of Gruler's work?" Angus asked one night after he'd tracked me down at a coffee shop in the Village.

"Which one's Gruler?" I said, resigned to having Angus, whose skin was as pale as my own, sit across from me. His eyebrows came together like an arrow pointing toward a thin but prominent nose. I noticed he wore a gold ring with an emblem on his pinkie, an ascot tucked into a worn, monogrammed shirt.

"Of the ongoing *Suppers?*" Angus said in a vaguely English accent, offering me a Galoise. Angus's gray-green eyes looked rheumy as if the life of a displaced aristocrat condemned him to literal jaundice.

"Ah. *That* Gruler." Of course, I knew exactly who Ian Gruler was, having watched a full semester of footage showing variations on Leonardo's *Last Supper* ranging from a child's birthday party at Chuck E. Cheese to a society dinner at "21." Ian was one of the few students I'd looked at twice. He had a Midwestern twang and was converting to Judaism with unconvincing piety. "I think he's brilliant," I said to Angus. "Why?"

Angus leaned in conspiratorially. He had combed his dark hair straight back and slicked it down. In spite of myself, I leaned in, too. The smoke from our Galoises merged. "They say he's Brando's son."

"As in Marlon?"

Angus nodded with eager satisfaction. "His mother was a junkie. He hates women."

I replied that as far as I could tell from the footage we'd watched all semester, *everyone* in the class hated women—especially the women.

"Yeah," said Angus, blinking rapidly, "but we're not all Brando's kid." From the look on his face, I could tell he found this disappointing, as if being the progeny of someone famous would be the ultimate wild card, transcending the need for talent and work. "In my country, Brando was a god."

"And what country was that, Angus?" I said, knowing there was little hope in stopping him from telling me what I'd already overheard him telling everyone else.

"Rhodesia."

"You mean Zimbabwe?"

"I mean *Rhodesia*. Before they took the farm away."

Thus the accent. Again, I took in the ascot, the ring, the family crest. Angus Farley, son of Rhodesian farmers, raised to herd cattle, and educated in a British boarding school. His father had died. His mother had brought him to the States. His early promise led him to art school, then NYU.

"And here I sit before you," he said. "Hapless, landless, and at your mercy."

It took me more than a year to fully comprehend the truth of this, and by then it was too late. I was living in a loft on the East Village near Tompkins Square—enough of a hovel to be romantic, but saved from dreariness by huge, divided-light windows and a view of the Williamsburg Bridge. I scuttled to classes and screenings, and back to my own little world, where I hid out—reading, smoking, drinking alone. How Angus found me was a matter of connecting the dots. A sizable rent, no roommate, and no apparent means of support. Had I had my wits about me, I might have seen him coming, but at twenty-six, I was more or less an unenlightened inebriate, and thus a sitting duck for Angus.

After our first conversation, Angus kept showing up like a toe fungus. My strategy shifted from ignoring to insulting him, but he was relentlessly ingratiating, always there to say, *Nicely done, Addison. Nicely done*. Once or twice, I saw Ian roll his eyes, but by then Ian was wearing a yarmulke as well as eye shadow, so it was hard to take him seriously. Drinking made it all sublimely comic or tragic, depending. But through my art, I was able to project my pathos onto film.

"You should call it 'Dreaming of Kafka,'" Angus said of my ten-minute film of a girl running through a train station. I had shot footage at Grand Central of a professor's child who was about the age I'd been when we took the Super Chief to Michigan. The camera I used was a 35mm Hasselblad with a 200mm lens to be discreet. Over and over, I filmed her running through the crowd. Ian played the father figure turning toward the child, reaching down in a denouement of rapidly edited hands clasping, unclasping, being wrenched away. The result was a grainy image with an off-kilter angle resulting from being jostled.

"It's so Dr. Caligari," said Angus, leaving the theater after the critique. "It's so oedipal. Is it memoir?"

Ian tagged along beside us: "More referential than oedipal, I'd say. At least, I'm hoping that was your intention." When I said nothing, he went on. "The Lumière Brothers in 1895? One of the first films ever made . . . ever . . . was about a train."

"Thank you, Moshe Dayan," said Angus.

"Really?" said I.

Ian sighed. "And you should have used Super 8. But I liked that thing you did with the handheld. It was like a home movie, you know. That's what memory's like. For me, anyway. Just one drawn-out home movie."

The yarmulke looked ridiculous on Ian. I tried to see the resemblance to Marlon Brando, but his blue-shadowed eyes, sunken cheeks, and wispy, straw-colored hair spoke more of the heroin-addicted mother than the famous movie star. "And what are *your* memories, Ian?"

Ian gave me a blank, sad stare. Even then—before I knew about the Percodan and the alcohol and the smack, the joyless, relentlessly religious upbringing, the townies who violated him and left him in a field to die—I knew there was something creepy and brilliant about Ian. What caught my attention, however—more than his alleged relationship to Marlon Brando

or his quixotic conversion to Judaism—was his ostentatious sobriety. I had
never met anyone so resolutely abstemious as Ian. His latest *Last Supper* had
been staged in a cafeteria in the Bowery, his camera lingering on half-eaten
plates of chipped beef and mashed potatoes, the can of soda in Christ's
hands. A hooker stood in for Judas. Had I known he would someday become my best friend, I might have asked Ian more about why he didn't
drink, but Angus had locked his arm with mine and was pulling me away.

I t was a week before graduation. I had put the final touches on my
version of the girl in the train station. Most of my classmates were
interviewing for jobs either in New York or Los Angeles, though a few
were considering Canada. Angus was moving out west and pestering me to
come with him.

"You're a California gal," he said, the word *gal* sounding particularly
odious when coupled with his accent.

"I don't know, I don't know, I don't know."

That evening I headed across Washington Square. It was late spring,
and the streetlights had yet to come on. A flock of pigeons flew up, then
radically and without apparent reason switched directions.

"Maddie?"

The voice came from behind. My hair bristled even before I identified
the source. It was as though a chill wind had broken through the warmth
and revelry of a city emerging from a too-long winter. I turned.

He wore a jacket with a hood. His shadowed face looked altered, but
what struck me first were his tobacco-stained teeth. I hadn't seen him in
years, but he had always been reasonably fastidious. My mother told me
that he'd gone back into the military, the implication being that he was involved in covert operations in obscure and nameless countries.

"Edward," I said.

He took a step toward me, and I moved away. He removed his hood.
Fine, livid lines were tattooed from the edges of his hairline, down across

his cheeks, meeting at his mouth. It was the eighties and New York City, and I was accustomed to grommets, tattoos, artistically shaved heads. But nothing I'd seen outside of *National Geographic* resembled this fierce topography of self-vandalism. I could see where he'd cut deep—with a razor, perhaps—the scarred skin waxy and florid. Involuntarily, my hand flew up to my own cheek as if the same wounds marked my flesh. There was much to ask, and nothing to say other than, "God, Edward."

"You don't look so good," he said, and then, seeing my expression, Edward smiled one of his utterly rare smiles. I didn't know whether to laugh or feel insulted that someone this damaged was commenting on my own disturbed appearance. Maybe I had been sitting too long in dark theaters, analyzing edits, the cutting of scenes, but all of Washington Square took on a surreal, filmlike quality, as if Technicolor had faded to black. A passing couple glanced our way in slow motion, their deep, bottom-of-the-ocean voices indecipherable. A juggler next to a park bench stopped spinning his pins and mimed for me to come away. I could feel corpuscles throbbing in every capillary, nerve endings winnowing for air. Edward spoke, but his words sounded like "ta, ta, ta." I shook my head to clear it.

My urge to flee was overcome by curiosity. "Edward, where have you been?"

Edward jerked his head. Reluctantly, I agreed to sit with him at one of the tables where the old men play chess. As Edward talked, I watched his hands jumping from the table to his knees to the side of his face.

"It's hard to keep traction," he said.

After Vietnam, it had not been unusual to find Edward combing through wastebaskets or taking photographs off the wall, running his fingers along the back. He now reached into his pocket and pulled out a container of pills, spread them on the table, carefully placing them in the white squares of the checkerboard. As he hopped one pill diagonally over another, I wondered if he felt, as I did, a lingering sense of mortification. But Edward seemed to have no memory of what had passed between us. Again, I asked him where he'd been all these years. Like the glacier receding from the cornfields, Edward had ebbed out of our world, leaving a rubble-strewn gash. At any mention of his name, the family grew silent. Even my mother didn't express her opinion anymore.

"I've been out of commission," he said. "Locked up. Lassoed. Lavaliered."

"What does this one do?" I said, pushing the pink pill across the table. "And this?"

"This one's for anxiety," he said. "This one's for the voices. You got any money?"

I gave him what cash I had. He kicked back the pills, one by one, got up, and turned to leave. Remembering how he'd grunted and heaved with nothing between us but our clothes and a sheet, my mind tumbled back to an earlier summer.

"Edward," I said, "what happened to Chippy?"

"Chippy?" he said, turning back. "Chippy? Look"—he threw up his hands—"I'm not even here."

And with that, my chipmunk's fate was left, as it had always been, to my imagination, The other question—the bigger question—remained unspoken.

"Where are you going?" I said to his back.

Making the motion of a golf swing, he said, "Beneath the surface," and walked away.

I t was dark when I found Angus with a group of friends in the bar. I walked straight to their table, where Angus's laughter rang louder and more braying than the rest. "Angus?" I said, and he turned. The look he gave me was of appraisal. It was a look I would come to know well. *What state of mind is she in? Has she been drinking?*

"Sit down, Addison," he said, jumping up from his seat, pulling out a chair with perverse gallantry. "You don't look so good." It was the second time I'd heard it that day.

I ordered brandy—not my usual drink—but I wanted something to scald and sear as it traveled down my throat. The conversation around us had stopped. Everyone was staring. If Ian Gruler had been there, perhaps he would have stopped me. As it was, I was on my own. Downing the snifter in two gulps, I turned to Angus and said, "Let's go."

FOURTEEN

I went to California with Angus Farley because I was scared. Scared when I woke up in the morning, scared when I looked into the mirror, scared I was losing my mind. I was drinking too much, and seeing Edward in that condition had rattled me. We drove to California in Angus's beat-up red Alfa, checking off the state-line signs like numbers on a bingo card. Ohio—where my father grew up; Missouri—the floodplain of my mother's youth; Oklahoma, Texas, New Mexico—where we had once traveled by train. Somewhere in Arizona, a swirling dust devil moved toward the car and pounced, making us jump two lanes. After that, it took Angus half an hour to calm me down.

While we drove I started talking. It seemed to bubble up out of nowhere in the parched, Southwestern sun. Perhaps it was because we were so far from Michigan, but Angus was the first person I told about what had happened in the summer of 1974.

"You've got to be kidding," he said. "Your *cousin?*"

I sucked on my cigarette, turned away, and looked out the window. "I knew you'd understand."

"I mean, did he do it with you? Did you actually fuck?"

"Jesus, Angus."

"Well?"

That night, we reached Nevada and checked into a Motel 6 on the out-
skirts of Las Vegas. Angus was keen on saving money, and what we spent
was mine. I wouldn't let him touch me; it was a condition of my compan-
ionship. I would go with him to L.A., see if we could get jobs, provide financing for the duration of the trip. In exchange, he was to keep me
company and his hands to himself. The week had been a series of sterile
motel rooms with Saran Wrapped glasses, grilled cheese sandwiches, and
the local news talking about head-on collisions and drought. Angus flipped
the remote control. Motel 6 had cable and air-conditioning and beds that
vibrated when you put quarters into them. We always got two queens.

Angus had played the slots in the lobby, yielding about two dollars in
quarters that he was now using to make his bed swerve and buck. MTV appeared, and Angus hummed along to Duran Duran's "Hungry Like a Wolf"
above the din of his whirring bed. "So what you're saying is he diddled . . .
or tried to diddle . . . his cousin."

I began to wish I hadn't confided in Angus. I knew he'd misconstrue the
information and hoard it away like a coin. I picked up a map, using the scale in
the legend to calculate the miles left to go. Angus reached over from his bed
and took the container of fries, went back to humming. He changed the channel. The news came on to say there was a hurricane heading toward Geor-
gia. It was almost June, the season of packing trunks. I licked some ketchup
from my fingers, snapped the Styrofoam container of french fries shut.

"Tell me," Angus said. He chewed on a fry, his stare fixed on the television, but I knew his concentration was totally on me.

"Screw you," I said. Angus laughed; french fries flew.

Angus was going to stay with friends from New York when we got
to Los Angeles, I at my sister's house. As he drove off, Dana
looked at me and said, "He's kind of cute. What's the story with him?"

By then, Dana and Philip had been married ten years. Marrying Philip seemed like the most spontaneous thing that Dana had ever done. They had dated for less than six months when Philip proposed, checking first with my father to get his blessing. Everyone thought it was a rebound from her tennis player, but Dana seemed to put Bruce Digby behind her like yesterday's bell-bottoms. Her earnest conversion to Catholicism coincided with her schedule of bridal showers and luncheons, and by the time they married in December of 1975—halfway through her junior year—Dana was confirmed into "the one true faith." They moved to La Cañada while Philip went to business school, moved into a bigger house when they adopted Jessica.

"Love the accent," Dana said as Angus drove away.

"It's always thicker when he wants something," I said.

Dana picked a dead head off the azalea bush by her door. She'd cut her long hair shoulder length and pulled it back in a headband. The perfect widow's peak she shared with my mother gave her forehead a deceptive serenity. "What are your plans?"

The question begged a number of answers. Did she mean my plans for the next few hours or the next few days? Or was she asking for something more existential regarding my purpose—something she could hang on to, like a railing or a guidepost, a concrete assurance that everything would be all right?

Ignoring her, I went into the house to find my niece.

"MaddieAunt! MaddieAunt!" Jessica screamed when she saw me. She was six years old, her straight, dark hair in pigtails, her brown eyes saucer-wide. In her plaid jumper—the uniform of her school—she looked precious as a China doll.

"*Ma petite choute!*" I said, scooping her up. Dana's house was so tidy it made me want to cry. The kitchen gleamed, the fabrics matched, her clothes were folded and hung. In the front hall were footlockers that she was packing for Sand Isle. It was an oasis, this house—so clean and safe and sane.

"How was your trip?" asked Dana.

Outside of Bakersfield, Angus had reached over and stroked the inside of my thigh. I hadn't responded, but I hadn't made him stop.

"Long," I said, burying my nose in Jessica, smelling her delicious, foreign skin.

A ngus Farley was nobody's fool. He knew enough to leave me alone and maintain the pretense of detachment. And he had a knack for finding great situations for himself. Not surprisingly, he found a place to stay in Bel-Air, a suburb even more upscale than neighboring Beverly Hills. Now Angus was living in an acquaintance's pool house with a wet bar and a view of downtown.

He called me every other day to report on his job status or, more specifically, everyone else's. Who was working as a grip, who was an assistant editor. Ian Gruler was doing okay. And two of our classmates had headed to the Bay Area to work on an animated film combining real actors and cartoons. "The technological implications," said Angus, "are staggering."

Angus was more equivocal regarding his own prospects. He had, it seemed, landed a series of interviews involving long lunches at restaurants with valet parking.

"I've got to get a better buggy," he told me.

I twirled the phone cord in my fingers, scanned Dana's list of items to be packed. She and Philip had left the day before, saying I could remain at their house, but Dana had urged me to come to Sand Isle for the summer.

It's not like you have a job, she had said.

"Why don't you downscale to a bicycle?" I said to Angus. He had bought his Alfa-Romeo Spyder, he told me, because it was the car Dustin Hoffman drove in *The Graduate.*

"A bicycle?"

"People will think you're eccentric."

Angus scoffed at the notion, but I could practically hear his thought processes as he weighed the pros and cons.

"And you, Addison? What's up?"

Tra-la-la, I wanted to say. *What's the hurry?* But the truth was I was paralyzed. School, at least, had provided structure. I knew where to go, what was expected of me. But this business of having to line up interviews and sell oneself like a hygiene product was problematic. To tout one's own abilities and skills seemed presumptuous and brazen, totally contrary to the notion of modesty I had acquired from my parents. One doesn't brag or swagger, but one could hope that one's talents might be noticed without one's having to point them out.

"I'm writing my résumé," I told him.

"Forget the résumé," said Angus. "I'm having lunch with a producer who knows Spielberg. Why don't you join us? Bring your train film?"

It was two in the afternoon. The morning fog had not so much burned off as morphed into a forbidding brownish haze. My sister's house looked north toward the mountains. It had been a dry spring, and the hillsides looked eerily combustible. I had never stayed in L.A. for the summer; now every cell in my body was longing for the deep, dewy greens and the clear blue waters of Michigan.

"I'll think about it."

After hanging up on Angus, I pulled out a bottle of tequila and Triple Sec, some Rose's Lime Juice, poured them into the blender with a scoop of ice. It was scorched here, uninhabitable. Dana and Philip's swimming pool and patio were built into a hill that was held back by a tall bougainvillea-covered wall. I sat on the Brown Jordan with my margarita, wondered if there were rattlesnakes in the wild dirt beyond. Purple petals from the jacaranda tree littered the ground, and at one point, I got up to sweep, then poured another drink. Lying on the chaise longue, I thought vaguely about my life as the heady poison of smog filled my lungs. The pitcher soon was empty. I must have slept. When the sun went down, the sky became the livid crimson of bloodstained cloth.

So lovely, I thought, seeing it through filmmakers' eyes.

. . .

Angus took me to a party somewhere in the hills. Down the street on Wilshire Boulevard, a Saudi prince had painted the statuary in front of his house in obscenely realistic colors. It had been a scandal in the early eighties. A year before, the house had burned to the ground.

"Arson," someone told me as I leaned against the column of the pool pavilion, scrutinizing the horizon for a glimpse of ocean. The house was sprawling, and all the walls were glass. There were young women like myself standing by the pool in cocktail dresses, scanning everyone who came in to the party to see if they were someone. *I'm no one*, I wanted to tell them.

I downed my glass of wine, and went to look for another. The June night screamed with sirens and crickets. A man grabbed my arm and pulled me into his conversation. "Where's Blue Jay Way?" he asked me urgently.

"Above Penny Lane," I said, tossing off the answer, but I had no idea. The man pointed at his friends and said, "See? See?" Angus had drifted off, and the pool lights were making the pretty young women look alien and sickly. I had difficulty breathing. There was a sense of closing in.

But this was different. The ground beneath my feet seemed unstable as if the earth had tilted, though no one else seemed to notice. The lights of the city reeled. Somewhere from the middle of the ocean, a tidal wave was heading to the coast.

"There you are," said Angus. He found me tottering on the edge of the terrace. Taking my arm, he gently steered me back toward the pool. "There's someone I want you to meet."

"I want to go home."

"She's a producer."

"I don't want to meet anyone."

Angus stopped, looked me in the eye. He was wearing an ascot and

Men's Wearhouse faux-Brioni. His hair was slicked back, but when he put on his Wayfarers, I started to laugh.

His mouth twitched. "What?"

"Angus, it's *dark* out."

"What are you talking about, Maddie?"

There was a crescent of white just beneath the edge of his left nostril. I took off my shoe, rubbed my toe where a blister was forming.

"Where'd you get the cocaine?" I said, alert to a possible reprieve from this purgatory. Angus pretended not to hear me, but behind his Wayfarers, he did the calculations. He knew I was tenuous, knew I could easily shatter. Not that he minded. It was a matter of timing, he told me later.

"Come meet this producer," he said evenly, "and I'll get you the blow."

The producer was an edgy, fast-talking woman with short black hair who wasn't much older than I. She was amazingly thin. Every time she put her hand on my arm, Angus looked eagerly from her to me. I must have smiled convincingly, must have nodded in the right places, because the woman, too, was smiling and talking even faster, stroking me with her hand. I clutched my wine, pretending to study the horizon. When she momentarily turned to signal the waiter for a drink, I hissed at Angus, "Get the coke."

Later, we were driving in a huge car with leather sofas. "You've got to see this," the producer was saying. She was amped up about showing us something—her apartment, a movie set—I wasn't sure. The night was going nowhere in a haze of brake lights and Madonna on the stereo.

And Angus, nodding, said, "Show us what you got."

The situation was cinematically seedy. The crystal decanters, the marquee lighting, the fake pine smell of air freshener. My heart was in my throat, and I wanted to tell the chauffeur to drive faster, faster, back through Arizona, straight through to the heart of the country.

"Jewish section," said the producer as we passed the kosher delis and clothes stores along Western Boulevard. "This is where I grew up."

Angus smiled benignly. He put his hand on my knee. "Addison grew up around here," he said. "Tell her, Addison."

"Pasadena," I said dully, staring out the tinted windows, my heart racing from the coke and the bleakness of the landscape.

"Practically neighbors," said the producer, her hand caressing my other knee.

I said nothing, but didn't remove her hand. I had always thought Angus would make his move—was, in fact, resigned to it, but the tongue that slid up my neck in the back of the limousine wasn't Angus's. I closed my eyes. My breath became sharp and shallow. She removed the spaghetti straps of my cocktail dress, nuzzled my chest. My eyes rolled toward Angus, who looked on placidly. *I'm drowning,* I tried to tell him, longing for his help. He nodded as if he understood, held the coke spoon to my nose, gently pressed one of my nostrils shut. Instantly, Angus looked like my only hope. I inhaled deeply just as the producer grasped me, found me with her lips. Even Angus looked surprised.

Adele's here with Guthrada," Dana was telling me, "and Sedgie's coming tomorrow."

Pacing with the cordless phone, I stared out the window in hope of deciphering the outline of mountains. I had had two hours of sleep, and my brain felt like seared tuna in the noonday sun. "Is she pregnant?" I asked.

"Huh!" Dana said impatiently. "Adele has ten percent body fat. You *know* she'll never get pregnant." Dana knew all about infertility and the quest for pregnancy, having gone through years of testing. For whatever reason, she and Philip had failed to conceive. "Jamie's here," Dana said.

Oh God, I thought, remembering the back of the limousine. I had extracted myself from the producer, pulled up my dress, said something lame and witless about having been raised in Pasadena. When they dropped me off around 3 A.M., I'd staggered into the guestroom bathroom and thrown up.

"He's engaged."

Nausea seized me again, but before I could say anything to Dana, there was a clicking on the line. "Wait a minute. I got a call."

I depressed the cradle on the wall phone.

"Addison? You hungry?"

"I'm not talking to you."

"Listen, I've got someone here who—"

I punched the cradle again and got Dana on the line. "What do you mean, 'engaged'?"

Dana cleared her throat. "Aunt Pat said they're taking the tiara out of the vault."

"We-ll . . . it could be for one of his cousins?" I said hopefully.

"He's here with a woman, Maddie."

Click, click, click. "Hang on." I took a long, deep breath. "Angus, what do you want?"

"Hellooo?" said Dana, perplexed.

"Damn." I depressed the cradle with my thumb, held it down an extra second, then put the receiver cautiously to my ear. "Angus?"

"I'm coming over," said Angus.

"No, you're not." But Angus had hung up. Again, I punched the cradle. "Dana, can I call you back?"

I could hear muffled voices, then my mother's voice saying, *She's being ridiculous. Tell her to come.* "Maybe Mom can tell me that herself."

Again, the muffled voices, and my mother got on the line. "Maddie? Your father would love it if you'd come."

I wondered what my father would say about that pretty little scene last night. I started to tell my mother that I was in trouble, that I was overwhelmed. What was I doing in California? I wanted to tell her that the world had provided me with too many choices in no apparent order. But before I could say, *I'm drowning*, the incessant click of call waiting began again.

"You'd better answer that," my mother said.

H onestly, Addison, I had no idea."
Angus had appeared as promised, and now we were seated beside Dana and Philip's pool on chaise longues, drinking Bloody Marys. He seemed suspiciously perky given the amount of drugs and alcohol we'd consumed the night before.

"Seriously," he went on, "I thought she was interested in *me*."

"No, you didn't." It was three in the afternoon but, as my mother would say, it had to be five o'clock somewhere.

"I was quivering, Addison. *Lit*-rally quivering."

I sipped my Bloody Mary. My headache was subsiding by fractions. *Hair of the dog,* Angus had said as he marched through the door of Dana and Philip's house, helped himself to their liquor cabinet.

I wanted Angus to go away, but he continued to babble. "I know she'll call you. I know it—"

"I just want to forget about it—"

"You can put it on your résumé. 'Felt up by famous producer.'"

"You're disgusting."

Angus looked at me and smiled. I was beginning to recognize that particular smile—a combination of pity and complicity. "I wish I'd had a camera."

"Oh, please."

Angus sipped. His hair was slicked back as if he'd just washed it. "You're not really into sex, are you?"

"Spare me your boarding-school prurience."

Angus reached over and touched my stomach. I shifted uncomfortably as his fingers played around my navel like butterflies. "It's okay," he said. "It's one of the things I like about you."

His fingers continued to move in circular motions. My belly rose and fell. Something creepy was happening in my toes. Angus licked his lips. His fingers slipped beneath my shirt.

"Stop it," I said.

But he didn't. He kept stroking until my eyes closed, and I started to feel like I was floating. I had that same sensation I'd had the night before of needing him—the way one needs a life preserver when one is going down. I was terribly sleepy, my eyes like stones, my skin sucked dry by the California sun.

"I can't take much more, Addison," Angus said.

I waited for him to kiss me, or to get up and take me by the hand, lead me into the house. But he didn't. He just touched me as if he knew that's what it took. I wanted to say, *You bastard.*

But Angus, his voice thick, his accent even thicker, spoke first. "Marry me, Addison."

I yelped with laughter, but when I opened my eyes, I saw he was serious. He wasn't gorgeous like Jamie, but his eyes were green like Derek's.

Ultimately, I didn't say yes out of audacity or whimsy or even righteous conviction. I was a child running through a train station, searching for sanctuary in my father's hand. Angus was rubbing my stomach, and I, soothed by vodka and the feel of his touch, suddenly longed for him as if he was my salvation. He seemed to understand. If Angus wasn't exactly like the boys I'd grown up with, he was a damn good imitation—down to the pinkie ring on his left hand. He was familiar, and his familiarity promised safety. So when I said *maybe*, which Angus took as saying *yes, yes, yes,* I virtually climbed into a car and set off down a highway with him driving, pedal to the metal, our speed approaching ninety as we hurtled toward a nonnegotiable curve.

FIFTEEN

Ultimately, Angus *did* make his move, and I *did* let him touch me. There was a delicious, toothachy inevitability about it all. Within a week, he was staying with me at Dana's house. By August, we were engaged. "We're a team, Addison," Angus said before we made the call to my parents. "We drive our own train."

I had the phone in my hand. It wasn't as if I *had* to marry him. But the possibility of choices eluded me—partly because of my drinking, partly because of Jamie's engagement, partly because, to my horror, I exhibited a degree of fertility unknown to my sister and Adele.

"Anyone who wants to can climb aboard. If they don't, we'll just pass them by," Angus went on, expanding the metaphor. I had no idea what he was talking about, but it was not an altogether unpleasant image. I had never thought of myself as a driver of trains, a passer of others. Angus seemed confident and assured, absolutely certain he knew what was right. As far as he was concerned, the deal was sealed. He took a can of nuts from Dana's pantry, popped it open while I dialed the Aerie in Michigan.

Chewing on cashews, Angus said, "Tell them it's a synergistic marriage of artistic intention."

The phone on the other end was ringing. No one was picking up. I could imagine the empty house abandoned for the lake.

"Tell them," Angus went on, "I'll support you in the manner to which you're accustomed."

A click. A voice on the other end. "Addison residence."

"Louisa? It's me, Maddie."

"Ooohhh, Miss Maddie. What's wrong now?"

It wasn't the greeting I'd hoped for. "Louisa, is my mother there?"

"No one's here, child."

"Dana?"

"Uh-uh."

"Hmm," I said.

Angus went on. "Tell them we can all be there by Labor Day."

"Louisa, look. They've got to call me at Dana's. I need to speak to them."

Silence at the other end. Then: "Girl, you sound strange."

Knowing there was little hope in putting something over on Louisa, I whispered loudly into the phone, "I'm getting married."

Louisa made some kind of "Oh!" that could either have been joy or agitation. She dropped the receiver. I heard rapid footsteps and, in the distance, Louisa shouting someone's name. Minutes seemed to pass. Then Dana picked up the phone. "Maddie?"

I took a deep breath. "Dane—you know that guy who dropped me off at your house in June?"

"Louisa just told me you're getting married."

"Tell her," said Angus, "we'll get the ring later."

"Yeah, well," I said.

"The guy with the accent?"

I braced myself for one of my family's pronouncements about my choice of partners. "His name is Angus."

"Who *is* he?"

I found myself reciting Angus's story of the confiscated farm, the dreary boarding school, the long-dead father.

"How long have you known him?"

"Years," I said, though the first time I'd ever talked to him was maybe eight months earlier.

Pause. "Are you pregnant?"

I was stunned. Put so baldly, the fact of my pregnancy took on a new lucidity. I felt my future crystallizing out of germination, mitosis, the replication and differentiation of cells.

Dana was breathing heavily. "When?"

"Um," I said, "Labor Day. We thought the end of summer would be good. Everyone will still be in Sand Isle."

"No. When's the *baby* due?"

I did the math and, with reluctance, said, "April, I guess."

"So you're not showing?"

"I've barely missed my period."

Dana didn't laugh. She was all business. "Don't tell Dad."

"Are you *kidding*?" I said.

We went to Sand Isle in the middle of August. My parents seemed rather taken with Angus. I, on the other hand, felt sucked into a vortex from which I couldn't emerge. My father, who had never been to Africa, pressed Angus for details. Angus was quite a storyteller, weaving images that would have impressed Dinesen about the blood-red African sky. My mother sipped her drink, laughed at Angus's jokes, seemed particularly pleased that he, in turn, laughed at hers.

"So," she said, turning her attention to me. I noticed that, for the first time, she hadn't come up with a derogatory name for my boyfriend. "Bridesmaids?"

I hadn't thought about it. I was feeling nauseated most of the time. My listlessness seemed epic. I stared back at my mother in dumb, addled silence.

"Dana, of course," my mother went on. "And Adele. Don't you have any college friends?"

"I've got *plenty* of friends," said Angus, who doubted my ability to produce a guest list. His mother would be appearing. An old friend from boarding school would be his best man. Derek was living in France, and Edward was institutionalized. But Sedgie would be an usher. Hurried phone calls, the stamping of envelopes, the frantic perusal of catalogs. My mother and Aunt Pat would separate the worthy wedding gifts from the "shovundas" that were to be returned or given away. It would all come together in a blur of fabric swatches and the sickeningly sweet smell of lilies.

Three weeks later, I was standing in the bathroom, dressed in my great-grandmother's antique lace. There were no full-length mirrors in the Aerie—a legacy of our Protestant aversion to vanity—so I stood on the toilet to catch a glimpse of the total effect in the medicine cabinet. The effect was not good. I looked undercooked, the depravity of June having spilled into July before it was preempted by morning sickness and a marked absence of vitality. My eyes were holes; my collarbones protruded; my skin looked sallow and prematurely old.

"Will you hold still?" said Dana. She was trying to cinch in the sash of the dress we'd rescued from the costume box. Ringlets and a parasol would have completed the picture, but my hair hung drably, in spite of my mother's efforts to tease it into something more buoyant.

Dana was dressed in peach moiré, as was Adele. Neither of them looked delighted. Adele had been married for six years to a holistic shaman who went by the name Guthrada, and was trying desperately to have a baby. Lack of body fat, Dana insisted, but here I was, as skinny as Adele, yet indisputably with child—a fact I had shared with no one but Dana.

"I'm going to puke."

"Don't you dare, Maddie. Don't you dare!" Dana's eyes glared ominously as if to say, *Haven't you caused enough problems?* Words from my mother's mouth. Words from Aunt Pat. Dana grasped my sash so tight, I thought she would never let go. She would walk me down to the croquet lawn at the yacht club, see that I didn't pass out from nausea or heat or from being utterly overwhelmed by my situation.

"Nerves," pronounced Adele. And then nodding as if the reason was obvious, added, "Your mother-in-law."

Aunt Pat had been looking smug ever since the arrival of Angus's mother, whose appearance and demeanor cast into doubt the authenticity of Angus's story about the farm. *All the English have bad teeth*, my mother said. *Besides, she's a widow*—as if this explained the state of her clothes. But when Aunt Pat inquired about her deceased husband, Mrs. Farley was taken aback. "Passed away, you say? More's the pity."

Later, Aunt Pat had remarked that Mrs. Farley was very "interesting."

"Not very evolved," said Adele, examining her cat's eyes in the mirror. Adele was reveling in the recent assertion by a channeler that she was the reincarnation of Mary Magdalene. It boded well for Adele's karma—the one fly in the ointment being her inability thus far to produce a child. Within a year, Adele would find more flies in the ointment in the revelation of Guthrada's mistress, but in that summer of 1986, she felt her course was set.

"I'm going to have a baby," I blurted out before I could stop myself. Dana glared at me, but I wanted to see Adele knocked down a peg for that comment about Angus's mother, who, in spite of her dreary clothes and bad teeth, I rather liked. Adele's smile didn't drop, but I heard the quick intake of breath, saw the flicker of an eyelid, and knew I had hit my mark.

A dance floor had been laid out on the croquet lawn, tiny lanterns strung overhead. The wedding was late in the day, the shadows long and heralding autumn. Once—many summers before—my mother, Dana, and I had stayed through Labor Day after Dana and I had come down with chicken pox. We had watched the other families on Sand Isle leave, watched Harbor Town empty of summer people while the lake turned from blue to green. For a week, the Aerie and the island became our own private universe. My mother taught us how to play spit and bathed us in calamine lotion. To this day, Dana bears a scar just below her ear.

As I stood at the altar the florist had fashioned from an ivy-draped trellis, I longed again for that quarantine. Dana was standing so close beside me, her breathing became my own. A decade earlier, I had stood beside her in a Catholic church, the priest's mutterings indecipherable, the service unbearably long. Dana had looked pale and tired; her hands had shaken. Now our places were switched. I had sworn I would never have a conventional wedding, but here I was. There was no praying to a pantheon of gods, as we'd done at Adele's wedding to Guthrada. No tossing flowers off the edges of cliffs. I pledged my troth with the most pedestrian of promises. The only hint of anarchy was to come later—not from me or from Angus, but from my mother, who went swimming in her evening dress. It was quite remarkable. She hated water.

Time has a way of attenuating like a piece of Silly Putty, stretching the transferred image of unpleasant memories until the cartoon becomes a cartoon of itself. Focus in with a long shot from the lake, the little gathering of seventy or so distant at first, the tent and the yacht club barely distinguishable. One long, unbroken shot, and move in closely, panning the ladies in their St. John's Knits, the gentlemen in linen jackets, the four or five black-clad film-school friends looking uncomfortably hot in this sea of pastel. Focusing on the wedding party, you linger on the face of the groom (delighted), the bride (pinched), the matron of honor (earnest), the best man (sloshed), and the bride's parents (inscrutable). Over the background of the Presbyterian minister's admonishments about God's intention and cleaving together, dub the bride's interior monologue: *Oh God, just let me get through this. Please, dear Lord, don't let me go crazy.*

Afterward, my father gave a silly toast about how I used to train chipmunks using peanuts, and now I had Angus eating out of my hand. I daintily sipped my champagne, pretended to laugh, but I had lost my taste for alcohol. It was like a reprieve, this abstinence. It lasted for a year.

Soon we were all dancing under a ceiling of lanterns. The sun was setting lower in the west, staining the sky an improbable red. "Sailor's delight," Angus whispered into my ear as he spun me around.

It was during the break that I found myself standing alone. The music had stopped; Angus had disappeared with his old friend from boarding school; Adele, who'd had too much champagne, was sitting at a table with robed Guthrada, crying, "It just isn't fair." My mother's eyes met mine, and she opened her mouth to say something, but changed her mind.

"Six *years!*" Adele wailed.

"Well, then," my mother said to no one in particular. She grabbed up the hem of her peach chiffon and, drink in hand, flounced down the lawn and straight into the lake. For a moment, no one said anything. Then Mrs. Farley, who was more than a little tipsy, let out a braying laugh identical to Angus's, grabbed my father by the arm, and said, "Come on, ducks. We're all going in!"

SIXTEEN

Angus and I moved into a ground-floor apartment in Santa Monica. We could see the ocean from the roof. The apartment building was Deco/Nautical, built in the twenties. Angus ran his fingers across the turquoise tile above the sink and said, "Quintessential L.A.," as the realtor showed us around. There was a central courtyard with palm trees and pampas grass, but no place for a child to play.

While Angus went on job interviews I'd walk the four blocks to the beach to watch surfers in the distance while the derelicts on benches tried to get some sleep in the harsh light of day. The owner of the taco stand asked me what my husband did, and I said, *Oh, he makes movies,* but I was never quite sure where Angus went from nine to five. He no longer mentioned my train-station film. There were no producers for me to meet. The searing autumn heat of Los Angeles gave way to the gray sort of nothingness they call winter.

Angus still had his Alfa, so I bought myself a used Volvo—a hideous car with an orange interior—but I loved the way it made me feel secure and anchored, the wheels gripping the road, its guarantee of traction. I'd grown up only thirty miles from here, but now I drove on freeways and cut into neighborhoods where I had never been. Oil derricks sprouted from moon-scapes. Mexican kids in cars mounted on bloated wheels cruised La Brea in the afternoon. Onto the freeway, then off again, I was cruising, too—past the parched brown lawns of South-Central, through the oily haze of Long Beach, up Interstate 5 into the upscale malls of Northridge with its sea-vast parking lots and freshly painted curbs.

"I found a place in Pico Rivera we can get the nursery furniture," I said to Angus after a day of cruising the barred facades of Latino discount stores.

"Are you serious?" said Angus. "Your sister's giving you a baby shower."

"Good cheap stuff," I said. *"No crédito necesario."*

Angus stared at me. "Maddie," he said, eyebrows in a V, "what's with the slumming?"

Eventually, Dr. Anke would ask me the same question using different words, but then, as later, I was unable to describe how I was gripped with the fear of running out of money. This whole movie thing seemed impossi-bly indulgent. Everyone in California was making films. Each day Angus came home, smelling of smoke, his hair slick behind his ears, talking as if something was about to happen.

It was the Zeitgeist of L.A., this about-to-happen-ness. An earthquake or a fire or a nine-car collision. Even in February when the rains came, turn-ing oil slicks into traffic hazards, there was a sense of impermanence bor-dering on quicksilver. It could have been my pregnancy. It could have been my mind. I was purposefully avoiding the well-fed lawns of Pasadena. Whenever I went to visit my mother or my sister, they would ask me ques-tions. Was I eating well? Did I have a diaper service? How would we make a nursery if Angus insisted on using the second bedroom as an office? I was driving farther afield, radically changing lanes before veering off into Torrance.

"Names, Maddie," my mother said. "You've got to come up with a name."

"Did you know," I told Angus, "that there are no white people in Comp-ton? I drove around for hours and didn't see one other white person."

Angus mixed himself a martini. He had begun looking at my stomach with something between possessiveness and horror. "I don't understand you. Did you lock your doors?"

But I was seeing everything through filmmakers' eyes—the faded-beauty-queen loveliness of downtown, the vibrant perishability of the farmers' market, the chain-linked vastness of concrete rivers—even the red aorta of brake lights that tracked down the 405. Together, the baby and I would explore new neighborhoods. We followed track-house cul-de-sacs into dead ends in the foothills, traversed Melrose looking for movie stars. At the top of Angeles Crest, we drove to the observatory that was built before smog.

By April, my belly was big, and the baby was kicking constantly. And just as cells individuate and become lungs, skin, and heart, I, too, was differentiating, finding a purpose all my own.

"I met Coppola today," Angus said.

"Did you get a job?"

"I need to work my ideas into the conversation." He looked at me. "Are you opening tuna for dinner?"

"Protein," I said, eating directly from the can. Chewing, I jabbed the fork at him. "*I* have some film ideas. Picture this," I said, going on to describe a shot of a man on a street meridian conducting an imaginary orchestra segueing into the chatter of girls in a shopping mall. Fade out. Fade in to an appliance-store window, rows of televisions showing Reagan giving a speech that sounds like the voices of teenage girls.

"I wouldn't mind a steak," said Angus.

I licked the bottom of the can, eyed my husband across the lip of it with such disdain that he shrugged and suggested we go out.

"I was thinking of showing him your train film," Angus said as we drove down Santa Monica, looking for a steak house.

Besides the fact that Angus hadn't mentioned my train film in months, I wasn't sure it was the kind of thing Coppola would go in for—the clatter of Mary Janes, the blur of grown-up legs. Later, I would make documentaries about physicists and musicians, but then I was conceiving of something more discordant and oddly juxtaposed: the catcalls of Spanish at the local burrito stand becoming the plink of tennis balls at the Hotel Bel-Air; the bullhorn of a Santa Monica lifeguard blaring at surfers turning into shop-girls with voices like leaf blowers.

We pulled into a Sizzler. I heaved myself out of the Alfa. My belly was so big now—so full of baby—I almost toppled over. Angus, eyeing my rounded front, my ballooning breasts, said, "Moo."

"Very funny," said I.

"If the shoe fits."

Arching, I pressed into the small of my back to relieve it. "Nothing fits," I said.

B y May, the baby had dropped, and Angus was working for White Bread Studios. Dana insisted on throwing me a shower and taking up collections for a stroller and a crib. No longer able to walk along the beach in Santa Monica, I went to movies, but was unable to sit. I wore espadrilles with the heels squashed down. My one dress was a tent. Food stains collected above my breasts. Angus, fastidious as ever, made comments about my appearance, the one benefit being the copious amount of hair that began to grow as soon as my hormones changed.

"It all falls out," said my mother at the shower. Dana had assembled an assortment of my mother's friends and her own, along with a few of the girls whom I'd known in high school. They, too, were mothers, having cho-sen that route years before I stumbled into it by default. I knew we were dif-ferent species. They shared their stories of childbirth, each more gruesome than the last. *You need to rest*, said one of my old friends. *You'll hit the ground running.*

Babies isolate you, another friend said.

I didn't know how to tell her I'd been isolated for years and that my life was nothing like theirs. I was already deep in the forest, far from the sunny wisdom of their poolside lives. The look my mother gave me betrayed her concern. Was she still worried I would run onto the train tracks? Did she think that I was odd like Edward?

I drove back to Santa Monica, my car full of baby gear and tiny under-shirts, my head full of admonitions about epidurals and episiotomies and post-partum blues. Heading for the freeway, I passed the train station where we used to depart for our annual pilgrimage to Michigan. The train station was boarded up and abandoned. Its irrelevance hit me like a slap. The morning's overcast had burned off into smog, and even the mountains had disappeared.

I was driving on the Santa Ana Freeway, listening to KOLD, the oldies station, rocking to "Stairway to Heaven," when my labor began. I was in a retro-seventies mode that day, empowered by my Volvo and no clear exit strategy off that particular freeway. I had turned up the volume at the part where the acoustic goes wired and Robert Plant shrieks when, suddenly, I felt the low-belly wrenching of a uterus stretched to the size of a beach ball.

Two hours later, I was in the hospital, and they were trying to find An-gus. "Try White Bread Studios," I said, "in Burbank."

He wasn't there.

"Try Killer Post-Production in West Hollywood."

They'd never heard of him.

"Try Zeno's Pub on Beverly."

Angus was on his way.

Seven hours of labor and pushing. No drugs. I pleaded for them, but the labor nurse said, *You're doing fine, honey. Go!* The labor nurse had a pierced nose and eyebrow. She spread my thighs and looked right up my vagina. "Now push!" she shouted. "Push!"

Angus and I had come up with names—ridiculous movie-star names like Marlon, Troy, or Winston if it was a boy, Zaza, Lana, or Jemima (An-gus's favorite) if it was a girl.

Sounds like a syrup, said Dana.

After seven hours in the riptide of contractions and pushing, Angus, for once, deferred to me. When our daughter came out, even the nurses wept. They laid her on my chest after cleaning her up. There was still a spot of blood on her head, but otherwise, she was perfection—wizened, fidgety perfection. No movie-star names for this girl baby. No cute little handles better suited for jewelry stores. I saw my family's genes in the turned-down edges of her mouth, her eyebrows already mobile and ready to judge. I must have had a premonition.

I named her after a ghost.

H appiness is an elusive sensation when you're not intrinsically prone to it. I'd awake with a start to a baby crying, a keening imitation of an ambulance siren. My world smelled sweet from breast milk. I cried, I sweated, I continued to bleed. Dana and I discussed how our mother delivered—oblivious in twilight sleep while the doctors yanked us out with forceps, then prevented her from nursing by swaddling her breasts. The fifties, we agreed, were Gothic. Years later, when Dr. Anke explained maternal projection—the mother's need to identify with the child springing from her own desire for reassurance and approval (seldom offered by my father)— I experienced some degree of compassion for my mother. But I couldn't help wondering if I wouldn't be a different sort of mother—one who looked at her daughter with unadulterated pride, each of us whole and adequate.

I got a diaper service because someone told me disposable diapers were clogging the landfills. I wouldn't let my baby touch a drop of formula lest her digestive system be contaminated with gunk. My breasts hurt. I was ravenous for water and rest. *It's perfect,* I thought. *Perfect, perfect, perfect.* But in my heart, I didn't think it would last.

A ddison here," said Angus, "has been auditioning for the part of cabdriver." He was talking on the phone to his mother, drinking a martini and slunk into an imitation Le Corbusier chair we'd bought at a furniture store on Sepulveda. Angus wanted our apartment to look steely and modern to fit in with his image as a film editor.

I was nursing Sadie and ignoring him. The more I ignored Angus, the more he tried to goad me into a response.

"I kid you not. All the time she was preggers, she kept driving around. Her parents marooned her in Pasadena. She's trying to reclaim her misspent youth."

"Ha ha," I said.

Angus's eyebrow shot up. "She evidently disagrees."

I moved Sadie to the other breast. In point of fact, I was no longer driving aimlessly. I felt perfectly happy staying home, feeding and strolling the baby. Some mornings Sadie woke me at 4 A.M. Together we would lie on a blanket in front of the television watching *Sesame Street* reruns. I was besotted with Elmo. "El-mo," I said over and over to Sadie. "El-mo loves Sadie."

My mother had offered to hire a baby nurse, citing my tendency to isolate, but I had refused, telling her that Angus's mother would be coming out.

"Make sure she washes her hands," my mother had said.

"What have you got against her?"

"Nothing. She's perfectly delightful."

"Did Aunt Pat say something?"

I could hear my mother lighting a cigarette, thinking things over. "We're packing the trunks. Do you want me to send anything ahead for you?"

"You didn't answer my question."

"Maddie," my mother said, "when have you ever known Aunt Pat to say anything nice about anyone?"

Now Angus was talking to his mother, who was telling him when she was arriving. She was going to spend the latter part of June and part of July with us, sleeping on the sleeper sofa (also a Corbu knockoff) and ordering out for Chinese.

Angus set the phone back carefully on the cradle. He looked at Sadie and me. "It warms me cockles," he said.

. . .

Angus's mother was mad for Oprah. And Sally. And Jenny. She would eat Reese's Peanut Butter Cups and watch daytime talk shows for hours. Other people's troubles thrilled her—the more grotesque, the better.

"Will you look at that gargoyle?" she said. "Not even her stepfather would sleep with her." Without glancing my way, she held out her hands and wiggled her fingers, saying, "Here, sweetie. Pass her to me."

But whenever Mrs. Farley held Sadie, her perfume would linger on my baby's skin. Once, she handed Sadie back to me with smudges of chocolate on her tiny cheek. I began to see Mrs. Farley through my mother's eyes. Even Adele's sly comments rose uncharitably in my thoughts.

Mrs. Farley flicked the remote, surfing her way through news till she found an old movie. "*The Best Years of Our Lives,*" she exclaimed. "I *love* Jimmy Stewart."

"It's Dana Andrews," I said, nuzzling my child. It was almost 6 P.M. There was no dinner on the horizon. Angus tended to go out with his friends or work late, the most productive time in film editing being when everyone else was asleep. My mother-in-law had little inclination to cook. I assumed it was because of all those years in Zimbabwe when she had staff doing everything for her.

"It must have been hard," I said.

"What's that, dearie?" She blinked into the TV for a second, an expression on her face that betrayed how she must have looked as a teenager. Dull, snaggletoothed, but eager.

"Losing the farm." I was starving now. I realized I would have to put Sadie in the car carrier and drive to Safeway if we were going to eat. The lenses of my eyes felt furry from lack of sleep. I regretted not taking my mother up on her offer of a nurse. My mother had only come once to see Sadie, the west side of L.A. being foreign territory. She preferred the valet service and predictability of Pasadena to the Santa Monica hodgepodge of bodybuilders, fake breasts, and men holding hands.

"The farm?" said Mrs. Farley. Her eyes were fixed on Dana Andrews. Suddenly she roused herself and, with a little shake of the head, said, "The farm, dearie, is a bit of a stretch."

I stared at her blankly.

"Angus just having his fun."

This was the first I'd heard about it. Whenever the farm was mentioned before, Mrs. Farley had vaguely said, *Ah, the farm, the farm.* In an instant, I saw in her and Angus the same qualities I'd seen in L.A.—orchestrated, shallowly rendered, the colors not quite right. For weeks, I had lain awake at night, wearing the Southern California heat like skin. The sirens on Santa Monica Boulevard had made me pull my pillow over my head. My body wasn't my own. Sometimes, there were popping noises amid the lurid night sounds—backfires or gunshots. I'd lift Sadie from her crib and take her into our bed. I felt the same longing I had a year before. The need for water. The need for green. I craved to be back among the familiar smells and stories of my family in a house where I could count the stairs and knew which ones would creak.

"Mrs. Farley?" I said. I wanted to ask her which part *was* true. Had they lived in Rhodesia? Had Angus gone to boarding school? His love and his lies were wrapped in paper fine as tissue. Clutching Sadie to my chest, I picked up the baby carrier and headed to the car.

Take the I-10 to the I-5, head north to the 134 that turns into the 210 at Pasadena. Do not exit. Let your parents sleep. Head east on the 210, the mountains to your left along with the silhouettes of oleanders lit by strip malls and gaudy fast-food signs. Roll up the windows. Turn on the fan (there is no air-conditioning in this used car because you were too cheap to buy a decent one). Slam *Dreamboat Annie* into the tape player and sing at the top of your lungs, imagining you are one of the Wilson sisters, the one with the stronger voice and the broadest range. You sing "Magic Man"; you sing "Barracuda" as if your life depended on it. You blend with the perfect, cranked-out voices of the Wilsons while your own sister lies asleep in the La Cañada hills.

You know if you can make it as far as the Continental Divide, you will make it all the way. At the tipping point, water splits. If you can break to the east, you will flow in that direction. You have a credit card. You have some money. You can buy clothes and diapers en route. You pass Arby's and Macy's and Taco Bell. They keep passing you, like the caves and palm trees and rocks in *The Flintstones* when Fred is chasing Barney. Ahead lie Nevada, Utah, Colorado, Kansas, Missouri, Illinois, Indiana, Michigan. The song changes to "Crazy on You." East, you think. East.

Let me go crazy, crazy on you . . .

Sadie starts crying. She is inconsolable. You reach over the back of the car seat and paw her reassuringly. It doesn't help. You fast-forward through *Heart's Greatest Hits* to find "Dog and Butterfly" because it's sort of a lullaby, and it might work, but it doesn't. You get as far as Riverside, and then you turn around.

SEVENTEEN

Sadie smelled like me. Her skin, her sour-milk breath, even her baby farts—all familiar in a visceral way. I would bury my nose in her neck, and Angus would say, *What are you doing?*

Don't they smell babies in Zimbabwe? I asked him.

Rhodesia, he said. *And no.*

I'm sure Angus loved Sadie as much as I did. I'm sure that her smells and her cooing and the grip of her tiny fingers stirred him as much as me. But it was I who had carried and bore her, I who held her to my breast five times a day. When she cried—which was often—I was the one who walked her or put her in the car seat and drove her around. Down the freeway I drove, through Anaheim, pointing out the Matterhorn, telling her that in a few years, we'd go there as a family.

Sadie is brilliant, I told her. *Sadie is perfect.*

I would never have put her on a leash.

I pushed her down the sidewalk on the Santa Monica beach in the baby carriage my mother had given me. The derelicts and the bodybuilders admired her and called me Susie Q. The man at the taco stand said, "*Bonita bambina! Pero, señora, se aparace nostálgica.*"

"*Nostálgica?*" I asked.

"Homesick."

"*Sí, es verdad.*" Once again, the season of packing trunks had come and gone. I would fold a blanket around Sadie or tuck her ears into a hat, wonder if, unlike me, she would grow up to be a girl who could clearly find her way. After I was born, my mother took to her bed. They had wrapped her breasts, handed me over to a nurse, and apologized to my father for my being another girl. My father was indignant. *What did I care that you were a girl?* he would say. *You had ten fingers, didn't you? Ten toes?*

But I felt he mentioned this point too many times.

I want to take Sadie to Sand Isle," I said to Angus.

"You know I'm too busy." Angus was working overtime on a project at White Bread Studios—a miracle of postproduction revisionism involving an actor's acne. This intricate manipulation of pores into flawlessness, frame by frame, took hours. Often, Angus returned home well after midnight—his eyes red with the fine work of close editing, the scent on his skin betraying baser pastimes. *Hairline,* he told me, citing the area they'd been touching up. *The pores around the nose.*

I wasn't altogether indifferent to his straying, if that's what it was. If I'd had more passion for Angus, I might have been undone. But as it was, I was tired. And though I relished her tiny body upon my chest, I was always holding Sadie. Touching was constant. There was a heavy, clinging weightiness about my skin—the way my breasts draped, the fullness of my thighs.

"Mommy used to make films," I told Sadie. "When you grow up, you'll get to do something, too."

Have you thought about the Junior League?" my mother said when I told her I was coming to Michigan without Angus.

I was packing hastily. Not for us the fine old leather trunks with compartments for shoes and hats. I stuffed anything I thought we might need into a duffel—diapers, pacifiers, the baby monitor, Desinex, and a change of clothing into the quilted bag decorated with cows. The phone tucked under my chin, I said, "That's not the issue."

"How will he cook dinner if you abandon him like that?"

"I'm not aban . . . Mother, Angus knew how to feed himself before I met him."

"Is something wrong?" I could hear her light a cigarette. "I mean, is there a problem?"

"It's almost August. Don't you want Sadie to see Sand Isle?"

"Have you talked to Dana?"

I had talked to Dana, and Dana had pointed out Mother's concern that showing up without one's spouse the summer after one's wedding was unseemly and boded badly for our marriage.

"Our marriage is a paradise," I said to Mother, holding a black leotard up to the light, then tossing it aside.

"You're not becoming like Adele, are you? Because when you think what she gave up . . ."

Mother and Aunt Pat were still reeling from Adele's divorce from Stephen Reed thirteen years before. He was a lawyer from a good family, and an impressive dancer to boot. But Angus was none of these things. Angus was a prevaricator of the worst sort—the kind who told you what you wanted to hear. What would I be giving up by leaving Angus?

"It's only for three weeks," I said.

"Are you bringing a nurse?"

"A what?"

"Who's going to watch the baby?"

In the living room, Sadie was happily asleep in her swing. I'd put on a tape of any kind of music (Pink Floyd, Lou Reed, Bach), and she would stare dreamily off into space like Derek on peyote. I had given birth with no drugs, breast-fed her, kept her with me day and night for four straight months. What could my mother teach me about parenthood?

"You can sleep in the nursery," my mother said. "When are you coming?"

"Tomorrow night."

I could hear the surrender in my mother's voice. No doubt she was worried about the effect my showing up for a month without Angus would have on my father. I wanted to remind her that many women of her generation had coped while their husbands were off at war, but I knew this was different. Theirs was a sacrifice born of virtue—a temporary widowhood to be endured until the men returned to assume their roles. I had seen the photographs on the walls of the Aerie—Aunt Eugenia and my mother next to Uncle Halsey and my father in their uniforms staring impassively at the camera. Their reunion seemed inevitable as sunrise—their marriages preordained. My marriage was a different sort of paradise, and, like a wayward Eve, I was breaking out.

"Assuming I don't get stranded in Detroit," I said, zipping the duffel shut.

We slept in the nursery where I had slept as a child with Louisa. My great-grandmother's shadow had walked here. My cousin and, later, Jamie had pressed themselves upon me. Yet the room felt safe as a sanctuary. I knew the patterns in the wood grain; the faded geraniums on the curtains; the squeak of the mattress; the smell. It was a room of dead moths and lavender. How many children had breathed into these pillows or nestled beneath the covers on a chilly summer night? The toilet in the WC next to us ran constantly. I checked the crib for spiders, judged the width between the rails to be safe. Derek's son had slept here, as had Sedgie's children. As a baby, Jessica had lifted her head like a turtle; later, when she could stand, she would shake the bars and scream. A pillow needlepointed by my mother read *Shhhh! Baby's sleeping!* The rail pad had Winnie-the-Pooh and Tigger doing somersaults, flying kites, and being chased by bees. Into this downy nest, I laid my child.

· · ·

The wonderful thing about Tiggers," I sang, cupping Sadie's head in my hands, her legs propped on my chest as we twirled about the Aerie's living room, "*is Tiggers are wonderful things . . .*"

"So, is he coming at *all?*" said Aunt Pat. She and my mother were sitting in the card room playing double solitaire, trying to concentrate while I bobbed like a maniac in front of the fireplace.

"*Their tops are made out of rubber . . .* I *told* you, he has a deadline. For which he's getting paid."

Adele was back in the Love Nest that summer. Following her breakup with Guthrada, she was working with a past-life regressionist to understand her proclivity for dominant males of questionable virtue. The regressionist had suggested Adele spend some time in the Aerie getting in touch with the vibrations of our ancestors, and now Adele was driving everyone to distraction by stopping suddenly, holding up her hand, and saying, *There! Do you feel it?*

"Even so," said my mother. "They should give him time off to be with his family."

"*Their bottoms are made out of springs.*"

Aunt Pat, I noticed, was keeping her eyes on the cards as if she was determined not to look at Mother. She had already screamed at Jessica that morning for coming in with sandy feet. When she turned her back, Jessica had stuck out her tongue.

"What kind of work is he doing, anyway?" Aunt Pat succeeded in sounding nonchalant, but I wasn't deceived. A careful scorekeeper of lives as well as bridge rubbers, Aunt Pat had been delirious that Adele's first husband had gone to Harvard Law School. *Bidding and strategy are critical*, she once told me, *but nothing beats being dealt a great hand.*

"Pores," I said. "The occasional stray nose hair."

Pat's obsessed with her obituary, my mother used to say. *She wants it to read like one of her Christmas cards.* Reading Aunt Pat's legendary Christmas cards, one might think Adele had been married to a Supreme Court justice and that Sedgie was up for an Oscar.

"Honestly, Maddie," said my mother as she moved a row of cards and flipped the remaining one over. "Angus is a film editor—"

"—who alters reality," I said.

"Well," said Aunt Pat, rearranging cards as if they were errant children, "we could all use a little of *that*."

If Aunt Pat had known Sedgie was going to be divorced from his wife, Elaine, by this time the following year, she might not have been so smug. But she was busily managing everyone's lives as usual: her husband's, her children's, her children's spouses', her children's children's, and anyone else who got in her path.

"*And bouncy, bouncy, bouncy, bounce . . . and, oh! So much fun!*"

"Your mother tells me your old beau is about to be a father."

"Mmm," I said, determined not to give up points. "Which one?"

Aunt Pat shot me an incredulous look that suggested I'd had only *one* beau worth mentioning. "That divine Jamie, of course."

"Ah," I said, blowing raspberries at Sadie. "The married one."

My mother stubbed out a cigarette that she seemed to have forgotten, so long was its ash. She lit another one, blew out smoke, and gave Aunt Pat a long, appraising look. Later, I would get that same look from Dr. Anke— a look that said, *You're up to something, but I'm going to stay very quiet until I'm sure exactly where you're going with this line of thinking.* My mother was a veteran of Aunt Pat. She had made her peace by fitting in, by generally agreeing with her, and, by all appearances, giving up.

But I was damned if I was going to let Aunt Pat use my marital choices for fodder. Opening my mouth to say something disparaging about Jamie Hester (I wasn't sure what), I was beaten to the punch by my mother, who said, "No child, Hester or not, will be as beautiful as little Sadie." She then smiled in a superior fashion. If Aunt Pat had said anything to contradict my mother on this point, my mother would have played her ace: in this case the fact that Aunt Pat's grandchildren—Sedgie's Jason and Patricia—

had been found in the boat room smoking bongs with Skippy Swanson's daughters, who both went to Farmington and whose records had been exemplary until this lapse with the Hadley grandchildren.

I was as dazzled by Mother's audacious trumping of Aunt Pat as I was by this surprising display of loyalty. I suddenly realized I had my own trump card, and her name was Sadie. My mother was seeing me in a different light. Only last night, she had presented Sadie with a silver monogrammed brush that had been my father's as a child, telling me it was good for cradle cap.

I started to bounce again. *"And the best thing about Tigger,"* I sang, feeling for the first time in years that I actually belonged, *"is he's the only one."*

I t started out as one of the best Augusts in memory. I hadn't been this happy in Sand Isle since I was a child. Sand Isle, I realized, was made for children. If I thought of Angus, it was only in passing. The Aerie had taken on a pronounced female energy since Philip had gone back to California to meet with his client. The only cousin besides Dana and me was Adele, the only grandchildren, Jessica and Sadie. My father and Uncle Jack spent most of their time on the boat or the golf course. Louisa, who was getting old, stayed in the kitchen watching her "shows." Against my father's wishes, my mother had bought her a portable TV. Between *All My Children* and *One Life to Live*, she'd get up and stir the soup.

From the storage room, we had resurrected an ancient wicker baby carriage that had carried my father and his siblings. My mother and I would perambulate Sadie down the sidewalk, my mother smoking, her bracelets jangling, her feet moving cheerily in Belgian loafers.

"She's adorable. *Ab*-solutely adorable!" said Bibi Hester when we wheeled her by the tennis courts. Her eyes met my mother's, and they both sighed.

Mrs. Swanson, who was married to the "Drape Man," called from across the net, "Evelyn, aren't you thrilled? Finally, a grandchild!"

"I have *two* grandchildren," my mother said coolly.

Mrs. Swanson shielded her eyes over a toothy smile that implied, *But Jessica isn't blood.*

We walked on. My mother smoked and jangled. After a while, she said, "Bitch."

My mouth filling with the minty memory of Addison's Antiseptic, I laughed out loud. My mother tossed down her cigarette, ground it out, kicked some dirt over it with her fuchsia shoe. It was a cloudless day, warm but not hot. Shadows of leaves pocked the sidewalk as we headed home.

"Don't tell your father."

"Well, she *is* a bitch, Mom."

My mother smiled. "She is, isn't she?"

Sadie's eyes shot open. She gave my mother the studied, sober look with the preverbal wisdom of a four-month-old. *Fresh from the divine,* Adele had said about babies. *They're already missing God.*

"Look at her," said my mother, still smiling. "She looks just like you. Even when you were a baby, you looked like you'd already figured it out."

Maybe when I was fresh from the divine, I knew more. But nothing seemed so sharply focused now. The world was shot through a Vaseline haze of postpartum bafflement. I would wake up in the night and wonder where I was. *You were colicky,* my mother told me as if that explained why she had taken to her bed after I was born. *You always cried.* But I wondered, too, if it hadn't been my infant scowl, already accusatory, that was the final straw in a world that measured my mother and happily found her wanting. She navigated it as best she could—with a stalwart smile and cordial, empty words, the occasional utterance under the breath.

"How did you do it?" I asked suddenly.

Without asking me to elaborate, my mother lit another cigarette and pressed her gray, cotton-candy-stiff hair. I waited for an honest answer, one that would explain her compromises, but in the end, her smile wavered, and she said, "I was lucky to have your father."

· · ·

That night, I made a videotape of all of us dancing. After a dinner of veal cutlets, stewed tomatoes, and green beans, someone had put on Herb Alpert and the Tijuana Brass. The album was crackly and familiar, the horns and the beat sufficiently contagious to override our reticence and inspire us to move. Jessica, who was only eight and still good-natured, showed off her break dancing. Aunt Pat and Uncle Jack did the fox-trot, my father tapped his foot, and even Adele joined in—communing, no doubt, with the spirit of our great-uncle who had ridden across Turkey on a camel. My mother lifted Sadie from her bouncy seat and held her to her cheek. Together, they waltzed her around the room.

In the shadows, Louisa clung to the doorframe. When I moved the camcorder toward her, she waved me off, but I could see she was pleased, even when she covered her face with her napkin. Playing peekaboo, she revealed her eyes, her mouth. Her face was wrinkled from chronic smiling and the steam of countless soups.

"Louisa," I said, "how old is your latest grandchild?" I focused the camera on her.

Every summer, Louisa still left her family to come live with ours. While she was gone, her daughters and grandchildren fished in the Ohio River and caught fireflies in a jar. A smile cleaving her face, Louisa jerked her head at Sadie. "Same age as her." In the fall, when she returned, they would open the jar and present her with the luminescent memories of her missed summer days.

I panned the camcorder back across the bookshelves, the fireplace, and the swaying heads of my relatives. But it was on Mother and Sadie that my lens finally landed—the folds of Sadie's neck; my mother's throat swanning over her. My mother was humming something in three-quarter time, waltzing to music that bore no resemblance to Herb Alpert's south-of-the-border beat. Sadie had cried the hour before dinner, but now she was half-asleep, lulled in my mother's arms. That morning, we had held her up to the wall in the dining room and measured her. She stood as tall as my grandfather had in 1887.

"Let me have her! Let me have her!" Jessica said to my mother. Everyone wanted to hold Sadie. Had my mother ever danced this way with Dana and me? Or had Louisa whisked us off for a bath? I couldn't remember—could remember only hands pulling me from my father, my outstretched arms. Now the camcorder felt good in my hands. I tightened my grip, focused closely on my daughter's face.

S adie was napping, as was my mother, but everyone else was on the beach. The day was muggy and buzzing with insects' shrill chorus, and Louisa was baking cookies—strange since everyone had been too enervated with the heat to finish the vichyssoise she had served for lunch. I had wrapped a towel around my bathing suit and was waiting for Sadie to wake up so we could go down for a swim. The phone started ringing. As I ran to answer it, my flip-flops made a thwacking noise across the floor.

"Addison?"

"Angus," I said. He had been calling me daily, asking when I was coming home, telling me he missed us, and that he wanted to see Sadie. *You don't know what you want,* I started to say. *You can't even tell the truth.*

"I miss you," he said.

"And the project?"

"We'll be finishing up in a day or so, and I'll have a week to play."

I stared at a photograph of my grandfather at the helm of the *Green Dragon.* Next to it, a tintype of my great-uncle, my grandfather, and their sister Elizabeth, who died. Beyond the doors of the butler's pantry, I eyed the monitor on the kitchen table. There is a clucking sound a baby makes, along with apparently random mews and trills. One becomes totally in tune to this symphony of noises, the way one becomes engrossed in a baby's smell or the way her face contorts like an inebriate upon waking up.

"How's the Unit?" Angus said—Unit being one of his favorite names

for Sadie, along with Cheese Breath and—for some unfathomable reason—
Ebenezer.

"She cries a lot," I said, adding rather testily: "She's asleep at the moment."

"*Still* crying?" I could hear him smiling three thousand miles away.
"Can't Louisa fix that? Hasn't your mother put vodka in the formula?"

"Ha ha."

"And I"—he made a clucking noise—"cad that I am, sleeping through
the night."

"So . . . what do you want?"

"Are you seriously asking me that question, Addison? Because if you
are—"

"Why'd you make up stories, Angus? Your father is living in Las Vegas."

But Angus didn't seem to hear me. "What I want is to see you looking a
little less like Joan of friggin' Arc." He paused. When I had no comeback,
he said, "We don't all get fathers like yours, Maddie."

On the wall, the photograph of my grandfather in a sailor's cap, jowls
resting on a starched shirt collar. Next to it, a photograph of my grandmother with her children arranged according to height. A picture of my
parents, their arms around each other, gazed happily at the camera, meeting my eye.

"Perhaps," I said, "I need a job."

The line crackled. In thousands of miles of telephone wires from here
to Los Angeles, electrons like tiny messengers were shifting and pulsing at
warp speed, carrying our voices, our silence.

When Angus said nothing, I pressed on. "I do, Angus, I really do." The
tediousness of it all, the barren lack of creativity at not having something—
something!—outside the home that required some degree of vision or intellect or, God forbid, effort. "I'm suffocating," I finished. The smell of cookies
filled the house.

A pause. Electrons waited, panting, then were once again activated by
Angus saying, "Have I ever told you *not* to work?"

My father was coming up the front steps. His thinning hair glistened—either from perspiration or the mist of lake. Through the dining-room window, I could see him resting his hand on the banister as he caught his breath. For the first time, I realized, *He's getting old,* though he was not yet seventy. I'd seen him board the *Green Dragon* that summer, pulling himself gingerly out of the dinghy, coiling lines deliberately with arthritic fingers; his famous squint as he set the sails, barked the orders, called for the proper trim.

"It's not you," I said to Angus.

My father came through the front door, a look of distress contorting his face.

Angus said, "Then what in God's name *is* it?"

"I need to get to the bathroom," my father said. "I feel sick."

I cupped my hand over the phone. "Dad?" I screamed for Louisa. To my father, I said, "Sit down. Sit down!"—as his knees buckled, and he slunk to the floor. *"Louisa!"*

From the phone receiver swinging like a pendulum, Angus's voice was indecipherable. Louisa scurried in, shrieking *Mrs. A!* at the base of the stairs.

"Damned ulcer," said my father.

Then I remembered Angus. The receiver was still dangling like a noose, the air thick with the smell of burned cookies. "Angus?" I said, picking it up. "Angus?" But the line had gone dead.

I n retrospect, I can find omens in the slightest thing. A burned batch of cookies. My father's sudden attack. Like a palm reader, I could have decoded stains on the tablecloth or a cobweb glistening with dew. But what would they have told me?

My father had spent the rest of the afternoon in bed, but showed up at breakfast the following morning. Dana and I sat at the table facing him with Sadie in the bouncy chair between us.

Wiping Sadie's nose, which had been running constantly, I said, "Tell us about this ulcer."

He rustled his *Wall Street Journal*. "Nothing to tell."

It was the family's common response to illness. Uncle Halsey's shrinking away to nothing before expiring on vomited blood; Uncle Jack's eventual demise from an unnamed pathology involving insufficiencies in the heart—all described in terms of how well the surviving aunts had behaved. The highest praise my father could bestow on someone facing a crisis was to say he was a "brick." Upon hearing me describe this years later, Dr. Anke would observe with some irony that my family was prone to denial of unpleasant facts.

My father turned the page. "No use having *you* worry."

Don't talk to us as if we're children, I wanted to say, but something in my father's demeanor stopped me. My father was only seven when the market crashed in '29, and though there followed long lines for the soup kitchens, everyone still used Addison's cough medicine. Indisputably effective (its alcohol content was thirty proof), it was in great demand by the Prohibition-parched, economically depressed masses. In this way, the family had profited from despair.

"Angus is coming," I said to no one in particular, wiping some spit up from Sadie's chin.

"Glad to hear it," my father said. "Another hand in the regatta."

Dana said nothing. I focused keenly on my father, searching for his true opinion of Angus.

His eyes tracing columns of numbers, my father cleared his throat. "Good, good, good."

I lifted Sadie out of the bouncy chair. She was wearing a stretchy terry-cloth jumpsuit with a high collar that made her look like Elvis. From the kitchen, the rattling of dishes. Louisa—God bless her—entered with a platter of sausages. My father cleared his throat.

"Here, Louisa," I said, replacing Sadie in her chair, "let me help you."

Together, Louisa and I stocked the sideboard with that morning's fare.

Aunt Pat appeared, wearing a quilted robe. A caftan-clad Adele emerged from the Love Nest bearing shadows under her eyes as if she was becoming deranged from conjuring too many spirits.

"Someone needs her diaper changed," said Aunt Pat, setting her coffee down in its saucer and digging into a plate of sausage.

Your daddy's coming," I whispered as I carried Sadie upstairs. "He's going to nibble your toes." Sadie, of course, didn't remember who her daddy was. Her world, like mine as a baby, was the sound of relatives talking, the clink of china, the lap of waves. I set a towel on the bed in the nursery and stripped her down. Naked, her arms and legs jerked like deep-sea coral ruffled by the tides. Her eyes were fixed on the windows, and I wondered how far away she could see. Could she make out that squirrel on the tree outside? The clouds? Only four months out of the womb, and she was already holding up her head. Those tiny toes. Those grasping hands. I made a raspberry on her belly and dressed her in something pink my mother had given her—embroidered rosebuds and smocking. We lay together on the narrow bed while I nursed her, her eyes heavy with the deliciousness of it, both of us peaceful. Just us.

"Shhh," I said. The horse and carriage clomped by. It was our own little world. No one could find us here. *"Your daddy's rich, and your mama's good-looking,"* I sang. And Sadie, who didn't know my voice was dreadful, fell asleep.

Hospice was right. Death comes slowly. It is the eight restless hours of night, the sixteen of day. It is muffled talk, slamming doors—or worse—one gently closed. Telephones ring, the slow descent down the stairs. Words become air bubbles, winnow for the surface, effervesce, pop, and vanish. There's too much light; there's not enough.

And then there's the reliving that consumes hours, days. You find your-self emerging from the subway or getting out of a cab, and you don't recall the ride. Or the conversation. Or the person. This is years later.

In cinematic progression—the low rumble of a train, rain on a window, the taste of consommé and 7UP Louisa used to give you when you had the flu. None of these have anything to do with what is happening. You buy flowers. You think, What's the use? In the screening room, the film winds down to test numbers.

How long is a heartbeat?

Dying goes on for years.

E ven before I opened that door, I knew. Maybe it's instinct or pre-monition. Your skin tingles, and you suddenly feel sick. People of-ten say they don't remember a traumatic event, but certain details haunt me. The rosebuds on the smocked dress my mother gave her. The tiny cres-cent of nail, slightly peeled, the skin beneath it blue. Her head was pushed into the corner of the crib between Tigger and Pooh, and she didn't move. One of her booties was off. Hearing my screams, Dana thought a raccoon had gotten in. Mother was in her dressing gown, and her hair wasn't combed. Down by the bicycles, Aunt Pat yelled, *"Dickie? Is it Dickie?"* My father's low voice on the phone—was that before or afterward?—and that horrible sound in my mother's throat. To this day, I can't remember yanking Sadie from the crib, trying to rattle her eyes open, but I remember the taste as my mouth closed over hers, the crust around her nostrils. Later, it was Dana who clutched me in her arms.

T he doctor prescribed for me. Everyone was kind. The Swansons and Aunt Bibi sent flowers and soup. The phone rang. I could hear them saying, *Not now.* My mother played solitaire, her bracelets jarring everyone. Adele sat with me, telling me stories. *Keep your religion,* I told her.

I insisted on going to the beach. Feverish, I wanted to get into the water. I tracked sand back into the house, and when I saw Aunt Pat, said, "I'm sorry," and she said, "No, honey, *I'm* sorry." She put her hands on each of my shoulders and gazed into my face until I looked away. Then she pulled me into her chest. "It's going to be fine. Perfectly fine."

Angus wasn't suited for tenderness. He sat on the porch and smoked. He was a fish out of water—superfluous, an outsider. We weren't his family. He called his mother. He needed explanations. I heard Aunt Pat talking to him in the room off the kitchen. I was taking spiked tea back to bed. She said, "This is nobody's fault."

After that, Angus tried to bully me with his charm. Since my mother and aunt had made all the arrangements, there was nothing else for him to do. "Come on, Addison," he said, "get out of bed."

The house was tainted with mourning. I was inconsolable. I tried to be a brick. My mother's eyes were red, and I knew she wasn't sleeping. My lips were parched with salt. My father had no words. If it had been in our nature, we all would have howled.

PART THREE

EIGHTEEN

Sometimes, I dream of Edward. I usually wake with a start. He cut off contact with the family over a decade ago, but I believe his ghost is here. The Edward I knew was unpredictable, hair-trigger moody, and dangerous. But in my dreams, he's the most rational of us all. He says, *The thing is, Maddie, no one really sees each other. If they say they do, they're lying.*

I hear a buzzing sound coming from my mother's room—almost a hum. Poking my head in, I see a prostrate figure on the floor at the end of the bed.

"Adele?"

She doesn't answer. Her hairless head is bent forward so that her forehead touches the floor. The back of her neck is thickly grizzled, more muscular than one would expect in a woman. I wish I could wake my mother just for the pleasure of having her see Adele kneeling before her. In my mother's opinion, Derek's pacifism and hippy clothing were nothing compared to Adele's two divorces and what my mother called her "serial exhibitionism." She had been my father's favorite niece—well mannered but fun, athletic, popular with boys. *Too* popular, according to my mother. *Like flies to flypaper,* she said.

After she took up with her Italian, Adele became exceedingly glamorous. *A throwaway,* said my mother. *Unseemly,* my father said. No Addison should be caught dead with Gucci luggage, much less gold-framed designer sunglasses and necklaces that spelled AMORE in diamonds. Adele wore pink high-heeled mules with jeans, had her colors done and her chart read, dumped her Italian for a Hindu, went with him to Bombay. She came back wearing gold bracelets up to her elbows, and set up an altar in the Love Nest, complete with candles, incense, flowers, and a picture of her guru.

I think about asking Adele if she brought a wig.

Mother, her left side permanently placid, seems oblivious to Adele. Perhaps she is ignoring her. More likely she doesn't know Adele's here—the way she's forgotten her hand or her foot.

Adele lifts her head like a cobra. I notice that the sunflowers I put in her room are now on Mother's bureau. She finishes her half-whispered chant, sits back, claps her hands together, opens her eyes and fixes them on me. "Why have you stayed away so long, Maddie?"

"Why did you move the flowers?"

In 1980, when Adele married Guthrada, my mother said, *Guthrada, my foot. He's Jewish.* The ceremony was held on a bluff in Bolinas overlooking the Pacific under the proper alignment of planets. We all threw flowers off the cliff, prayed to seven or eight gods to bless the union. Later, when Guthrada pulled me close and ingratiated his tongue into my mouth, I knew that Adele was in trouble.

Adele rises to her feet. Like the fast-forward animation of plant life, she seems to unfurl and blossom. She is undeniably regal, even with her shorn head. Thin as she is, she should look like a cancer victim. But there is too much life in Adele. She pulses with it.

"She needs flowers," Adele says briskly, steering me out of the room. "And air and music and prayers."

Again, I feel that twinge of guilt, as if everyone else knows what's best for my mother. I want to tell Adele that it's too late, that Mother's needs were abandoned long ago, that what she wanted was to be recognized, heard, to be taken seriously, but I'm not sure if I'm speaking for my mother or for myself.

I follow Adele into the hall. "She brought this on herself," I say, flinching at the harshness of my words.

"It's because she's a Taurus," Adele shoots back.

"A-dele," I say, drawing out her name, "it's because she's an alcoholic."

Adele caresses my cheek. Most of the household is still asleep. Once again I shy away, whether at Adele's beauty or her compassion, I'm not sure. I don't want her to touch me, but I stand perfectly still, my eyes fixed on a light switch by the door. I brace myself for some irritating assertion of incarnations and karma. "Sadie's still with us, you know," says Adele. When I say nothing, Adele nods wisely. "And she's not the only one."

"Please," I say.

"She's waiting to come back."

I want to slap her, but Adele has a way of making a believer out of us all. I want to touch her head where her beautiful hair used to be. It must have lain in chunks around her feet when she hacked it off. Did the nun who shaved her do it lovingly? Was there a ceremony—like the Brownies moving up to Girl Scouts? And with this transcendence, this baptism, was there *gnosis*, insight? Like Edward falling into mirrors, I try to fall into Adele's all-knowing eyes, but my beliefs are limited, and I can't share her certainty.

Philip has come up from the beach to announce that the sailfish was washed down to the neighbors' last night, even though he pulled all the boats up and secured them. "Nothing's ever as secure as you think," he says, running his hand through his now-frizzy hair and glancing at the hard line of blue that has formed on the horizon beneath the dissipating clouds. "A lot of branches down."

"Did they clear out the view?" says Dana. The three of us are standing on the porch. Not for the first time, I marvel at Dana's anxious hopefulness.

Philip nods. "We can either have those branches hauled, or let them mulch over the winter. The garden's trashed anyway."

Philip, securer of boats, assessor of damage. We have had our differences. I have raged at him about policy and politics. He always calmly rebuts me. *You are so predictable*, he says. And so it goes, each of us wrapping ourselves in the cloak of Addison righteousness, a cloak that, were I to be honest with myself, fits Philip as much as me.

"Why don't we haul them ourselves?" I cast a look at him. "Oh, come on, Philip. No one will see."

But Philip has his own ideas, and Dana usually capitulates. "Why don't you two hash this out," Dana says, turning on her heel, "and let me know what you decide."

I peer over the edge of the railing and nudge Philip. "Look."

Below us, Derek is already hacking at the fallen branches. Squatting, he shoulders an immense birch limb, complete with leaves, and begins to drag it down the path.

"What the hell—?" says Philip.

I watch Derek disappear beyond the dunes. For the first time in years, I feel a visceral desire for a drink. Branches and twigs have flattened the sunflowers. The sandy soil has washed over what's left of the boardwalk. Slowly, the forest is reclaiming us. It will take fortitude and will to beat it back, tame the sands, and wrestle the unruly tendrils into something resembling the summer garden of our great-grandmother. I would have sworn that I'm more drawn to the beauty of wild things, but the crushed, surrendered artifice of Grannie Addie's garden makes me sad.

I pour milk onto my cornflakes, listen to plans for canoe rides and tennis, jam sessions in the afternoon. Jessica is going to sing, accompanied by Beowulf. There is a striking musical talent in their generation, and I wonder where it came from.

Miriam comes out of the kitchen, carrying a tray of Ensure, Snapple, and toast. She draws a bead on Adele as if she still can't believe what blew in the night before. Clearly, Adele is the result of a séance gone bad.

Jessica is examining the charms on Adele's bracelet—a seated Buddha, a jade Ganesh, a Celtic cross, a heart, praying hands, a bug of some sort, possibly a beetle—all having to do with her latest religion. "I *love* it," says Jessica, fingering each charm like beads in a rosary. "Love it, love it, love it."

"It has nothing to do with anything," Sedgie says. He has had a long talk with Adele that morning and decided that the whole religion is bogus. *Just watch,* he told me. *They'll get her dough.*

I thought this was a little rich coming from Sedgie.

Adele's eyes settle on Jessica. "Your wrist," she says, nodding at Jessica's tattoo. "It's Celtic?"

The seduction is beginning. I recognize the signs. *Like flies to flypaper.*

"Tell me," says Adele, mesmerizing Jessica with honeyed attention, "are you drawn to the Celts?"

Sedgie chimes in from across the table. "She's a wanton little pagan, Dell."

Adele, her eyes not leaving Jessica, says, "There's nothing wrong with paganism. You just have to know your gods."

"Mammon," says Sedgie. "Now, *there's* a god."

Adele gives Sedgie a long, cool look. Nothing ruffles her.

"But you're probably thinking more of Gaia," Sedgie persists. "The earth-goddess thing. Or the one with all the arms and tits."

"Betty," I say.

Sedgie and Adele look at me.

"My friend Ian calls God 'Betty.'"

"Who's Ian?" says Sedgie, but the spell is broken. Pulling her wrist away, Jessica snorts with laughter.

The hours of summer days on Sand Isle seep into one another. Meals pass the time. The sun moves overhead, leaves stir, the wind on the lake kicks up. One has the vague impression of morning, and then suddenly it is afternoon. The desultory feeling of a languid Midwestern summer overtakes me, and I meander from room to room. For a while, voices drift up from downstairs—the sweet harmonies of Jessica and Beo. But that sound, too, ebbs, disappears, drifts off to the beach or elsewhere.

Mother is sleeping. Miriam has rolled her onto her side, and her knees are drawing up, her back rounding as if she is receding into her birth. Her breath is uncannily steady for someone who has smoked for years. *If there's a heaven*, she once said, *I'll be able to smoke there.* A soft curl of gray hair falls across her forehead, and I tuck it back. Leaning forward, I smell her skin.

In my mother's bedroom, as with most of the rooms of the house, there is a little desk fashioned between the wall studs. A pull of the knob, and it opens to reveal slots for mail and pens, scissors, and Post-its. In a drawer are sheets of yellowed paper: *Evelyn Petrie Addison, The Aerie, Sand Isle.* One-cent stamps from the forties with pictures of Teddy Roosevelt. Stamps from the fifties with soldiers waving a flag. I reach into the drawer, discover a gold thimble, an ashtray with scraps of beach glass, a pearl earring, a lipstick, a miniature bottle of vodka that my mother squirreled away just in case. I can imagine Grannie Addie writing her friends in her beautiful scrawl, describing summer pastimes, the evolution of children. I pull up a chair and sit. Taking an old ballpoint and a sheaf of stationery, I begin a letter to Dr. Anke.

I don't agree with what you said about Angus, I write. *What was to be gained by marrying him? Certainly not salvation. My father led us down that path of virtue as if there was no other, and yet look what happened to me. Perhaps you are right. Perhaps I wanted to redeem my mother.*

The morning after I married Angus, I knew I had made a mistake.

It didn't work, I write. *The redemption thing. My mother's gone downhill twice as fast since my father died. If freedom is what she wanted, she certainly didn't take to it. If you saw her now, you'd understand. She's lingering between living and dying. She's lingered there so long.*

Behind me in her bed, Mother breathes. I chew on the pen. Outside,

the sunlight bangs off the water. I think I make out our sailfish sail skitter-
ing westward. It's been years since I sailed, years since my father died.

Dr. Anke told me she was trying to get me to reconnect with my feelings. She said this the same way my tennis coach used to say, *We're trying to
get some spin on that serve of yours.* They both made it sound as if my life depended on it.

*Do you remember the story of when I went into treatment? We had lost
Sadie, then Angus and I divorced. After Dad died, Mother simply turned away as
if it had all been my fault. Do you think it brought home the uncomfortable fact
that we all have choices?*

Dr. Anke and I have covered this ground countless times. You break
rules in families like ours, and they close ranks. Better to be quietly drunk
than flagrantly sober; better to be miserably married than wantonly divorced. The fact of my cousins' imperfect lives didn't deter my father from
judging his own children. But after he was gone, my mother had a choice.
And her choice was harsher than his.

Mother gives off a sudden, loud snore. Her arm is reed thin. The ten-
dons in her neck protrude like fallen branches beneath the snow. When I
was a child, I crawled into her lap, let her enfold me in her smoky perfume,
her spangle-covered arms. She would rest her chin on my head, rock me,
sing the song about mockingbirds and diamond rings, even when I was too
big and my legs touched the floor. I knew who I was then. I knew I was
alive.

I ball up the letter to Dr. Anke, toss it into the wastebasket. In the mirror, I smear some lipstick from the drawer on my lips. Revlon Passion Pink,
#421. The effect is eerily incongruous with who I think I am.

I find Miriam in a room off the kitchen. It is a room of projects waiting to happen. There is a bed and a sewing machine. An old, broken
rock tumbler sits on a table amid a battlefield of unpolished rocks. In the

closet are shoe boxes of photographs to be stuck into albums, framed or pitched out. In an armchair in the corner, bent over a gateleg table sits Miriam, sorting flowers. Between leaves of paper, she is laying down snippets of Queen Anne's lace. The room is quiet except for a low, rhythmic snore that I identify as coming from the receiving end of a baby monitor that Miriam has clipped, walkie-talkie style, to her lapel. It reminds me that Mother is with us, even as I sit on the old spool bed that groans under my weight.

"What is it?" says Miriam. She doesn't look up.

"Nothing." I used to go down to Louisa's room until I was a teenager. At some point, I became aware enough to understand that this was exclusively Louisa's territory, and although I was tolerated, I was no longer wholeheartedly welcome. After that, I lost interest anyway, preferring other company to that of our cook. But there was a time when I asked Louisa a million questions—questions about her children (two), questions about where she grew up (Louisville), questions about cooking (*you jes' look at the recipe, child, but nothin' is rule*). She took her tollhouse-cookie recipe with her to the grave, but we've made our stabs at it, melting the butter or substituting lard, halving the baking powder, stirring by hand instead of by blender. But Louisa held her magic close, and the memory of her cookies exceeds in virtue those that we have eaten since.

"What are you doing?" I ask.

"What does it look like?"

I can see Miriam's pressing flowers, but I want to understand why.

"So I can remember," she says.

It seems so Victorian to embody memory in the flattened and parched remnants of flora.

She says, "Don't you have any hobbies?"

I consider telling her how, when I was pregnant, I used to drive aimlessly, waiting for ideas to come. Sometimes a scene would catch my eye, stirring my imagination in such a way that I could envision it on film. "I'm not a hobby person."

Miriam places the pages into a viselike contraption and says, "Then what kind of person are you?"

We got Miriam through an agency. Nothing on her résumé mentioned her tendency toward bluntness. My mother would have liked her—probably *does* like her. Except that Miriam would never have put up with my father. She would have looked him right in the eye and said, "If *you're* so smart, why don't *you* run for president?"

"I tried to knit once," I say. "Dana taught me." I remember that pink yarn, the tiny pattern, those four pieces I never sewed together.

"Why'd you stop?"

I concentrate on the snoring coming from the monitor clipped to Miriam's breast. I am struck by the absurdity of my mother's persistent breathing. It takes me back to a time when I'd ignored the monitor on the kitchen counter while talking on the phone.

When I was a child, Louisa would fold me into her outstretched arms and tell me I was special, but I can't fold into Miriam, nor she into me. I want to ask her why she went into nursing, why she cares for the sick, and if along the way she has made her peace with death. I want to ask her what she sees when someone takes his or her last breath. Is it something to be feared or welcomed? Is it no more eventful than finishing a meal? I want to know what Miriam knows, but the moment passes, broken by a halting snore. I can see Miriam's age in the tender way she lifts to her feet. Her stockings are rolled down, and the pink quilted slippers are crushed at the heel.

"You should get one," she says. "A hobby, I mean."

J essica and Beowulf are singing in clear, harmonically perfect voices. Beowulf lies back on the couch, his eyes closed, his fingers occasionally plucking an articulated chord. Mostly, though, they sing a cappella. Their voices blend, swerve, match in mysterious ways—Jessica's high and singsongy, Beowulf 's raspy—in a song I recognize from *Godspell*.

Where are you going? Where are you going? Can you take me with you?

It strikes me that they hardly know my mother, that for the last ten years while they were growing up, she was practically a ghost. She'd sit at the table and smoke, mutter something to the help—a different person every summer after Louisa died—push her food around on her plate while all around her swirled random conversation. At least, that's how I imagine it for the last decade since I've been here. The cousins and the cousins' children must have fled the table as quickly as possible in search of talk and laughter away from the glum gaze of my mother.

"Would you sing that for Evelyn?" I ask. The request surprises even me. Jessica breaks off and eyes me inscrutably. I wonder what Edward would have made of my niece's brand of jungle eyes.

"Mom said we weren't supposed to bother Grannie Ev," says Jessica.

Beo produces a languid chord. "Do you think she'd even know?"

"Why not?" The proper music nourishes the soul, or so they say. Even plants seem to thrive.

Now it is almost evening, and the house is filled with unfamiliar smells. Odors as succulent as sautéed onion and garlic, tinged with something even more exotic like ginger and basil that don't mesh with my memory of Louisa's cooking. It's actually Dana's turn to make dinner tonight, but coming into the kitchen, I hear her laughing with Sedgie and wonder where they found such ingredients when all I could find were dreary lettuce and American cheese. The two of them are standing over the old Magic Chef stove, Sedgie with a dishtowel wrapped turban-style around his head, brandishing a pan and speaking in a dead-on East Indian accent, "You must not bruise the basil like so."

"I'm going to pee," says Dana. Tears are trickling down her face.

I look at Sedgie, who continues in the melodious accent. "What is one to do, sahib?" I must have done the eyebrow thing because Sedgie suddenly looks exasperated and drops back into his normal baritone. "Oh, Maddie, lighten up for once."

I feel affronted. I want to protest that it's Dana, not me, who's the serious one. But Dana can't even catch her breath, and every time she looks at Sedgie, she starts to laugh again.

"Where'd you get the basil?" I ask.

"*Fabulous* basil," says Sedgie. "Farm stand out the shore."

"I've never heard of it," I say, my glance falling on a stained, amber-colored bottle with *Extra Virgin, Cold Pressed* written on the label. "Where'd you get the olive oil?"

Sedgie looks at me patiently. "From New Yawk, cuz. Sometimes, you've got to bring your own."

I sniff. It seems a little unseemly, this bringing of one's own ingredients. We've always made do with Crisco and locally grown produce like parsley. Now the table is stocked with an array of tomatoes and lettuces and beets.

Dana, who seems to have composed herself, says, "We're making a pasta sauce." Over the backs of chairs, they have strung long strands of flattened, homemade noodles. Obviously, Sedgie has brought his own kitchen equipment as well. "And check out these tomatoes," Dana adds. "*Heir*-loom."

Dust motes swim in blades of fading light cast from the venetian blinds. Dana flips on a switch; the fluorescent light pulses on. She holds a cookbook, but Sedgie takes it from her and, in an uncanny imitation of Louisa, says, "You jes' look at the recipe, but nothin' is rule."

"Dana," I say abruptly, "what do you think about Jessica and Beo singing to Mother?"

"What do you mean?"

"You know. Music."

Dana's eyes narrow. "Is this Adele's idea?"

I cross my arms. "Did you know Mother used to play Mozart?"

Dana has that same suspicious look she had the other day when Miriam and I dressed Mother up.

"I read the hospice brochures," I say. "They suggest music to soothe the patient."

"What do you mean, she used to play Mozart?"

I hold up my hands. "Evi-*dent*-ly, it's what she told Miriam when she was still talking."

Sedgie adds a dollop of red wine. The sauté pan sizzles maniacally. "I remember Evelyn playing the piano when I was a kid." He yanks the pan, and the onions hop in unison. "I wonder why she stopped."

I can imagine all sorts of reasons for stopping. Maybe it was something my grandmother said. Or my father. Or the aunts. Maybe she decided there was no point in going on. There are myriad reasons for walking away from something you love. "Remember how she used to sing 'Raindrops Keep Falling on My Head'?" I say.

"Dancing," Dana says, shuddering, "in her bedroom after dinner."

"She'd had too many cocktails. Besides," I say, running the arugula under a faucet, "she was capable of better."

Dana warily eyes a cluster of beets. "I hate beets."

Sedgie is still dancing around the kitchen like a deranged swami. Already a little drunk, he deglazes the pan with a spatula, then twirls to the sink, where the pots and pans are soaking. Years ago, a vole or a mouse got into the pipes and died. For a week, flies kept swooping out of the drain whenever Louisa turned on the faucet. By the time the plumber fixed the pipe, the flypaper we'd hung over the kitchen door was coated with tiny black corpses.

I stare at the mound of suds, pondering the mystery of Chippy, my long-vanished chipmunk. After a brief hesitation, I say, "Why do *you* suppose she stopped?"

"I don't know." Dana sounds depressed, but it could be the beets. "Why do people stop doing anything? Why do kids stop talking to their parents?"

I know she's worried about Jessica. They were close when Jessica was a child. Then Dana could read her, but now her daughter is as inscrutable as runes.

"You, for instance," says Dana. "All those years you just stopped talking to Mother. Or Edward."

I shake out the arugula, pat it with a paper towel. Sedgie hums, up to his elbows in suds as he swizzles dishes and tosses them into the drainer. It's been a long day, and I suddenly want to lie down in the hammock and rock myself to sleep. I feel inevitably forty, my past dragging behind me like a train. I can't remember the last time I marked my height on the wall behind the door in the dining room. The calendar on the kitchen wall depicting the lighthouses of northern Michigan tells me it is August 14, 1999, but it could be the summer of 1987 for all my failure at moving on. I run my hand across my breast, remember how tired I was that August. Sadie was a colicky baby who cried a lot. I would walk her up and down the hall. No one could sleep on those hot, crying nights. *You've got to get her on a schedule*, my mother had said. *When you were a baby, we always let you cry.*

Sometimes we stop speaking to our parents the way we stop speaking to our friends, our lovers, our spouses. The throat closes, and no sound comes out. Rust forms. Like the pipes in these old houses, clotted with the minerals of hard water, words become a trickle if they come at all.

The last time I spoke to Edward was after we lost Sadie. I had furled into myself the way Mother is furling into herself now, but my pathology wasn't physical. I made myself sick with longing and guilt and wine, thinking, If you try to remember your baby, and you can't see her face, but can still smell her, are you crazy? At the time I thought maybe Edward could tell me, but I didn't know how to find him. It was in the days when no one was talking about Edward. I called Aunt Eugenia.

Honestly, Maddie. I'm not sure where *he is.*

When Derek phoned from France to tell me how sorry he was about Sadie, I asked him how I could find Edward. He gave me a number with a Boston area code. I called it for days. On the fourth day, Edward answered.

How do you know if you're going crazy? I asked him.

If you ever hear voices, he said, *don't tell anyone. I don't give a shit about what you've seen, or who she was, or if she smelled like lavender or dead fish, do you hear me? It's the voices they'll use against you. Trust me on this one.*

"I saw him, you know," I say. "Right before I went to California with Angus. I ran into Edward in Washington Square."

"What on earth was he doing there?"

"He'd gotten out. He'd fooled his doctors, or gotten the meds right, and flown the coop."

"Which coop was it that time?"

"I don't know. Menninger or McLean. One of the Ms."

A month or so later, he emerged in Boston. Aunt Eugenia had him recommitted, and when he was released, he disappeared.

Where are you going, Edward?

Beneath the surface.

"No one told me he'd disappeared," I say.

"You had your own problems," says Dana succinctly.

"Still, someone should have told me."

"Whoops!" says Sedgie as he drops a cup. It shatters on the floor. He picks up a shard as if he's examining a broken egg from a rare bird's nest. Then I see the name painted in red—*Sedgie* rendered fastidiously, lovingly in our grandmother's cursive. For a moment, I think he's going to cry, and it strikes me again how much stock we put in our memorabilia, our evidence of having had a past, a family member who cared enough to trace our name.

"Oh, Sedgie," I say, seeing his eyes glisten as he cradles a piece of the shattered cup.

"Crazy Edward," Sedgie says, but Dana is quiet. I can tell she is hurt as if I'm reprimanding her, and I suddenly want to reassure her that it wasn't her fault. If I can stem *her* anxiety before it starts, I won't have to feel anxious myself.

"*What kind of schmuck am I . . . ?*" sings Sedgie slurrily to the tune of "What Kind of Fool Am I?"

"You mean schlemiel," I say, remembering Ian's brief flirtation with Judaism. *We all have our mishigas, Maddie,* Ian would say. We all have our craziness.

"I would have been scared," Dana says.

For a moment, I don't follow her. "Scared of what?"

"Oh, you know Edward. He was in and out of nuthouses. We were *all* scared of him."

From the wall, the portrait of Louisa looks down, her pasted-on smile rendered by Derek. I still have a torn piece of one of his drawings. In it, I am looking back over my shoulder, my lips parted, but my right side is torn away.

"Let me see that cup," says Dana. She takes the broken pieces from Sedgie, pulling them close to her eyes. "Philip might be able to fix this."

Beo and Jessica are practicing their duet in the living room; the spaghetti sauce on the stovetop exudes its rich aroma; and for a moment I wonder if, given the right adhesive, our world could be glued together again. I pick up a gargantuan tomato, the product of sand and manure. It is the size of a baseball and veined with streaks of green. I grab a knife and begin to slice it, saying with affected indifference, "Edward wasn't scary if you knew him." The red juice and seeds spill onto the cutting board. "He never bothered me."

D inner is over, and Mother is holding court, lying propped up on her pillows, her hair combed up into a Pebbles Flintstone sort of swirl. Diamond clips fastened, rings on her fingers. Miriam has even attempted lipstick.

Mother's right eye beadily regards this sudden influx of children, nieces, nephews, and grandchild. I search her face for a reaction—the mere suggestion of a smile or a frown. Does she approve? Or would she prefer to dismiss us? Even if she could comment, Miriam doesn't give her the chance as she briskly informs her that her *family* (Miriam emphasizes the word) would like to sing to her. "And you know how you love music, don't you, Evelyn? Isn't it lovely they're taking the time?"

Again, I search Miriam for signs of sarcasm. But Miriam regards us placidly beneath her painted eyebrows. She cocks her head to the side.

"Okay," I say. "So. Mom—" I have to fight to address her directly and not in the third person. "This is a song we thought you'd like." I glance at Dana for support, but her eyes have that out-of-focus look they get when she leaves her body. "Anyway, I thought you'd like it, and Jessica and Beowulf are the only ones with musical talent, so they're going to sing. Okay?"

Mother's diamond pin seems to twinkle, but otherwise she's still as a statue. Strokes can rob their victims of facial expressions along with verbal responses, leaving the impression that the person has no idea what's going on. For all we know, Mother's mind is a veritable symphony of thought— her world as incandescent and as artfully rendered as a Degas pastel—but any conversation is left to our imagination and thus becomes the sound of one hand clapping.

"O-kay," I say. All the cousins are gathered. Sedgie's arms are crossed; Adele is standing across from Miriam at the head of the bed; Derek is at the window looking out on the lake; Dana and Philip are next to each other, but do not touch; Jessica and Beo with his guitar stand at the foot of the bed. I lean against the bureau for support and give them the nod.

Jessica clears her throat and makes a sound that is haunting and pure. To a backdrop of waves breaking on the shore, her chest expands as she draws the note heavenward. Then Beo joins in, plucking a tune that supports this ladder of redemption that asks where we go when life is done, and their two voices wash over us like a fountain. I can make out the words *For my hand is cold, and needs warmth*, but it is as if there are no words— only achingly beautiful harmonies that speak of loss and hope.

To which there is no response—only the wet eyes of cousins looking on—until Miriam begins her own version of what they are singing, the essence of the Mississippi River Valley pouring out of her. Then, as if her past lives are rushing to lend their voices, Adele starts to sing. A moment later, Derek joins her, and, after several measures, so does Sedgie. All the cousins are singing—everyone but Dana and me, who believe we can't, that our gift isn't song. Dana and I would rather lip-synch than vocalize the words to "Happy Birthday" and "Silent Night." But the tender harmonies of our family are eddying around us, and Dana and I are caught up in the tide. We, too, begin to sing, jerkily adding our off-key voices until they meld into music and make some crazy sense.

NINETEEN

This morning, Miriam seems snappish, and Mother is mutely agitated. Derek has removed himself to the basement to rummage around in the remnants of his former studio, and I have a headache. Whatever serenity was conjured the night before by the sonorous duo of Beo and Jessica has been replaced by the strange energy of directionless weather and too many days of togetherness.

When the phone rings, everyone runs for it. To my irritation, Dana gets there first. "Hello?" She mouths *Dr. Mead* at me. "Well, she was calm until today. Now it seems like she can't get comfortable." She listens for a while, and then says, "So what dosage do you recommend?" Pause. "Uh-huh, uh-huh." She writes something on a pad. "And for the constipation?" Scribbles something else. "I'll send someone in."

Now I'm heading into Harbor Town to fill a prescription along with Jessica and Beowulf, who are on a clandestine run for hamburgers. As Mac ferries us across, we assess a monster yacht that has anchored here—Jessica with puppyish enthusiasm, Beo and me with contempt. She's the kind of yacht that goes to the Bahamas for the winter—a white, shiny hundred-and-twenty-footer with a transom proclaiming her to be the good ship

Eureka! I remember the furtive way I used to stare at Mr. Swanson's racing yacht when we raced the *Green Dragon*, secretly admiring the *Swan Song*'s lines, all chrome and fiberglass, built for speed. It had felt clandestine, this comparing of boats—a small betrayal that exposed my inadequacy. Virtue lay in the fact that things stayed the same. You didn't buy new boats; you inherited them and kept them up and nursed them through races in spite of the changing technology. You didn't raise membership dues at the yacht club because people like the Baileys or the Hobsons might be replaced by the new people who came up from downstate with their freshly minted fortunes.

"Sweet," says Jessica.

But in a tone worthy of my father, I say, "We never used to have boats like that around here."

Which isn't exactly true. Besides the *Swan Song*, there was the *Little Annie* that belonged to the Baileys since the thirties. She was an elegant white yacht with a glossily varnished cabin and two staterooms paneled in cherry. She'd been in the harbor forever. Rumor was she'd been given to the Prince of Wales, who'd sold her off as soon as he abdicated the throne. My cousins and I regarded the *Little Annie* with a sort of collective pride by virtue of her tenure in the harbor.

Now we rumble across the channel, silently regarding the much-larger *Eureka!* Cirrus clouds have congealed into gauze, and Mac offers me an umbrella to take into town, again reminding me that I've achieved matron status, albeit with none of the accoutrements like children and a ring. I reject the umbrella. I have no hairdo to protect. "It's just water," I say.

Spray spits up from the bow of the boat, misting us. Beo has tied a bandanna gypsy-style around his head, and Jessica's bleached hair is showing an inch of black roots. These two won't fit into Harbor Town. They lack that corn-fed openness, the easy smiles and sunny coloring of a people whose genealogies trace back to Holland, Germany, and Poland.

Jessica is eyeing Mac. "I love your uniform," she says.

Mac's eyes are hidden behind mirrored Ray-Bans. He says, "It's just a summer job."

But Jessica is determined to engage him. She wants to know what he does in the winter, where he grew up, what his "real" life is like. We never used to ask guards or workmen about themselves, but here is Jessica in a tank top, her almond eyes wide, looking for the world as if she's genuinely interested. Even Mac seems surprised by this proffered intimacy. Fixing his Ray-Bans on the *Eureka!*, he tells her he goes to school at Michigan State. He straightens his shoulders, deepens his voice, but from the flush creeping up his neck, one would think Jessica has asked him to drop his pants.

Jessica doesn't seem to notice the effect she has on people. She says something to Beowulf, who throws back his head and laughs. We have almost reached the other side. Seagulls swoop and squawk in our wake. Mac weaves his way through the moorings, reaches the pier, casts a line, and jumps up, fending off, offering me a hand. I ignore him and hop up, sprightly.

It's a short walk to town; we won't need the car. There is brightly colored clothing and art (mostly seascapes) hung in the windows of storefronts. I remember when it used to be a real town with a five-and-dime, a dry-goods store, a hardware store, a movie theater, and a pharmacy. Other than the pharmacy, the former businesses have given themselves over to T-shirt shops and antique stores selling the "look" of cottage life.

Jessica and Beowulf peel off to a hamburger joint while I go on to the pharmacy. Tourists clutching shopping bags clog the sidewalks, gazing into realtors' windows. The air stinks of fudge. Navigating through a crush of bicycles and strollers, I work my way to the pharmacy that used to have a soda fountain and a newsstand.

As I push through the door, a bell rings, and I am suddenly thirty years younger. It smells exactly the same—sugary water with the hint of chocolate crunches combined with Bactine and castor oil and eucalyptus salves. The fluorescent fixtures dangling from the pressed-tin ceiling buzz cheerfully. Shelves of shampoos and cold remedies—many of them Addison products—line up in rows leading to the soda fountain and the newsstand that are, to my amazement, still intact. I used to be a regular customer as a child, allowance money jingling in my pocket for cinnamon gum and *Archie* comics and, when I was older, *Seventeen*. Now *Yoga Journal, In Style*, and *Wired* have been added to the display. When I see a *New York Times*, I practically leap for it.

The headlines predict hurricanes, presidential candidates, the ominous coming of Y2K. I move on to the business section, start to scan the stock pages to see if what's left of our fortune is still intact.

"Maddie Addison?" says a voice.

I look up and, for a moment, it could be 1968 with the kind face of the pharmacist blinking at me from behind the soda counter.

"Mr. Marks," I say.

Grayer and a little stooped, he beams widely, and I shuffle the paper, guilty to be perusing without purchasing. When we were kids, Mr. Marks used to come across us reading furtively in the shelves and gently inquire if we wouldn't be happier buying that comic book and taking it home. I quickly fold the *New York Times* and hand it to him, scanning his face for judgment concerning my absence and the reasons for it. Harbor Town is small; there is no such thing as privacy. Marriage and divorce, rumors of indiscretions, health problems, births and deaths filter through the ether like radio waves.

Yet Mr. Marks betrays no disapproval. He holds out his hand, seems delighted to see me. I offer mine. I am nine years old buying bubble gum; eleven with a comic book; sixteen buying Cover Girl blush; twenty-eight filling a prescription for Valium.

"Good to see you, sir," I say.

"Gee, I'm sorry about your mom." He says it perfectly, emphasizing the word *sorry* ever so slightly and dropping his voice. How many times has he uttered those words? More *sorrys* than *happys* from the look of him—that bit of downturn at the edge of the eyes (although they still twinkle), the yellowing of teeth that speaks of cigarettes snuck in the alley behind the store.

"Yes," I say, muttering the usual platitude about Mother being, at the very least, *comfortable*, and thank God for that. Then I gaze at Mr. Marks, suddenly hoping to find in him help and solutions. "You *do* think she's comfortable, don't you?"

Mr. Marks, who grew up in Harbor Town, a contemporary of my father's (though slightly younger), who watched the summer people wash in like the tide, patronize his father's store (later his), who saw us grow up, age, grow feeble, die, looks blandly back at me and says, "Of course."

The answer doesn't entirely satisfy me. Mother seemed restless this morning, twitchy. She lifted her hand, seemed to be plucking something off an imaginary shelf. I tell Mr. Marks this, press him for answers. The hospice brochures are inadequate. Surely she's frightened at what lies ahead; surely she feels some remorse.

Mr. Marks gives a little chuckle and shakes his head. "She's on thirty milligrams of morphine. You can't get much more comfortable than that."

Morphine is a drug I've never tried, but perhaps should consider—the concept of maximum comfort being particularly appealing at this moment. I nod, feign agreement, ask him about the prescription Dr. Mead phoned in.

"Ah," say Mr. Marks, "the laxative." He disappears behind the drug counter, briskly searching for whatever Dr. Mead has decided is just the thing, all the while asking me about where I live now. When I tell him, he says, "New *York?*" as if it's exotic.

He hands me the bag, a smile fixed on his face as he says, "That'll be it?" I expect he will ask if I wouldn't like some ice cream, but instead he reaches out and grasps my hand. I start at his touch and his abrupt, raw earnestness. "If there's anything I can do. Anything. Your family . . . all these years . . . your mother was my favorite."

"Thank you," I say, withdrawing my hand.

M ac is waiting at the pier when I get back. I scan the parking lot for Jessica and Beo, but there's no sign of them. Earlier today, a halo around the sun predicted trouble, and, sure enough, a bruise of black clouds has been conjured out of nothing. The wind kicks up; the spars of the sailboats ting madly, and even the seagulls are hunkered down.

Two figures in yellow slickers jog toward us from the parking lot, gesturing madly at Mac to hold the boat. A man and a woman arrive breathless, bags in hand, and I recognize Jamie, who sees me and waves. But before he can introduce me to his wife, I have begun the inventory. Taller than I (markedly so); long auburn hair; dazzling smile; and on her left hand one of the biggest Hester tiara diamonds I've ever seen.

"Maddie, this is Fiona. Fiona, Maddie Addison."

As I shake her hand, my glance drifts down Fiona's legs, alights on alligator loafers that must have cost nine hundred dollars. I raise my eyebrow at the extravagance; I can just imagine what my father would say.

A low roll of thunder, and Mac suggests we get going. We climb aboard, Jamie and Fiona with their shopping bags, me with my mother's laxative and my *New York Times*. The channel has grown choppy, and the eyesore yacht to the east seems to strain at its anchor. Jamie mutters something about the Dusays' skipper working overtime, and I say, "You *know* them?" Fiona beams, and it occurs to me that she probably *would* be a friend of these yacht-owning Dusays, builders of shopping malls, wreckers of cottages. No doubt she cruises with them, creating huge wakes that pummel the beaches—that is, when she's not imperiling small children on Jet Skis, or flying around on Learjets or—

Easy Does It, I can hear Ian saying. *Let go and let Betty.*

I breathe.

"How's your mom?" Jamie asks, dropping his voice to tell Fiona that my mother is ill.

Fiona drops her smile and shakes her head sadly. For the first time, I realize she has no idea who I am. I find this disturbing. At the very least, she should see me as a rival, although with my pitiful hair, my oddball clothes, and my freckles, I can see why this may not be so.

I look at Sand Isle, at the Dusays' yacht, at the threatening sky. At the worst, Jessica and Beo will spend the afternoon shopping for T-shirts if they become marooned by the storm. Waves slap the bow, and the wind plasters Mac's hair back. With the sharp focus of a filmmaker coupled with the desperate desire to look anywhere but at my old boyfriend and his wife, I notice that Mac's hair is receding. I envision him at forty, fifty, and wonder if he'll still be ferrying families to and from Sand Isle. Fiona has wrapped her head in a scarf that looks uncannily like the Pucci ones my mother used to wear. Out of the corner of my eye, I see her whispering to Jamie, see Jamie respond with a vehement shake of his head.

The driver, Mac, clears his throat. "I've seen your film."

"Excuse me?" I can't tell where Mac's eyes are fixed behind his mirrored Ray-Bans that he insists on wearing in spite of there being no sun.

"The one on Ralph Feingold."

Ralph Feingold, theorizer of universes. He named all his children after galaxies and constellations—Andromeda, Pleiades, and Cassiopeia that he mercifully shortened to "Cassie." Ian and I documented Ralph's life, his early obsession with telescopes, his vampirish sundown to sunup existence. "Where on earth did you see *that?*"

Mac pushes his sunglasses back on his head. We are almost to the other side. His eyes are alert, excited, and, to my mind, highly intelligent. "I'm a physics major. *Everyone* in the department is into that film."

"Wow," I say, torn between the urge to preen and that of distancing myself from my other life. In Sand Isle, I am Maddie Addison, daughter of Richard and Evelyn, sister of Dana, granddaughter of the formidable Bada, great-granddaughter of Edward, who was the son of Josiah, maker of cough medicine and suppositories. Like all the *begats* of the Bible, we know our place. It is heretical to expose it as otherwise.

I notice Jamie monitoring the conversation. I wonder if he'll comment on my filmmaking, my divorce, my absence, or any other component of my life. But Jamie is too polite to inquire beyond the health of my mother.

"Pleiades," says Mac, naming Ralph Feingold's second child. "How could you live with a name like that?"

. . .

Almost four o'clock when the squall hits, and still no word of Jessica and Beowulf. Against Dana's wishes, Philip has set out in our old Boston Whaler to retrieve them. As a wall of white moves toward us from the west, we drag in cushions, rush to fasten windows, place towels along the sills. I remember my mother years ago in her bra and girdle struggling against the French door in the master bedroom, her hair blowing straight back, a cigarette clenched in her lips as she tried to wrestle it shut. It took the two of us to secure that door. We were both drenched and laughing. We never would have laughed like that if the weather had stayed calm.

Miriam plants herself in a chair next to Mother, and swears she's never seen weather like this in all her days. And the weather *is* odd—so much rain this summer, and now the eerie calm before the storm in which the lake fuses with the sky. The change in barometric pressure is so sudden, our ears pop. The gutters whine and keen. The trees come to life. Possessed by the wind, they buck, twist, rend their hair.

"Damn it, Philip," says Dana, her voice almost inaudible against the wind.

Thinking back to that Indian woman we picked up hitchhiking so many years ago, I remember her prognostications about the astronauts and the changing climate. I mention this to Dana.

"What Indian woman?" she says.

Derek, who spends much of his time up in trees with a chisel, seems unconcerned. He is trying to match the tone of the wind with his recorder—a bent B-flat, he tells me, but the sound is so creepy, I think it will conjure ghosts. Water strafes the windows facing the bay. I watch the trees rocking and hope that most of the weak branches already came down in the storm two nights ago. Most summers, we get only one violent patch of weather, but this summer seems to be under the spell of distant hurricanes or tidal shifts, the ill-omened approach of the millennium. The lake is leaden and mottled with whitecaps. The darkest part of the storm moves through, followed by a barely perceptible lightening of the sky until, like the gradual ebbing of a labor contraction, the wind lets up. A few rays of sun spike off the drenched leaves as Philip blows through the door with Jessica and Beowulf. The three of them are soaked.

There is much fussing and huzzaing around Philip, who grows progressively more patriarchal as the twenty-year-olds gush about the rough crossing. Philip strips off his jacket as Dana rushes toward him, exasperated that such an endeavor even took place. The kids could have stayed in town. And what was he thinking taking that old Whaler?

"You could have drowned!"

Stalwart Philip, rescuer of wayfarers, repairer of cups, stares at Dana. He starts to speak, then stops. For a moment, I feel a rare allegiance to Philip—our kinship sealed by the common experience of Dana's disapproval and aversion to risk.

"He was just trying to help, Dane. He didn't want them stranded."

Clamp-lipped, Dana shakes her head and turns away.

The French doors have failed to keep out the rain. The sheets on Mother's bed are damp. Before mopping up the puddles that have seeped through the windows and doors, I help Miriam change the covers. We pull back the top sheet. Mother is wearing a pale pink satin nightgown, exposing her arms and legs upon which bruises have blossomed like septic roses.

"How much does she weigh?" I ask Miriam.

"I'd put her at eighty-five."

My mother was never heavy. She had gorgeous long legs that survived the cut of Bermuda shorts and pedal pushers, broad shoulders and lovely breasts that filled sweaters and jackets to perfection. Now I can practically see through her, her skin like the filmy sheath shed by a snake.

"Can we move her?" I say.

Together we lift Mother, who feels light as a fallen leaf, up onto the pillow. For a moment, I hold her right hand—her "good" hand. I detect (or imagine I do) the faintest clasp of fingers. While Miriam flings open a clean, dry sheet, I let Mother's hand rest in mine.

We cover her with a field of pink cotton that matches her nightgown, replacing the damp blanket cover with fresh white piqué edged with faggoting. "She looks ready for the Queen," I say.

"You hear that, Evelyn?" Miriam says. "Her Highness has given you the seal."

Miriam gathers up the old bedding, shoots me a stern but vaguely amused look, and flounces out of the room.

I sit on the bed. I study my mother's face. "I saw Jamie today," I tell her.

Her right eye flickers. I've always wondered how my mother felt about Jamie. Does she think I should have married him? Was she glad when we broke up?

"His wife was wearing very expensive shoes."

Mother makes the palest wheezing noise. I wonder if the laxative is working. She used to laugh so hard with Bibi Hester—their off-color jokes at other people's expense. Now Bibi won't come to see her, Mother being a grim reminder of what's down the road.

"Do *you* think I should have married him?" I ask Mother. I've never asked her before. Did she see me as the wife of a bag baron? Or did she want something else for me?

When my parents were first married, my father gave my mother a little pendant fashioned like a scale: the Addison & Sons logo. She wore it for years.

"I saw Mr. Marks today," I tell her. "He asked after you." I pause. She'll never tell me her opinion on Jamie. Or on Angus. She stopped giving me her opinions after my father died. Since then, as far as she was concerned, my business was my own. "He said . . . Mr. Marks . . . he said you were always his favorite." I study her intently for a reaction. A flicker. "You got something going on with him?" Now the corner of her mouth twitches slightly. I nod. "Just as I suspected." I cross my arms. "Is he good enough for you?" I shake my head. "It'll be a scandal, you know."

Dana appears at the doorway. She looks from Mother to me. "Who were you talking to?"

O nce again, the rain is falling steadily, we have a fire crackling, and it's too early for dinner. Miriam has gone for a "lie-down" after being rattled by the squall. The lights have flickered off and on. A puzzle is splayed out on a table—shards of the *Mona Lisa* with a few truant pieces gone missing. Derek is in the Love Nest, playing his recorder; everyone else picks desultorily at a book or a backgammon game. Sedgie paces up and down the room, reciting lines from Ibsen. Every now and then, he tries to get the attention of a meditating Adele, who sits cross-legged, eyes closed, in front of the fire.

Finally Sedgie throws up his arms and, in a melodramatic voice, says, "Sardines!"

Dana puts down her knitting and quickly says to Sedgie, "You're it!"

S edgie has hidden. We clustered in the living room, eyes closed and counting while he disappeared. Once the count was finished, we began to roam the house. Now we steal glances at one another as we open cabinets, look under beds. After checking the coat closet off the dining room, I start downstairs to the maids' rooms and the storage, avoiding Miriam's since she is resting. I examine a trunk containing a Venetian mask, polka-dot bloomers, chiffon scarves, wraps made of dead, furry animals of indeterminate species, and a large sombrero that must have come from California. From there I check Louisa's old room. It is a narrow room with one window looking out into the woods. When Louisa was alive, she covered her bureau with pictures of her two daughters, who grew up invisible to us except for those photographs. We saw them go from wearing tiny braids to straightened hair in the sixties. I remember one daughter in cap and gown, the pride in Louisa's voice when she told us that daughter was going to the University of Cincinnati. It meant little to me at the time. All of us were going to college. It was as inevitable as sailing classes and dance school.

Adjacent to Louisa's room is Derek's old studio. The walls are now bare; the shades are drawn. An old glass jar, caked with dry paint, sits on the window ledge. I open a drawer to find a couple of Strathmore tablets, a packet of unused brushes, a watercolor sketch of a boat. No lingering smell of linseed oil. No Derek to sing "Suzanne." All traces of my fourteen-year-old self are expunged. That long-ago morning, Derek had found me sitting in a flotsam of shredded paper. I had started with the nudes, but once I got going, I tore at everything—art-school portraits of models, sketches of the lake. None of them escaped my fevered tearing. The room had become a ticker-tape parade of body parts—torn elbows and faces, genitalia and hands.

I head into the boat room, where Edward used to sleep. A couple of faded and useless life jackets hang from a wall while other hooks fix oars to the ceiling. Edward's cot is still there. I try to imagine what it was like to see the world through Edward's eyes. Did it all appear bent and threatening? The panes of glass looking out onto the garden are lacquered with grime. They make the outside world seem dark, subterranean. I have the urge to find a cloth and wipe them clean, but I remind myself that it is Sedgie, not Edward, I'm searching for.

I move on to the bathroom, pushing back the shower curtain hanging over the claw-foot tub. A peppering of mouse droppings dots the floor. The bathroom smells of mildew and dry rot. Someone has left an ashtray full of butts on the windowsill. There is rust in the toilet and a skid mark where the sink faucet drips. In this house, pipes appear randomly—protruding from a ceiling, disappearing through a wall, reappearing in the room below. When winter comes, they will be drained and bled out like ancient Egyptians for mummification, the shutters across the front windows like coins upon the eyes.

I push through a door onto an outside landing connected to my grandfather's office. Philip uses this room as his office these days. It is neat and

square, with windows on three sides, some files, and a rolltop desk covered
with stacks of yellow legal pads and sharpened pencils. Mainly, Philip looks
after his client's affairs, moves her money into treasuries and stocks, makes
her monthly transfers, advises her on charitable remainder trusts, philan-
thropic bequests, generation skip trusts, and probate. She has been planning her death for half a century. Thanks to Philip, when she finally goes,
it will be a thing of beauty.

There is a comforting gravitas to my grandfather's desk. With its drawers full of leather-bound ledgers, it gives the impression that someone is
still in charge. Anchoring a copy of yesterday's *Wall Street Journal* to the ink
blotter is a coffee mug that reads THINK BIG on the side. I wonder where we
came by such a mug at the Aerie and make a note to ask a friend who does
ceramics to make a new cup for Sedgie with his name on it. Surely someone in the family must have "thought big" at some point (why else this
house?), but the philosophy is as out of fashion with our generation as the
bathing costumes and woolly knickers in the photographs of my ancestors.

Leaving the office and feeling expansive, I pledge to get new cups for
everyone. I travel up the next flight of stairs to the porch, where I peer under the glider, then slip through the French doors into the living room.
The house is thick with quiet. The three downstairs bedrooms appear
empty, as does the kitchen, so I make my way to the top floor. I pass the
linen closet filled with antimacassars and blanket covers anchored by the
letter A, delicate sheaths for baby pillows, and the garish lime-green-and-
yellow Marimekko sheets my aunt bought in the seventies. Beyond the
linen closet is the laundry chute, where Sedgie got stuck during a similar
game when we were children. I remember his shrieks as Aunt Pat tugged
on his legs. Wherever he's hiding now, I'm sure it affords greater spacious-
ness, but when I check the bunk room, the Schooner Room, the Lantern
Room, the Jack Russell Room, I feel the presence of no one. The only
sound I hear is a squeak in the master bedroom, and I wonder if Miriam has
risen from her nap. Standing in the doorway, I see Mother lying where
Miriam and I propped her last, her head turned slightly toward the window

as if she's watching the rain drip from the gutters. The oppressive, almost tropical air that preceded the storm has lifted. She seems to be sleeping, but in the light of the window, I make out that half smile that appeared briefly when I kidded her about Mr. Marks. Her blanket has fallen partially off the bed and is spilling onto the floor. Then I notice a sneaker-clad foot and realize where Sedgie has hidden.

It hadn't occurred to me that this room wasn't off-limits. We are always taking pains to let Mother rest, to preserve her serenity. Now I stride into the room, pull away the blanket, and lean down to see seven people jammed beneath and behind Mother's bed. Everyone screams with laughter. Like college kids jammed into a phone booth, they unwind themselves with relief. "It took you long enough," says Sedgie, obviously pleased at having chosen such an unlikely place. "God, what is it about Sardines that always makes you have to pee?"

Mother's calm seems beatific, given that she has loathed large groups for years. Now she can't get away from us. We bang loudly on the piano downstairs, come into her room to sing, use her bed as a hiding place.

"Your turn," says Dana, citing the Sardines rule of the last remaining person being the next one to hide.

"Fine, fine, fine," I say, still dazzled by Sedgie's audacity and the memory of my underpants upon his head.

Everyone scatters.

I look back at Mother before I leave the room. She still seems to be smiling as if secretly delighted. "What?" I say.

While everyone is counting outside, I head down to the coat closet off the dining room. It's been used countless times, but if I can insinuate myself far enough into its depths behind layers of slickers and windbreakers and tennis rackets and lacrosse sticks and rain boots, I might disappear. The closet is unbelievably musty and full of the rubbery smell of rain gear. Generations of clothing are crammed together, forming a nearly impassable barrier of garments and sports equipment. I whack my knee on a tennis racket. A can of tennis balls and a hat tumble from the shelf. With a lacrosse stick jammed into my rib, I feel the low-belly panic that grips me in confined spaces. *Breathe,* I tell myself.

There are footsteps in the dining room. Someone opens the closet door, pauses, and then closes it. I have become invisible after all. People bang up the stairs overhead. I hear someone say, *Did you try the laundry chute?* Silence. Then the door reopens, and a hand reaches in, shuffles the boots and the rackets till it touches my leg. I know it is just a game, but it feels as though there is more at stake. I am Anne Frank hiding in that attic. I am Patty Hearst locked in that closet.

Derek has found me.

Slowly, firmly, he pushes back the coats. Like Houdini, he snakes into a space barely big enough for a child. The closet is pitch-black; I cannot see his eyes. But I feel him. I feel his breath, his chest, his leg against my thigh. When he puts his fingers to my lips, it is all I can do not to moan.

The phone outside the closet door rings and rings and rings. I hear cousins calling in the distance, but they sound impossibly far away. I want them to call *all-ye all-ye oxen free,* but they don't. It is quiet except for Derek's breathing and the deafening pulse of my heart. In such proximity to Derek, all the feelings, memories, expectations, and disappointments I have managed to avoid are jamming into the closet like lost relatives. The ghosts of my father's terse words; the impotent echo of my mother's responses. The ghost of Aunt Pat by the hose bib as she peeled off our bathing suits to wash us down, sending us naked upstairs to dress. I press myself against the wall, recoiling from recollections of Derek's drawings of a self-consciously nude fourteen-year-old; memories of Edward saying, *No one really sees you.* I am prodded in my sternum by Jamie's wounded, angry eyes; Sadie's soft head nudges my chest; my throat is gripped by the hot relief of vodka. Dread is upon me in this closet. Five middle-aged cousins still acting like children—we have played this game for years.

In a low whisper, Derek says, "They can't find us. It's too obvious."

To which I can say nothing. This is the Aerie, after all. *Sanctus sanctorum por pueris eternis.* We'll never really grow up.

There are voices in the dining room. Someone is saying, *Did you check the closet? I checked it,* someone says, but Sedgie says, *Check it again.*

The door swings open. A tiny bit of light streams in, and I can make out Derek's eyes. You can fall into those eyes. They are links to a new dimension. Boots are being pulled away. Tennis rackets. Hangers are stripped of foul-weather gear. Everything is rearranged until Derek and I stand exposed.

"Right under our noses," Sedgie says. "Christ."

I head to the kitchen for a glass of water. My hand is shaking, and my chest feels damp. The dining room looks like a rummage sale with everything pulled from the closet.

You've got to be kidding, Angus had said. *Your cousin?*

Maddie, said Dr. Anke, *where was your mother?*

I put my glass in the drainer, lean against the sink. Dusk is falling, and there's still no electricity. Soon we'll be lighting candles and setting out leftovers.

I shake my head to clear it. The tunnel recedes; my heart slows. Everyone seems to have gathered back in the living room. Slowly, I climb the stairs. I move through the Lantern Room, through the two adjoining bathrooms, coming out into a hallway just off the nursery that I prefer to avoid.

It's just a room, Dr. Anke told me. *Go in, breathe the air, touch the crib. Cry if you like. But go in.*

I push through the door and am assaulted by the scent of lavender. It sends me cartwheeling back to those nights with Louisa in my bed, shadows on the wall. Being in close quarters with Derek has disoriented me. Now I can hear breathing—my own, at first, then the breaths of someone else—in and out—as faint and indiscernible as that of a sleeping child. Hypnotized, I listen, wondering if there are ghosts. But there is nothing unworldly about this breathing. It comes from the bed. I rise, stride over, and pull back the sheets, see my fully clothed niece entwined with Beowulf. They could be two small children holding each other, afraid of the storm. They could be twins like Derek and Edward reaching for each other in their mother's womb. There is nothing menacing or untoward in the way they are pressed together, but in a flash, I snap. I hear myself saying in a voice not my own, "Oh, my *God*, what are you *doing*? Get *away* from her! What are you . . . get *away*!"

"What is the big deal?" Jessica's eyes are practically popping as she sits up.

My voice. Again. Even shriller. "Oh, my God. Oh, my *God*."

"What the—!" Sedgie has run into the room, followed by Dana and Philip.

"Maddie, we heard you—?"

"Don't you touch her. Don't you *touch* her!"

"It's because of Sadie," says Dana crisply. "Get Maddie out of this room." She wheels around to Philip. *"Now!"*

Philip grabs my arm, but I shake him off. I am shouting. "She wants to get pregnant! He's her *cousin*, for God sakes."

"Easy," says Beowulf.

"Maddie!" Dana's voice is sharp, authoritative, and as effective as a slap to the face.

I stop midstammer, my eyes meeting Jessica's. "You . . . I'm . . ."

"*Sorry?*" says Jessica sarcastically. If Dana's voice stopped me in my tracks, Jessica's makes me flinch. She shakes her head in disgust and, pushing past me, says, "You think you know everything, MaddieAunt. You really do."

No one spoke much at dinner. Sedgie tried Hamlet's soliloquy, but no one seemed to care. The conversation was whispered and subdued, suitable to candlelight. We couldn't see one another's faces. It was better that way.

Now I am lying in my bed, listening to the dripping of gutters. By midnight, the electricity has come back on. The rain stopped hours ago, but like a wound that won't heal, water hemorrhages from the eaves. Even now, I am haunted by the smell of ghosts and lovers and babies who die. There is madness in the scent of it. It's how I know we're not alone.

Adele says there are souls that linger in between. Neither here nor there, they are dust balls clinging to the lacy casements of our minds. Dr. Anke calls them introjections. People in AA call them the wreckage of our past. Whatever they are, they have me by the throat.

The dripping becomes the incessant beating of a pulse. My lids are pricked with light. Is this the beginning of the relentless sleeplessness that Dana has described? Unconsciousness eludes me. In a slumbering house, I lie awake.

I pull off the covers and rise, leave my room, and go into the hall. Most of the doors to the bedrooms are closed. Downstairs, Derek sleeps in the Love Nest, his wife of twenty-two years halfway around the world bivouacking above Tanzania. I can hear Mother snoring, wonder if it echoes in Miriam's room via the monitor. I glide down the stairs, avoiding the creaky one. The table has been cleared, the closet put back; the kitchen is spotless thanks to the teamwork of cousins. There is cereal in the upper cabinet, jam in the refrigerator, scotch and vodka under the sink in the pantry. That's where I'm headed, pulled into the gravity of a black hole, the event horizon rushing at me.

Where is God to help me now? Or for that matter, Betty? *Half measures will avail us nothing,* the AA Big Book tells us. *We stood at the turning point.*

I reach for the vodka, unscrew the cap.

Alcohol is a molecule that binds quickly to the blood. The digestive tract recognizes it as a sugar and, with a burst of insulin, rushes to incorporate it. The taste buds rebel while the prefrontal cortex, the corpus luteum, the hippocampus, and, finally, the reptilian brain all say, *Yes!* And if you are alcoholic—not a "problem drinker" or an occasional drunk—but if you're the bona fide real thing, you don't break alcohol down like everyone else. It sticks in your system; you reek of acetaldehyde; the residue, as it hits your nervous system, is like morphine in its potency.

And for a period of time, you feel absolutely normal.

I know what it is like to approach the turning point. I feel like it at this moment. The past rushed by me in that closet, the Doppler-warped sound crashing as it sped into the future. I want to call 911. I want to cry out for help. In a minute, my hemoglobin will be bejeweled with intoxicants, and the receptors in my brain will be screaming for more.

Slamming the bottle back under the sink, I stride into the dining room, pick up the phone, and call Ian.

TWENTY

As you first stir awake, you struggle between what was dream, what was reality. Dream, you pray. Please let it have been a dream. The sky is lightening to the east, and you think, Did you drink or not?

Ian says he's not afraid of taking the first drink; it's all the subsequent drinks he'll have to take once he begins that keep him from starting. As soon as the residual trauma of flirting with disaster wears off, I'm sure I'll feel idiotic. Now all I feel is a dull wonder that the sky is lightening, and that Ian has agreed to come. In New York, I have friends who know me by my work, not by my family ties. I think, Why don't you die so I can go back to my life, but I'm not sure whom I'm addressing. My mother? My memories? My self?

Facing one's demons is overrated. I make a note to mention this to Dr. Anke.

A fresh morning breeze crosses Mother's room and catches me in the doorway. In the half-light, I can make out the form of a mahogany bureau, a Boston rocker, a pair of slippers, and a robe. Light falls on her pillow, and I see she has slipped down and rolled onto her side, her head bent as if she's ducking from a blow. I cross to her bed. On the night-stand sits one of those divided pillboxes that have compartments for days and weeks of medication—medication to thin the blood, medication to sleep, medication for the bowels, medication to keep the skin and teeth from decaying. Now that we have taken her off everything except mor-phine, the compartments are empty. There is a glass with a straw, and I sniff the liquid, but it is only water.

"Mother?" I say.

She draws a long, ratchety breath, and I decide to pull her up on the pil-lows. I come around to the other side, bend down, and, as if I am lifting a child, hook under her armpits and heave. She moves so quickly, and her head jerks, that I am startled and unnerved. "I'm so sorry!" I say quickly. "Did I hurt you?" Her right eye drifts open. Again, that rattle of a sigh.

"Ian's coming," I say once I'm assured she's all right. "I showed him a picture of you with your garden club." I speak briskly, now, knowing my mother has no choice but to listen. "He said you looked like you would never smell."

I tell her if it weren't for Ian, I would never have stayed in filmmaking. We've made three documentaries and a short. Our criterion is that it be about anybody and anything unorthodox. And that we get the funding. In the meantime, Ian still works as a freelance editor to make ends meet, and I've nearly run through my inheritance.

I sit on the side of her bed. Rented from the hospital-supply company, it is rigid and, unlike the rest of the beds in the house, gives little. Ian started drinking when he was eleven. His family in Minnesota treated him like a freak because he loved art and beauty and music and women's clothes.

"He got me into AA," I say.

My mother told me never to mention those meetings again, but what's the harm at this point? I'm sure it's my imagination, but it feels as though she is hanging on my words. She once asked me with great embarrassment how homosexual men managed sex. I remember hesitating, then dissembling, uncertain if *fellatio* and *anal intercourse* were in my mother's lexicon. Now I tell her how Ian practically flunked out of high school, how he sniffed glue and chomped on Percodan and drank beer for breakfast. When he was eighteen, he was beat up and raped, but he doesn't even remember or, for that matter, hold it against anyone. He spent a month in a hospital. When he got out, he left for New York, where he shot up drugs while working as a film grip. By the time he landed at NYU, he'd been sober for three years and was determined to overcome the Lutheranism of his childhood by converting to Judaism—a plan he later aborted, pleading fear of circumcision.

"He's a brilliant filmmaker, Mom. He says if it weren't for Lee Remick talking about that oil slick in *The Days of Wine and Roses,* he wouldn't have gotten sober. You know that part, don't you? The part when Lee says that, when she drank, she saw a beautiful rainbow instead of an oil slick?"

I look at my mother's symmetrically perfect profile. I think she knows exactly what I mean about oil slicks and rainbows and the elusive quest for joy. She was a shy girl who grew up thinking the river was going to swallow her. She drank because she was terrified. She drank because she was bored. She drank because she was married to a man whose inviolable virtue put him out of reach. She drank because it's what they did, these postwar wives with their postwar babies and their postwar husbands who had reclaimed the world. She had a diamond circle pin and a pearl necklace and a big beautiful house with a cook. She told Dana and me that we should aspire to the same. What did that treachery cost you, Mother? The words should have stuck in your throat.

"Ian's compulsive about germs, and he's convinced he's HIV-positive, even though the test keeps coming back negative," I tell my mother. "Dr. Anke calls it survivor's guilt."

I look out the window at the silver dawn lake. Survivor's guilt is something my therapist and I discuss frequently. We rank it right up there with shame. My mother once threw up in a revolving door after a wedding reception at the Ritz-Carlton in Boston. Whenever she recounted that story, she made it sound hilarious, but I don't think I can make almost drinking vodka straight from the bottle after years of sobriety seem even remotely funny.

I notice someone standing at the door. Dana, still in her flannel night-gown, is peering in.

"I'm talking to Mother," I say preemptively. "I'm telling her about my life."

Dana raises her eyebrow. "Do you think that's a good idea?"

"Do you think it will kill her?" I say irritably. "My poisonous life?"

"That's not what I'm saying."

"What, then?"

Dana considers, then shakes her head. "I don't know what I'm saying, Maddie."

Dana looks so suddenly vulnerable, so completely overwhelmed that I want to go to her and take her in my arms and rock her and sing, *Hush little baby, don't say a word*. But the argument from the night before still stings. All I can come up with is a pathetic, "I'm sorry."

I'm sorry about what I said about Jessica and Beowulf. I'm sorry I disappeared.

"Ian's coming," I tell her. "I called him last night, and he's catching a flight this afternoon."

"Ian?"

"My partner. You know, the filmmaker?" The impatience in my voice is full-blown now.

Dana says quickly, "I know who Ian is." A pause. "But why?"

"Why is he coming?" I look out the window. There are whitecaps on the bay, and the sun is shining furiously. Soon, Miriam will arrive upstairs to prepare Mother, to administer her morphine and try to get her to eat, at-tending a decaying shrine long after the gods have left.

"I nearly drank last night."

Crestfallen doesn't begin to describe the look on Dana's face. Alarm, betrayal, possibly disappointment. I can't even say *I'm sorry* again. I can't even tell her why. I want to protest, *It's the disease*, but Dana doesn't see al-coholism as a disease, rather more as a failure of will. Even with all I have learned about addiction, I tend to agree with her. It's as if my character is flawed, as if my father's suspicions about my lack of virtue were confirmed. Had I done a better job of polishing the winches, coiling the lines, suppressing the feelings of envy and longing when I looked at the newer boats, I wouldn't be cursed with such spinelessness.

You realize there's a genetic tendency? Dr. Anke once asked me.

To which I responded that it was consistently demonstrated to me that drinking was a viable coping mechanism.

So you blame your parents?

Yes. No. Doesn't everyone?

"Was it because of Jessica?" Dana says.

The summer I was fourteen, my cousin came to my room. I thought about telling my mother, but she was too concerned about Dana, so cavalierly treated by that tennis-player boyfriend. If I try to explain to my sister how my life changed that August out of disillusionment and embarrassment combined with a saucy, rebellious pride, she will be utterly baffled.

"No," I say. "It wasn't because of Jessica."

I 've stood in this airport a thousand times, waiting for planes. When we stopped taking trains, we started flying on a twin-engine prop that was guided in by a man waving flashlights on the ground—the same man who then hauled our baggage off the plane and carried it inside. Molded-plastic chairs have replaced the splintery wood benches; video games the pinball that earlier replaced the Foozball. There is a hamburger joint but no shop in the airport, no place to buy a magazine—only local real-estate brochures and road maps and tourist brochures advertising the Mackinaw ferry and the A-*maaaaz*ing Mystery Spot.

Ian has to catch the 6 A.M. flight out of JFK to make his connection to northern Michigan. When he gets to Detroit, he will have to wait for hours. He will scan the flight-departure monitors, looking for the name of an obscure and sparsely populated town and be directed to a gate in the

G concourse, miles from where he disembarked from his New York flight. He will walk endlessly to get to the gate and, when he gets there, find it as desolate as a bus station. The only other flights leaving from that part of the airport are heading to Escanaba, Manistee, or Sault Ste. Marie. There will be no Starbucks, no newsstands. Only a vending machine with the Snickers sold out. His flight will be delayed. Unable to find a latte or a *New York Times*, Ian will try meditating because AA encourages it. He's terrible at meditating; worse at praying. Nevertheless, when there's nothing else to distract him, Ian surrenders and tries.

When they finally announce his flight, he will walk outside and find a tram that will take him to a prop plane at a distant locale on the tarmac. At this point, his resolve will be tested—not because he is unfamiliar with this kind of banishment, but because it will feel like a regression to the wastelands of his youth. Only the promise of the Shangrai-la of Sand Isle at the other end (that and the duty-bound need to rescue his friend) will prod him on.

When his plane comes to a stop, I feel that leap of excitement I've always felt when people arrived. It is like meeting the stagecoach after it has crossed the Sierra, or Lindbergh's plane after his transatlantic flight. Slowly, the propellers wind to a stop. Everyone looks tired as they step off the plane; they blink blearily at the sky. Then they inhale the sweet Michigan air, and all is forgiven.

Ian is the fourth person off, after a businessman and an elderly couple. I wave at him frantically through the sliding-glass doors. I can tell he sees only his reflection in the windows because he's squinting desperately as if he's not quite sure he's landed on the right planet.

"You're here!" I say as he pushes through the doors.

"And where is 'here' exactly?" says Ian, peering around. The gritty terrazzo floors and general seediness of the airport bode poorly in his assessment, but I tell him it gets better, that this is just an outpost, a place for landing planes.

"I brought a *huge* suitcase," he says. "I packed everything. Three pairs of khakis, every cashmere sweater and Lacoste shirt I own."

He's taken his earring out, I notice. I also notice he is sockless, and that he is wearing loafers with buckles.

"You're looking a little straight, Ian."

"Actually, it's *you* who looks a little . . . God, Maddie, you look awful." He bends down. Ian is quite tall—well over six feet—and his eyes are the palest, saddest gray I've seen in a human being. But now he's studying me, searching my face for answers. There are no answers, I want to tell him. Just the stupid fact of my nearly unraveling after eight whole years.

"MaddieAddieAddie."

"Let's go," I say.

L ord, what a trip," Ian says as we pull out of the airport parking. He jerks his head at the fleet of private jets on the other side of the chain-link fence. "How do we get one of those?"

We turn onto the highway. I refrain from mentioning that one of "those" belongs to my former boyfriend Jamie. Irritated with Ian for even bringing it up, I say, "Everything's changing."

"This is *definitely* not the Midwest of the plains," says Ian as we speed down country roads.

I wait for Ian to start in with his "you're only as sick as your secrets" lecture about doing the twelve steps (even if he *does* call God Betty)—although, right now, he is busily behaving half like a tourist, half like a filmmaker, pointing out wildflowers and picturesque barns.

"Ian," I say, "what's with the Gucci loafers?"

"An attempt, Maddie dear—albeit a pathetic one—to fit in."

Ian has this picture of my family as shabby gentry, but no one (other than my ex-husband) is running around with ascots and smoking jackets. Our family's fashion flair expired with my mother's generation—unless you count Adele, whose own sense of style has evolved into a combination of Jean-Paul Gaultier and Elvira.

"You're very cute, Ian. Even when you're jet-lagged."

"You're not still on the 'I'm thinking of having a baby' kick, are you?"

"If *you* were straight . . ."

"Lord help me. With your hideous taste in men?"

"Not all of them."

"Angus Farley?"

"Who doesn't count. I was drunk."

"That's a lame excuse."

"And since when have *you* been so picky about men?"

Ian doesn't answer. He is taking in the scenery. I can almost see it through his eyes: expanses of green velvet edged by dense woods or pocked by thistle and Queen Anne's lace, the occasional stupefied cow. We roll and wind; forest becomes marsh, clotted with cattails and the drowned carcasses of trees. Only a few white clouds smudge the sky. If Ian finds it beautiful, he isn't letting on. He may find it reminiscent of the plains, but surely this is lusher, greener, less susceptible to the expansive flatness of his youth. "God," he says with plaintive resignation bordering on disgust. "Bovines."

Ian has a face designed for a billed hat and a piece of straw sticking out of his mouth, but he thrives on the pungent fumes of traffic, screeching and blaring, twenty tongues spoken at his neighborhood market, the table reserved at Paolo's, the hustle and negotiation of cabs, elevators, and doormen. I assure him that we're still far from Sand Isle, that the farmland is just a warm-up act. Besides, I tell him, it's not as if he's *never* seen the countryside.

"I was drunk," he said. "Doesn't count."

"Lame excuse," I say.

"Touché." Ian crosses his arms and leans back, taps his improbably expensive shoes on the dashboard of the Malibu. "Are they excited I'm coming?"

I don't know how to break it to Ian that my family barely knows who he is. I have explained that there is an insulated quality to Sand Isle, but Ian hasn't yet fathomed that it applies to him. Even my cousins' spouses (what's left of them) seldom come. Only Philip with his plodding loyalty— and even Philip has constructed a boat-centric universe all his own. I have no idea how my family will respond to Ian. I suspect they will scrutinize him, test his humor, his wit, his politics; Adele may try to convert him; Derek may find in him a connoisseur of art. If Ian has musical talent or a penchant for sailing, he may be accepted, but as far as I know, he has neither. He *does* have a gourmet streak born out of rebellion against the bland and the canned, so at the very least, he and Sedgie, his big-screen crush, will have something in common.

"You'll *love* Sedgie," I say.

"Are you trying to mitigate my culture shock? Because it's very condescending."

I shake my head, but maybe I am. A residual shame dogs me about Sand Isle; I hover between penitence and protectiveness. Ian is holding up his hands, making a screen with his thumbs and forefingers, looking for angles in the bucolic expanse. As a filmmaker, Ian's vision veers toward the telling detail, while I am more drawn to stories of clashing contradictions and seamy undersides.

He turns and levels me with his stare. "So . . . *what* is going on?"

Ian is known for his tight shots—the nuances of the forefinger, the protruding tongue, the blinking eye. The subject's eyes betray worlds. An upward glance to the left shows they are lying. Two or three sharp blinks means your question has hit home.

I take a big, dramatic breath. "It's harder than I thought."

"What's the worst part? Your parents? Sadie?"

"It's not just Sadie. It's everything around Sadie, and who I thought I was at the time. I mean, why *did* I marry Angus?"

Dr. Anke likes to say I was doing the best that I could at the time, but the fact remains that I should have done better. I say this to Ian, who rolls his eyes.

"You and everybody else. Look, Maddie—"

"I know, I know, I know." I just can't make traction, I tell him.

Ian studies me for the longest time.

"Don't look at me like that."

But he persists. "So tell me about Derek and Edward."

Here is where I choke. Like Ian, I am prone to voyeurism, so his curiosity comes as no surprise. And I agree with him in theory about our secrets being our downfall. But I can't reconcile my youthful attraction to not one but *two* cousins, each of whom I confused with the other. Even now I can't say if it was Derek or Edward who enticed me more.

So, like my father, I say, "Nothing to tell."

As we pull up to the ferry, an early-evening calm has settled on the channel. The hard mirror of water reflects the few clouds that remain after yesterday's storm like boorish guests who won't leave a party. I introduce Ian to Mac as my partner.

"Oh, man, you worked on the Feingold film?" says Mac.

Ian's eyes meet mine, and I fight to keep from smiling. There is a comforting, familiar smell of leather in the old teak boat. The houses sit like regal dowagers swelling with expectancy as Mac motors us across.

"Oh, my God," says Ian when we get to the other side, and the horse and carriage pull up.

"I told you."

"No, you didn't, Maddie. You really didn't."

The last time I brought someone to Sand Isle, it was Angus. He, too, accused me of understatement. Angus was treated with cordial politeness and a modicum of interest and seemed to avoid the scathing labels of his predecessors like the Criminal or the Chinless Wonder. Angus sailed with Philip, drank cocktails with my parents, and apparently fit in with my family better than I. *Charming* was a word often associated with Angus. I've been suspicious of that adjective ever since.

Riding to the house, Ian looks sanguine. "Whose house is *that?*" he asks when we pass the big one with the columns. When I tell him it's the Swansons' and sing a few bars of *Where there's a swag, there's a Swanson*, Ian double-takes. "Curtain rods built that house?"

The Aerie, I assure him, is nowhere near as fancy, but when the carriage stops, and Ian sees my family's grand old house on the lake for the first time, he leans over and says, "I have no sympathy for you, Maddie. I really don't."

Lutherans, Ian once told me, are too parsimonious for ambiguity. Whereas I read everything as words within words, Ian expects people to mean what they say. It's one of the few benefits of growing up among people with a limited capacity for invention. Ian, for instance, is unembarrassed about picking up a vase and turning it over and saying, *My God, this is Rookwood!* Or looking at our umbrella stand and saying, *Delft!* With this proclivity for collectibles, he turns a connoisseur's eye toward my family. It's the Addisons he's interested in—the Addisons whom I've described to him as eccentric relics, my odd assortment of cousins and a dying mother to whom I've barely spoken in years.

We're on our way to Ian's room when we run into Dana. "You're going to put him in there?" she says. She smiles embarrassedly at Ian. "I'm not sure it's even clean."

"It's clean," I say evenly.

"Really?"

"As a matter of fact, *I* cleaned it."

"Maddie," says Ian, "is quite the domestic."

"You should have seen her room when we were kids."

"I can just imagine," Ian replies in a chummy tone I could do without. "Well!" he says after we close the door behind us. "Not much faith in you, has she?"

"It's genetic," I say, trying to heave his massive suitcase onto a luggage rack whose needlepoint straps were stitched by my mother. "Aunt Pat used to kneecap Mother with nasty comments."

"Like?"

"Like, 'Why won't you come for a swim, Evelyn? Are you worried about your *hair?*' Or *'Peut-être le francais, n'etait-il pas parlé dans le Missouri?'* "

Ian, fingering the lilies I've put on his bureau, says, "Meaning?"

"Meaning my mother was afraid of drowning, and my aunt went to boarding school in Switzerland."

"*Pauvre* Evelyn."

"But she outlived them all, didn't she?" I unzip his suitcase and start pulling out khakis, shirts with embroidered polo players, cable-knit sweaters in the softest wool. Ian buys clothes like a dying man—which is what he believes he may still be, given how many friends he's lost. *Why not enjoy life?* he always tells me. *We're all going down in the end.* "No wonder you're always broke," I say.

"I've been meaning to speak to you about that," says Ian as he folds his boxers into perfection. "These arcane subjects that nobody but us cares about. I'm over it. I just can't save the world anymore, Maddie. I'm tired." He takes me by the shoulders, looks down at me with those overcast eyes. "Let's make some money, Maddie. Let's go hog wild. Merchant and Ivory did it. Damon and Affleck, for God's sake."

"Hey, Mac the ferry captain *loved* the Feingold film. If anything, we should push ourselves. When was the last time either of us did a story on disease or war?" Meeting a blank if incredulous stare, I go on. "Besides, Merchant and Ivory have financing and access to talent. Not to mention the fact that I'm immune to making money. Another genetic defect."

We've had this conversation before—Ian wanting to go more commercial, me angling for another direction. *Why are you so afraid of making money?* Dr. Anke has asked. It's a subtle point, one I can barely articulate—the relative merit in *having* money as opposed to *making* it.

"*Somebody* made some," Ian says, waving his arm around like a helicopter.

"Anomaly," I say. "He was looking for a way to patch his roof and came up with a palliative for chest colds."

"And the rest is history," mutters Ian, picking up a plate on the bedside table. "Herend."

Out of habit, I fold Ian's clothes and lay them on the bed. Equally out of habit, Ian redoes my handiwork. It's the way we work together—me laying out the broad strokes, Ian fussing with the details. We're made for each other, I often tell him. Including our shared attraction to men, he counters.

"What's that smell?" he says, suddenly looking up.

"Mmm," I say. "Sedgie."

Sedgie?" says Ian, visibly perking. He is padding after me toward the kitchen. For the entire day, I've managed to avoid the cousins. When I left to pick up Ian, everyone was down on the beach. I don't want to face Jessica. I don't want to face Derek. Derek, I've decided, doesn't remember what I remember: the entrails of paper, myself forlornly in their midst. It's like Dana forgetting the Indian woman we picked up. Sometimes, according to Dr. Anke, we block experiences out, relegating memories to separate compartments that we seal and never revisit.

We push through the kitchen door. It looks like a party with Jessica wearing the "Kiss the Cook" apron, and Sedgie still in his bathing suit, a Hawaiian shirt thrown on out of respect for Louisa, who didn't warm to half-naked men in her kitchen. Jessica's boom box is blasting Bob Marley, and Sedgie's hips are undulating. "Me some badass Don Ho, what say, niecy cousiness?"

"Whatever," says Jessica. She eyes me coolly.

Sedgie's eyes are half-closed as he spins around the kitchen. He's obviously stoned. Ian, smiling slightly, cocks his head. I want to ask him if he still sees Harrison Ford potential in Sedgie, but from the expression on Ian's face, I think he sees more than that.

"What's for dinner?" I say.

"Mmm," says Sedgie. "Mmm."

Which apparently means new potatoes in pesto, grilled whitefish, string beans with arugula, and popovers like Louisa used to make.

"Incredible," says Ian. "You could open a restaurant."

Sedgie buttons his shirt, straightens up. "Finally," he says, "a man of vision."

. . .

One by one, Ian meets all the cousins. Adele doesn't let him down. She glides down the stairs in a violet satin tunic over gauzy see-through pants. She has charcoaled her eyes. Without her hair, the effect is reminiscent of Nefertiti (one of her incarnations, we find out later). When he meets Derek, Ian studies him intently the way he studies someone we're about to shoot. I've told Ian all about Derek. As Ian shakes his hand, I stand behind Derek and pantomime a swoon.

At dinner, the heavy mood from the night before has lifted. Even Jessica and Beowulf seem to have gotten over my outburst. Nevertheless, they sit apart. Dana seems slightly withdrawn, but everyone else is talking animatedly, expertly dancing around any temporary awkwardness last evening may have produced. I compulsively gulp water as if to purge myself. Perhaps because Ian's here, I feel a sense of relief. At the same time, I feel slightly resentful, as if he's an intrusion I have to accommodate. I can no longer be left alone to my thoughts. I have to incorporate him into my life—although, as evidenced by how convivial my family is acting, there should be little problem in this.

As the potatoes are passed, Philip asks Ian about the films he makes. I want to remind Philip that Ian and I collaborate, but Ian, by virtue of his outsider status, seems already to have more credibility. Ian sends them into peals of laughter describing Ralph Feingold's oddly named daughters. Had I told them about our musician friend from Hoboken? Now, *there* is a subject. Not to mention the herpetologist from Brooklyn who looked exactly like one of his frogs. "*Hyperolius Marcus* we called him," says Ian, "after his own buggy eyes."

"And his tongue," I add.

But no one seems to hear me. Everyone seems riveted by Ian, so I give up, stare at my plate, stab my whitefish. With Ian, there are nine people—not nearly as many as there used to be at the height of summer when we used to add a leaf to the table. When my father was a child, they had to "dress" for dinner. In our generation, at the very minimum, we were forced to wear shoes. No one had tattoos or piercings other than in their earlobes. No one shaved his or her head.

"What are you working on now?" says Jessica.

I open my mouth to say, *Zip*, but Ian says, "Something more commercial. Something that sells."

I let my eye wander to the ceiling. For the first time, I notice there are stains between the beams—not just one stain, but several idiosyncratic and concentric outlines left by water damage. They could have been there for ages—like circles in a tree trunk marking the years.

"You're selling *out?*" says Beowulf.

"If possible."

"I did a movie once," says Sedgie.

I don't much remember the dinners where my grandmother presided. I have a vague memory of taking a carrot from a passed plate of crudités, my mother whispering, *Take just* one. After Uncle Halsey died, my father became head of the table, grilling us on politics and sports and social responsibility. *What have you done to justify your existence today?* he would ask. To which there never seemed to be a brilliant or even adequate answer. Even if one of us *had* worked for world peace, as Derek believed he was doing by going conscientious objector, we hadn't done it *correctly.* CO stood for *cop out,* according to my father. You go, you serve your time, you stand up for your principles. *America is a great country,* my father said. *Hear, hear,* said my mother.

Life was simpler then.

"I was Amish," says Sedgie.

"I saw that film," says Ian, nodding sharply, his mouth full of pesto and potatoes. "Flawed, but *you* were brilliant."

Kiss-ass, I think.

"So," says Dana, "what are you doing tomorrow?"

"Is Maddie taking you swimming?" says Philip.

"I'm a terrible swimmer," Ian says.

"So's Maddie," says Dana.

"I'm taking him on a tour," I say. "Ian has been fetishizing about Sand Isle for years, so I want to debunk his romantic notions."

"Too late," says Ian. "I'm already besotted."

I have taken Ian to see Mother. He stands at the door, taking in her diminished size, her staring eye, her sacrosanct stillness, and her improbable hairdo sticking straight up from her head.

"It's okay," I say, nudging him in. "She hardly knows we're here."

"She's so . . ." His voice trails off.

"Mother?" I say.

She takes a sudden, deep, shuddering breath. Ian clutches the doorframe. I cross to where Mother is lying, beckon him over.

"This is Ian," I tell her.

Her right eye drifts toward him. The clot that traveled to her brain, stealthy as a thief, landed in her right lobe, and robbed her of oxygen. The X-rays showed a small white mark the doctors called an "infarction"—the kind of word that would have made me snigger as a child. This mark— barely perceptible as an aberration in the folds of the brain—is, in fact, the epicenter of her disease. From it, paralysis reverberated like an aftershock. Deprived of its ability to instruct her left side, her mind interacts only with her right. Her left eye, therefore, remains closed.

"Mrs. Addison?" says Ian. He leans in close, takes her hand. "I'm so pleased to meet you."

For the first time in weeks, the right side of Mother's mouth draws upward into something resembling a jack-o'-lantern smile. Her eye beams around and settles fixedly on Ian's face. She makes a sound like "Ga." It is the first sound she's spoken in my presence since I've been here. It is as profound an utterance as I have ever heard. I say so to Ian.

"It's my winning smile," he says as he meets Mother's gaze. "You know a good man when you see one, don't you, Mrs. Addison?"

"Ga."

"Don't call him names, Mother," I say, glancing up at Ian. "She was always calling my boyfriends dreadful names."

"I'm not your boyfriend, Maddie."

"Except for Angus. No name for him." I look back down at her. "He was a 'no-name' husband, right, Mom?"

Her lopsided smile doesn't waver. Her gaze bounces off me, but I swear her eyebrow drifts up. It's nearly nine, and the horizon is glowing red. Sailor's delight. From downstairs, the clatter of dishes being put away followed by a jazz riff on the piano. Outside, the drumbeat of waves. Ian and I stand on either side of Mother like acolytes. I touch her hand. The hospice ladies said that dying seeps in from your fingertips and toes. Mother's once-vivid nails are cold and brittle as mica.

"I'm *not* her boyfriend, Mrs. Addison. Maddie's got to get it through her thick skull. She's incredibly dense about these things." He winks at me, but elicits only a pale smile in return. This pattern of amusing Mother at my expense is frighteningly reminiscent of Angus. But Ian doesn't stop. He leans into Mother. "The thing about Maddie is she doesn't realize that she's smart and funny and beautiful, and she doesn't have to be such a bottom-feeder, don't you agree?"

Mother starts as if an electrical pulse surged through her. I think Ian has alarmed her, but when I look at her face, I see a facsimile of glee. She's having a marvelous time. In her heyday she might have mocked Ian's Adam's apple, his thin blond hair, his uncanny resemblance to Ichabod Crane; now I can see she adores him. She used to say she'd take up with a gay man if something happened to Dad. *They're so much more fun*, she said, *and they never bother you in that way.*

You're a hit," I say to Ian as we sit on the deck drinking coffee under the night sky. "Everyone thinks you're brilliant and witty and fascinating." I look at him. "Yesterday, they didn't know who you were, Ian. I swear to God."

"Ye of little faith, Maddie."

"I've never had faith. You know that."

"Ye of little hope, then."

"What's the difference?"

"Ah."

"Tell me."

Ian considers this while gazing out on the horizon, where Venus hangs like a Hester diamond. From the living room come hoots of laughter, Dana's exclamation of, *Where'd you find* that? Bats dart and dance in the dusky sky, predating insects. "Hope," Ian says finally, "is the acknowledgment of infinite possible outcomes."

I blow the steam from my mug. "You sound like Ralph Feingold."

"You asked."

I take a sip. Someone has put on an old record, but I can't quite make out the music. Stars are awakening in the night sky and winking madly back at us. If there are infinite possibilities, why did everything always feel like it was written in stone? There were no choices, only acceptable and nonacceptable paths. Possibilities, perhaps—but few alternatives.

"Then I hope . . ."

"What?" says Ian.

"Good question." I recognize the music now—one of Dana's old Traffic albums. *"Seems I've got to have a change of scene . . ."* I sing along softly.

"You have a terrible voice," says Ian.

"But someone's locked the door and took the key—" I break off. "What do *you* hope for, Ian?"

Ian smiles inscrutably, raises his eyebrow, and rocks his chair. "MaddieAddieAddison. You know better than to ask."

"You're not dying, Ian. You're not even sick."

"Ah, yes." He looks at me. "What I hope, Maddie, is that, in the meantime, you can lighten up."

It seems to be a running theme. If I could unclench my fists, life would be better. I would have more fun, not to mention friends. I might even date. Instead, I change the subject. "So, what do you make of Sand Isle?"

"Sand Isle?" The name sounds exotic coming from Ian, like some far-off place he's visited. Inside, someone starts the song over. The light from the house is reflected in Ian's eyes, making them almost feverish. I hear Adele laughing, and Derek saying, "No, no—the other one!" And over it all, Sedgie bellows to the music. The air is sweet with the perfume of lake and leaves. Ian sets down his coffee, folds his arms behind his head, and kicks off his loafers. "Sand Isle is a dream, Maddie. Like some strange, beguiling dream of childhood. You could sit right here and think the world makes sense." He looks at me. "It's crazy."

"Exactly," I say.

TWENTY-ONE

For the first time in two weeks, I awake feeling rested. It's a peculiar feeling, reminiscent of some long-ago place in which I was completely happy. A memory of cards spread across a table between Mother and Dana and me, my mother's throaty, smoke-filled voice as she laughed and said, *You two!*

I stretch, squint, and only then realize that the room is ablaze with sun. The yardman has swept and gone; the horses are making their rounds; and from downstairs—the sound of Dana laughing hysterically and the smell of something buttery.

Ian, I think.

Pulling a sweater on over my nightgown, I head down to the dining room. Ian is telling Dana a story about how we shot ten times the normal amount of tape on Ralph Feingold, ". . . just so we could find something—*something!*—that we could make sense of. Everything the man said was obscure. You didn't know whether to fall on your knees and worship the guy or call 911."

I take stock of the stacked pancakes on the sideboard; the heap of scrambled eggs with herbs; something that looks like runny brains but which, I suspect, is Irish oatmeal. It's still too early for Sedgie to have risen, much less play chef.

"You?" I say.

Ian winks. I have told him about the breakfasts Louisa used to make, getting up at 6 A.M. to slice strawberries or wash blueberries for pancakes. As a child on Sand Isle, I never once rose without the smell of coffee brewing and bacon frying.

"You'll spoil the group." For the first time, I notice how big Ian's hands are. Farmer's hands.

"I told everyone to be here by eight-thirty," Ian says. "Miriam's taken Evelyn's Ensure up to her, and Philip's down on the boat."

I cross my arms. "Anything else I should know?"

"Adele and Derek have gone to meditate on the beach. Sedgie, alas, is still asleep."

I try not to laugh. "Oh, Ian, you think you can corral this bunch?" But just as I say it, Philip pushes through the front door, and Jessica comes downstairs. Ian looks at his watch. Within minutes, Adele and Derek have materialized, along with Beo and Jessica.

"Oh, my God!" says Jessica, staring at the sideboard.

It seems to be the universal sentiment. Even Sedgie, staggering down at the last minute, seems impressed.

Ian has assumed the superior look he gets when he tells his life story at AA meetings—a saga that is generally met with a similar level of disbelief. I, myself, didn't believe it at first—a debacle full of such delirious highs and gut-wrenching lows as to make my own story of taking to my bed to drink myself into oblivion pale by comparison.

You actually woke up in Barcelona?

Madrid, he said. *And yes.*

For three years after Sadie died in her crib, I would wake up after a night of drinking unsure what day it was. Sometimes, I didn't know the season. I found an apartment when I left Angus and crawled into sodden hibernation like a bear.

"Look at these!" says Jessica, fingering the pale pink place mats edged with lace.

"There are drawers full of linens," Ian says. "And silver that needs polishing."

And in the pantry—china. Place settings for twenty or more, ten different patterns. Simple white breakfast china with fluted edges. Flowered tea china. Gold-edged dinner china. Pyrex pitchers mixed in with the Waterford, orange-and-yellow plastic next to the Minton. Chipped cups. Useless cups. Bowls for consommé and fingers.

Ian points out the tea set that sat on the sideboard for years until Aunt Pat announced it was a nuisance to maintain and insisted it be put away. Now Ian has resurrected it along with my great-grandmother's gold-and-turquoise dessert plates, a silver toast rack, and the Salton hot plate my mother bought in the seventies.

"No finger bowls?" says Sedgie.

Everyone is standing around with their hands in their pockets, looking like hick guests at a too-fancy wedding. However accustomed our parents may have been to being served—and graciously at that—time has scoured the taste for luxury out of our generation like plate off base metal. We could no more have a Louisa in the kitchen than a chauffeur in livery. None of us knows exactly how to respond to Ian's charming but weird replication of our childhood family breakfasts.

Except for Adele, who has shown up in a batik sarong and with sandy feet. With less than a moment's hesitation, she grabs a plate and starts enthusiastically piling it. I notice fine fuzz forming on her scalp.

"Thatta girl," says Ian. "Got to keep your energy up for all that transcendence."

Adele throws back her head and laughs. One by one, we follow her to the sideboard, reverentially selecting eggs and melon balls and curly, crisp bacon as if it were Communion. We pour coffee from the ancestral silver, use a monogrammed spoon to ladle oatmeal. We take our seats, each of us naturally gravitating to where we sat as children. Ian takes the head of the table, bestowing his presence like that of a revered minister. Pulling up his chair and shaking out his napkin, Ian announces that, since early this morning, he has been talking with Adele about reincarnation, and that Adele has informed him that her inheritance is karmic, having to do with past-life experiences of impoverishment and destitution.

"We were talking about guilt," Adele says, serenely chewing on eggs. "And who we were in previous lives."

There is a moment of silence, and then everyone chimes in about who they think they might have been. Jessica insists she was Vietcong, now forced to live with American capitalists. Beowulf thinks he perished in the Holocaust because his music is so morbid. Adele calmly informs us she was Mary Magdalene, Nefertiti, and, after an interim stint as a maid in medieval Japan, David Livingston's wife. "At least, those are the lives I have hits on."

"A *maid*, Adele?" says Sedgie.

"Don't people always assume they were someone important?" says Jessica. "Like Mother Teresa?"

"Mother Teresa's not dead," says Dana.

"Whatever," says Jessica.

"What-*ever*," Philip says, mimicking her. "Fine talk for a Communist."

"What does this all have to do with guilt?" I ask.

"Money," says Sedgie. "Filthy lucre. The ill-gotten inheritance of wastrel scum."

"Good estate planning," says Philip.

"And you, Maddie?" Ian asks.

I push a melon ball around my plate like a tiny head. "What past life caused me to end up in this one?"

"Make a stab," says Sedgie.

But I'm at a loss to explain what past-life scenarios would manifest in my now being among cousins in a too-big summerhouse, waiting for my mother to die.

"C'mon," says Dana.

A vision or a memory: I am seated in a canoe, shaded by a fringed bit of silk. There is a bundle in my lap. A baby in a blanket. With my free hand, I stroke the water and smile into the face of my husband, whose mutton-chop sideburns, mustache, and high-collared shirt speak of a different era.

"Grannie Addie?" I say weakly.

"Foul," says Sedgie. "You can't be the incarnation of a family member."

"Isn't that, like, incestuous?" Jessica says.

My eyes flicker to Derek, who seems to be regarding his oatmeal. Who was that husband in my dream smiling back at me? Who was that baby in my lap?

"You're all nuts," says Miriam from the landing on the stairs, where she has been listening to the last few minutes of our conversation. "Do you really think that once you're through with this life, you'll get another try?"

"Sit down for a change, Miriam," says Sedgie. "Have a plate."

"You *do* believe in the transmigration of souls?" says Adele, her eyes following Miriam's dark head as she approaches the sideboard.

"Mmm," says Miriam, her attention riveted on the remaining pancakes. She fixes a brimming plate, joins us at the table.

"Life after death?"

"Oh, yes I do," says Miriam, digging in.

"Do you realize that before the Council of Nicea in the fourth century, reincarnation was an accepted premise of Christianity?"

Miriam's eyes narrow. "The council of *what?*"

Adele leans forward eagerly. "The bishops met to select the gospels—"

"The *bishops?*" says Miriam, outraged. "Girl, that is the *Word* you're talking about, and the *Word* says we're going to be raptured, and those who aren't are going to be left behind."

"That'll be us," says Sedgie happily. "Stewing in our own juices."

"The heretical Presbyterians," says Ian the Jewish Lutheran, nodding solemnly.

"Infidels," adds Sedgie.

Again, I feel that peculiar sensation of happiness. In a past life, Ian woke up in Madrid and spent the day at a bullfight with a man whose name he didn't know. Upstairs, with glacierlike tenacity, Mother moves toward a new incarnation that is seemingly open-ended. Reincarnation is something I used to think about, seeing Sadie in giggling, hair-tossing girls who were the age she would have been. Thus my fixation on a Band-Aid-covered knee, the scuffed sneaker, a raveled braid, a cry of *Mommy!* Even though I suspect it is a fantasy, I flirt with the notion that her soul somehow appeared in another baby just after she died. I wanted to believe Sadie was still with me. I want to believe it now.

L eaving the cousins to do the cleanup, I finagle Ian to myself. We make our way through the ruined garden. I push down the collar on his Lacoste shirt, but he flips it back up and picks the dead head off a sunflower. The boards on the walk are loose or rotted. Some have completely broken away. Virginia creeper encroaches; worse—poison ivy. I steer Ian around a particularly virulent-looking patch. Decades ago, after contracting a vicious case of poison ivy, Sedgie drew a map showing the way to the beach. Since then, his drawing has been pinned next to the refrigerator, yellowing and curling with age. It depicts a bird's-eye view of the house rendered in colored pencils, the flight of stairs, the flagstone path through the myrtle. *Beware the spiders!* it says. *Beware the poison ivy!*—with a arrow drawn to a scribble of green covering the dunes.

Ian crosses his arms and stares up at the facade of the house. Rising from the sandy soil of the garden is the boat room. Above that sits the porch and the tower room, where carved garlands once decorated the fascia. Three stories up, a bank of bedrooms, including Mother's, overlook the lake. This is the south side of the house, baked by the sun in summer, battered by storms in autumn, gutted by ice in winter. It wears its face like a once-beautiful woman who has known sorrow and happiness, and who wasn't afraid to live.

"It needs paint," says Ian.

"Every three years."

"Not recently, from the look of it."

It occurs to me that perhaps we've missed a cycle—that after Aunt Pat died, Mother forgot to call the painters. It also occurs to me that after Mother goes, the task will fall to us.

"Adele tells me she has no money."

I push back my hair. It needs cutting, and I'm sure the gray is coming in. "Yeah, well, you know the situation."

Ian shrugs. He knows the details of my own finances as intimately as if he were my spouse—more so, in fact, given that when Angus and I were married, I kept the stark facts of my inheritance to myself. It wasn't until we signed our first joint tax return that Angus said, *Bloody hell, Addison. Why do you want to work?* By the time I left him, Angus had ferreted out every detail, and he wanted to be compensated.

But wealth is relative, and what seems like a windfall in your twenties looks paltry when you need serious money to produce a film. Ian and I have leveraged my meager fortune to garner grants, loans, investors. Still, we make our films on shoestring budgets, and the fact of our house needing paint seems daunting.

"What do you suppose it costs?" says Ian.

I, too, cross my arms and scan the building. It's more than paint; it's corroded hardware and broken panes and lost shingles and dry rot. The Dusays allegedly spent millions to build their shiny new house. Even split among six cousins, our old house will require thousands from each of us to maintain.

"Kiss our budget good-bye," I say.

Neither Ian nor I has ever owned a home; we are both chronic renters. But own the Aerie I will when Mother dies—along with Dana, Sedgie, Adele, Derek, and the long-absent Edward. Together, we will have to decide when the dishwasher needs replacing, the stairs repaired, a piece of furniture tossed.

"It's too depressing to contemplate," I say.

"Can't we rent it out for movie sets?"

I stare at him in disbelief. "And what's with this *we?*"

We continue down to the beach, passing through the cedar and overgrown lilac that form a gloomy cave around a landing. *Enter at your peril!* Sedgie wrote on this section of his map. From here, the stairs trace steeply down the dune and end at a boardwalk that disappears altogether as we come out on creamy sand edged by rock and the lapping waves of Lake Michigan.

Ian gasps. "It's lovely, Maddie. It's as beautiful as any beach I've seen." The tenacious pulse of waves, the rattling rocks. Seagulls catch the wind, caw, dip. The air is fragrant with pine and fish. "Imagine your Victorian ancestors kicking off their shoes and stockings, hoisting their skirts, and showing a bit of flesh."

"And bloomers," I say.

"How did they pee?"

I try to imagine my starchy Victorian ancestors hiking up their ruffled taffeta and lowering themselves over chamber pots. They took umbrellas to the beach, had staffs of seven or more, but the call of nature was unavoidable, and the plumbing, such as it was, allowed for little dignity.

"What's this?" Ian says, regarding Derek's burgeoning mound made of rock and wood. "A beehive? A *stupa?*"

"C'mon."

We make our way up the beach, scrambling over wooden cribs that were built to retain the sand. The windward side of the island is overgrown with scrubby pine, beyond which oak and maple and alder stand nobly. The houses of Sand Isle are perched on the hill, half-obscured by the trees. A few leaves have started to turn.

"A Republic Steel family lived there," I say. "One of the boys had a crush on Dana. And that was the Birchmeiers'. Beer." I point out each house to Ian, tell him who lives there, how many generations have owned it, and which ones are still called by the name of the original family, the current owners notwithstanding. "Still," I add, "there's not a lot of turnover."

Pharmaceuticals, glass, bags, toilets, banking, manhole covers, curtain rods, and buggy whips.

"The Dusays," I say as we come around the west side of the island toward the channel, where a colossal white shingled house, newly built with a tower and a widow's walk and fan-shaped windows and three porches, spreads out like the skirts of a Southern belle. "Shopping malls."

"Ghastly," says Ian—bless him. "And the buggy-whip people? What happened to them?"

"Half the family refused to diversify. The other half wisely invested with Henry Ford."

Don't touch the principal, our father said to us repeatedly. I, however, have sold off chunks of my Addison stock with the furtive abandon of a dope fiend.

We start up the concrete stairs at the portage alongside the yacht club. I pause at the landing to point out the *Green Dragon* among the vessels of various vintage and seaworthiness. The gleaming racing machines seem to quiver at their moorings like Thoroughbreds. The *Green Dragon* looks docile as an old cat.

"Maddie Addison!"

The voice appears to be coming from the yacht-club deck. I spot a frantically waving napkin and a soufflé of blond hair. "Oh God. Sunday brunch."

Eleven years since I've seen her, and the last time is too embarrassing to dwell on, involving a teary (mine) conversation on our porch involving a maudlin confession (also mine) concerning her son.

"Hello, Aunt Bibi," I say, waving back with a smile, regressing into the insincerity that was a mainstay of my youth.

"Jamie told me you were here, but I couldn't believe it. Come here so I can see you."

It's useless to pretend I'm late for church or bridge (she'll believe neither), so I surrender and climb the remaining stairs with Ian in tow to say hi to Jamie's mother. Bibi looks exactly the same. I wonder if she's specified on her driver's license, along with various organ donations, that her skin be used for a second life as an alligator purse. The hair, itself, is magnificent. A miracle of backcombing and lacquer, it has achieved a topiary wonderfulness reminiscent of humpbacked tortoise.

"Maddie Addison," says Bibi Hester through Coral Sunset lips. "Maddie Addison," she says again, as if repeating it will conjure some notion of me from the past. "How's your mother?" Her eyes flicker onto Ian, the smile unwavering even as her gaze drifts back to me with an unspoken, *Well?*

"Aunt Bibi, this is Ian Gruler, my business partner. Ian, Mrs. Hester."

Is it gratification or relief on Bibi's face? And is it my imagination, or is Ian suddenly becoming swishier as he says, "Delighted!" and kisses her hand. "Maddie has told me so much about you." On her other hand, the prune-size diamond glitters. Ian, who has spent the day before reminding me he's *not* my boyfriend, suddenly throws his arm around me and says, "Isn't she beautiful?" He gives me a little squeeze and smacks me on the cheek. "And this is one talented lady, Mrs. Hester. But you already know that."

Aunt Bibi strains to keep smiling. "Have you met Jamie and Fiona?"

Tra-la-la, I want to say. *No need.*

"I'm dying to," says Ian.

I shoot him a look.

"Then again . . ." says Ian.

"Here they are!" says Aunt Bibi.

And indeed, they are—Jamie in pale yellow linen with an Hermès tie, Fiona in . . . well, Hermès everything. I swallow so as not to blurt out, *God, Jamie, what's with the clothes?*

Ian is smiling (inanely, in my opinion) and pumping Jamie's hand and telling him that Hester bags are his favorite. "I love that little clip thing."

"RidCo," says Jamie.

"Excuse me?"

"The company's RidCo. Not Hester. My grandmother was a Ridder." As he says this, I notice Jamie brushing his hand against his pant leg. Not exactly wiping it. Just a little sweep as if he is brushing off lint.

"*You* make the movies!" says Fiona. The lightbulb, I see, has gone on.

"Films," says Jamie, correcting her.

Jessica would say, *Whatever,* but Fiona drops her voice and obediently says, "Films."

That could be me wearing that outfit and having my choice of words corrected. In a trice, my attitude toward Fiona softens. Not that I'm a thing of beauty in my old shorts and sandy feet and a T-shirt that shows the New York skyline above my breasts, but at least Ian (who's *not* my boyfriend) isn't saying, "*Film,* darling. Not *movies.*"

"Ta," says Ian, wiggling his fingers as I drag him away.

C ould you possibly get any gayer?" I ask as we cross the porch of the yacht club to the bayside, where the lawn tumbles down to the windward side of the island. It is the lawn where I was married. The dance floor was over there, the ivy trellis to my right. And from that beach, my mother took a swim.

"She's a type, Maddie. She's perfect. The whole thing. It's so . . . summer. It's so . . ."

"WASP-y?"

"But with a Midwestern flair."

"*Midwestern* and *flair* are oxymoronic."

"Okay," says Ian with a sly, sideways glance, "the daughter-in-law isn't too bright. But the son!" Ian shakes his head. "You could have *had* that ass!"

I feign shock. "Actually, he's quite a decent person."

Ian wags his finger at me, evoking memories of Aunt Pat. "Those were *very* well-cut slacks."

"He used to wear jeans."

"Roots, Maddie, roots." He pronounces *roots* with a roll of the R, only half kidding as he goes on to make a point about continuity and shared history. "To have people who've seen you grow up. Who grew up with your parents. These people *know* you, Maddie."

"And since when have you gone all gooey over people who've known you forever?" I ask. "The cow-milking Larsons who've known the cow-milking Grulers for a century, yet who look at you like you're some kind of anti-cow-milker?"

Ian crosses his arms and nods. "Point taken. But it's different. That's not what they see when they look at you."

"They don't see a cow-milker?"

Ignoring me, he says, "They see your family history. They see someone who was formed by this place and by generations of tradition."

It occurs to me that Ian is going to be of little help.

"And yes, there *is* some cow-milker in me," he goes on. "And those farmers do, in fact, understand that . . . aspect of myself." He rattles this off quickly as if it pains him to acknowledge it. "Soooo, in some ways, the people at that yacht club know you better than I do."

I concede his point, but only slightly.

We've reached the sidewalk, heading west again along the bay. The Hobsons' gray cottage fronts here, almost as battered and in need of paint as the Aerie. Now, according to Dana, Larry Hobson's wife wants it in a divorce settlement.

Next to the Hobsons' sits the Baileys', whose daughter, Deb, was killed with Tad Swanson in a car accident. Beyond the Baileys', the Swansons' pillared Victorian with its boxes of begonias and a lawn jockey. Ian and I pause to examine the statue, its arm extended as if for a handout, its painted face like Al Jolson in blackface singing "Mammy."

Ian crosses his arms and wags his finger. "Now *that* we're going to have to fix."

We arrive back at the Aerie, brush the sand off our feet before heading up the three flights of stairs. We're not even halfway to the front door when Jessica bursts out. "MaddieAunt! Something's wrong with Grannie Ev!"

By the time we get to Mother's room, Derek and Dana have joined Miriam, who has climbed onto the bed with Mother and draped her over her shoulder the way one would burp a child. She's hitting Mother on the back, and every time she smacks her, Mother's head whiplashes like she's having a convulsion. Jessica starts crying, and I say, "What happened?" and Dana shushes me, which makes me mad.

"Don't shush me," I say.

Miriam signals Derek over, and Ian, too, rushes to the bed. Miriam says, "Hold her under her arms." And they take her, and Miriam squeezes her from behind, and in a gush, Mother vomits. For a second, I have an image of Mother throwing up in the revolving door of the Ritz-Carlton Hotel. Ian cradles her head, and Derek strokes it.

Miriam takes out a stethoscope, listens to Mother's chest. "Maddie, you need to call Dr. Mead and tell her your mother's aspirated."

"On *what*?" I say. As far as I know, she only drinks liquids. What could possibly stick in her throat? Words? Memories? Unuttered expletives at my father?

"Ice cream," Miriam says.

"Chocolate chip," says Jessica.

Dana runs to get clean sheets, but Derek and Ian are still by Mother's side, Derek on her right, Ian on her left. This triptych of Mother and my idolized cousin and my homosexual-recovering-film-partner makes me woozy. Perhaps past lives and current incarnations *do* collide. Perhaps, as Ralph Feingold posits, there *is* no separation between universes. Or perhaps God/Betty, unable to resist the juxtaposition, has a tweaked sense of humor after all.

D r. Mead has come and gone. Once more, I have marveled at her taste in clothing and her wonderful hair. *It's inevitable*, she said. *Swallowing becomes impaired. Digestive functioning shuts down, and food is no longer ingestible. The process could take days, but this is usually the last leg.*

So what should we do? Dana and I asked.

Keep her comfortable. Say what needs to be said. Wait.

Now Dana and I are alone in Mother's room. Out of deference to our mother-daughter-sister status, everyone else has left.

"Have *you* said everything that needs to be said?" asks Dana.

"I wouldn't know where to start."

After a pause, Dana says, "Me neither."

The two of us are sitting on chintz-covered chairs in the tower room across from Mother's bed. From here, we can see the horizon—a patriotic line of blue in the afternoon sun. What an idyllic place to die, I think. Little wonder there are lingering ghosts. If my father were alive, the *Green Dragon* would be slicing up the bay. Now there are Jet Skis and some kind of "cigarette" boat cutting every which way, unfettered by sails. We Addisons are a wind-tethered bunch. Like the leash of my childhood, the wind gave us only so much leeway, determining our course, the rate of speed, the distance one could cross in an afternoon. Instead, these turbocharged demons make short shrift of the bay.

Downstairs, Beo plays dirges on the piano. Sedgie is in the kitchen making soup—leek, from the smell of it. I wonder if Mother feels hungry, and if this inability to eat will leave her famished. The only option at this point, according to Dr. Mead, is to intubate, and all of us agree that Mother would rather die. So, too, have we agreed not to treat with antibiotics if and when this aspiration becomes infected. Pneumonia will set in. She will find it hard to breathe.

"It's hideous," I say, "this playing of God."

Dana, the converted Catholic, says, "We do it all the time."

From the kitchen, cackles of laughter—evidently Ian and Sedgie.

"I like your friend," says Dana. "It's hard to imagine . . ."

"That he used to geeze up?" I shrug. "It's hard to imagine a lot of things about people. Like Derek. Hard to imagine him as anything other than a hero, right?" Dana looks at me sideways, but doesn't ask me to expand. I try another angle. I'm irritable, and I'm tired, and I'm looking for a fight. "Take me, for instance. For about two minutes, I was a wife and a mother. Then I was a drunk."

I can tell from the look on Dana's face that my pedantry exhausts her. Truth is, it exhausts me, too, but I cling to it like a piece of fabric that was once my baby blanket—because I know the smell, know the texture, and the familiarity makes me feel secure.

"You were always hung up on Derek," Dana says.

I gape at her, but she doesn't elaborate. Finally she says, "We were a *lot* of things. Some of us played God and lived to regret it afterward."

"Dana, if you honestly believe Mother wants to be kept alive through a feeding tube . . ."

"I'm not talking about Mother. This isn't *about* Mother. And it isn't always about you either, Maddie. You're not the only one who has regrets."

But I *do* have regrets. Oodles of them. They sit on my shoulders like drooling gargoyles. A neglected baby monitor, eerily quiet. That first drink after a year of abstinence. "I should never have married Angus. I should have had an abortion."

A scrap of an étude slips up the stairs, meshes with the crash of waves. "I had one," says Dana. "It doesn't solve everything."

For a moment, the light refracting off the lake makes me dizzy. I'm sure I heard her incorrectly. One wave breaks. Two. "You and . . . Philip?"

"Philip?" Dana shakes off the question as if I couldn't be more off base. "It was that awful summer when Bruce Digby dumped me. Don't you remember how hysterical Mother was?"

"You were *pregnant?*"

"By a jerk-aholic tennis player who hasn't thought of me since."

"So you . . ."

"Exactly. And then I couldn't get pregnant again. That drug Mom and Aunt Pat took for morning sickness? Better living through chemistry, but it made your daughters more or less barren, Adele and me case in point. If I'd known, I'd never have had an abortion."

I think back on that summer, my mother's edgy nervousness, the way she'd looked at my father, the way she'd looked at me. The Aerie had been quivering with hormones, shooting like arrows, missing their targets, hitting the wrong ones altogether.

"But the religion?"

"Oh, Maddie. Don't we all get religion when we're in trouble?"

I think of Ian, our tight-lipped refusal to say the Lord's Prayer at the close of AA meetings. An uncomfortable urge to laugh rises like gas in my chest. Just as I clamp my hand to my mouth, someone with movielike timing clangs the triangle for dinner.

I f Sedgie was brilliant in the kitchen before, he's a genius when partnering with Ian. Together, they've done something fantastic with chicken involving tuna and capers.

"And mayonnaise," says Ian with a flourish. "Only it's homemade."

Sedgie is serving us like an Italian waiter, a towel draped over his arm, his sleeves rolled up, hair slicked back, his accent impeccable as he describes *il tonnato, e pomodoro, e mozzarella*, and so fourth.

I should find it funny, but I don't. "This is Michigan," I say.

"MaddieAddie," Ian says under his breath. He knows I can spiral into a crankiness that takes days to dissipate. The rest of the cousins seem oblivious, pleased to have abdicated anything culinary to Sedgie and his new assistant. Even Dana seems perky, as if she's confessed, repented, and atoned.

Did Mother know about your abortion?

Dana had smoked like a fiend that summer and sobbed in her room. We drove out the shore and picked up an Indian woman. Elton John's *Yellow Brick Road* was our favorite album, and it was the first time we'd seen Edward since Vietnam. I had flirted with Derek on the beach while he took peyote and talked about rocks. It was the summer of dented moons and dented hearts.

Yes. But not Dad.

"Adele, *what* are you doing?" says Sedgie, looking appalled.

Adele looks up guiltily from her plate, where her chicken lies barren of sauce.

"Oh, God," says Sedgie, "you've scraped off the *tonnato*."

"It's mayonnaise," says Adele.

"You're anor-EX-ic," says Sedgie. He looks around at the rest of us. "Please, somebody. Confirm this."

"Delicious chicken," says Dana.

"Mmm," says Beowulf.

"Mmm," says Jessica.

"She *is* anorexic," I say darkly. "She used to throw up when she was a teenager."

Adele's eyes narrow. "I used to *what*?"

"It's the truth."

Beo looks from me to Adele. "You barfed?"

"I didn't . . . barf." Adele looks at me. "You're a fine one to talk about barfing. As I recall, you spent a whole summer barfing."

I meet her gaze. "Mitigating circumstances."

"You were a lush."

"That's true. Lush, drunk, sot, juicehead—"

"Stop it!" says Dana. "Eat your chicken."

"I feel better," I say.

Across the table, Adele sits with her uneaten food, her eyes tearing up. I want to attribute my testiness to the pressures of a deathwatch, a near relapse, or too many family meals, but Adele's smug self-starvation and spiritual chauvinism have annoyed me for years. She is her own version of Aunt Pat—dogmatic, righteous, trembling with virtue. Now, seeing her tears, her despair around food, it occurs to me that, balancing on the fulcrum between malnutrition and vigor, she, too, has been tyrannized by expectation.

"Can we have a little prayer?" says Dana. "Hold hands and go around and say what we're thankful for?"

"Oh, Christ," says Sedgie.

"Yes!" says Ian. "A twelve-step meeting right here in the Aerie!"

We awkwardly take hands. No one says anything. We wait for a de facto leader to present him- or herself, but everyone is staring at their plate and waiting. Finally, Philip clears his throat and says, "Well . . ."

"State your name," says Ian.

Philip looks at Ian questioningly, but says, "Philip?"

"Hi, Philip!" Ian and I bark in unison.

Philip looks nonplussed. He seems to have forgotten what he was going to say.

Silence descends, only to be broken by Adele, who says, "How about we send some energy to Aunt Ev? Let her know it's all right to go."

Oh please, I think, but everyone else agrees this is acceptable, so, with eyes closed, we hold Mother in our minds and hearts. It's one of those moments that make me ache with discomfort. I peer through slit eyes, but the whole group—even Ian and Sedgie—has their heads bowed, and I feel a wrenching inadequacy due to my lack of solemnity. I wait for a sign—the squeezing of a hand, a cough, but the only sound I hear are cousins breathing. Then Dana's stomach rumbles—the great gurgling rumble she used to produce as a child.

"A sign if there ever was one," says Sedgie. "Let's eat."

No one else seems inclined to confess anything or speak the truth— mercifully, since I'm still reeling from the news of Dana's terminated pregnancy twenty-five years before. Letting go of one another's hands, we pass the tomatoes and mozzarella and move on to other subjects like film and politics and who's doing the dishes.

"I have to leave in a couple of days," Sedgie says. "Ibsen calls."

Four or five days at the most, Dr. Mead said.

"You can't leave now," I say.

"Truly," says Jessica. "We'll have to start eating takeout again."

"I have to work, you guys."

Everyone shifts uncomfortably. No one talks about work in the Aerie. We park our vocations and our everyday lives on the other side of the channel so that we can give our full attention to games and sports and conversation.

"It's only acting," says Dana, poking at her chicken.

Right, I think. It's not physics. Or banking. Or law. "But it's what he *does*, Dane."

"What I was going to say," says Philip abruptly, "before I was so rudely interrupted"—he looks pointedly at Ian and me—"is that it behooves you all to discuss the fate of this house once Evelyn goes."

This pronouncement seems even more intrusive than Sedgie's mention of work because (A) it presumes Mother's death, and (B) we will have to talk about money. Dana rolls her eyes; Derek sets down his fork; Beo and Jessica look at each other blankly; Sedgie groans; and Adele says, "Count me out."

"Excuse me?" I say.

"It's a nonattachment thing."

"You've run out of money?" says Sedgie morosely.

We all turn to Adele for confirmation. Her head is high and handsome. "I haven't 'run out.'" She makes quotation marks with her fingers. "I've dispensed with it."

"Oh, that's rich," says Sedgie. "Well, two ex-wives, and I've done my share of 'dispensing' as well."

"It was mine to lose."

Philip sighs a long, deep sigh, and I realize I've never thought of it as "mine to lose." I was raised to dip into the font, but not drain it lest the next generation ends up railing like Blanche DuBois about the kindness of strangers. We've stretched our dollars, hoarded our airline miles, done our best to live within our means, but taxes, alimony, and issue take their toll.

Seeing our glum faces, Ian looks alarmed. "But this *house*!"

"We could turn it into a B&B," I say, aiming for irony, "like they do in England."

"Or a retreat?" says Adele, sounding more upbeat.

"Sedgie could cook," says Jessica.

"In that case, I have dibs on Louisa's old room," says Sedgie the way he used to call dibs on the bunk room.

Obviously, no one realizes I was kidding.

Dana looks at Philip, then at me. "Well?"

Suddenly Philip takes on a new significance in our family hierarchy. We turn to him as if to an oracle. "There's some money in a trust, right?" I say. "To keep it up?"

"It's my understanding," says Philip, "that all the remaining principal gets distributed along with the shares of the house. In other words, it's up to each of you to commit to ownership or not."

"You mean we have the *option*? Why wasn't this explained?" I say.

"I believe your father thought he was going to live forever."

"So what *does* it cost?" asks Beowulf.

Philip clears his throat painfully. There is something sage and grave about his expression. "The taxes alone will be exorbitant."

" 'You take my *house* when you doth take the prop that sustains it,' " says Sedgie, quoting *The Merchant of Venice*, more or less.

Philip folds his hands together and begins to hold forth about taxes, assessments, maintenance, and upkeep. I can see why his client employs him. His air is as authoritative as Ralph Feingold's about the transient-dimensional plasticity of space. We are transfixed and confused. Even divided by a factor of six—no, *four* without Adele and, presumably, Edward—the reality of the transience and plasticity of our net worth smears like numbers on a chalkboard.

"This is horrible," says Jessica. "Grannie Ev is dying, and you're talking about money."

"Oh, lofty one," says Sedgie, "do you suggest a bake sale?"

"It seems disrespectful."

Philip looks at his daughter with the same gratified expression that used to cross my father's face whenever one of us demonstrated some semblance of virtue. Clearing the table. Speaking politely to our elders. Manners were so much the social currency on Sand Isle that I had since dismissed them as anachronistic, but nine years in New York have made me long for their company as for that of an old and familiar friend.

"You're right," I say to Jessica, while wondering if Philip has ever considered electrolysis for that hair on his shoulders. "It seems crass. But it's important. If we never talk about money, we won't have any left."

"So what are we going to do with the house?"

We all look at one another. The question, as disputable as the origins of the universe and the meaning of life, hangs in the air.

W ake up."
       I rustle, groan, turn over as if I was dreaming, but Ian gives me a sharp shake and tells me to get up.

"We're heading out," he says.

In the dark, Ian is invisible, but a floating glob of pale hair implies that Jessica is with him. "C'mon," she says.

Yawning, I say, "What do you want?" which comes out *wa-wee-won*.

"We're on a mission," says Ian.

"A little art project," says Jessica.

Minutes later, we are heading down the bayside, Ian in some kind of Chinese lounge outfit, Jessica in boxers and a T-shirt, me in my white flannel nightie. I glow like a ghost. In the lamplight, our shadows grow long on the sidewalk. Fractured moonlight splits the lake, but most of the houses are dark. Jessica is carrying an old can of white paint and a brush. She skips along, so suspiciously comfortable with the task at hand, I wonder if she has actual graffiti experience.

"*Where are you going?*" she sings. "*Where are you going?*" The paint slops cheerfully in the bucket.

"Some things, Maddie," Ian says, "are unacceptable."

In a daze, I follow. The whole thing is as unreal as a dream. In fact, it occurs to me that I *am* dreaming, and that Ian hasn't come to Sand Isle at all. Ian on Sand Isle seems incongruous; my half-Vietnamese niece with a can of white paint seems downright subversive. As if in a dream, I glide above the sidewalk, my feet not touching the pavement. Any minute now, we could spread our arms and fly—Ian, Jessica, and me—like the children from *Peter Pan*, a book I find disconcerting given its subject matter of lost children, Never Never Land, and parents who entrust their offspring to a dog.

"I'm flying!" I say, my nightgown swooping around behind me.

"Why aren't you wearing shoes?" says Ian.

"Shhh," I say. "We're on a mission." But I have no idea for what, and Jessica has stopped singing.

We arrive at the Swansons' house. It is pillared in an antebellum style, although all of the houses on Sand Isle are decidedly postbellum, having been built by fortunes made during the Civil War. Nevertheless, the Swansons' tries to evoke nostalgia for mint juleps on the plantation porch, ladies in wicker swings, darkies in the field.

No light comes from the Swansons' house. It is about three in the morning, and the only stirring comes from waves and a few malingering crickets. Surely, the Swansons are asleep and have no idea marauders are standing on their lawn. I look around nervously for Mac or one of the security guards who might be patrolling.

"We've got to act fast," says Ian. He jerks his head toward the lawn jockey and says to Jessica, "Get its face and hands."

"You've got to be kidding," I say. "This is vandalism."

"It's racist," says Jessica. "We're painting."

"Actually," I say, holding out my hand before she wields her brush, "I don't think it is rascist. Weren't these things used in the Underground Railroad or something to signal escaping slaves?"

"You're thinking of quilts," says Ian. "This"—he jerks his head at the jockey—"demeans black people and trivializes the horrors of slavery."

"Remember that fat mammy cookie jar that was in the Aerie kitchen?" says Jessica.

"Now *that* was definitely slave art," I say. "Louisa told me."

"Those are *very* collectible," says Ian, his acquisitive inclinations momentarily trumping his urge toward social justice.

"So what are we going to do with the paint?"

"Hmm." Ian strokes his chin. "Is it racist or not?"

"Totally," says Jessica.

"Shall we ask the Swansons?" I say. "We could knock on their door and say, 'Excuse me, but do you intend your lawn ornament to be a symbol of white supremacy and the oppression of blacks? Or is it merely an artifact, reminiscent of our once-divided nation, the wounds of which have never healed, but without its manifest tensions, our struggles would be meaningless? Even futile?'"

"We *could* ask them that," Ian says slowly while Jessica dabs away at the lawn jockey until it bears a creepy resemblance to a mime. I start to freak out. I am nearly forty, dressed in a nightgown, engaging in an act of defacement, the significance of which is debatable. My bravado evaporates. I know security is on its way. "They're calling the cops," I say. "Let's go."

"Just a minute."

I swear to God, I can see his flashlight! "Give me that," I say, grabbing the brush.

"Done!" says Jessica as I slap one last dab on the jockey's cheek.

We fly down the sidewalk, leaving the defaced jockey to stand guard in front of a house owned by a person my mother used to call the Drape Man.

"Lose the paint," says Ian. "It'll lead them back to our house."

Sure enough—like Hansel and Gretel's crumbs, dribbles of paint trail after us. Jessica shoves the can into a cedar hedge, and we continue on through the night, giddy with anarchy and a sense of possibility that recalls a twenty-five-year-old memory of picking up an Indian woman hitchhiking home.

We bound up the stairs, shushing one another and stifling laughter. When we reach the landing, I see the light is on in the tower room. Mother's room. It's barely 4 A.M. It occurs to me she must have had a restless night for her light to be on, but no sooner have we pushed through the front door and come into the dining room than I hear Miriam's voice at the top of the stairs saying, "Is that you, Maddie? You'd better come."

TWENTY-TWO

Her breaths are so far apart—each one seems like the last. Everyone's awake now. Sleepy, tousled, they've filed into the room. It will be dark for another hour or so; then, the sound of a broom will start. Mother is under her pink blanket cover, her hair combed back from her face. She is pretty like this—here, on the cusp of dying. Sadie, too, was in pink.

I want to tell her we painted the Drape Man's lawn jockey white. Mother would laugh. She could see the fun in iconoclasm—especially when my father wasn't looking.

But I don't think she can hear me now. Ever since yesterday, she's been hovering somewhere else. No one speaks. Adele touches her, and I realize it's okay, that it will not hurt her. Is it easier to leave this world with people holding you? Or to be left alone?

There—a breath. Dana's eyes trace foggily over mine, and I nod. I hear everyone breathing, hear the shift in their weight, feel their focus pressing in. For once, the solemnity in our family isn't forced.

I left Angus during the Christmas of 1987, less than a year and a half after we were married. I didn't return his or my mother's calls. There would be no service, no memorial. Later, Angus stood outside my new apartment and hollered. By May, Sadie would have been walking.

Let's talk about how you related to your family after Sadie died, Dr. Anke said. *Why did you remove yourself?*

I was expected to be a brick, and alcohol was the surest way. It was either that or go crazy.

Dr. Anke flinched at the word. *But you couldn't prevent it, could you?*

Which? The death of my child? Or going crazy?

Mother breathes in a sudden, raspy breath. Her mouth opens as if she's gulping air.

"What's that?" I say to Miriam.

"Soon," Miriam says.

Keep the Corbu furniture, I told Angus when I opened the door. He slapped me and called me an ungrateful bitch. It was a good excuse to keep drinking.

"Is she suffocating?" asks Dana.

"She's shutting down," says Miriam.

I was pulled over for driving under the influence. I was booked, finger-printed, spent the night in jail with a woman who had knifed her boyfriend. We spent hours consoling each other. Her body was bone-thin and smelled of fried fish, but she leaned into me, and I held her as if she were my child. In the morning, they released me. I didn't have enough money for a cab, so I rode the bus from Laguna to Santa Monica. All those months of driving aimlessly had paid off. I knew my way around.

"She's releasing," says Adele.

Jessica says, "Shouldn't we say something to her? Sing?"

Eventually, I was drinking because I had to—not because of my marriage or my child, or that Jamie broke my heart, or because it made the oil slicks look pretty. I drank because every cell in my body demanded it. Adele would say another spirit had moved in. She may be right. There is no redemption in losing a child.

"We should light candles," Adele says. "And incense. It will calm her spirit."

I touch my mother's skin, placing my hand across her clavicle, where she used to trace Joy perfume. A dead branch. A twig. Even her blood runs like the sap of a diseased tree. I want to ask her if she's sorry. I want to explain to her that alcoholism is an illness and that you don't have to die from it.

Adele and Jessica bring candles from all parts of the house. The hiss of a match, the air fills with pyrite, and the walls take on a golden glow. Slow deaths allow opportunity for ritual. It's the sudden ones that rob you of the ability to prepare.

I'm sorry I hurt you and Dad.

I'd returned to Sand Isle alone the summer after Sadie died. If there are ghosts in this house, I was one of them. It was a summer of murky, edgeless days. I threw empty bottles down the laundry chute. I hid them under my sweaters. I was an animal. It was an embarrassment for my parents—to have a grown child go to pieces like that. It is one thing to get tipsy at parties—another to pass out.

Unacceptable. Absolutely unacceptable.

I don't remember if they said I had to go, or if those were my words. But I left. Eleven years is a long time to bleed.

I feel as if I'm doing my mother's breathing for her. She was always afraid of water, and now her lungs are drowning. I suddenly gasp for air. It's lavender I'm craving, the evidence of ghosts. But I can only smell the fresh Michigan morning, the faintest scent of fish. She is so still. Not a single breath. Like Sadie, her eyelids aren't completely closed. The slightest lightening, and the sweeping starts. The ghosts are gone.

I an finds me in the nursery. It is almost lunchtime, but no one has made any plans. Philip has called the undertaker, who will be coming later to take my mother's body across the channel. The arrangements seem suddenly overwhelming—where to have the service, what prayers to say, what hymns to sing, who to give the eulogy. We're none of us religious—except for Dana and Adele—and Adele's suggestion of the

Buddhist practice of chopping up the body and feeding it to the birds, while exotic, is met with skepticism.

Everyone has retreated into whatever gives him or her solace. Derek has returned to the beach to work on his structure. Downstairs, piano music starts and breaks off. I hear Dana in her bedroom talking to Philip, arguing even. It came sooner than we thought it would. I don't know how I imagined Mother's actual death, but it was correlated with the packing of trunks. Not that there are trunks anymore—they've been long put out to pasture—but the ritual of packing up and closing down provides the coda of the summer. We would have dragged up the boats, stripped the beds, pulled in the wicker, closed the curtains, emptied the refrigerator, covered the furniture. Before the crew from the Sand Isle Association arrived to drain the pipes, we would have said to Mother, *There, you can die now.*

But she's jumped the gun.

"So what are you doing?" Ian asks.

"Sitting."

He curls up beside me on the bed. The springs, like all of the box springs in this house, squeak. How can you have privacy in a place where you can hear snoring through the walls? Perhaps there is a tacit agreement to ignore certain realities: bodily functions and parents fighting, screaming babies, or a young man touching his cousin who has braces on her teeth.

"When I was little, I played with chipmunks," I say.

Ian says, "Most of *my* friends were imaginary."

"At least you *had* friends."

Ian studies me with a sideways look. He knows when I tumble into self-pity. *I have no sympathy for you, Maddie Addison,* he has said to me more than once. *Your cup runneth over.*

"Do you have any ideas? Because this service is going to be a travesty if we don't get our act together."

Ian adjusts himself to sit cross-legged on the bed. "Not for Evelyn's service, no. But I *do* have an idea for a film."

"My mother just died, Ian."

"Yes, and I'm rarely appropriate. So I was thinking—" Ian's face has that intensity he gets when he's tracking a subject. "Let's make a film about your family!" He leans back as if he's just bestowed me with a brilliant gift.

I fight my eyebrows, but there's no stopping them. "My family? How fascinating. I'm sure it will have mass appeal."

"I'm being very serious, Maddie. Think of an Altman film. Think of Chekhov."

Ian can cajole me out of a mood like a parent distracting a pouting child. "We just . . . follow them around with a camera?"

"Actually, I'm thinking of moving away from documentary and more into dramatization. Sedgie, of course, can play himself."

It occurs to me that Ian isn't being entirely flippant. I try to wrap my head around the concept, but the creepiness of using one's family as material notwithstanding, why would anyone be interested? Every summer, we return to our childhoods to play charades and Sardines. As a family, we're prone to substance abuse. We fret about an old house and argue points to which none of us is qualified to speak. Besides, everyone hates rich people. Even when they're not rich anymore.

As if he's read my thoughts, Ian says, "People use their families as material all the time, Maddie. That's what artists do. And you don't give your family enough credit. You underestimate them."

"Oh, please . . ."

Ian sighs and shakes his head. He rolls over and lies back on the pillows. The bed creaks. Through the window, he regards the woods. "The *Appassionata*."

"Excuse me?"

"Beethoven's *Appassionata*. Miriam told me it was one of your mother's favorite pieces. Someone should play it at her remembrance."

I lie back with him, marveling at Miriam's ability to resurrect a mother I never knew. Side by side, Ian and I stare at the ceiling. "Does it smell like lavender in here?"

Ian closes his eyes and inhales deeply. Then he sneezes. "And dust." From behind his head, he yanks one of the old throw pillows that have lain on the bed since the beginning of time. The pillow is flattened and so barren of stuffing it doesn't warrant the name. Ian sniffs it. "There," he says, tossing the offending object away. "Lavender. The Victorians made everything into a sachet."

I cast my eyes around the room. The Tigger bedding is gone from the crib. Someday, another baby will lie here. It was just about this time of day that I found her. Midmorning. I had been talking on the phone to Angus. For years, I blamed him for keeping me on the line. For years, he blamed me for not noticing the monitor was too quiet. Mother strained for every last gasp of air, so why does a baby simply stop?

Where do they come from, your ghosts? Dr. Anke asked.

Are they memories that cling like cooking smells? Or are they our lost children, our lost selves, beating like moths against a window? When I was a child, I thought I knew.

"God," I say, regarding the scented pillow on the floor. "Not even the ghosts were ghosts."

I t is not Beethoven that Beowulf is playing when I come into the living room, but something dense and marshier that fits the heaviness of the house. "What's that?" I say.

"Berg. *Wozzeck*."

The sequence of discordant notes describes exactly how I feel. It seems appropriate that Beowulf has chosen an opera about madness. From time to time, someone goes upstairs to visit Mother's body. At the moment, Derek and Adele are sitting cross-legged on the porch like bookends, their hands resting palms up on their knees. I make out Adele's shorn head next to Derek's shaggy one backlit by the lake. Whatever they are meditating on, I'm sure it has to do with a reinterpreted reality. Maybe we're all looking for our separate universes—mine one of celluloid and videotape; Sedgie's ablaze with klieg lights; Dana's orderly sequence of stitches. Edward disappeared altogether. And now Ian wants to make a film.

I find Dana in the kitchen making peanut-butter sandwiches. The counter is patina'd with years of cooking and cursory cleanups. Dana sets out a plate depicting one of the buildings of Princeton University. The edge, I notice, is chipped.

"I didn't know you could cook," I say.

She looks askance, but I smile to show I'm kidding. Ever since she made her confession the other morning, I have seen her through kinder eyes.

"It must be exhausting," I say, dipping my fingers into the peanut-butter jar, "to have to be so good."

"What are you talking about?"

I lick my forefinger. "Mom and Dad had such high expectations for you."

Dana cuts the sandwiches in half, sets them on the blue plate. "Like they didn't for you?"

"It wasn't the same."

Dana raises an eyebrow. She takes a paper napkin from the little holder on the counter, folds it into a triangle, tucks it under the sandwich. "I'm not doing a very good job," she says.

"You *are*," I say, meaning it. "You're doing a wonderful job. Jessica's fine." I pause, waiting to see if this small dart of praise can pierce my sister's stoicism. When she doesn't budge, I press on. "I wish we'd had *half* the support that she does."

Dana gives a faint, defeated smile. "And now they're all gone."

"The last of the grown-ups," I say.

"I don't suppose the cousins will be able to afford to keep the house. Adele's broke, and Sedgie's run out of money. His last divorce . . ."

Yet Ian—who's not a part of this family (but who seems to think he is)—sees gold in our stories.

"Dana," I say, "would you ever go see a movie about a family like ours? You know, a family on the cusp of . . . something." It occurs to me that we are on the brink, like the dinosaurs with their pea brains that had no idea of what was about to transpire when the meteor hit.

Dana chews vaguely at the crusts of her sandwich. "You mean a big family of cousins who are forced to live together for a few weeks each summer in a once-grand house?"

Weather reversals, apocalyptic geological upheaval, the demise of life as we know it. "Something like that."

Dana picks at the bread. I find myself waiting too eagerly for her verdict. "Maybe," she says finally. "But to make it interesting, you'd have to have a murder."

D ana thinks we have to have a murder," I tell Ian as we walk along the sand. I have dragged him down to the beach to get out of a house where everyone seems at sea.

"Hmm. Are there any that you know of?"

Scanning my family's history for trauma and scandal, I come up with Grannie Addie's breakdown, Uncle Jack's alleged wartime cowardice, and Edward's psychosis. Other than that, not much. Derek's tower shimmers in the sun. "An abortion?" I say hopefully.

Beneath the straw hat he stole from Sedgie, Ian is slathered in sunscreen. "*Who* had an abortion?"

"Dana. When she was nineteen."

"Ah," says Ian. "That explains it," as if it all makes perfect sense.

I marvel at his ability to intuit things I miss entirely. At the same time, I'm annoyed. "Explains what?"

But Ian is regarding Derek's construction of wood and rock with an expression similar to the one he assumed when he first saw the lawn jockey. He crouches down like a golfer gauging a putt. Then he rises, stands back, and shakes his head. "How people betray their secret histories," he says. "Dana is very, very careful."

"Oh, she's always been like that."

"I'll bet she hasn't," says Ian. "People often project the opposite of what they feel."

"Thank you, Dr. Anke."

"Organization compensating for chaos. Virtue for shame." He stares at Derek's mound. "God, what *is* this?"

I think of those pictures of our parents, those fading testimonials to happiness, smiles forever fixed, arms thrown around one another as if they can't believe their good fortune, and I realize that Dana and Philip provide a center—something immutable in an ephemeral world. Exhaling imaginary smoke, I study the lake. It looks cooler today, potentially autumnal. "Did you know," I say, "that when you have a stroke, you actually lose awareness of part of your body? Think about it. How exquisitely perfect for my mother, who did exactly that. For forty years, she kept denying, denying, cutting off part of herself with booze and cigarettes and naps until—ta-da!—she finally lost awareness altogether." I pause to punctuate what I consider to be a brilliant analogy concerning the moribund facets of my mother's self. "And what did my father amputate in the service of marital longevity?"

"Ever the philosopher, Maddie," says a voice from behind. Sedgie, in his Hawaiian shirt and a towel around his hips, works his way down the dune and lands on the sand beside us. Beowulf tags along wearing cutoffs and a T-shirt that says THE END IS NEAR. GET SERIOUS. Sedgie takes a long look at Ian, starting at his toes, finishing at his head. "That's my hat."

"Is it? It was just lying there."

"Hmm," says Sedgie, his eye still on Ian.

Beo tells us they are going to bond over a "lithesome doobie." Perhaps we'd like to join them?

"Alas," says Ian, fanning himself with Sedgie's hat. "We're abstainers."

"You're getting high?" I say.

"Until the bartender comes," says Sedgie. "We *are* having a bartender?"

The first thing Dana did after Philip called the undertaker was to call hospice. Then she called the yacht club.

"We're getting high and looking for heart-shaped stones to put in Eve-lyn's grave," Beowulf says. "It's a tradition."

"Whose tradition?"

Beowulf thinks about this. "Well, it *should* be."

Practicing serenity, I fight not to say, *Why don't you two grow up?*

"By the way," says Sedgie, "the phone's been ringing off the hook. Your sister's looking frantic."

I look at my watch. It's already 2 P.M. The news must be spreading. And I feel the inexorable pressure of having to work out details. When my father died, Mother took to her bed, relinquishing the details to Aunt Pat. Not yet sober, I wasn't even in Sand Isle when they threw his ashes off the stern of the *Green Dragon*. Years ago, we used to time Coke bottles we'd chucked off the stern, counting the seconds until they sank beneath the waves, someday to wash up on the shore as smoothly sanded shards of emerald or aquamarine.

"I'm heading up," I say, turning to Ian. "You coming?"

Ian shakes his head. He's going to help Sedgie and Beowulf search for rocks. As they head down the beach, Ian trails them, holding up his hands as if he's framing "the middle-aged guy and the kid getting stoned" scene— the one that we'll put toward the end of the film when the family starts to unravel.

Mother has been dead for less than eight hours, and the flowers have started to arrive. In the kitchen, I see a Portmerion casse-role and a plate of cookies wrapped in plastic. Upstairs, I find Miriam in Mother's room. Seeing me, she slams shut the book she's holding and shoves it back on the shelf.

"Where's Dana?" I ask.

"Resting. She's rattled."

I look at Mother who isn't Mother. When life leaves the body, the dif-ference becomes eminently clear. And when someone is as emaciated and frail as Mother, it's hard to recognize the woman who used to decoupage with the aunts, tipping her cigarettes with kisses of pink. Now her teeth and cheekbones are exaggerated like the bold lines of a caricature. Miriam has already picked up all of her pills and removed them. The bedside table looks unnaturally empty. Mother used to cover its surface with photographs and ashtrays and Kleenex boxes and glasses of water or vodka. She always kept See's candies in the drawer.

I had moved to New York before my father died. It was September. Like most of us, Dad wanted summer to go on forever—but he dutifully returned to Pasadena. A portrait of my grandfather hung over his desk alongside a nautical chart of northern Michigan and a barometer. His secretary, who at first thought he was taking a nap, dropped the glass of water he'd sent for, splattering his desktop. She was mortified, she told me later. His desk was always so neat.

At the time, I hadn't seen him for more than a year. It had been such an awkward departure from Sand Isle the summer after Sadie died that I couldn't face him. *I found your detritus in the boat room*, he told me, referring to the bottles I had hidden. As demoralized as I had felt then, I wonder why I even bothered.

Miriam's voice is brisk. "You're going to have to tell that undertaker what to do. She wanted to be cremated."

Cremation is a family tradition. There is something unseemly about lying intact and allowing nature to take its course. Still, they wouldn't allow me to go with Sadie to the crematorium. I was at home, sedated, secured to my bed by well-meaning relatives who thought they knew best.

"Can I be alone with her?"

"Of course," says Miriam. She looks around the room and, with a sweep of her arm, indicates the vases that have been arriving from the florist since this morning. "All these flowers. This last year I've been with her, I'd never know she had so many friends."

After Miriam leaves, I sit by the bed. Although I've talked to the dead many times in my dreams and my imaginings, it is another thing to speak to a body. *Where are you, Mother? If you're with Sadie, will you do a better job watching over her than you did watching over me?*

My mother's corpse doesn't answer. If her spirit is in this house, I can't find it yet. Her hair is combed, but her lips are pale. Except for her wedding ring, she wears no jewelry. The early-afternoon sun spikes on the lake and, for a moment, I can imagine she is napping. Aside from the hospital bed, all of the trappings of sickness are gone. The lilies have the strongest smell. They remind me of my wedding. Soon, the undertaker will be coming. I take my mother's hand, remove her ring, and pocket it.

C arnations," says Dana, standing over the pantry sink, plucking the carnations out of a vase of roses and baby's breath. "Mom would have croaked."

She starts to laugh, and I join her, both of us quaking with the absurd-ity of attributing Mother's demise to a tasteless flower arrangement.

Suddenly Dana stops. "The undertaker will be here any minute. Jessica's gone. I have no idea where anyone is." A few indigenous-sounding notes drift in through the window from no specific location. "And that damn recorder. Where's Philip?"

I tell her that we have plenty of time, and that Mother will stay dead.

"But they'll take her out of the house. Doesn't everyone want to be here?"

I see her point. There should be something more ritualistic about re-moving a body. What would the Irish do? The Sufi mystics? Can't we ulu-late and rend our hair?

"*I'm* here," I say.

The doorbell rings, and we jump. No one ever rings the doorbell; they just walk in.

"Where's Miriam?" Dana says.

If Aunt Pat were alive, she would immediately take charge and gather the forces, but the best I can summon is a paltry whistle that no one will hear from the porch. I go to the door. It is not the undertaker but the hospice ladies standing like Mormons, earnestly paired.

"We're so sorry for your loss," says the older one.

I wait for the platitude I know is coming. Death is a natural part of living. They see it all the time. Their job isn't to deny death, but to steward it. "Come in," I say.

Ten minutes later, we are drinking tea at the kitchen table. The two ladies knowingly nod when we tell them how the last breath was such an anticlimax; how Mother seemed so small; how final it was to witness the cessation of life and know she's not coming back. *Yes, yes,* the hospice ladies say. *That's how it is.*

"Ghosts," I say.

The white-haired one looks at me. "Pardon?"

"In this house."

"*I've* never seen them," says Dana.

"The world is a mysterious place," says the younger hospice lady with the dyed red hair. She is wearing loads of turquoise. The look in her eye strikes me as ghoulish. Who would go into this kind of work? Who would pretend to translate death? They are necrophiliacs, the two of them, getting off on our loss. I decide to give them nothing.

"Maddie lost a child," Dana tells them.

Traitor, I think. But if it weren't for the tattooed initials on the dining-room wall, I might wonder if I imagined the whole thing.

"Ah," says the older one.

"It's a huge loss," says the one covered in turquoise.

How does your loss feel? Dr. Anke asked. *Does it remind you of something else?*

"How old?" the older asks.

"Four months," says Dana.

"Meningitis? Flu?"

They remind me of Aunt Pat and Aunt Eugenia, efficient know-it-alls miming concern. *Do you feel threatened by authority?* Dr. Anke once asked.

"The death of a child . . ." says the turquoise one, her voice trailing off.

"So difficult to get closure," says the other.

I almost spit out my tea at the word. Where's the closure when you look at other people's children and feel both repelled and fascinated? What kind of closure is it when each year hinges on a birthday in May, the years marked off by what grade she would be in, what she would look like, if she would be athletic, pretty, smart? Will I finally have closure when I go through a day without having to scrub the idea of her from my mind like a stain?

"Never completely," says the turquoise one.

I look at her sharply. The ladies sip. Again, the doorbell rings. This time, it is the undertaker. He is surprisingly tan. For a moment, he and I stand blinking at each other. His suit is linen, like Jamie's. "You rang?" I say.

They all come eventually. Glistening from sweat, reeking of pot, WD-40, suntan oil, and incense, they make it back to the house. Mother's corpse is laid out benignly on top of the sheets, dressed in peach chiffon.

"She wore that dress to my wedding," I say.

"It's a beautiful dress," says Miriam.

"Peach?" says Ian, looking at me.

I shrug. "It was the eighties." I examine the fabric for stains. She walked into the lake in that dress, and now it will be reduced to ash.

"Are you going with her?" Ian asks. Ian is no stranger to protocol, having made countless trips to various mortuaries over the past decade and a half. He knows how the body disappears from view in the crematorium. He's seen the miracle of makeup in disguising Kaposi's sarcoma on sunken cheeks.

When I die, just push me into the East River, he once said to me. *Anything but send me back to Minnesota.*

"Just to the pier," I say, as if the island is enchanted and to leave its gates would condemn me to the Hades of reality.

The tan undertaker and his beefy assistant cover Mother with a sheet and lift her onto a stretcher. Light as air, they carry her down the stairs, knocking some of the photographs askew. My grandfather's stern face, now crookedly hung, stares down on us. When they took Sadie, they wouldn't let me watch. I had bruises on my arms, and Aunt Pat had pulled my face into her chest to muffle the sound. They move through the dining room, the living room, out the front door, and start down the labyrinth of steps that twist to the sidewalk below.

The carriage is waiting. By design, there are no other passengers. The two men work efficiently. They set the stretcher across the seat, one of them sitting with her to brace it. Dana and Adele climb aboard, but the rest of us walk behind. Occasionally, we have to jog a little to keep up. When we were kids, we'd run after the carriage at night, darting in and out like Indians, shushing one another, trying not to giggle at what seemed a radical act of delinquency as we climbed aboard the luggage rack. *Woo, woo, woo!*

"Whoa," says Sedgie, dodging a fresh pile of horse manure.

All afternoon, I've had the urge to call someone, but it's Saturday. Dr. Anke won't be in her office, Ian and Dana are here, and anyone I know in New York would say, *I didn't know you were close to your mother.*

As we pass the tennis courts, people wave. Bicyclists pull over. We're an odd little procession, heading to the channel. Too soon, we reach the pier. The mortuary has its own boat—a sleek Boston Whaler that they probably use for fishing when not needed for official business. Mac has stopped the ferry and is standing by the Whaler. I think he might salute. Sedgie once told me that the Odawa used to bring their dead to Sand Isle to bury them, but no bones have been found, and I'm sure he said it just to scare me. In India, the Hindus take the corpses down to the river and light them on fire. This is not so different, I think as they load Mother's body onto the boat.

I have come to the beach to be alone. It is nearly evening, and the house feels claustrophobic in its silence. We walk past one another, unsure what to say. We knew she was dying, but we are stunned nonetheless. No one has any appetite.

The sand is cool beneath my legs. I throw a handful of rocks into the lake. Derek showed me how to skip stones when I was almost fifteen. *It's all in the wrist,* he said, putting his arm around my waist, pulling me close from behind. His hand left a mark on my belly, and his chin was rough as he showed me the stroke. Afterward, my neck had a red spot matched by two flushed dots on my cheeks.

The rocks make a gratifying plop when they hit the water. They will sink and nestle among other rocks, become covered with algae before they are churned up again when the frozen lake melts and rages upon the shore. *Plop. Plop.* The waves break and pull back. There are no tides on Lake Michigan, huge as it is. You don't have to factor in shifts in the current when you set your course. *Watch the wind,* my father told me. *Check your sails.*

Goddamn it, Maddie, Jamie said. *You're fucking crazy.*

No amount of stones. Not enough years. I throw back my head and let out a wail that pitches to a howl and dies in a croak—a sound that no one in our family has ever dared to make.

TWENTY-THREE

F an-friggin'-tastic," says Ian, reviewing footage in the viewfinder of his video camera. I feign disinterest.

Sedgie, however, is enthralled. He is draped across the back of the couch, looming vulturelike over my film partner and friend. The two of them could be brothers, both in need of sun. Sedgie's hair falls forward, nearly touching Ian's head. Backlit by the window, there is a haloed beauty to the tableau.

"That's my bad side," says Sedgie. "I look better from the right."

"You look better when you're sober," says Ian, unable to resist didacticism.

"*Nothing* looks better when I'm sober."

Ian and I exchange a glance like a secret handshake. I'd given up "twelve-stepping" my family years ago. In 1988, I moved back to New York with nothing but my clothes, my drinking problem, and the box of Sadie's ashes.

You had the most talent in the class, Ian told me after he heard about Sadie's death and my split from Angus. *The train film was exquisite.*

The conventional wisdom in recovery is that alcoholism is the disease that tells you that you don't have one, but I knew what I had. It didn't look exactly like my mother's gin-and-tonic-with-a-lemon-twist form of alcoholism, or the depraved Mad Dog–guzzling of the bench dwellers along the Santa Monica beach. Instead, my alcoholism looked like a desperate move to New York to take a film job with an old acquaintance, dragging out of bed each morning in my monk's cell of a midtown apartment, retching and wretched, sleep-deprived and overwhelmed by a crushing depression that could only be remedied by several glasses of wine at the neighborhood bar, then another bottle to keep me company once I got home.

And I vomited.

Nonalcoholics don't understand why you would persevere when your stomach rebels, but to an alcoholic, it makes perfect sense. At first, you're trying to keep the bad feelings at bay—wipe them out altogether by pressing the restart button and moving to New York. Only it doesn't work. You then resort to your old standby of drinking yourself into a different reality, but all you get is sick to your stomach. Still, you persist. The end justifies the means, and the end (dissociation from reality) is eminently worth it. Imagine the pull generated by a black hole—the gravity of a billion imploded suns. Now try turning around.

This was the kind of alcoholism that caused Ian, after half a year of working together, to say, *Maddie, dear, there are a thousand reasons for the way you've been acting, and none of them is good.* He took me to the outdoor flower market in Battery Park. He held freesia to my nose. *Smell them.* Picking up tuberoses, he said, *And these. And these,* he said, holding a fistful of Rubrum lilies. They dusted my face with saffron; my face became rust-streaked with tears. *Maddie,* Ian said, *Maddie. You've got to live.*

Ian was an expert on recovery, having OD'd on vodka and speedballs when he was twenty-five. His veins were near collapsing; he was seeing locusts (like any good Bible-banger, he told me); and the numbers on his liver had gone through the roof. By the time he arrived at NYU, he'd been in Narcotics Anonymous for over three years and was starting to convert to Judaism. That he tested negative for HIV after all this led to his begrudging belief in Betty.

Another conventional wisdom in AA is that you bottom out only when you're ready. My last binge consisted of me not leaving the apartment for days, too semiconscious to answer the phone, or—when I did—too incoherent to talk. I went through three bottles of wine, a bottle of Harveys Bristol Cream, and a six-pack of Heineken. Toward the end, if there had been vanilla extract or mouthwash in my cupboards, I would have consumed those, too.

In the fall of 1989, when my father died, I had flown back to California to stay with Dana for his service. I was thin again, and dressed in the perpetual mourning that constitutes the New York wardrobe. It felt like everyone was watching me—a not-altogether-paranoid thought given that my sister smelled my breath, and my mother said, *You're not going to fall apart, are you?*

Ten months later, I had consumed every drop of alcohol in my apartment and was unable to call the market to deliver more. After twenty messages from Ian, several from Dana and my mother, Aunt Pat's voice appeared on the answering machine.

This is not acceptable.

It was summer 1990. The family was going to toss my father's ashes off the *Green Dragon*. I was cowering in a corner when Ian found me and called the ambulance that took me to detox, where they tied me to a bed. It took an eye-shadow-wearing, quasi-Jewish Lutheran junkie to tell me what I already knew. If you asked me how a young woman such as myself—from a good family—got to this place, I would respond: *How could my mother throw up in a revolving door at the Ritz?*

When I was sober for a year, I finally filed the divorce papers. *Half measures avail you nothing*, the AA Big Book tells us, but when I repeated this to my mother over the phone, there was a long, significant pause. I heard her puff on a cigarette as she considered what I had said. Then she suggested Valium.

This AA is ruining your life, she said, adding that the divorce would have killed my father. But by then he was already dead.

The wonderful thing about AA is that you can speak in shorthand about nightmarish experiences, and everybody in the room knows exactly what you mean. You can talk about your desperation, your embarrassment, your awful choices resulting in awful consequences, and everyone laughs.

I wasn't brought up to consider dry heaves and car wrecks the stuff of polite conversation. I wasn't brought up to be an inebriate or marry the first person who proposed. I was brought up to hold my head high and have dignity and carry the noblesse oblige of my family like a torch into the next generation.

When I relayed this in earnest to Ian, he practically convulsed with laughter. *Unlike the rest of us slobs. Is that what you mean?*

It's different, I said after Ian recovered (it took several minutes). I'm *different*.

Oh, Maddie, Ian replied.

Now Ian holds up the camera and focuses on me. I stare him down with steely resolve, but it is only a matter of seconds before I can't help myself and start to mug. The tongue comes out; the eyes loll. I stand up and do my ghoulish zombie dance around the room.

"Maddie Addison," narrates Ian, "brain-dead descendant of drugmakers. Little did they know the pharmaceutical influences that would permeate the family ethos for generations to come."

"Aarrgh-guh-guh," I say.

Dana comes into the room and eyes us suspiciously. Our laughter seems untoward in the postmortem atmosphere. But we have always dealt with loss through humor. Even our father used to joke how they misplaced Bada's ashes after she was cremated and shipped back to Cincinnati.

"The mortuary called," says Dana.

"That mortician looks like George Hamilton," I say, resuming my place among the living. "What kind of undertaker gets that much sun?"

"We need to pick out a receptacle."

Receptacle is a cold word. I prefer *vessel* or *container*—the simple metal box that holds my daughter. I remember my father handing it to me.

What did your parents do when Sadie died? Dr. Anke asked early on in our sessions.

My mother drank and played solitaire. My father polished brass on the Green Dragon.

And you? Where did you go with your grief?

The answer I gave to Dr. Anke was the same as Edward's when I last saw him in Washington Square.

Beneath the surface, I said.

For seven years, I saw my family sporadically—mostly when I had to go to L.A. for work. Each time, I was confronted by feelings of such unbearable guilt that I would flee back to New York and my friends, my meetings, my therapist. To Dr. Anke, I described my sister's sighs and my mother's smoke-filled silence.

So let me get this straight. You felt guilty about your father's death and your mother's agoraphobia? You don't see these circumstances as being, at the very least, out of your control?

"Grant Us the Serenity" and all that?

Maddie, isn't it possible you were profoundly angry and disappointed in your family for not understanding you? And that, rather than express these feelings directly, you turned them on yourself in the form of guilt?

I must have read the book spines in Dr. Anke's office a thousand times. Freud, Jung, Miller, Sacks. I would come to know all about repression, isolation, displacement, and projection. Dissociation, depersonalization disorder—now part of my lexicon.

I knew something was wrong before I went into that room. Perhaps if I'd gotten there sooner . . .

Dr. Anke gave me such a long, sad look that, for a moment, I felt I should comfort her. *You've been sober, what, five years now . . . ?*

Six.

What are the odds of that? I'd put them at one in fifty.

Anyone can stop drinking.

No, said Dr. Anke with a vehemence that startled me. *Not anyone.*

The mortuary is veneered in mahogany, brand spanking new five years ago, a Sears Roebuck Oriental carpet, a gaslit fire, a stage set for the dead. Families are sequestered from other families so that grief remains private. It is like being in a fancy men's club to which most people would never belong. The hallway smells of oil and pine. I keep sniffing for formaldehyde or something worse. Babies who die of SIDS are taken not here, but to the coroner. There has to be a reason for sudden death.

Death due to cessation of breathing, the coroner's report had said.

Dana and I stand in the lobby, unsure where to go. There are prints on the walls of hunting scenes and sailboats, barns in a field, Mary Cassatt's oft-reproduced *Mother and Child.* The prints promise places that are happier than here. Tranquil, mindless fields. Cool rivers. The warm embrace of a mother.

"Mother wanted to be a seagull when she returned," says Dana.

"A seagull? She hated water."

"That's what she told me."

The gulls were cawing on the beach yesterday when she died. I clear my throat. "Have we run this by Adele?" I make my fist into a microphone. "Earth to Adele. Incoming incarnation . . ."

Dana jabs me in the ribs. George Hamilton, the undertaker, has entered the room. We assume correctly sober expressions. "Ladies," he says. "Would you follow me?"

Dana and I glance quickly at each other, and then follow him, obedient as dogs as he leads us into their showroom that is a mishmash of Victorian wallpapers and cut velvet upholstery and damask curtains. Heavy mahogany case-goods—the ultrashiny kind—show off a variety of containers, from the simple to the sublime, the most elaborate being one of inlaid marquetry like the kind found in stores selling gilt statues of Mercury and elaborate chandeliers. Dana and I peruse the choices politely. There is a plasticine-marble number with a bas-relief of angels, selling for nine hundred dollars. Another receptacle mimics burled walnut for less, but has the feel of Formica.

"What are we doing here?" whispers Dana.

I shake my head. Sadie was returned to me in an unadorned metal box cloaked in a velvet sack like a bottle of Chivas Regal. For the last ten years, she has sat on my bookshelf, holding up my twenty-volume set of Shakespeare.

"Excuse me," I say to George Hamilton. "My sister and I need to talk. Outside."

He nods knowingly, appreciative of the virtue of conferring over diffi-cult and painful decisions. He offers us a private room, but I tell him the parking lot will do. When we get outside, we breathe in the fresh air and sun like divers coming up from the depths.

"Where are we going?" says Dana.

"Trust me," I say.

B y the time we return to the mortuary, it is late afternoon, and the undertaker comes into the hallway with a look of impatience. He is reknotting his tie, and it occurs to me that he was probably hoping to go fishing and get his daily dose of rays. When he sees the decoupaged letter box we've brought from the Aerie, he looks even more distressed. At first, I assume it's because he's lost a sale, but his discomfort transcends mere commerce or the desire to get out on the lake.

"It's too small," I say, reading his thoughts.

He nods.

"You can't fit all of her in here?"

Again, he nods. Dana and I exchange glances.

"We-ll," I say, "can you put as much of her in as possible and dispose of the rest?"

Beneath his tan, George Hamilton blanches.

T he memorial service is set for the following day. Tonight we're having take-out pizza that arrived half-cold, having crossed the channel by ferry. Since none of us has attended church in Harbor Town for

years, we have decided to forgo the services of a minister. The format for
Mom's memorial, we have decided, shall be that of a luncheon "To Celebrate the Memory of Evelyn Addison" instead of a cocktail party—those
endless soirees that constituted our parents' life.

We're going to bury Mother's ashes in the cemetery on the bluff. The
rest of her remains—the ones the undertaker couldn't fit into the letter
box—Dana and I will keep. "Because you missed tossing Dad," Dana says,
picking some cheese from the corner of her mouth.

Since hitting upon his idea of using my family as his subject, Ian has
barely put down his camera. "Inheritance," Ian says to my assembled relatives, holding up the video camera to tape their reactions, "is more than
money and genes. It is a vocabulary of shared concepts passed from one
generation to the next. Like a liturgy."

"Bullshit," says Sedgie. "I had nothing in common with my father."

My memory of Uncle Jack is of a jokester—the loudest and crassest of
the uncles, seldom serious, flaunting the virtues of his wife's family the way
a rebellious teenager mocks his parents. I refrain from pointing out the sim-
ilarities to Sedgie.

"Weren't Uncle Jack and Uncle Dickie, like, Republicans?" says Beowulf, picking off the pepperoni. "I mean, they had that company."

"That *company*," says Philip, "has been very good to this family."

Ian has focused in tightly on Sedgie, who has a dab of grease on his lips.
I fiddle with my fork. The camera drifts from face to face.

"At least Uncle Halsey was a war hero," says Sedgie, referring to Derek
and Edward's father. "He didn't weasel out like *my* father."

We all knew the story about Sedgie's father's bum back that kept him
home pushing papers. Aunt Pat defended his contribution as an essential
administrator, but my mother told us Uncle Jack never got over women
handing him the white flower of cowardice, assuming him to be someone
who had "bought" an exemption.

"What do *you* think, Derek?" says Ian, focusing on him.

"I think," says Derek, his voice assuming moral authority as he stares directly into Ian's lens, "that evolution is arbitrary, not purposeful. We don't consciously select for our environment. Our environment selects for us."

We chew our pizza contemplatively.

"Buddha says that corporeal life is a mirage," says Adele. "As opposed to the spirit, which is constant."

"Expand," says Ian, caressing Adele's exquisite features with his camera. "In your own words."

In the final edit, Ian may feature Adele's fiddling with her spoon or the slightly blank look on her face. The down on her head is filling in, and I notice it's flecked with gray. "Aunt Ev, for instance," she says finally. "Where is she now?" She looks from me to Dana. "Is her spirit still flowing within us?"

"We're nothing like our parents," says Sedgie.

"I don't even know who my parents *are*," says Jessica. Ian cuts quickly to her.

Philip clears his throat and opens his mouth to say something, at which point Dana jumps in and, much like my mother, changes the subject. "We need a new dishwasher," she says.

"We don't need a dishwasher," says Adele, the pizza uneaten upon her plate. "Louisa did for years without a dishwasher."

"Louisa, my darling, *was* the dishwasher," says Sedgie.

"What about *paper* plates?" I say.

"*Miriam* needs a job," says Sedgie.

We look around. Ever since they took Mother's body, Miriam has been almost invisible. It occurs to me that this is Miriam's loss as well. How many people has she ushered through the last stage of life, making it possible for them to transition with a minimum of discomfort?

"That is so racist," says Jessica.

"Work is work," says Sedgie.

"The most successful systems," Derek says, nodding, "find a way to adapt."

I wonder if Derek should be shot from below to give him authority? Or from above to diminish his stature?

"Yeah?" says Sedgie. "How much money do *you* have?"

Derek opens his mouth to respond, but before he can, the racket of a vibrating knife stops us all short. Wedged into the table seam, the knife crescendos deliriously while Beowulf—the apparent mastermind of this prank—shrieks with laughter.

O h, God help us," says Sedgie, holding up an album with Neil Diamond on the cover. "Whose is this?"

Dana holds up her hand and confesses to having gone through a major Neil Diamond phase. Tossing it aside, Sedgie seizes on another album, whisks out the disc, sets it on the turntable. With a skip of the needle, the voice of Steve Winwood fills the air. "Get down!" says Sedgie, who jumps up and sweeps me into a clumsy waltz, the two of us, in giddy three-quarter time, twirling around the room to "Heaven Is in Your Mind."

At first, we're the only ones dancing, then Adele and Jessica grab each other's arms in a sort of hip-hop minuet. Sedgie throws me back as the instrumental takes over. In slow motion, I fall into the arms of Derek, who catches me, our bodies colliding like galaxies. His arms are strong and familiar. I freeze, but he turns me and lifts my arms into a dance position the way he used to pose me. The guitar and percussion of "Dear Mr. Fantasy" starts.

My feet don't move.

Dear Mr. Fantasy, play us a tune . . .

Derek sways me. I stare into his eyes. It's the sort of song that sent me reeling as a teenager, full of base and plaintive lyrics and a rock-me-baby tempo. Derek's hips brush against mine; our bellies touch.

I break away.

Ian has filmed all of this. For a moment, he lifts his head from the viewfinder and follows me with his naked eye. I pretend to study another album cover while Derek stands alone in the middle of the room. Angus wasn't much taller than Derek. At our wedding, he twirled me around. Jamie and I danced together in my dorm room, our bodies locked, my head crooked in his neck the way Sadie's was crooked in my mother's. But this is the first time I've danced with Derek.

What does Ian mean by that look? Is he adding up the pieces of the story I tell at AA meetings?

My name's Maddie. I'm an alcoholic . . .

The resounding response of, *Hi, Maddie!*

And then I would tell them. About the train times. About hiding in the wood room, the comfort I found in darkness.

Our father was stern. My mother cut her nails.

I'd tell them about Angus. I'd tell them about Sadie. And sometimes I alluded (but only vaguely) to this thing I had for my cousin.

Ian keeps the camera running as I stride toward the stairs.

Adele's question stays with me. Where *is* my mother? Is this world one of our imagining where we all transcend existence? Now I search for meaning in the empty room of my mother. It is where my great-grandparents slept, even after the death of their daughter when Grannie Addie wrote to her friend that the view from the room was wasted. After she died, Bada and Banta slept here until they, too, were gone (their essence, according to Adele, immutable, but assuming other forms). At one time or another, the Halseys, Aunt Pat, and finally, my parents—all denizens of this room.

If it was up to me, I would tear down the window coverings, move the bed (the old mahogany one, not the hospital rental) close to the window, where I could see the lake. I would fill the room with flowers cut from my great-grandmother's garden. Those that currently adorn the room are store-bought, tight-knit arrangements of Johnny-jump-ups and bachelor's buttons. Like demons, I will cast them out in favor of the Victorian beauties of my ancestors.

Already, the bureau is filmy with dust, the initialed ivory brush set of my great-grandmother cracked. Opening the little desk, I rifle through its contents. The tiny bottle of vodka stares back at me. My mother, the pragmatist, must have stuck it into her purse during an airplane flight. Derek's touch has brought back memories of longings and awakenings, and I crave that vodka, its shill's siren song of hope. Making a silent plea to Betty, I slam the desk shut.

Above the desk is a bookcase filled with an assortment of old and venerable titles along with a smattering of John Grisham and Danielle Steel. I trace my fingers across the spines of the books. Between *Little Women* and *The Late George Apley*, I find a small, leather-bound book that, when I open it, is filled with my great-grandmother's arabesque. I look at the date of the first entry. July 1890. Downstairs, someone has put on Frank Sinatra singing Cole Porter, but there are shouts of protests, and Frank is replaced by Cat Stevens's *Tea for the Tillerman*. I pocket the book.

I scan the titles, remember Miriam replacing one on the shelf. *For Whom the Bell Tolls. I Heard the Owl Call My Name. The Untenable Teen.* I pull down this last one, page through it, and find a dog-eared chapter on "Sex and Pregnancy." Did my mother look to these pages for hope and solutions when she discovered her elder daughter was with child? I can see her smoking and poring over the fine print. It must have been a hell of a summer. Adele and her Italian, me and my Harold Robbins, Dana in hysterics because she was in trouble, and it was going to kill our father. Did they plot together, Dana and my mother? Did they call Mr. Marks and ask him for a doctor's name? I have a vague memory of my sister coming home that fall, but it is convoluted with another, earlier memory of her saying, *I don't need the Pill.*

I open *For Whom the Bell Tolls* and out falls a flower. Not even a flower—
the mere silhouette of one. I hold in my hand, like a dead butterfly, one of
Miriam's pressed, desiccated memories. I open more books, and more flowers fall out. Book after book, until the floor around my feet is strewn with
the paper-thin shards of our lost summer days.

TWENTY-FOUR

Once again, I wallow in the delicious sleep of childhood. Usually, I wake an hour before dawn, but last night I stayed up until after midnight, reading the purloined copy of Grannie Addie's diary, especially the entries from that unhappy summer.

> AUGUST 4TH, 1890—Dr. Stillman insists that Halsey be sent away now that Geoffrey is showing symptoms. We have sent him with Winnifred and the Baileys to stay with a Dutch family named Van Dam on a farm outside of Grand Rapids. It would be a sweet mercy if I were to grow sick and die myself. It distresses Edward when I do not speak.

> AUGUST 6TH—It seems the summer has been abbreviated. Everyone has packed up their trunks and fled Sand Isle, driven off by the plagued Addisons! I do not blame them. Had I seen the infection coming, I would have bundled our family away.

AUGUST 10TH—The doctor has prescribed something to help me sleep. I did not tell him I hear voices. At first, I thought it was the girls below the stairs, but it was so late, and everyone was asleep. The medicine gives me a slight headache, but I float through the next day, which is fine.

AUGUST 13TH—I have a received a letter from the Van Dams with a scrawled note from Halsey asking his mummy if he can come home. He misses his boats and his chipmunk.

We are considering boarding up the house soon. I don't suppose I shall return.

AUGUST 16TH—Bea has introduced me to an Indian woman who has visions. I felt so foolish riding in the carriage to the little cabin up the shore, but it was the most precious place, although it had a dreadful smell. Under other circumstances, it may have been a great adventure— the two pale-faces and the Ottawa lady huddled around a stump! But we'd heard of the Indian problems out west, so I didn't tell Edward, as it would have made him nervous.

The Indian woman's name is Lucille with an unpronounce-able surname—four or five syllables. Her children run wild, and when I asked her if she'd lost any, she said six!

"This is why I can talk to the dead," she said. I could barely understand her. Poor woman, her husband drinks when he's out of work. There is need for plenty of lumber to be cut these days, so she says it's not too bad. I told her my husband drinks as well. I've never told anyone.

I turn the page, skip entries that describe housekeeping problems and the weather, pause at her entry of August 20, in which my great-grandmother describes the beauty of going back up the shore that, in happier days, she might have appreciated.

> We passed a cunning church that is separated from the lake by a section of woods. The Franciscans built it to "edicate" the Indians. I had never set foot into a Catholic church, but this one was as simple and pure as our beloved First Presbyterian. Except for a garish statue of the Virgin in the altar, I would have felt at home.

I know that church. It still stands today. The Indian woman Lucille lived close by in a square-logged cabin that smelled of smoke and wet wool not far from where Dana and I dropped off our hitchhiker in 1974.

> She has the most serious face, this Lucille. She told me that Elizabeth is hovering over my left shoulder. She said it as matter-of-factly as she would spot a robin. I would have laughed and thought, Superstitious Catholics! Except that her description of my Elizabeth was true. And she reassured me that Geoffrey will be fine, but sees no children in his future.

> AUGUST 23RD—Edward has called Dr. Stillman to see me, and Bea confessed to him about Lucille. I defended my visits, saying they give me comfort. But Edward will not hear of it, and has accused Bea of being a bad influence. "A bad influence!" I said to him. "Your breath smells of whiskey!"

> AUGUST 28TH—An Indian came to the kitchen door today and asked to see me. Winnifred tried to shoo him off,

but when I heard the ruckus, I got up from my bed and
went downstairs.

Lucille had sent him with this message—that our daughter is safe and wants to stay in the house.

The voices seem to have diminished lately. They're like
cobwebs that tangle in my hair.

AUGUST 29TH—Edward was so pleased when I told him
I no longer wanted to sell the Aerie.

According to the diary, early in the summer of 1890, the Miners from
Louisville stayed in the Lantern Room, where I am sleeping now. The Miners
raised horses and dogs, and gave my great-grandparents a gift of a Jack Russell
doorstop that became eponymous for the room down the hall. They stayed
less than a week. The brief, rather chilly entry in my great-grandmother's
diary reads, *Elizabeth is running a fever. We have sent the Miners away.*

Was scarlet fever the gift of the Miners?

A knock on the door, and I rise, squinting fuzzily through the windows
at the glorious, blue-drenched day.

"Morning, sunshine," says Ian, who is mercifully bearing a tray of coffee.

"Bless you," I say as he climbs into bed with me, the two of us side by side,
adjusting our limbs and our steaming mugs, protecting the old stained quilt
from yet another indignity. "Why couldn't you be straight, Ian? You'd make
the perfect husband."

"Straight men never make perfect husbands, Maddie."

"They have their virtues," I say, sipping daintily. I push the diary toward
him. "Look. It says here my great-grandfather drank. And they put
Grannie Addie away."

Ian touches the book like a holy relic. "Put her where?"

"I don't know. I suppose they had a nicer name than 'madhouses' by
then. A sanitarium?"

"She writes about it?"

"Barely. After her baby died, she stopped writing for nearly a decade."

> MAY 10, 1899—After what seems like an endless hiatus,
> I am home again. My hand feels shaky and uncertain, my
> fingers full of rust. I could not write. It was not permit-
> ted. "Too disturbing," they said. But Edward says I seem
> so much better after my rest. He follows me from room
> to room like a puppy, more enthralled than our sons who
> are practically men. Edward, too, looks better. But I know
> his eyes—those beautiful green eyes! He cannot disguise
> the sadness.

"God," says Ian, nuzzling me.

People in New York think Ian and I are lovers because we often walk hand in hand. But we are merely playing at it, both of us afraid of the real thing.

"Can't we smoke in here?" he says.

"No."

"Shoot heroin?"

I shove him away. "And listen to this!"

> I cannot bear to look in the mirror. My hair is almost gray.
> Edward has promised to reopen the Aerie after almost
> ten years. I am overjoyed to be seeing Elizabeth again!

I extract an ancient photo from the diary. It is of my great-grandfather Edward, standing beside a canoe. His pale sepia eyes could have been gray or green. A hundred years later, they have reappeared in Derek.

"You know," says Ian, placing his cup on the bedside table and scrunching up a pillow behind his neck, "Virginia Woolf had relations with her half brother. And look what happened to her."

A vision of myself filling my pockets with stones and walking into the lake. At the far end of the island, there are drop-offs. The descent would be sudden and swift; the light from the surface swallowed by the darkness.

"I didn't have 'relations' with . . . Why are gay men obsessed with Virginia Woolf?"

Ian throws up his arms in exasperation, hitting his coffee cup. A new stain blooms on the bedspread. "You barely share at meetings. You barely share with anyone."

Wounded, I say, "I share with you. I share with Dr. Anke."

"Maddie," says Ian patiently, "don't you think you're the tiniest bit repressed . . ."

I slam the diary shut. Today is the day of my mother's memorial service. Everyone will come together on the lawn of the yacht club. The Hesters will be there. And the Baileys and the Hobsons, and the Drape Man and his wife. My wardrobe may be bereft of Lilly Pulitzers, but for today, at least, the appropriate color is New York black.

D ana is on the phone. "I don't want a European one," she says. "You can never get them repaired." *Dishwasher,* she mouths at me as I come downstairs.

Sedgie is at the dining-room table in his Hawaiian shirt, the *New York Times* crossword in front of him. "I told her we should have a meeting to discuss this. But, no."

"At least someone's taking charge," I say crabbily.

"What got into *you* last night? You disappeared before the fun began."

"I guess I already had my share."

"You *are* dreary, Maddie."

By midmorning, all the cousins are scrubbed and ready for the burial and the luncheon. I find Dana in the kitchen, leaving a note for the appliance installer. "Only in Harbor Town could you call and get same-day service," she says.

"Only at the Sand Isle Yacht Club," I say, "could you put together a luncheon for two hundred in one day."

"Or a wedding."

I watch her write. Her handwriting is flawless and lovely.

"You know, Grannie Addie didn't have a kitchen for thirteen years," I say. "Much less a dishwasher."

"Grannie Addie was nuts," says Dana.

"How much?"

Dana finishes the note, weights it down on the counter with an eggcup. "Seven hundred. And sixty. Installed."

I whistle and pat the old dishwasher. "Soooo, how much money do *you* have . . . more or less?"

We were always told to "never touch the principal"—that core investment on whose yield we rely. If you touch the principal, the well could go dry. It is a cardinal sin. But what *is* the principal, exactly? Our Addison stock that has limped along, but, unlike buggy whips, survived? Or is it an abstract number from which a percentage is drawn to underwrite our varied and profligate lives?

I, for one, have been touching mine for years.

Making a little moue of disgust, Dana finally quotes a number. It is substantially greater than my number. Hers is a number born of frugality and reinvestment, the staid and conservative La Cañada life. Mine is not a negligible number, but it has been eroded by divorce and disaster, not to mention what Adele would describe as "following my karma." Nevertheless, I do the math, estimating the sum total of all the cousins' numbers. Philip, who seems to have the clearest idea of these things, has told us what it will cost to keep the Aerie. *More or less,* he said. *Count on more.*

I bite my lip. I have the sudden, desperate yearning for a family member who can make some real money. A movie star or a rock star would be nice. "Dana," I say, "you're going to have to touch the principal unless we're all in this together."

Dana scrunches up her face. "I know. And what are the chances of that?"

. . .

An hour later, we have buried most of Mother's ashes in the cemetery on the bluff. At the bottom of a hole the size of a wastebasket sits a heart-shaped rock, retrieved by Beowulf from the beach. Ian
filmed the whole thing: Sedgie trying to look tragic, then breaking down
into genuine sobs, the rest of us following, until we were all huddled together, weeping. No grown-ups there to tell us otherwise, no one to tell us
to stand straight and be a brick.

"A stone heart," whispered Ian afterward, wiping his eyes. "Think of
the symbolism."

"At least it *was* a heart," I said.

It is just past noon. Already, people are gathering. My parents'
friends come in two types. There are the "old shoes," who have let
time and gravity take its course. Their hair is gray, their footwear practical,
their sweaters (draped over their shoulders on this hottest of days) cabled
in pink or green. The Hobsons (Aunt Dottie and Uncle Paul) fall into
this category, as do the Baileys. The men have lost their vigor due to mal-
functioning prostates, and the women (always tough, but disguising it under an ebbing tide of estrogen) have come into their own. They speak
their minds in loud voices, saying, "Good Lord, Maddie! It's like seeing a
ghost! If I was your mother, I'd have written you off." They own large, happy
dogs that bark.

Then there are the "well preserved." In this group, the women, especially, have defied time. Take Mrs. Swanson. Hair insistently ash blond,
teased into full volume. That little brown sheath of a dress, spiked heels,
gray eye makeup, and skin stretched into seamlessness. She wiggles her fingers at me. Jewels ignite like flashbulbs. "Soooo sad, Maggie."

"It's Maddie."

Ian sidles up with an iced tea and introduces himself to Mrs. Swanson.

He's looking very Turnbull and Asser with a monogrammed shirt, red tie, blue blazer, and those ghastly shoes.

"A director?" says Mrs. Swanson. "How divine."

I notice a run in my nylons. I know better than to wear black stockings on Sand Isle. Sand Isle is a bare-legged place, regardless of the occasion.

"I was an actress—well, a model—when I met Gerald," Mrs. Swanson tells Ian.

"You didn't give it up, did you?"

I can see Ian framing Mrs. Swanson's face as she tells him about her life. What Ian doesn't know is that Mrs. Swanson's son Tad wrapped himself around a tree in the summer of 1974. The Swansons and the Baileys do not speak. I have half an urge to warn Mrs. Swanson that Ian's portraits are not necessarily flattering, but she has a ravenous look in her eye. The ice clinking in her glass, she leans into Ian and whispers. After a minute in which I am ignored, she throws back her head and laughs. Ian, too, laughs—a spastic expulsion. He wipes his forehead with his cocktail napkin, watches as all ninety pounds of Mrs. Swanson slither away.

"Well!" he says.

"Well, what?"

"She thinks . . ." He starts laughing again, which annoys me. This is a memorial service, after all. Just because Ian goes to so many funerals doesn't give him license.

Across the crowd, Jamie and Fiona are talking with Dana. "These people hold very narrow views," I say.

"Unlike you."

"My mind is so open, birds fly through it," I say.

"Really?"

"Absolutely."

"Then why are you acting so churlish?"

If we were filming a scene, all these people would be extras, the buzz of their conversation simulated by the verbal repetition of *nutsandboltsnutsandbolts*. It is reminiscent of my wedding, and I suddenly feel a profound longing for my mother—her graceful figure draped in peach as she elegantly and without hesitation walked into the lake.

"Churlish?" I say. "There's a word."

People approach us, say a few things about my parents. But mostly they want to ask what we'll do with the Aerie now that the grown-ups are gone. Aunt Dottie Hobson with her bulldog eyes who grew up with my father, and Uncle Paul of the gaff-rigged Mallard; their son Larry—bald now, and going through a divorce (*Still single are you, Maddie?* says Aunt Dottie); Brett Bailey, whose sister Deb died with Tad Swanson and whose mother was a friend of my mother, but with whom I have nothing in common; Mr. Marks looking sad and pinched; the needlepoint types and the tennis types; the golfers and the sailors, and the people with whom they played bridge. They're all here, buzzing like heat bugs with their own mortality. And now Adele, shorn-haired, her tunic glistening, is ringing her glass with a spoon and standing up on a chair.

"Brava!" yells Ian. "Brava!"

"Oh God," I say.

Conversation trails off as people become aware of Adele. The discreet clink of forks on plates as everyone comes to attention. I look around wildly, expecting to see the raised eyebrows, the barely repressed laughter, but everyone looks at least politely interested.

"*Namaste,*" says Adele in the traditional Hindu greeting.

She waits, but only Derek, Beowulf, and Jessica *namaste* her back. Adele clasps her hands together, as if in prayer, above her head. Everyone must be grasping for a cultural touchstone—some point of reference like a yacht christening—to give a context to Adele's display.

"Today, we celebrate a transition."

I wonder where Dana is, and who, if anyone, encouraged Adele to take charge.

"Our bodies are but one manifestation of the divine."

My eyes light on Dana talking to Jamie, who looks amused. Aunt Dottie

Hobson has lit a cigarette and is absentmindedly flicking the ash into her husband's drink.

". . . and when we go to the Land of Bliss, we will find a lake of pure, sparkling water whose waves lap softly on the shores of golden sand."

Everyone nods with relief and dawning comprehension that Adele is talking about Sand Isle. I spot Jessica off to the side, standing next to Mac watching from behind his Ray-Bans. Her dark skin set off against a bright-patterned dress she has taken from my mother's closet, Jessica resembles a fierce punctuation point in the midst of otherwise bland prose.

". . . where we find Infinite Light and Boundless Life."

"Maddie?"

I turn to see Jamie. He has extracted himself from Dana and is staring down at me with eyes that used to make me recite poetry. Itching from the black summer wool of my dress, I have the urge to touch the hairs on his wrist.

"In this world of lust, a person is born alone and dies alone; and there is no one to share her punishment in the life after death," says Adele.

Jamie makes the same face he made in my freshman dorm when he saw my roommate's "If by Chance We Meet, It's Beautiful" poster. The mole on his cheek quivers as we try not to laugh. For the briefest moment, I feel like I have landed.

"Are you going to be around later?" he whispers.

I incline my head. "Later?" I repeat the word as if he has asked me something complex and significant. "Yes."

As he touches my shoulder, a fleeting expression recalls that long-ago look of wounded anger, but then he nods and drifts away. Adele seems to be concluding her remarks, but before she finishes, I feel another presence at my elbow: Aunt Bibi Hester, Jamie's mother, in gray ultrasuede and silk. Her sun-spotted hand, adorned with the faded but gargantuan Hester tiara diamond, is wrapped around a drink. She jerks her head toward Adele, and through her smile says, "Your mother would have been charmed."

Given that my mother called Adele a "throwaway," I doubt it. "Mmm," I say. I look around to find Ian, who has drifted off to get a better angle on Adele.

"The law of cause and effect is universal," Adele drones on. "Each man must carry his own sin to his own retribution . . ."

"Speaking of sin," says Aunt Bibi, "did you hear about the Swansons' lawn jockey?" Aunt Bibi's eyes are electric blue. I've seen pictures of her in her twenties, along with my mother, looking gorgeous and dangerous.

"Can't say that I have."

"Painted," Aunt Bibi whispers, the red of her lipstick creeping into the lines above her lips. "Defaced."

"Seriously!"

"Gerald suspects sour grapes. Someone he trounced in the regatta."

"You think?" I still flinch whenever I recall my sodden confession to Aunt Bibi that I was still in love with her son.

Adele concludes with a flourish about everlasting light and love and the divine reinterpretation of souls. Everyone amens as if she has just read from Psalm 23.

"No," Aunt Bibi says flatly. "I don't." Then she smiles the conspiratorial smile that used to amuse my mother (the two of them gossiping on the beach) and, to my amazement, winks.

Conversation resumes—the Sand Isle denizens and the handful from Harbor Town, all of them engaging our oddball family as matter-of-factly as if we still belong. They touch our arms and look into our eyes, their light but enduring friendship binding us. Like a lifeline. Like a leash.

O ne by one, we peel off from the gathering and return to the Aerie. The house smells of flowers whose water needs changing, and there is nothing left to do but pack.

We'll all be leaving in the next few days. Sedgie is starting rehearsals, and Derek needs to get back to France. Beo is heading into his final year at

Oberlin, and Jessica will be starting her junior year at Cal State. According to Dana, Beo is moving out west after graduation to start a rock band. Dumping out the water from a bouquet of zinnias into the kitchen sink, Beo looks at me with surprise. "A band? Who told you that?"

I could swear it was Dana, but perhaps it was in the ether.

"Given the financial exigencies," he says, "I'm going to apply to law school." This from the young man who said school was a "temporal sop to the sublime." He lifts his eyebrow. "I know. Who'da thunk it?"

I tell him that's wonderful, that we need a lawyer in the family. *And* a rock star. And by the way, what's the situation between him and Jessica?

Beo picks the dead head off a zinnia and stares at me with such a knowing expression that my assessment of his legal ability improves on the spot. "Kissin' cousins, MaddieAunt. Surely you understand."

There is a rank smell of old water. The refrigerator hums. I stand accused—though of what, I'm not sure. Could something have filtered through the airwaves? But whatever happened between my cousin and me was so long ago. Besides, no one knew.

I hang up the phone and run to find Ian, who is in his bedroom packing. "We are so busted."

Ian folds a shirt, inserting tissue, and places it into the gaping mouth of his open suitcase. "For?"

"Bibi Hester knows, Ian. She winked at me."

Ian holds up a tie. "Bibi Hester knows *what*, Maddie?"

I narrow my eyes. Ian was the one who seduced me into a world of crime and painted lawn ornaments, and now I'm going to pay the price. "The Sand Isle Association has to approve even a bequeathed stock transfer. How will it look when this gets out?"

"Not a problem," says Ian.

Fine for him. Ian's not the fourth-generation family member who will end up disgraced because of a momentary lapse in etiquette, if not judgment.

Perhaps awareness of his own mortality renders him cavalier, but I have no such luxury. I am bound by obligation.

"They'll decline us," I say miserably, wondering if we have any brown paint in the basement.

Ian picks up the video camera and, focusing on me, says in a stentorian voice, "The Addison family who has resided on Sand Isle for more than a century? Declined? That's absurd. It won't happen. Besides, I thought you hated this place."

"That doesn't mean I won't keep coming here."

Ian squeezes one eye shut and continues to film. "Tell me, does Dr. Anke know about this destructive urge to repeatedly subject yourself to situations in which you're uncomfortable?"

Ignoring him, I go on. "And now *Jamie* is thinking of buying the Aerie. He just called. I thought he wanted to see me, but Dana has talked him into looking at the house in case we want to sell. Aunt Bibi implied that she knows *exactly* who painted that jockey, and now Jamie's sounding very confident that the house *is* for sale, and that we have no other choice."

Ian flips off the camera and tosses it to me. "Here, get some more footage after I'm gone." He shakes out a cashmere sweater and pulls it over his head. "What did Jamie Hester say, exactly?"

"He said, 'Hi, Maddie. Wondering if I could bring Fiona by to see the house.'"

Pause. "From which you deduced all of the above?"

"This is Dana's doing."

"You're jumping to conclusions. Besides, Mrs. Swanson thinks the Hesters did it."

"What?"

"That's what she said to me. Something about her husband and the regatta . . ."

"Why would she tell *you* that?"

Ian checks his watch. It is time to take his pills. He flips open the compartmentalized plastic case that is labeled by days of the week, hours of the day. He shakes out a handful of vitamins, slams them into his mouth, and gulps them down with water. It takes him a moment to catch his breath, but when he does, he says to me, "Who better to talk to at a party than a quasi stranger you'll never see again? Unlike you"—he looks at me pointedly— "I don't fit in here, Maddie. That's my virtue."

J amie and Fiona are in the living room talking to Dana. I crouch at the top of the stairs the way I did as a child, trying to overhear the grown-ups when they argued or gossiped. Dana is saying something about family history and letting go, but I'm sure she's got it wrong.

Jamie makes a comment about the plumbing in these old houses. When he asks how many bedrooms there are, I cover my mouth. We used to cohabitate in a tiny dorm room, and now twelve bedrooms mightn't be enough.

"What are you doing?" says Miriam, appearing behind me at the top of the stairs in an olive-green pantsuit.

"Shhh," I say, indicating for her to sit down.

I jerk my head toward the base of the stairs and pantomime listening. "They're looking to buy the house," I whisper.

Miriam—bless her—looks alarmed.

Dana's voice grows louder. She is laughing with Jamie and Fiona, saying, "This crazy great-uncle brought this silk back from Turkey. We always thought if we tore it down, the whole house would collapse."

Miriam hits me in the arm. "They're coming."

I hear the creak of the dining-room door. Dana is showing them our marks measuring a hundred years of family growth, and I can see the top of Fiona's auburn hair pulled into a French twist. No one has looked that elegant in the Aerie for years. Not since my mother was young. Not even Adele.

"What are you doing?" says Jessica, coming out of the bunk room.

"Shhh," I say.

Miriam mouths, *Selling the house.*

Jessica looks horrified and sits down quickly.

I hear Sedgie's baritone from below, followed by Dana making introductions. Sedgie says something indecipherable and starts up the stairs. When he sees us at the top, his expression doesn't change. Slowly and elaborately, he steps over Jessica, turns around, and joins the huddle. Below us, Jamie, Fiona, and Dana disappear into the kitchen.

"Granite countertops," says Sedgie. "I can see it now."

"She's going to paint," I say.

"We'll have to kill them," adds Jessica.

"Hmmph," says Miriam. "All's you got to do is tell them the place is haunted."

The three of us gape at Miriam.

I intercept Jamie, Fiona, and Dana in the Love Nest. "Kind of a pigsty," I say, glancing at the unmade bed covered with Derek's clothes. "Squishy mattresses."

Jamie says, "I've always loved this house." He's still wearing his blazer from the luncheon. Beneath his bushy blond eyebrows, he looks feral and proprietary.

"It has a wonderful view," says Fiona.

"The weather slams it."

Dana cuts her eyes at me and tells Fiona and Jamie to follow her upstairs. I trail after them. Fiona has knotted a cashmere wrap about her neck. Her satin mules click on the treads, and her arms are tan and lovely.

"Ignore the mouse droppings," I mutter.

"Maddie's feeling nostalgic," says Dana briskly as if I'm not present. "We're *all* feeling nostalgic. I mean, we grew up here, learned to swim. Well . . . some of us learned to swim."

"How many bathrooms?" says Jamie.

"Ignore the hospital bed," I say as we enter the master bedroom. Out of the corner of my eye, I see that some of Adele's clothes are already hanging in the closet.

"Oh!" says Fiona, clasping her hand over her mouth. "This is where she died?"

"A lot of history . . ." I say.

"We'll have it cleaned," says Dana.

"Crazy great-uncle. Crazy cousin. Crazy great-grandmother."

"I mean, it's—"

"Crazy, crazy, crazy," I say.

Jamie makes a snort that seems to indicate he agrees with my assessment.

"You'll need to burn sage," I say as Adele comes into the room. "Tell them, Adele."

Fiona turns to Adele and holds out her hand. I'm surprised she can lift it with that ring. "I loved what you said today. About the infinite light and all."

Adele clasps Fiona's hand as I explain that Jamie and Fiona are interested in the house. "*If*"—I pause—"we're going to sell it." I gaze beseechingly at Adele. "The feng shui?"

Adele's eyes graze across mine. "Ah," she says. She nods at Fiona. "It's problematic."

I silently bless her.

"Can we fix that?" says Fiona.

"Honey," says Jamie, "we can fix anything."

M addie?"

I turn to see Fiona, who has followed me into the dining room while everyone else is in the kitchen, talking to the Sears installer. She eyes the light fixture, runs a long, painted nail, reminiscent of my mother's, along the table, tracing the gouges made from years of the knife-in-the-crack trick.

"I suppose you'll want to paint *this* out," I say, indicating the initialed measure marks on the wall. My voice sounds harsh and peevish.

Fiona cocks her head. "Why would I want to do that?" Her cornflower eyes widen, and I can see that I scare her. I suddenly feel embarrassed for both of us.

"I'm sorry," I say. "It's all been too much."

"No," she says, shaking her head. "It's a beautiful house. I would love to have grown up in a house like this." She makes a goofy face that I begrudgingly find endearing. "If you saw where I grew up . . ." Fiona points to our tattooed measurements with her flawless nail. "How could you let something like this go?"

Why not? I let Jamie go. He screamed at me on the beach, and Aunt Pat told me I didn't try hard enough. Years before he became Fiona's husband, years before he became president of RidCo. In the kitchen, I hear Jamie talking to the Sears guy about trash mashers, and what it would take to get a Sub-Zero up these stairs. Fiona listens to him for a moment, and looks me in the eye. "Talk about nostalgic. Why do you suppose he's even looking at this place? I mean . . . our marriage is fine and all. We have kids. But *you* were his great adventure."

S he said that?"

I am sitting with Dana on the porch. The lake is a swath of sapphire, and the air is filled with the preparations of one last great meal.

"I should have said 'his great *disaster*.'" I swat away a mosquito. "Look at my clothes. Besides that, I like his wife. It kills me to admit it." Dana laughs. "So, do you think they'll buy it?"

"It depends," says Dana. "Do *you* want to sell?"

"Would that it were so simple."

"But it *was* simple once. When did it change?"

"I don't know. After Dad bought the TV for the moonwalk. Or when we stopped coming by train."

"Or the summer Tad Swanson died," Dana says. "*That* was a summer." She is knitting something green and complicated. It spreads before her like a lawn. She had her abortion; life went on.

"Can you even imagine us together?" I say. "Jamie Hester and me?"

" 'The Mole'?" She shakes her head. "No."

"Ah yes. The Mole. Did Mom ever call any of *your* boyfriends names, Dane?"

"I believe she had something biting for Bruce Digby."

"Ha! No doubt." I inhale the fragrance of leeks and morels. Tomorrow, Sedgie and Adele are heading out, then the rest. I'll stay on an extra day to help Dana pack the house; then we, too, will evaporate. "But she must have liked Angus Farley. She never came up with a derogatory name for him."

"Actually," says Dana, "she did."

I jerk my head around and look at her. Knitting, avoiding my eyes, Dana mumbles something.

"Excuse me?" I say.

She clears her throat. "The Dreadful Bloodsucking Faux Brit." Her mouth twitches. The smell of sautéed garlic and onions rushes past us, along with a suggestion of mint.

"Well, they could have at least told *me*."

"They knew you were pregnant."

I am taken aback. "No, they didn't."

Click, click, click. "Yes, they did."

"Did *you* tell them?"

Dana gives me a sideways look as she counts her stitches. "You know, Maddie, parents see more than you think. Half the stuff we used to do? They knew, Maddie. Parents *know*. You think *I* don't know about Jessica?"

To which I say nothing.

"Besides," Dana goes on, "Jessica's a big talker. You can't believe half of what she says."

"Parents don't know everything, Dane."

"That's not what I'm saying."

"There're lots of things they don't know."

"And things they don't *want* to know," says Dana, scratching her eyebrow with her knitting needle. For a moment, I think she's going to stick herself in the eye. Two squirrels race each other up one side of the oak tree and down the other. "Why do you hate it here, Maddie?"

"I don't hate it here."

"You do. You treat it badly, like an old doll you don't love anymore. Like you don't love *us*."

"But I do love you! Besides, *you're* the one showing it to prospective buyers."

I hear Sedgie calling for Adele, and somewhere in the house, Beo laughs. From the Love Nest, the thin trill of Derek's recorder, and I think, I *love* it here, now more than ever. Maybe because Mother is gone. It's a wobbly, awful house that surely will bankrupt us, but I'll fight tooth and nail to keep it.

"Maddie, what *happened* to you that summer?"

The question is so unspecific as to be meaningless. Perhaps she means the summer of the convention or the moonwalk; the summer Sadie died; the summer I got drunk; the summer I broke up with Jamie; the summer my chipmunk disappeared. But from the look on her face, I know what summer she means. The summer of hitchhiking Indians and cast-off rings. Dana was pregnant, and I had grown silent and furtive. I scratched at my arms. I could have peeled away my skin. I pretended nothing was happening. For Edward's sake and mine, I was a brick.

There is a moment in truth telling when one recounts a story told in one's head so many times that it suddenly sounds false. Memory has a surreal quality, as if experience, perception, and interpretation don't quite mesh. What is the boundary between intention and consequence? At what point does a natural loving embrace between cousins cross the line? In our family, truth was never legal tender. To speak the truth, you have to trust, and how can you trust if you think you'll be called "a throwaway"? But now, in the twilight of a dying day, with both parents gone and no one left to reject us, I turn to my sister and tell her.

After I finish, I say, "You see, he was so damaged. It wasn't really his fault."

In a flicker of recognition, we had chosen each other. No one else had any idea of what Edward really saw in Vietnam. *The waste*, he said. *The stupid,*

*stupid stupidity. The thing is, I don't know anymore. I don't even know what's
what.*

What happened between us felt as intimate as if we'd taken each other.
Afterward, Edward had clutched my wrist. My instinct was to pull away,
but I had learned about patience by trailing nuts along a path and holding
very still. If you wait long enough and quietly, shy, defenseless things will
come to you. When I wrapped my arms around him, Edward wept.

Dana inspects me through the corner of her eyes. I wait for her to say,
That's really weird, Maddie.

Instead, she says, "Oh, Maddie," in a voice so compassionate it makes
me wince.

I find Derek on the beach. The structure, as far as I can tell, is complete. It stands about twelve feet high—a mound of branches and
driftwood and rock. Ian told me to get some footage, and that's what I
intend. Less detail-oriented than Ian, my style of interviewing consists of
dialogue punctuated by the provocative question.

"What is it?" I ask.

"Whatever you want it to be."

With Ian's camera slung over my shoulder, I ask Derek about his structure and if it represents his current artistic direction or a new departure
altogether. He ruminates for a moment. The evening is warm and brushed
by the tame light of a dwindling season. I hold up the camera, set the auto-
focus, fix Derek through the lens. He blurs and grows sharp. Sometimes,
that's the way life is—the small things coming gradually into focus. Other
times, it takes the panoramic shot to give perspective and context. Derek's
face, reminiscent of Edward's, is the kind the camera "loves." Plain faces
can appear handsome or beautiful when photographed; the beautiful sometimes appear plain. But Derek, handsome to begin with, seems to come
alive when seen through the lens.

"A fortress? Or a funeral pyre?" I suggest.

"A phallus, maybe. An object of desire."

"Eye of the beholder," I say.

The thing looms like some alien visitor alongside the beached sailfish and the canoes. My internal narrator's voice describes it as *the incongruous manifestation of a fertile mind.*

Derek readjusts some rocks. Out of the blue he says, "Why do some marriages make it? And some go preposterously bad?"

"You're asking me?"

The camera keeps whirring. Derek stands back, assesses the change, begins to circumnavigate once more. "Your parents, for instance. Do you think they were happy?"

Tracking him with the lens, I say, "They were married for more than forty years." Of course, there was that vein in my father's neck when my mother was tight at dinner; the clipped way he said, *Evelyn*; my mother's naps and endless cigarettes.

Through the camera, his eyes meet mine. I, who have craved nothing more than being seen, have spent the last fifteen years seeing others through a lens. Now I'm studying Derek, casting about for the proper angle, the proper light. Ian says you can tell if someone is lying by the way his eyes dart to the left. Hold still, I think to my own shaking hands.

I say, "Do you remember that day I trashed your studio? Just you and me sitting on the floor and all those strips of paper."

"My entire portfolio was in tatters."

"I had such a vicious crush on you."

"Maddie," he says, "turn the camera off."

I continue to film him. Derek turns back to his tower of rock and wood. Picking up a can, he douses it with lighter fluid and, with a strike of a match, sets it ablaze. The flames take hold, snake into a rage. Sparks drift down, burning holes in Derek's sweater, touching his hair. I reach out and brush them away. Moths swoop in like deranged fairies. I want to ask him why he stopped painting, but, pushing the camera away, he pulls me in roughly and kisses me.

For a second, I can't breathe. "Whoa," I say, pulling away. We stare at each other. In the shimmering light, he could be his brother. Derek and Edward. *Virtute et Veritas.*

"You were just fourteen," he says, his palms turned up like a beleaguered Jesus.

I wipe my nose with the back of my arm. "Look," I say, "my life is fine." For some reason, I think this will comfort him as if he needs to be absolved. We all crave absolution, but who is left to give it in any meaningful way? Derek shimmers, whether from heat or because of my dazzled eyes. Again I say, "I'm fine"—this time with a kind of surprised assurance that, for lack of a better word, seems to come from grace.

"Hey!" someone yells. "Hey!"

Smoke or steam is rising from Derek's sweater. Mac the ferry driver, singular fan of our Feingold film, is running down the beach. He is waving something. At first, I think he has drawn his gun, but then I realize it's only his flashlight.

"You're on fire," I say to Derek.

Solemnly studying the jewels of embers studding his sweater, Derek doesn't seem to notice either the smoke or Mac's shouting. Then with a start, he begins swatting himself, dancing about in an absurd jig. As bedazzlement gives way to panic, I pick up fistfuls of sand, flinging it at him to smother the flames. He holds up his hands as if I am hitting him, and maybe I am. Batting away embers and lashing out at my cousin Derek— lashing out even at Edward—expressing my fury at what was lost that summer when I last stood on the edge of innocence and everything was possible. As the flames subside, replaced by the acrid smell of burning wool, a sudden squall of laughter rushes up from deep within my belly. My old obsessions, my self-pity, my intractable antipathy toward Sand Isle—all of it caught up in a tide of convulsing shoulders, hiccups, and laughter. The spell broken, I am overcome.

"Ma'am?" says Mac, looking from Derek to me. "Ma'am? Is everything all right?"

. . .

I s this party crashable?" says Sedgie, arriving on the beach with all the cousins to see what on earth is on fire. While Philip looks gratified that *someone* had finally cleared out the branches and disposed of them, Ian picks up the camera I have dropped. He presses the "record" button, preserving for posterity the exquisite moment as Derek's effort of the past week combusts and collapses. I hear Jessica shriek, taunting Beo as they gallop fully dressed into the water. Then Sedgie, in a dead-on imitation of my former mother-in-law, screams, "Come on, ducks, we're all going in!" Within minutes, Adele has stripped down, Sedgie and Ian following suit. Philip, with an amused half smile, says to Dana, "After you." Semidelirious, I follow them, tripping out of my clothes.

"Hey!" says Mac, watching our clothes pile up on the beach, trying very hard not to stare. "It's not even *nine P.M.*!"

"Come *on!*" we scream to him.

Beyond the waves, Ian shouts back at the shoreline, "Beware, you last bastion of the idle rich! Your days are numbered!"

Then Mac, too, begins to unbutton his shirt. Sedgie laughs his contagious baritone and throws his arm around Ian. Summer is almost over, and the sun is setting earlier. In years to come, we'll replay this film, our smiles proclaiming *our* time to be the best, the happiest, the most divine. Stripped of my clothes and the weight of my past, I plunge into the cold, resurface into the eternal summer of childhood. It is a moment glimmering with possibility, what Ian would call hope.

TWENTY-FIVE

Adele clings to me, her eyes glistening, her fuzzy head tickling my cheek.

When we were children, it seemed like forever until the following summer. I cried every year when it was time to go. We'd send the trunks ahead filled with Petoskey stones, but the train returning to California at the end of August was never as happy as the train heading east in June.

The horse and carriage are waiting. "Sed-GIE!" Adele screams in a dreadful imitation of Aunt Pat. In her current incarnation of destitution, Adele has no place to live, so she's going to New York with Sedgie. For a moment, I feel incongruous, unbearable love for her.

"Oh, Adele," I say. Her body feels like a broomstick in my arms.

Sedgie pushes through the front door with his duffel slung over his shoulder, Ian following him. Sedgie mutters something about the Citroën, then stares balefully at Adele. "Just when I thought I was single."

"You offered," she says, smacking him on the shoulder.

"Drive safely," we call after them.

"See you in New York!" yells Ian, blowing Sedgie a kiss.

"Really?" I say, turning to him.

. . .

The next morning, I take Ian to the airport. Standing at the gate, Ian shifts on his feet. Then he looks down on me with those gray eyes that have been anchoring me for the last decade, given me meaning and hope.

"Are you going to be okay?" he asks.

"Sure."

"I mean, when everyone leaves?"

I smile back at him while they call his flight number. "You're a kind man, Ian."

I watch his back as he climbs the stairs of the plane. In a couple of days, I'll follow him.

We're down to the last of us. Derek is going to push off with Beowulf and try to make Gary, Indiana, by midnight. I hear the last trills of a recorder before it is put into its case. In the living room, Beowulf picks out the *Appassionata*—his homage to Mother before he departs.

"I think she enjoyed your playing," I say as Beo leans down to kiss me good-bye.

Beo squeezes Jessica tightly. From where I'm standing now, it looks like the embrace of affectionate cousins, nothing more.

"Good-bye!" Beo yells as he heads down the steps. "Don't let Dana sell the house!"

I turn to Derek. "So."

He tells me he needs to work things out with Yvonne, but if she doesn't come back, he's going to go to Vietnam.

Derek, the Conscientious Objector.

"You're finally going?"

"I need to understand what happened to Edward. You want to come along?"

But what happened to Edward hadn't begun in Vietnam. If it began anywhere, it was here with the beady eyes of ancestors staring down from the wall.

Derek pulls a piece of paper from his jacket pocket and hands it to me. I take it from him, unfurling it to see an intact image of my childhood staring back.

"It's pretty good," I say. "When'd you draw this?"

"I call it *Maddie on the Stairs*. You must have been, what, ten?"

"Twelve," I say. The summer of Chippy.

Derek touches my head and descends to the sidewalk, turning back once to sing, *"But he's touched your perfect body with his mi-ind."*

I laugh. He heaves his duffel into the wagon and starts down the walk. I raise my hands and frame him. The camera pulls back; the film becomes grainy; the shot disappears.

B efore she left, Adele hauled Mother's hospital bed away and moved the original mahogany frame into the tower so she could overlook the lake. Adele's sense of entitlement endures regardless of her circumstance, and no one was inclined to argue with her.

"She's got the shrine thing going on the drop-lid desk," says Dana, sitting beside me on the rockers in the afternoon sun.

"Good thing I found Grannie Addie's diary on the bookshelf before she took that over," I say.

"What diary?"

So I tell her how our great-grandmother's loss of her daughter sent her into blackness and a sanitarium where she stayed for years. When she was "cured," she came home to her husband, returned to Sand Isle, built a kitchen, and wrote a cookbook.

"In a weird way, I relate to her."

"It's amazing how resilient people are," says Dana. "You, for instance."

It is as close to an acknowledgment as I have ever heard from my sister. We were taught never to praise each other because it would ruin our characters.

"Do you believe in lucid dreams?" I ask her. I could swear Sadie came to me last night, holding the hand of an older woman. They seemed to be telling me something. This morning I awoke with the resolve to send half of our daughter's ashes back to Angus.

"Your ghost?"

"Adele says ghosts are projections of our previous lives."

"You're not taking Adele seriously?"

"Why not?" *They're not so far-fetched*, Dr. Anke said, *your cousin Adele's notions about past lives*. But Dana and I have always seen things differently. When I showed her my train film, she said, *It's interesting, Maddie. But I don't remember it that way at all*. "It's hard to come home," I say.

"That's the difference between you and me," says Dana. "I find it hard to leave."

The sound of the screen door opening, and Jessica pushes through, dragging her suitcase, the door banging in her wake. Her roots have grown out, but she looks softer than when she arrived. Maybe I've grown accustomed to the tattoos. "You two look thick as thieves," she says. Fixing her eyes on me, she adds, "It's our 'pinup' girl."

I look from her to Dana. "Whatever happened to our time-honored tradition of keeping family secrets and letting them fester?"

Ignoring me, Dana says, "We should replant the garden. If we don't take care of this house, where will we come to find each other?"

"I thought you were worried about the cost."

"Are we really that broke?" says Jessica.

"It all depends on you," I say. "What are your prospects?"

"Me?" Her eyes widen. "I'm going to be a movie star. Just look at me!"

I have to admit she *is* beautiful . . . the most beautiful in our family. Probably because she's adopted. "Do you have any talent?" I say.

Jessica smiles confidently. Again, the virtues of adoption. "Ian says he's going to give me a screen test."

"Ian is totally grandiose."

Philip yells from below that it's time to go.

"C'mon," says Dana. "We've got to get you to the airport."

I rise with them, but Jessica puts her hand on my shoulder. "Good-bye, MaddieAunt." I can tell from her expression that she needs to be alone with her parents. For a second, it pierces me, but I reach out and grab her, embracing her as I might have held my own daughter, wrapping her tightly the way a mother should, telling her that she's fine, that it's okay to go. As she and Dana head down the steps, I ache for my mother. I wonder what she would have told me if she could have spoken at the end.

I won't miss this weather," says Miriam. "Not in the least."

Standing by the porch rail, we watch from the porch as Philip, Dana, and Jessica board the carriage. Miriam has on her "traveling" wig and is dressed in a double-breasted yellow pantsuit. Her eyebrows are sharper than ever, and her lipstick looks suspiciously like one of my mother's.

"What do you think, Miriam?"

"Oh," says Miriam, "she'll find her way. They usually do, even the ones who have to learn everything the hard way. You know the type."

"I wasn't talking about Jessica."

"Me neither."

After a pause, I say, "I was talking about the family."

The two of us flop down in the rockers. Miriam adjusts her wig so that it's even more crooked. "I've lived with plenty of families over the years. You get down to the bone—family is family. Nothing much special about this one." She begins to rock. "Your mother, though. She was something special."

Sitting next to the old, black home-care nurse who wiped my mother's bottom, I, too, begin to rock.

The last page of my great-grandmother's diary is smudged. I read until 1 A.M. and have woken before dawn to read again. Grannie Addie returned to this house, haunted by memories. She awoke to the sound of a child crying in the night. In several pages, she alludes obliquely to hearing voices, but like my cousin Edward, she grew cagey about whom she told.

About her own Edward, she said, *My husband follows me everywhere.*

Their life went on. Grannie Addie came to herself and persevered. She was, after all, a wife and a mother when that was a woman's highest calling. She watched the nineteenth century become the twentieth, saw the horse and carriage give way to the automobile, gaslight to electricity, the communal dining of Sand Isle replaced by a kitchen of her own. In 1915, Einstein crafted his Theory of General Relativity. The following year, Grannie Addie's older son rode through Turkey on a camel, but managed to avoid the war. To my great-grandmother's horror, he returned home with yards of silk, a hookah, and "a bit of a hashish problem." A year later, her second son, our grandfather, married our grandmother, thus assuring a lineage to uphold the Aerie.

By the time the vote was granted to women in 1920, Grannie Addie had lost a granddaughter (my infant aunt) to influenza. Throughout this loss, her mind stayed intact. In the meantime, appalled at the influx of Catholics to Sand Isle, Grannie Addie entertained the Presbyterian minister, stitched sachet pillows with her lady friends, and wrote down recipes for tripe. But in her scrawled prose, I detect the vestiges of trauma.

> AUGUST 1920—Halsey and Margaret have brought our
> granddaughter to the Aerie for a month. She is so sweet
> in her bonnet and curls. Indeed, I can barely bring myself

to look at her. At other times, I rush back into the room
to assure myself of her vitality.

Almost three decades earlier, while Grannie Addie was incarcerated in
her "rest home," two French brothers named Lumière created one of the
first motion pictures by casting light through transparent, contiguous images,
resulting in the film *The Arrival of a Train*. So realistic was the impression
of a train advancing toward them that the frightened audience fled the
theater. Ralph Feingold would say that film is an apt analogy for the sly
subterfuge of matter. But those Edwardian innocents, seeing the train conjured out of nothing, were convinced that they'd gone mad.

Soon, the sweeping will start, and then the first light. The house
creaks, whispers—the chatter of joist and shingle. In a few weeks,
it will be boarded up, and after that, autumn leaves will drop and languish
until spring. I, too, could lie here all winter, but I need to get up and pack.
The letters and diaries of my great-grandmother, themselves like fallen
leaves, clutter my bed. I fell asleep to Grannie Addie's description of the
shocking arrival in the harbor of the Baileys' yacht, the *Little Annie*. She
thought the vessel nouveau and garish. We, her descendants, perceive it as
a charming example of faded glory.

You can't go back to the train times. I breathe in deeply the Michigan
air. Tomorrow, I will be inhaling traffic fumes and New York heat, deafened
by the sounds of sirens. For a moment, I savor the lake and the pine, the
mildest aroma of lavender.

She's here with me. I can feel her all around. Dana says there are no
such things as ghosts, but I disagree. I have come to believe we are all part
ghost—full of archaic notions and the bequeathed DNA of skin and hair,
reconstituted beliefs like modified recipes, a mishmash of dishes, old photographs, and pen marks on the wall. Ghosts lap at us like the tongues of
small animals. I see ghosts in the lines of Grannie Addie's letters, in my

own habit of putting on shoes at dinner, in the imprint of a hand pressed against a window, in the needlework of women trying to cling to their minds.

There! Do you feel it? She is with me on the bed. A woman with muttonchop sleeves on a black lace dress. She leans over and pulls my head to her shoulder, embracing me like a mother would a child. She whispers words of comfort and encouragement. She says, *Dearest, let me tell you about the house.*

About the author

About the book

Read on

Insights,
Interviews
& More . . .

Terry Gamble on Family . . . and *Good Family*

The scholar of the first age received into him the world around; brooded thereon; gave it the new arrangement of his own mind, and uttered it again.

> —Ralph Waldo Emerson,
> "The American Scholar"

WRITERS ARE VAMPIRES. We feast upon and consume our immediate world, not so much because we are ravenous for experience, but because we are driven to digest and make order of life in all its messiness. Ten years ago my mother lay dying in the summerhouse on Lake Michigan that she had shared with my father for thirty years. Present were my father, my sister, and I, along with our husbands and children. Next door, in a house that was built by my great-grandparents in 1890, were several of my cousins and *their* spouses and children. On the other side of my parents lived my second cousin with her husband and child, and beyond that . . . a house owned by my father's cousin. My sister and I lived down the road, across from another cousin's house, and so forth. In this "family village" setting teeming with relatives, I conceived *Good Family.*

Observing the dynamics of my family, I became caught up in the humor, the details, the denial and unpleasantness of death, the peacefulness of acceptance, and the comfort of connection. There were new babies that year, my daughter included. The teenagers

> 66 That summer my cousin's daughter woke up to see the face of a woman looking down on her, only to hear later that the bedroom she'd slept in was rumored to be haunted. 99

were busy with their own dramas: boyfriends and girlfriends, swimming and waterskiing, playing music, playing cards. That summer we had a game of Sardines, a sort of backwards version of hide-and-seek, in the crazy mishmash of a house my great-grandparents had built. That summer my cousin's daughter woke up to see the face of a woman looking down on her, only to hear later that the bedroom she'd slept in was rumored to be haunted. That summer, the daughters of another cousin sang a song from *Godspell* to my mother, my sister and I tried to euthanize an ancient dishwasher that wouldn't die, and I danced deliriously to Aretha Franklin's "Respect" while holding my six-month-old daughter (videotaped by my cousin for posterity).

Why write about this? Moreover, why fictionalize it? Why not write an essay about the summer my mother died, how we were able to laugh, cry, and have fun in spite of it all, and how it changed our family forever? Anyone who has experienced the death of a parent surely understands the gamut of emotion—the grief along with the guilt, not the least of which is the guilt at feeling liberation and relief. But to fictionalize this experience is to tease out the deeper truth behind those tenacious memories, old jokes, and entrenched roles we assume when thrust back among our families. What history does each of us bring to the situation? What point of view? To unravel my own conflicts about my mother's death and the changes in our family, I instinctively turned to narrative.

When I finally began to write *Good Family* seven years after my mother's death, I wanted to write about loss and redemption, and about how silence and withholding are the ▶

Meet *Terry Gamble*

© Mary Pitts

TERRY GAMBLE is the author of one previous novel, *The Water Dancers*. Her poems, short stories, and essays have appeared in literary journals. She is a graduate of the University of Michigan, where she sits on the English Advisory Board. A member of the fifth generation of her family to spend part of each summer in northern Michigan, she lives in California with her husband and children.

Terry Gamble on Family . . . and
Good Family (continued)

undoing rather than the glue of a family. I
had written about a similar theme in a similar
setting in *The Water Dancers,* but that had a
more historic and cross-cultural arc. Now I
was ready to write closer to the bone. As the
narrator Maddie says, "You have to feel it,
and I never wanted to, none of us did,
anything but that."

So that was the starting point. Who was this
narrator who had fled her family in order that
she might avoid her own loss and pain and
thus survive? I had never left my family so
profoundly, nor had I lost a child. But I knew
what it was like to feel alienated, and had gone
through phases in my life when I felt unloved,
even unlovable. And I had this wonderful
summerhouse material to work with. Each
house was marinated in memories—the
history of our family. The houses provided
a touchstone connecting the diaspora of
our family members. No matter where we
were dispersed—China, India, the United
Kingdom, California, New York—we found
our way back each summer for those few
weeks or months on the lake.

Summer can be both the most vivid and
most unreal of seasons. From the vantage of a
porch, life is slowed down, savored, held close.
Those century-old walls provide succor and
support; so too can they stultify and suppress.
How many arguments about politics and wars
and presidents have taken place around that
dining room table since the late eighteen
hundreds? How many daughters were chided
for wearing that sweater or skirt ("You're *not*
going out looking like *that!*")? How many
spouses in earlier family pictures have

> 66 I had this
> wonderful
> summerhouse
> material to work
> with. Each house
> was marinated in
> memories—the
> history of our
> family. 99

disappeared? How many family members have died? Ritual, shared memories, the myth of security—it all lies here.

The biggest challenge was compressing the material—some of it true, much of it fabricated—into a more wieldy cast of characters (I am one of seventeen cousins). Characters were created, given a pulse and a voice, only to be killed off later or merged into other characters. An outspoken and often critical character was cannibalized for attributes to enliven Adele or Dana. Several cousins' children disappeared off the screen altogether. Limbs were lopped off the family tree. And then there was the problem of Maddie's life.

Why would this woman make such bad choices? Why, given her family and her background and her resources, would she spin out so spectacularly? As the youngest in a house full of adults and cousins preoccupied with their own lives, she suffers not so much from neglect as from negation—the death of a soul by a thousand cuts. Questions go unanswered, opinions are disregarded or sarcastically dismissed. Yet steering below the radar gives her a vantage point the more Olympian cousins cannot share. It also renders her unnoticed. She is left feeling unremarkable and perhaps in need of attention. If her sister is chronically well-behaved, the only thing left for Maddie is to misbehave (what a psychiatrist would call "acting out").

As Maddie confronts the consequences, not only of her own decisions but also those of the people she loves, she is stirred to a ▶

> 66 Why would this woman make such bad choices? 99

Terry Gamble on Family . . . and
Good Family (continued)

kind of acceptance similar to that which I experienced around the death of my mother. Writing *Good Family* was like coming full circle. Watching my mother die and watching our family move on, I—to paraphrase Emerson—brooded thereon, gave the experience a new arrangement in my mind, and uttered it again. ◞

A Conversation with Terry Gamble

Maddie states early in the book that she is not going back on account of her dying mother; instead, it is her sister who is calling her back. But what else is calling her back to a place she has basically shunned for over a decade?

She is returning to face her history and everything she has left unresolved. At nearly forty, Maddie is strong enough to take a look at events in her life, for better or worse. Prodigals are called home for a number of reasons, primarily to forgive and to be forgiven. In Maddie's case she's also called home to grieve. The Addisons are not a family who know how to grieve well. *Grievus interruptus,* you might say. Maddie describes it as literally being stuck in her throat. Only when she sits on the beach and howls after her mother's death does she begin to shake loose emotionally. Later, she is moved to laughter and hope on the same beach.

You allude to ghosts. What is the function of ghosts in **Good Family***?*

They are more metaphorical than literal, although some family members seem to have encountered actual ghosts in one form or another. The ghosts are more the shared family experiences, the memories, and the unprocessed grief. The Aerie is a ghost-charged house in particular because of the unexpressed emotions projected onto its rooms, its contents, and its history. As Maddie says at the end, "We are all part ghost." In a house in which many family members have ▶

> 66 Only when Maddie sits on the beach and howls after her mother's death does she begin to shake loose emotionally. 99

7

A Conversation with Terry Gamble
(continued)

lived, there are layers upon layers, each being incorporated into the present, reinterpreted, and redefined. There is a lingering sense of what went before, both literally in notes in a diary or markings on a wall, and figuratively in the smells and sounds and memories. During my research on scarlet fever, which killed Maddie's great-aunt, I discovered that a theory of the time was that the spores of the disease could live on and infect someone years later. I thought that was an amazing image for the pathologies of previous generations carrying over into those that follow.

Maddie recalls many memories of her past throughout the book. What points are you making about memory and perception?

Maddie arrives home with her own set of memories as well as her interpretation of them. In encountering her family, she is forced to reassess the accuracy of her recollections. Many events that loomed large for her were insignificant for her sister, and vice versa. The point is that every character has his or her version of the story. Most of us see ourselves as heroes or victims in our own dramas, failing to comprehend that those around us are dealing with their own challenges, their own realities. Maddie has made a career of using her specific interpretations of reality in her filmmaking. By going home Maddie moves toward empathy for her relatives, particularly for her sister and mother, and shifts toward seeing her story in an even larger context as she learns about her great-grandmother's tragedy. She compares her emerging sense of perspective to the craft of filmmaking, which requires the occasional panoramic shot as well as the closer view.

Given that the novel is written in the first person, people will inevitably ask how much of this is autobiography.

All authors bring some personal experience to their work. I can identify with Maddie, particularly because I came of age at the same time and with the same socioeconomic background. Starting in the sixties, women from that background were confused to some extent by the choices society was offering. Upper-class women are often bred to be hothouse flowers, and woe to those whose intellect, talent, or ambition propels them further. It isn't surprising that alcohol and sleep are so seductive to those who are attempting to sedate their true urgings.

And like Maddie I *have* lost my parents. I was particularly fortunate to be able to communicate my love and forgiveness before they died and to let them go. My father died a year ago, and within an hour of his death I had an experience—too vivid to be called a dream—in which he came to me as a thirty-one-year-old (instead of an eighty-one-year-old), announced that he felt *great,* and said that dying had been absolutely the right decision. It may have been his ghost; it may have been my projection . . . who knows? But it was as if I had his permission to live life fully and not to worry so much. ▶

> ❝ Maddie compares her emerging sense of perspective to the craft of filmmaking, which requires the occasional panoramic shot as well as the closer view. ❞

A Conversation with Terry Gamble
(continued)

So do you, like Adele, believe in reincarnation or an afterlife?

It's the big question, isn't it? *This* is the incarnation that counts, and our job is to live it with all the exuberance and joy and curiosity and experience that we can muster. Adele talks about children being "closer to the Divine," and maybe they are. But in my opinion the Divine isn't lurking out there somewhere, available only to those who haven't been born or to those who've died. It's right here and now for the taking.

> In my opinion the Divine isn't lurking out there somewhere, available only to those who haven't been born or to those who've died.

Read an Excerpt from
The Water Dancers

Below is an excerpt from Terry Gamble's first novel, The Water Dancers, *set in the post–World War II summer of 1945. The heroine, Rachel Winnapee, is a poverty-stricken sixteen-year-old Native American orphan who goes to work surrounded by wealth at the grand summer home of the March family on the shores of Lake Michigan. She strives to remain invisible, until she is assigned the task of caring for the family's emotionally shattered young scion, Woody March, a veteran haunted by his battlefield memories.*

Rachel is a young woman with no future; Woody's has already been mapped out in intricate detail: he is to run a successful banking business, marry the well-bred Elizabeth, and carry on the family name with distinction. Yet the weight of these obligations becomes unbearable as he finds himself inexorably drawn to Rachel. As the relationship between the two intensifies, it moves toward one pivotal event that will change their lives forever.

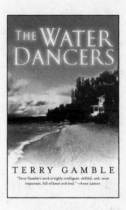

For six weeks, Rachel had been working at the Marches' house—six weeks of lining drawers, airing closets, carrying laundry, and she still couldn't keep the back stairs straight. One flight led from the kitchen to the dining room, the other up two floors to the bedrooms. Even the hallways confused her, twisting or stopping altogether. Wings and porches splayed out. Doors banged into each other. Twelve bedrooms and no one to use them but an old woman, the hope of one son, the ▶

"In this luminous first novel, Gamble . . . imparts a remarkable sense of place while launching a searing indictment of prejudice, all the while demonstrating a restrained, understated lyricism that only serves to heighten the novel's power."
—*Booklist* (starred review)

ghost of another, and a girl who had died in infancy.

Even Mr. March would only come toward the end of August, if he came at all. It was a house of women. Since the beginning of the war, women had prepared the food, cleaned the floors, kept the books, given the orders, folded the sheets, scraped the dough off butcher's block. Then there was the ironing. Rachel had scorched three damask napkins before she got it right. The Kelvinator in the pantry made her crazy with its humming. The oven smelled of gas. Something was always boiling, fueling the humidity. When she had left the convent that morning to come to work, the air was so close, the dormitory where the girls slept had grown ripe with sweat.

"Sister told us you could iron," said the cook, Ella Mae.

Her old, black eyes rested on Rachel's braids as though there might be bugs in there or worse.

"Remember," Ella Mae went on, shaking a finger, their dark eyes meeting, "the Marches have took you in for charity."

Charity. Even Sister Marie had made that clear from the start. *Our campanile, our statue of Mary—all gifts from Lydia March. You may think she has everything, but fortune is a two-edged sword. The Marches have given God a son and a baby girl. They will pay you four dollars a week.*

The Marches' house smelled of must, camphor, lilacs, and decayed fish that wafted up from the beach at night. Located on the very tip of a crooked finger of land, it had

> 66 Twelve bedrooms and no one to use them but an old woman, the hope of one son, the ghost of another, and a girl who had died in infancy. 99

the best view of all the houses on Beck's Point. Who Beck had been, no one seemed to remember, but one of the girls at the convent told Rachel it used to be a holy place where spirits dwelled and no one dared to live. Now it was chock full of summer houses, all white and lined up like pearls on a necklace.

Across the harbor, the town of Moss Village sat at the base of limestone bluffs, residue from an ancient, salty sea. Then came the glacier, molding and carving Lake Michigan like a totem of land, the Indians at the bottom, then the French, a smattering of Polish farmers, the priests, fur traders, fishermen, lumberjacks, and, later, the summer people.

And always the church. Even after the first one burned, the Jesuits built a second, then a third, its steeple rising above everything else. Next to it—a large lump of a brick building full of girls, some small, some older, all dark. All sent or left or brought by the nuns to learn American ways and to forget all things Indian. No more dancing to spirits with suspicious, tongue-twisting names. No more clothes of deerskin. Put the girls to work, and when they were big enough, some summer family—preferably Catholic—would take them.

Beyond the tip of the point, the water widened into a bay, the trees and hills beyond the town of Chibawassee faint upon the opposite shore. From the southern edge, the bay extended west toward the horizon. To the north of Beck's Point was the harbor—docks and trimmed lawns, raked beaches, moored boats—the best port between Grand Traverse and Mackinaw. From ▶

“ The Marches' house smelled of must, camphor, lilacs, and decayed fish that wafted up from the beach at night. **”**

every window, Rachel could see water, hear water, smell it, taste it. Not like Horseshoe Lake, which was small, tranquil, almost a pond.

"So much water," Rachel said to Ella Mae's daughter, who was helping her with the fruit.

"Like the flood itself," said Mandy, who could not swim. "Gives me the heebie-jeebies." A girl had drowned once, she told Rachel. Years before. A girl from the convent.

"I know how to swim," said Rachel.

Today, they were helping Ella Mae make cherry pie. Ella Mae worked the flour into butter until her thick, brown arms were gloved with white. Rachel pitted the fruit. It was July, and the cherries brought up from Traverse City were at their best. The juice ran down her arms. Whenever Ella Mae looked away, the girl hungrily licked them. She was always hungry, even when her stomach was full. As a child, she had sucked stones and dirt, ravenous for their minerals, as if she could consume the earth itself.

Mandy was watching her. "How old are you?"

"Sixteen," Rachel said, running her tongue around her lips. She was never quite sure.

"Sixteen? I thought you and me's the same age."

"How old are you?"

"*Seventeen*," said Mandy.

The air filled with sugar, butter, cherry. Because of the war, it had been hard to get butter these last few years. That and gasoline. Stockings. Things Rachel hadn't even known to miss.

> " From every window, Rachel could see water, hear water, smell it, taste it. Not like Horseshoe Lake, which was small, tranquil, almost a pond. "

"Chocolate," said Ella Mae, listing the rationed items. "Try to find *that*."

Ella Mae had taught Rachel to roll the chilled dough out thin and cut it so as to waste little. Rachel wadded up doughy crumbs and put them in her pocket to eat later. She wondered if Ella Mae would taste like chocolate if Rachel licked her. Same with Mandy and Jonah, Ella Mae's husband. Their skin was darker than hers, which was the color of milky cocoa.

Outside, Mrs. March, her gray hair coiled on top of her head, pointed to the empty fishpond. Victor, the gardener, followed her finger, shrugged. After the war, he seemed to be saying. After the war we will fill the pond with fish, the lake with boats, the house with laughter.

A guest was arriving that afternoon. "Before the war, we filled all five guest rooms," Ella Mae said. "The senator from Ohio stayed a week."

Mandy dipped into the bowl and swiped a cherry. Rachel almost reached out and touched Mandy's lips, they were so big and wide and black. Where'd you get those lips? she was about to ask, but Mandy spoke first, fingering Rachel's thick, black braids. "Where'd you get that *hair*?" Mandy said. "I could make it better."

Rachel touched her hair. Unbraided, it curled down her spine and spoke of something not Indian. French, perhaps. The fur trader who had taken her grandmother as his common-law wife.

"You're plain," Mandy said. "That nose of yours. Where'd you get that nose?" ▶

> **❝** Rachel wadded up doughy crumbs and put them in her pocket to eat later. She wondered if Ella Mae would taste like chocolate if Rachel licked her. **❞**

Even Rachel had to admit her nose was different, not flat and squished like most Odawa's, but longer and beaked like a bird of prey.

"And your cheeks!" said Mandy. She blew out her own until they were rounder than the girl's.

Rachel looked at Mandy's head—twenty tiny braids to her own thick two. It had been so long since someone had touched her, combed her hair. In the churchyard there was a statue of Mary holding the baby Jesus. Sometimes, the girl wanted to crawl right into Mary's arms, her face so sad like she knew she'd have to give her baby up.

Jesus died for your sins, the nuns told Rachel.

The Marches' daughter had died in the great influenza. There was an empty crib in one of the bedrooms, the curtains perpetually drawn. Had the Virgin Mary known her own sweet-faced son would die? Perhaps her own grief deafened her to Rachel's pleas to send her home to Horseshoe Lake.

"I wouldn't mind," Rachel said, letting Mandy touch her hair. Rachel's hands had grown sticky with cherries. Jesus bleeds for me, she thought as she picked up a towel, reddened it with her palms. ❧

> ❝ It had been so long since someone had touched her, combed her hair. ❞

Don't miss the next book by your favorite author. Sign up now for AuthorTracker by visiting www.AuthorTracker.com.